D1606406

Shades of Gray

Timothy R. O'Neill

SHADES OF GRAY

Viking

VIKING
Viking Penguin Inc., 40 West 23rd Street, New York, New York 10010, U.S.A.
Penguin Books Ltd, Harmondsworth, Middlesex, England
Penguin Books Australia Ltd, Ringwood, Victoria, Australia
Penguin Books Canada Limited, 2801 John Street, Markham, Ontario, Canada L3R 1B4
Penguin Books (N.Z.) Ltd, 182–190 Wairau Road, Auckland 10, New Zealand

First published in 1987 by Viking Penguin Inc.
Published simultaneously in Canada

Grateful acknowledgment is made for permission to reprint excerpts from the
following copyrighted material:
"Samhain" and "Liam" from "O'Riada's Farewell" from *The Celtic Consciousness*
edited by Robert O'Driscoll. New York, George Braziller, Inc., 1982. By permission.
Goethe's Faust, edited by Walter Kaufmann. Published by Doubleday & Company, Inc.
"The Waste Land" from *Collected Poems 1909–1962* by T. S. Eliot. Copyright 1936
by Harcourt Brace Jovanovich, Inc. Copyright © 1963, 1964 by T. S. Eliot.
Reprinted by permission of Harcourt Brace Jovanovich, Inc., and Faber and Faber Ltd.
"The Mist and Snow" and "To a Friend Whose Work Has Come to Nothing" from *Collected
Poems* by William Butler Yeats. Copyright 1933 by Macmillan Publishing Company,
renewed 1961 by Bertha Georgie Yeats. Copyright 1916 by Macmillan Publishing
Company, renewed 1944 by Bertha Georgie Yeats. Reprinted by permission of
Macmillan Publishing Company and A. P. Watt Ltd. on behalf of Michael B. Yeats
and Macmillan London Ltd.

LIBRARY OF CONGRESS CATALOGING IN PUBLICATION DATA
O'Neill, Timothy R.
Shades of gray.
I. Title.
PS3565.N55S5   1987   813'.54   86-40314
ISBN 0-670-81133-5

Printed in the United States of America by The Book Press, Brattleboro, Vermont
Set in Caslon 540

For Mary Ellen, Grail scholar

Samhain

Sing a song

for the mistress
of the bones

the player
on the black keys
the darker harmonies

ACKNOWLEDGMENTS

In the preparation of this work, I am indebted to many whose contributions on the lore of West Point have provided a mood and background, and to those former cadets, most notably Major John Feeley, whose knowledge of the ghost of the 47th Division formed the basis for the story's fundamental conceit. For information on ghosts of West Point in general, I thank Mary Kathryn MacIntosh of the Ladies' Reading Club—and hope my references to their membership are viewed with tolerance.

Most of all, my thanks go to John Calabro of the Department of English, whose merciless prolixity detectors reduced the bulk of the manuscript to manageable size; to Richard Curtis, whose definition of "manageable size" differed from John Calabro's; to my daughter, Mary Ellen, who provided notes on the Grail legend; and to those in the West Point museum who sent me a copy of the uniform regulations of 1825.

Shades of Gray

Prologue

*T*he sound was subtle at first, high above the highest discernible tone, then lower, then joined by other pitches. They came into the room in the silence before dawn, came with the cold, with the frost that touched the windows, the pipes, that sought out the lifeless things in every corner. The sound was now distant, now as close as the windowpanes that rattled in sympathy when the bass tones surged.

The fragile tracery of frost began at the edges of the window-panes, moving inward with a progress too slow to see, until only circles of clear glass remained and the cold floodlights from the new cadet barracks across the formation area was diffused, the clarity of the shadows muted above Barstow's bunk.

Barstow fought off the dream in those minutes, the dream he knew so well now; he knew it was a dream, but there was no comfort in that knowledge. He felt the cold in his dream, heard the shudder of the window frame, and made a soft sound.

Sleep was slow to release him, but after the passing of a long moment he was aware of a change from dream to a half-awareness, at once as soft and abrupt as if he had stepped unknowing through a looking glass. The dream was more vivid than his moment of waking. The light was dim, the commonplace landmarks of the room were somehow unfamiliar, and for an instant he thought the transition from dream to waking had been reversed in some wicked way, that the house and the woman were reality and this strange room a place of dreams.

But his eyes were only unused to the light, and as he lay on his side the texture of the partition between his bunk and Carson's gradually resolved, and the delicate pattern of shadows cast by the window gave the surfaces form and place.

1

Then the patterns of light moved, slowly and imprecisely, and Barstow knew where he was and knew with a resignation more terrifying than the fear what would happen. It was the hour again, between waking and the light.

As always, there was first and most urgently the feeling of panic; he felt the gentleness of the presence that held him fast, a soft, strangling pressure that was so strong his own strength was pitiful and helpless against it. He wanted to make a sound, but his throat would not obey; he tried to move, as he always did, but the weight was there, and his strength was sucked away by its unseen presence.

More than anything, it was the feeling of being utterly helpless in the presence of something just as utterly powerful. Once, when he was ten, he had paddled far into the surf on a blinding summer day, beyond the intrusions of parents, and felt the fright and exhilaration of being in water too deep to stand up in. Then he had felt a surge, a gentle pressure below the surface, and something had brushed his leg, something beyond his sight. He had panicked then, and nearly drowned, and even now there was a tightening in his throat when he felt the presence of things outside his sight. He felt it now. He lay on his side, and the source of the pressure, the enveloping presence, was above him.

Then, as always, the panic subsided. He knew the first presence; while he did not welcome it, he summoned his courage and in his mind he said Yes, I feel you, I know you, I welcome you.

And, as always, he felt the unsaid reply.

The sadness was there, he felt it through the terrible paralysis, the gentle invincible possessing pressure. The sadness, and the endless, bottomless weariness. I know you.

But he felt the rage as well, from elsewhere but also near, as always; and he thought of it in his half-sleep as a malevolent bird, flitting angrily about the benign shadow that held him. He knew it was not seeking him, the darting, unspeakable rage; but it awed him.

And he felt the fear, as always. Not his. The tiny fear that crept about and hid in the shadows. It was always there, quietly watching the sadness, cowering away from the fury.

With supreme will—he was more fully awake now—he turned over on his back. He had not pushed against the force; it had allowed him to move, as always. Only this and no more. It was always better when he could see it. And it was there, as always, quiet, watchful, remote.

Barstow looked back, and the cold light was reflected in his eyes, suddenly filled with tears. It was a pale light, a sad light, a cold light, incredibly distant. Was there recognition? He never knew for certain. Only a reflection of a reflection.

But tonight there was something else; not the mad, furious one, not the pitiful hiding one, not the sad watcher in the dark. He had seen it on other nights, almost hidden, a shadow behind shadows. It had no fear, no sadness, no anger for him. It was composed, it was known only to itself. Barstow knew, though, that if he saw it he would see the end.

Then, as always, the sad shape collected itself and turned—was there a last look? Then the lights were there again, dancing, swirling in the air as it left, following it to whatever errand called, and Barstow felt, now for the first time, a sense of an ending, of a change. Something was going to happen. There was no spoken message, only a feeling of expectancy, of something waited for, patiently, for an infinity of time. And the time was nearly at hand.

When the last of the lights were gone, Barstow felt the cold, sat up in his bunk with his shoulders wedged into the corner of his alcove. He faced the window, counted the panes aloud again and again as if the familiar recitation could anchor him again in a world he knew.

He wrapped his green blanket around his shoulders. The quiet had returned. Outside, on the formation area, he heard the quick, measured tapping of heels as the officer-in-charge walked back to Central Guard Room from a scheduled inspection. The familiar sound only added to the loneliness of the room.

He rested his head against the cold wall. Something's going to happen.

Carson was asleep on the other side of the alcove wall. Barstow had been breathing heavily, trying to drive away the feeling of constraint that still lingered; now he controlled himself to keep from waking his roommate. The luminous clock face on Carson's desk read three forty-two. But the night was over for Barstow. It would be a long wait. A lonely wait. His only ally was silence. Carson had stopped listening. The company commander wouldn't believe, looked at Barstow as if he were a fool. What could he say?

Three forty-five.

3

What had he seen tonight? It had always been the same until tonight, the same for nearly a month. There had been no words, only the increasing strength of the other one, the elusive feeling of a rising moment, something worth waiting for.

Three forty-seven.

He stared at the window and waited for the light.

1

Sam

Verfluchtes Volk! Was untersteht ihr euch?
Hat man euch lange nicht bewiesen:
Ein Geist steht nie auf ordentlichen Fussen?

[Damnable folk! How dare you make such fuss!
Have I not often proved to you
That tales of walking-ghosts cannot be true?]

—Goethe

1

The thing that set Sam Bondurant apart from his associates, other than his dry and irascible nature, was the fact that Sam thought a lot. West Pointers are by nature doers, not thinkers, and when they stumble upon a fellow sitting in his office, passive and immobile, and by self-report "thinking," they are likely to mumble something about wishing they had time to waste. They are trained from the start to value action over introspection, and if the action is the wrong one, they err at least on the side of aggressiveness, a desirable trait. Sam forgave them their impetuosity and they forgave Sam his inertia.

But then Sam was not a grad. By this we mean he did not graduate from West Point, though West Pointers are willing to concede that the verb "to graduate" may apply to other paths of learning as well. At any time a large proportion of the faculty—particularly the transient, nontenured faculty—is composed of non-grads. They are occasionally called "asterisks" as well, after the punctuation that once preceded their names on departmental rosters. The distinction has little substantive meaning, of course, because they were all army officers, and those of Sam's generation were graduates of Vietnam, a great leveler of distinctions. But Sam's kind of non-grad had more room for eccentricity.

Sam privately assigned grads to three categories: those upon whom the cadet mystique was indelibly marked; those who had matured into army officers and then regressed, to the consternation of their wives, into cadets again when they returned to West Point on faculty assignment; and those who were mature before the first day of Beast Barracks and who as a consequence never surrendered their initial issue of spirit. It was these officers that Sam valued most, for if they were no more courageous or efficient than their fellows, they at least valued their independence more than those by whom it was less dearly purchased.

Track Dortmunder was one of these, and his individuality was demonstrated on this morning when he entered Sam's office without ceremony, faced away, unbuckled his belt and dropped his green uniform trousers. Sam swiveled his chair back and regarded the scene, struggling to maintain a poker face.

Sam and Track had been friends for fifteen years. In 1969 they had served together in the 1st Battalion, 77th Armored, on and around Nui Con Thien in the far north of the Republic of Vietnam. Sam was C Company commander and Track was his first platoon leader. The battalion commander regarded Track as something of a lunatic, and had sent him to Sam's company from battalion staff as a present, for Sam was always begging for new talent. Sam knew the truth about Track. He *was* a lunatic, but the dry categories of the *Diagnostic and Statistical Manual for Mental Disorders* did not cover idiosyncratic adaptations to life in Quang Tri in 1970. Track was absolutely fearless and superb in a fight and his troops loved him because he spared himself nothing, smuggled beer to them in the field (with Sam's willing connivance) and made them laugh. Apparently the battalion commander based his own deathless definition of leadership on some other set of capacities, because he was always trying to settle Track's career. Sam had the job of rating him, though; the battalion commander only endorsed, and this image-conscious man would not make himself look like a horse's ass by contradicting Sam on an efficiency report. Sam made Track look like the incarnation of Joshua. Track prospered and Track's men prospered; but Sam knew that although a commander can love his men as a corporate entity, he courts disaster if he cares too much for a single man. Men have a way of being carried off in combat, and a commander cannot have too many holes in his armor.

Track's tank was hit by a B-40 rocket one day and he took a face full of spall. A scalp wound always looks more serious than it really is, because it bleeds a lot over the exposed face. Track was such a mess that the medic completely missed the more serious chest wound. Sam and the medic carried Track on a litter to the dustoff chopper and slid the burden onto the cargo floor. Track looked bad, and Sam, not practiced in the etiquette of saying goodbye in such a situation, asked Track if there was anything he could do. Track tried to gasp something, but the words were drowned out by the noise of the helicopter. Sam leaned close with a concerned, sympathetic look, and Track whispered "I could sure use a blow job."

Track led a charmed life, and his and Sam's careers crossed more than once. They attended the Staff College at Fort Leavenworth, Kansas, in 1975 with the same class, and no one but the witless personnel weenies at Department of the Army had been surprised when Sam went off to graduate school and then to a West Point instructor tour, and Track arrived a year later in the same department.

Sam pushed his glasses down the bridge of his nose, the myopic's last recourse when the world looks too grim to face without a merciful blur (and Track's behind was an uninspiring landscape). "Now," said Sam, "I've seen everything."

"Seen everything, maybe," said Track, buckling his trousers, "but you ain't heard anything yet. Just wait."

"I know that look. You didn't come here to bullshit, you want something. Have a seat while I get some coffee." Sam found his cup and walked out.

Track did not sit, but browsed through Sam's bookcases. Some people tried to find the key to Sam's difficult personality by assaying his books. Track knew better. Sam collected books for perverse reasons. One whole shelf was given over to texts on disorders of sexual behavior and child development. Sam was uninterested in sexual disturbance and indifferent to children, but he had once in a weak moment subscribed to a psychology book club that sent out the monthly special unless the member specifically provided a sworn affadavit, on the presumption that most subscribers are too lazy. Sam was too lazy, and most of the monthly specials had been on sex therapy or child development. Finally Maggie had pointed out that all those books on the shelf at home made him look like some kind of pedophile, and the goddamned things had to go. So Sam had taken them to his office to rest, unused, with the more important volumes; and by virtue of their obtrusive presence, Sam had become a de facto guru on sex and childhood. He had never read a single volume, but perpetuated this legend by happily handing the books out on loan on the promise that they be returned (and in the hope that they wouldn't). More revealing of Sam's

9

tastes were the bookends on the shelf reserved for his favorite books: a plastic replica of an Australopithecus skull and a human brain in a glass jar.

Track took down the brain and inspected it. The cadets in Sam's psychobiology course had dissected it into neat, flat slices, and the formalin was discolored and opaque. Sam kept it in plain sight, to the distress of visitors. He used it as a screening device for prospective students: a change in face color usually foretold troubles in the lab. The department head had complained about the dreadful thing more than once, which had only assured the brain of a permanent home on the shelf. Track sloshed the preservative around a little to moisten the drying surfaces of the cortex. Old Sam and his fucking brain.

Sam came in with a fresh cup of coffee and slouched in his swivel chair. Track replaced the brain and sat in the corner chair and grinned. "Good morning, sir. What do you have to say for old Track?"

"I know you well enough not to answer before I finish my first cup. Now, why did you feel compelled to moon me on a Monday morning?"

"You mistake me. I was furthering myself economically and educationally: my head was looking for loose change and my ass was taking private astronomy lessons." This was Track's way, boisterous crudity disguising an allusion to Aristophanes. He enjoyed the audience that was repelled by the grossness and lacked the erudition to catch the joke. Sam always did, and dismissed the ribaldry as an example of Track's inability to care whether he reconciled scholarship and soldiering.

"I know you were looking for me earlier this morning," said Sam, "and most of the time you don't bother trying again if I'm not around. What can I do for you?"

"One of the cadets I sponsor has a wee problem. Just a wee little bitty problem." Track stood and picked up Sam's telephone. "Matter of fact, I think Liam should hear this too."

"What," said Sam, "could Liam and I both be interested in?" Liam FitzDonnell was Sam's intellectual nemesis. He was the associate professor for individual psychology, and his instructors taught personality, counseling, and social and abnormal psychology. Sam was associate professor for human-factors psychology, concerned more with the technical problems of wedding men to machines, and his tools were computers, microscopes, and cathode ray tubes. Liam considered Sam a naive reductionist for whom the field of a microscope was a peculiar form of tunnel vision. To Sam, Liam was a neo-Shoshone medicine man.

Liam answered the intercom and Track invited him to step down the hall to Sam's office and listen to something interesting.

"What," asked Liam, "could Sam and I both find interesting?"

"Ghosts, Liam. Spooks, specters, haunts, púkas. No, Liam, I didn't know that. You would, though. That's why I called." Track gently replaced the receiver. "He's on the way. By the way, Sam: if you ever want to know, a púka ain't a fucking ghost."

"Of course not. It's a Celtic animal spirit that visits this one and then that one and how are you Major Dortmunder?"

Liam stood in the doorway and leaned on the frame. He was as tall as Sam, with the same lanky build, but his hands and feet were unusually large, and he walked with a lurching stiffness that was the only outward sign of a stretch of smooth burned skin from the small of his back to his shoulderblades. His hair was black-Irish-dark and ill-tended where Sam's was sandy and neatly trimmed. Liam looked like a poet except for the broken nose, relic of an indiscretion in plebe boxing that he had never bothered to have repaired because his girlfriend at the time (long forgotten) had thought it endearing. He had a soft, cadenced voice like a poet but, unlike Sam, no gift for satire, and a dark, quiet intensity that calmly deflected Sam's rapid-fire caustic sniping.

They were both tenured, having abandoned their original career tracks (Sam's had been armor, Liam's infantry) to remain at West Point; the correct term was PAP or permanent associate professor. In return, their personnel managers at Armor and Infantry had given up on them, regarding them disdainfully as mere schoolmasters who had escaped soldiering to hide out at the Military Academy. If Sam and Liam had anything in common, it was their reason for staying: they both loved West Point, though Sam referred to the place as "stones and clones" and Liam never spoke of it at all.

Liam smiled slowly. "Ghosts, Track? Last month Patti was up in arms about faulty plumbing. Now is it chains in the attic?"

"No, Liam—it ain't *my* ghost, I got better taste. This one's

11

in the Forty-seventh Division." The divisions were in the older cadet barracks near the gymnasium, odd, old-fashioned affairs with rooms clustered around stairwells.

Liam came in and slouched in the chair opposite Sam. He was incapable of *sitting* in the accepted sense because of his build and because of his injuries, and his arms and legs overflowed in unexpected angular excursions. His eyes were no longer their usual heavy-lidded ambivalent deadpan. They fixed on Track with a detached amusement that was Liam's approximation of curiosity. He's swallowed the bait, thought Track, now for just a little jerk to set it firm.

"One of the cadets I sponsor is company commander of G-4. He was over at my quarters on Saturday to watch the game, and he told me about this business kind of confidentially."

"G-4? That's Tetzler?"

"Tetzel, Sam. Anyway, he has this plebe in the Forty-seventh Division who's all wrapped around the flagpole and says he has a ghost in his room."

Liam stirred. "Don't I recall something about ghosts over there from years ago? A friend of mine lived over in the Forty-seventh Division."

"Yeah," said Track; "back in 'sixty-nine, after you graduated, there was some kind of strange shit over there, the same year the superintendent's wife got excited about a ghost in the basement of her quarters. I was a firstie then, and I was in Third Regiment, so I didn't know much about it firsthand. I was too busy trying to graduate to fart around with spirits—that kind, anyway." Liam smiled again. Track was remembered from cadet days as a gay rake of sorts who had marched a record number of punishment tours for overindulgent drinking. The commandant had been ready to throw Track out on his ear until in one famous interview the general made the mistake of pointing out that Robert E. Lee had never received a single demerit in his four years. Cadet Dortmunder had argued that Lee was remembered largely for being a gallant loser. The Com had been furious, but could not argue with Track's logic, reinforced by the evidence of Grant's reprobate ways as a member of the Long Gray Line. He had finally given Track another chance, and if Track's entire life had been like those last months before graduation he would have earned a place on the right hand of God. Once he'd graduated, however, his behavior had reverted to its old standards, and by the time he finished the officer basic course at Fort Knox his reputation among grads was right up there with Packer Porter, who painted Mickey Mouse on the clock face of East Barracks, and Charley Slade, who surprised various classmates and their dates at a company picnic by dipping his pecker in a pickle jar. Amid these traditions, ghosts were pale specters indeed.

"What happened to the ghosts that time?" asked Sam, who, since he was not a grad, had to rely on others for the unraveling of the cocoon of West Point lore.

"I think they quit bothering with it when *Time* picked up the story; besides, it was just before the Navy game, and there was enough horseshit going on to keep everybody busy."

"I was already in Nam when that happened," said Liam absently, "but I seem to recall hearing about it. Didn't they call in some kind of a medium?"

"Who?" asked Sam. "I can't imagine anybody over in Building 600 messing around with spoon-benders."

"I don't know," said Track. "They were too busy trying to kick me out to ask my advice. I think there was some group from a parapsychology institute in New York. Then they dropped it. We can't endure to be mocked for long."

"But you were talking about a cadet now," Liam reminded him.

"Yeah, John Tetzel, the indulgent"—Sam winced—"company commander of Company G, Fourth Regiment, which includes the infamous Forty-seventh Division. I've sponsored him ever since he was a yearling, and he comes over from time to time. He's in a kind of panic about this here business, and he doesn't want to go to his tac just yet."

"Who is his tac?" asked Sam. The "tactical officer" is an army captain or major responsible for a cadet company.

"Stu Broadnax."

"Stu's all right. Why is the kid afraid to go to him?"

"Well, look at it from Tetzel's point of view," said Track. "The plebe says there are ghosts. There's a limited number of reasons. One, there really are ghosts. Two, the kid is crazy as a loon, which will get him out of here in a hurry. Three, he's lying, which will also get him out in a hurry. John doesn't want to do anything rash."

Liam leaned back in the chair and regarded Track with a pensive stare. "Is this plebe in academic trouble?"

"No, I don't think so. John didn't mention it."

"Disciplinary problems?"

"Some time on the area, John said. Mostly small shit—tarnish, dirt, items displayed improperly, all that kind of world-stopping trivia. Gets a little spastic under pressure."

Liam pressed. "Does the company commander like the kid?"

"No. But he doesn't think he's a hopeless case."

"Then he should just take it to his tac and let the chips fall where they may," said Sam.

Track frowned. "I think he believes enough of the kid's story to be cautious."

Sam left to refill his coffee cup. His intercom buzzed twice, and each time Track picked up the receiver and said abruptly, "He ain't here." Liam was lost in thought. The whole business bothered him in some indefinable way; it was silly in a way, as if someone had "walked on his grave," and he resisted a trite name for his disquiet.

"Track," said Liam at length, "I don't like this business. You tell the cadet to take it to his tac."

"Why?"

"Because we're messing around with an adolescent under stress, and he should be going to the counseling center or mental hygiene."

"The kid won't do it, John says. He thinks the only people who go to the counseling center are fruits and nuts."

Sam returned just in time to hear this last comment. "The kid sees ghosts and he's worried about fruits and nuts?"

They all laughed. "For some reason John didn't think that was a good idea. I don't really know why, and he didn't elaborate. But something was really bothering him."

"I guess you're right," Sam said. "The typical cadet reaction would be to make a big joke about it or run the plebe straight to the headshrinkers."

"Hey, watch that shit," said Liam. He was a clinical psychologist by training.

14

"Or worse," Sam grinned. "The local parapsychologist is unlikely to be very sympathetic, either." The "parapsychologist" was Lieutenant Colonel Ward E. Lane, director of the Cadet Counseling Center. Lane was a former infantryman who was under great inner compulsion to shed a touchie-feelie image for the counseling center and prove that Medical Service Corps clinicians are just as tough as anybody else. He was a master parachutist, and in private his counseling staff had referred to him as the "parapsychologist" until a new officer had innocently asked Lane if he were really a parapsychologist, whereupon the nickname had vanished in an awesome detonation that left several wounded careers.

Liam began talking without his usual diffidence. "Look, messing around with a troubled eighteen-year-old plebe is folly. He may be a real cornflake . . ."

"Clinical term, Liam?" asked Sam

". . . or at best we'd be meddling with something that is very definitely the tac's business. It is also, I remind you both, the regimental tac's business. The regimental tac is, as I recall, one who once characterized our department as 'Bull Shit and Lies.' " The Department of Behavioral Sciences and Leadership was heir to an unfortunate set of initials. "Those are two—or three—good reasons for not getting involved."

Track was astonished to find that Sam, usually very reluctant to get involved in projects outside his own area, was in strong disagreement. "Hell, it can't hurt to talk to the man. If we see a real problem, we're qualified to refer him to counseling or back to Stu. Don't turn into a bureaucrat in your old age. You're the clinician in this merry band. You'd provide a service by assessing him."

"You mean you think the beanhead's steam pipes are banging?" asked Track.

"Or something. We don't know because we haven't asked. Or did your cadet give you more details, Track?"

"Yeah, he did. First, a lot of weird things have been going on in the division. People in the day room late at night hear kids running around the halls, and two cadets heard a little kid crying. Some vandalism, too. Broken windows. And there's one more little morsel. The guy's roommate went to the company commander a few weeks ago when this had just started and asked to be shipped to another room because his roommate was getting strange. He wouldn't say why at the time, but the reason John talked to me about it yesterday is because the roommate came to him again and asked to leave the room altogether and as soon as possible."

"The other guy was getting weirder?"

"No, the roommate was starting to see the stuff too. He was scared absolutely shitless."

Liam stirred again. "Just what are these people seeing?"

"John didn't really specify, but it made him get serious. The beanheads said they saw a sort of hazy human shape early in the morning, before dawn. Something about the room getting ice cold and then warming up again after the thing disappeared. That's about it."

"You said a while ago," said Sam, "that he half believed the plebe's story. Why?"

Track frowned. "I don't know. It's just an impression I had."

"Why didn't you ask?"

"Because I was trying to watch a damn football game."

"Marvelous."

"Look," said Track, "I don't know anything about ghosts. You two bastards probably do. You have the equipment and know-how to throw together some kind of a ghost detector, and everything Liam knows is covered with cobwebs. If there's a ghost in the room, you'll find the sombitch; if it's in somebody's head, Liam will."

This reasoning appealed to the vanity of both men, as Track knew it would. They agreed to talk to the company commander that week and decide what to do next. Track sent a message to Cadet John Tetzel and the latter agreed to meet them in Sam's office on Wednesday. Events, as it turned out, followed a less leisurely schedule.

Liam was divorced, and lived in the old bachelor officers' quarters on a cliff overlooking the Hudson River. The view, particularly in the fall, was magnificent, since his rooms were on the river side. On the far side of the Hudson he could see the town of Garrison, a view softened by haze and made splendid by the autumn hues, the colors muted by the last light of the sun.

West Point could be an ugly place, with its stone Gothic architecture and somber order. In the dead of winter it could be a setting for mad depression, the abode of demons called calculus and electrical engineering and social science papers; indeed, the days between the end of Christmas leave and the beginning of spring had long been called Gloom Period. In high summer, West Point is hot and breathless, overrun by crowds of tourists. But now, in mid-autumn, with the tourists gone and the weather fine, Liam judged it had been worth screwing up his marriage just to have this beautiful view.

He left the light off in the living room and leaned on the windowsill. Far below, on the flats that bordered the cliff and stretched about two hundred feet to the river's edge, he could watch the last activities of the day—intramural volleyball winding up, a modest crowd of Hasidic families from the city boarding their bus to get home before dinner. On the river a few sailboats beat upwind past the light on the point below Flirtation Walk, a wooded path where cadets escort young ladies in a welcome interlude of privacy.

It was getting dark fast, and he was hungry; but eating dinner meant the microwave. Liam was an utterly incompetent cook, and he preferred to eat out, even alone, rather than endure the private humiliation of ruining a frozen dinner against all the odds. He really wanted to be with Anna that evening, but she was in Boston. He thought of calling her, but knew himself and Anna well enough to have no illusions about the telephone's ability to reach out and touch anyone. Liam relied heavily on nonverbal things in talking to Anna, since her voice rarely betrayed any emotion stronger than impatience; and if he called and she didn't answer, the little demons started to nibble away at his spleen.

He was depressed for no reason and anxious for no reason, but he knew enough of man's incapacities to know that there is no more a thing called no reason than a thing called a free lunch. I'll see her this weekend, he said to the demons, and they chanted scornfully *Yes, Liam, yes, Liam, and when you leave we'll still be there, still be there.*

He saw it was really dark now, and he turned on the table lamp. The living room was small, but it was crowded with things inherited and things purchased and things slyly pulled from the talons of his ex-wife's smart fucking lawyer, may he fail to avoid probate. Liam's favorite was a carved cherry desk from China, circa

1880, with dark intertwined dragons, finely chiseled fretwork, and the most inefficient writing surface ever devised. It had a matching chair, known in his family as the Baron's Seat or the *leac na riog*, after the stone seat where the High Kings were once crowned in Ulster. It was carved in the same way, with a high back and arms; and, like the *leac na riog*, it was a supremely perilous and uncomfortable seat. It had belonged to his grandfather Roderick Fitz-Donnell, whose grandfather had been Ruaridhe Fitz Donnell of Fermanagh, who had insisted that Liam be so named. Liam is Irish for William, and so baptismal testimony remembered Willem Fitz Hugh Gilbert, the impoverished Norman adventurer from Rouen who had married Aoife ni-Donnaill to keep *her* father Con Mor uí-Donnaill from extracting vengeance for the loss of a snow-white bull. So Liam had been told.

It was an ugly chair and ugly desk, but Liam loved them. The desk had compartments with drawers that opened with carved pulls, and he opened one now and removed a leather bag. He examined it thoughtfully, then extracted, one at a time, three small fat stones. He put them on the desk top in front of him, right to left. Each had a curious linear design cut on its surface. Liam had found each stone on expeditions to a creek near Fort Sill, Oklahoma, while he was serving on the Field Artillery Board. He had rejected hundreds of similar water-washed pebbles until he was satisfied with twenty-one perfect ovals, smooth and symmetrical. On each he had carved a different rune.

He examined the one on the right: he had drawn *Man*, the Self:

Yes, where is it? Elusive little bugger. In the center was *Is*, the rune of standstill:

Yes, that's me. Stuck fast. On the left, he had drawn *Tir*, the warrior-rune:

And having cast the runes, Liam interpreted them so: I seek for the Self. Yet I am the warrior, full of impetuosity yet obedient to others, the warrior's ancient tension. And between these forces there is standstill, my soul hanging here from the life-tree like Odin, twisting slowly, slowly in the wind. He pushed the runes aside and drew another three from the bag and lined them up as before. *Wyn, Eoh, Nyth:*

ᚠ ᛄ ᛈ

Joy, defense, constraint. Well, hit me between the eyes, Old Woman of the Runes. Can't you be subtle? The runes have no magic beyond what they call forth from my chasm of despair; you work your sorcery on me, Old Bitch, *Voluspa*, and I'll throw you out the window onto the pathways of Flirtie. Joy: Anna. Defense: You can't hurt me again, never again. Constraint: I can't say it, not if you pluck at my tongue with hot pincers. No, Old Bitch, Old Sorceress, you don't get another chance tonight. Back in the sack you go, Rocky Horror Show.

He slammed the drawer shut on the runes in their leather bag and took a deep breath. Don't call Anna. This ghost business. What can we do? He got out paper and wrote:

First: Is the plebe suggestible? Stress, morbidity, autosuggestion? Hypnotic induction profile. The room-mate: *folie à deux?* Could be.

How to proceed? Profile, cadet and roommate: Whence the morbidity? Plebe's family life. Religiosity? Belief in the supernatural? Is the ghost a convenient escape from the private little purgatory between Mister Beanhead's ears?

One more question: Who in the hell am I kidding?
And he slammed into the bedroom and called Anna.

Sam was writing questions, too. He was propped up in bed with a note pad, scribbling away, and his questions were not Liam's:

1. Physical layout of room. Ventilation (coldness), pipes transmit noises?

2. Luminance levels during manifestations (bad word?). Telephotometer? Continuous readings, summed and averaged for long epoch? (How long "manifestations"?)

3. Audible? Ask J. T. Microphone, RTA computer?

4. Physio change in cadets? Parameters? Heart rate, GSR? Direct or IR telemetered?

Maggie glanced from the crossword puzzle in the Sunday *Times;* she was wearing her reading glasses and, as usual, filling out the words *in ink.* Snotty broad. She sensed his thoughts and said: "You married me knowing I'm a genius."

"Four-letter word for Celtic animal spirit," he said.

She smiled winningly and blinked her eyes. *"Púka.* Don't tell me you're doing research on invisible six-foot rabbits."

He laughed. "No, not even banshees. Just simple ghosts."

She put down the magazine and stared at him. "Ghosts?"

"That's not the first time today I've heard the word spoken with just that intonation. Actually, Track came to Liam and me with a ghost story." He recited the essentials of the meeting, and Maggie sat up on her elbow and faced him.

"You're actually going to *do* it?"

"Do what, woman?"

"Help solve the Great Ghost Mystery of the Lost Forties."

"It's 'Lost Fifties'; the Forties just have ghosts." The Lost Fifties were barracks divisions with numbers in that decade, so called because they were farthest from the centers of power and least likely to be inspected by the officer-in-charge. "And," he added, "I wouldn't touch it with a ten-foot electric cattle prod."

"You beast!" She sat up on her knees, fists on hips. "You have to do it!"

"Why do I have to waste my time on this nonsense?"

"It isn't nonsense! You've been scribbling away for hours, drawing diagrams, mumbling under your breath."

"It *is* nonsense. Track and Liam may do something about it, but if I'm going to hold my head up . . ."

"I'm beside myself with curiosity . . ."

". . . in the Psychonomic Society . . ."

". . . and you talk about holding your head up!" Her hair was fresh from the curlers tonight, and it tossed as she waved her arms.

"Well," he said reluctantly, "you might offer some small inducement."

She dropped her arms to her knees and smiled. "Five letter word meaning 'ready to negotiate.' "

"Loved."

"I was thinking of *horny.*"

"Close enough." He looked at the ceiling: "God, give me strength."

"Fat chance." She pulled her nightgown over her head and pulled the covers down and knelt over him. He reached up to touch her hair, the soft pale blond hair she maintained with many a rinse for his benefit, and she leaned over and kissed him, a long kiss with her tongue flitting around his, and he held her breasts in his hands and murmured "No promises, now."

She snorted in contempt and straightened up, took him in her hand and guided him, closing her eyes and smiling, first in amusement, then in another, more accustomed way, as he entered her.

"God," he whispered, "make me weak."

She settled down, taking all of him, and said: "Four-letter word, meaning 'man's greatest pleasure.' "

He got it wrong, and it cost him a pinch where it hurt.

Later she lay against him with her leg draped across him and her face on his shoulder, the blond curls slightly damp from their exertions. "Why are you such a pushover?"

"I was going to do it anyway."

"I know that. I mean why did you marry me?"

"You have nice tits."

"I know that, too, but you're such a beautiful man. You're a bad-tempered pain in the ass and conceited beyond all belief, and you're getting a little heavy around the middle, but you have the best mind around this pile of rubble, save possibly Liam Fitz-Donnell . . ."

"Watch it, woman."

". . . though of course he could never hope to match your performance in bed . . ."

21

"Thank you."

". . . unless, of course, he had an instructor like me . . ."

"You're figure-skating on profoundly insubstantial ice."

"Enough about Liam," she said. "Why did you marry me?"

"I told you—you have nice tits." He indicated with the tip of a finger where the nearest one was.

She was quiet, and he realized that this was one of those questions he was obliged to answer from time to time, and he had better stand and deliver or the stirring he was beginning to feel again was going to go begging. But he already knew the answer.

"Maggie, I married you because I'm a tired, disgruntled army guy who got educated beyond his and the army's requirements, because I didn't have anything to love until you loved me, because of reasons I don't understand myself. Why do you love me? That's a profounder mystery."

"No fair, Sam. I asked you why you married me, not why you love me."

"Okay, why did you marry me?"

"You have nice tits."

He reared up in the bed and she tried to protect herself, but he tickled her anyway until she screamed. The neighbors had known them too long to be alarmed.

2

*M*aggie was impatient for Wednesday, when the company commander was to have his interview with Sam and Liam. Her wait was shorter than expected, as Sam had a yellow telephone message clipped to his office mailbox at seven thirty the next morning requesting a callback to Colonel Pretorius. Pretorius was deputy commandant, a man with whom Sam ordinarily had no contact. There was also a message from Track. He visited Track first, and so was spared a surprise.

"Sam, the shit hit the fucking turbine blades big time last night. Tetzel decided to sleep in the plebes' room and see what all the ghost hoopla was about."

"I interpret all this colorful colloquial flourish to mean he saw something."

"You bet your ass. He called me this morning at oh-dark thirty and said he was so scared his sphincter was doing the peppermint twist. He called his tac in the middle of the night, and by lunchtime it's going to be all over the corps."

"Did you by any chance mention my name to Tetzel in the context of the ghost?" Sam was quietly folding and unfolding Pretorius's message slip, a momentary surrogate for Track's neck.

Track tilted his head back and smiled. "Well, I mentioned your names on Sunday, before the kid got this bright idea about sleeping in the haunted house."

"Could that be the explanation for a message to call Pretorius ASAP?"

Track grinned. "Certainly not. You'd never consider calling a full colonel a sap. However, I do recall Tetzel saying in the course of the aforementioned predawn phone conversation that the tac had ordered him to see Pretorius this morning just as soon as he could throw together enough gray wool to cover his nakedness. Whether he used your name in vain is, of course, a mystery to me . . ."

"In a pig's ass."

". . . but if I had made a recommendation about how to handle an investigation of a galloping ghost and a missing beanhead, why your name and Liam's would have been . . ."

"What do you mean, 'missing beanhead'?"

"Oh, yeah, I forgot to tell you. I just found out Barstow went over the hill some time Saturday night after taps. Placed our beloved uncollege in his rearview mirror and boogied. Did not pass go, collect his back wages, pack his bags or wire Mom to make up the spare bed. Vanished. Skied out."

Sam sighed. "Well, this ought to please Maggie, anyway; she was very insistent last night. This sort of thing fascinates her. Maybe she can write it up for some magazine." Before she met Sam, Maggie had been a budding specialist in medieval literature, happily working on a dissertation and grading essays and writing on the side. Now she was consigned to marriage, the ultimate tenure track.

Track sucked his teeth for a moment. "Maggie's bored out of her mind here, ain't she?"

"Well, it isn't university life. She's doing better now."

"How does she stand sitting in that damned Lee Road mausoleum of yours with a maid's room and a view and no job and only you to talk to?"

"It isn't easy, I guess," said Sam, oblivious to the jab. "She ought to have more to do. That word processor is a blessing, except I think she's getting crossed eyes and flat shiny fingertips from the hours she puts in. She sold another story to that mystery magazine."

"That's great. She's going to be the new Dame Agatha." Track looked at Sam seriously. "You know, Sam—and don't get offended—it beats me what a gorgeous woman like Mag sees in an asshole like you."

Sam laughed. "It bothers me, too. I guess patience wins in the end." Sam had been a confirmed bachelor for years, wedded to the army and dating irresolutely. He had met Maggie in graduate school three years before, a woman much younger than Sam and regarded as hot stuff in the English Department's covey of Ph.D. candidates. They were married within two months, to the consternation of her circle of friends, who were unwilling to the last to accept the idea of Maggie married to an older man, a psychologist, and an army Vietnam vet—probably a psychotic wife-beater as well, with a fascist personality and a string of mummified Viet Cong ears hung in the hall closet. Track also wondered about Maggie's wild love for Sam and sometimes wished idly that it was not as strong as it appeared. Like most other men in the department and a good portion of the male summer crowd at Delafield Pond, the local swimming hole, Track nurtured a private case of the hots for Maggie. Sam, on the other hand, displayed about as much emotion as the ugly pickled brain on his bookshelf.

"Look, Sam—John told me about all this last night, and he still wants to come see us on Wednesday. I've known him for a while, and I've never heard him talk like he did last night. There's something serious going on."

"Okay, Track. Let me give Pretorius a call." He paused at the door of Track's cubicle. "You're sure you didn't have anything to do with this?"

Track regarded him with wide, innocent eyes. "Would I do something like that to my old buddy?"

Sam's meeting with Colonel Pretorius lasted just under twenty minutes. The deputy commandant assured Sam that he had acted on Track's recommendation, and had full confidence in Sam's abilities. Sam was to conduct a brief, quiet investigation with whatever resources he had at hand. He was to avoid any contact with any outside agency; he was to approach no ghost hunters, no institutes for paranormal phenomena, no mediums, and, above all, no representatives of the communications media. The commandant of cadets, Colonel Pretorius promised, would give Sam any reasonable support he needed; in return, Sam would be discreet and avoid any cause for frivolity in the weeks preceding the Army-Navy football game.

Dismissed, Sam darted back to the department and called his quarters to break the news to Maggie. Maggie wasn't there, so he buzzed Liam and Track, but it was near lunchtime and Liam had left for the Officers' Club and Track was out jogging. Stymied at every turn, Sam settled down to some technical planning; but it was premature without the interview with the cadet, and he gave up after a few minutes and headed to the club to find Liam.

Liam was lunching in a corner of the main dining room with Doris Gilmer, an Air Force captain who taught abnormal psychology and so came under Liam's supervision. Sam didn't much like having to contend with both of them, but Liam had to know what Track had volunteered them to do so there was no helping it. Doris was hard to take on a busy day because she alternated between fits of femininity and kick-'em-in-the-balls assertiveness, as if suddenly awakening from a fugue state in one role and shifting in a panic to the other. This kept Sam off balance; he wasn't that skilled in dealing with women at the best of times and with Doris it was always the worst. He reckoned it must be hard trying to be female and a tough broad in uniform at the same time; some women descended into caricature, some tried to be all one or the other (usually without success), and some were very strong and independent women who didn't bother with role ambiguity. The last were almost always the happiest. Doris tried to be both, and if she did not manage her image the way she apparently wanted to, at least she kept men on the alert—which, Sam had decided, was a superb compromise.

Sam assembled a salad in the line and carried it to Liam's table. Liam greeted him with a subtle hint of relief; Doris had clearly been giving him hell about something, and Sam amounted to a diversion. If Doris practiced on Liam, she gave Sam the real treatment. She found him distant, dour, and dull, three *D*s which in Doris's alliterative lexicon spelled two-dimensional.

"A dull salad again," she observed, looking over the edge of Sam's plate as he stood by his chair. "What do you put on that stuff, Maalox?"

"It's blue cheese dressing, Doris. I'm not worried about keeping my weight down." That should shut her up, thought Sam.

Doris smiled with the warmth of an open door to hell.

"Well, Liam, it looks like we hunt ghosts," Sam said.

Liam closed his eyes for a moment. "Unlike you, I have a reputation to lose."

Sam looked at Doris. "Oh, really? I wouldn't have guessed."

"Eat your Maalox, Sam. You need it." Doris opted for the better part of valor and lavished full attention on her sandwich.

Liam grinned. "Track said you were marching to Pretorius the last time he saw you. He thought it was pretty funny."

"Track would have laughed at Little Big Horn," said Sam, "at least if he was an Indian. Pretorius wants us to investigate quietly, keeping a low profile. I get the impression we are not to allow sport to be made of West Point, particularly in light of the serious vein of the forthcoming Army-Navy game . . ."

"Don't worry," said Liam, laying a hand on Sam's arm, "in your next life you'll be a grad."

"Karma is karma," said Sam, "but I think I'm due to be a pig first . . ."

"Right on!" said Doris.

". . . so I can avoid the culture shock. Anyway, he also mentioned your name . . ."

"Thanks, Track."

". . . in connection with this endeavor."

Doris finally comprehended what was being discussed. "Ghosts? What ghosts?"

"The ghost of the Forty-seventh Division," said Sam. "Anyway, the project is ours to do with as we please. I think we owe it to Track to include him as well, if only to thank him for getting us into this."

Doris closed her eyes. "What ghosts?"

"I agree," said Liam. "The least we can do."

"What ghosts, damn it?"

"The very least," said Sam. Doris drew back her arm and punched Sam in the bicep. It was a well-placed shot, and Sam felt his arm go numb to the fingertips. "Shall we tell her?"

"I don't know, Sam. What do you think?"

"I think I don't want to be a paraplegic."

Liam told Doris about Track's cadet and the BS and L mandate to conduct a ghost hunt.

"Did you tell Maggie about it?"

"Yes, last night."

"That explains it." Doris sorted through her potato chips.

"Explains what?"

"What explains what?"

"Whatever you're talking about."

"Maggie." She examined a greenish fragment of something from her plate.

"What about Maggie?"

"I don't think I should tell you." She stared in fascination at the discolored chip. "You know, it's really disgraceful, what you find in processed foods."

"What about Maggie, Doris?" Sam nervously worried his salad fork.

"I agree," said Liam. "The food-and-drugs people should really do something about it. Pitiful, really."

"Look at it, Sam," said Doris in real earnest, holding the dreadful thing out for him to inspect. "It's *green* for God's sake."

"Is there anything you'd like to say, Doris, in these last few seconds before I rip your lips off?"

"Only that I saw Maggie over in the library today with about twenty books and some big old prints in front of her; she didn't even notice me."

Sam was pleased. Maggie was easier to deal with when she had a crusade in progress and less time to think about how dull West Point can be when you have given up scholarship to marry Sam Bondurant, aging boy experimental psychologist. "What was she reading?"

"How would I know?" asked Doris. "Am I in the habit of nosing into other people's business?"

"Yes!"

"Yes!"

Doris lifted her chin in venomous goodwill. "Lean over here, Sam—I'll whisper it in your ear."

Sam knew better, but today was a day for risks. Doris put her mouth to Sam's ear and said, in a slightly louder than conversational tone: *"Living With Herpes."* Officers at surrounding tables looked their way and saw Sam looking pale and Liam looking the other way.

Some blue cheese dressing had fallen from Sam's fork onto his lap, and he dipped his napkin into his glass of ice water and started swabbing vigorously, not relishing a walk back to Thayer Hall with a prominent stain on the crotch of his uniform trousers. Doris watched him, shook her head sadly, and said—loud enough to be heard—"I hate to tell you this, Sam, but that won't help."

As it happened, Maggie had been scouring volumes on the history of West Point, trying to find references to ghosts. When Sam got home, she was on the floor of the living room, surrounded by open books and large prints. He set his briefcase in the hallway and sat beside her on the rug.

She was primed. "Sam, look at this." She displayed a reproduction of an old watercolor of West Point at some remote time. Sam recognized the view as a perspective from roughly the position of MacArthur's statue over the roof of Eisenhower Hall to the Hudson Valley. Neither structure was there, of course; only a row of houses and various cadets, soldiers in quaint uniforms.

"Look, Sam. This painting was done in 1828 by someone named Emmeline Blood. This is the superintendent's house," she said, pointing to one of the buildings.

"Doesn't look much like it."

"Well, it's been modified a lot. And it's the last of these buildings left standing."

"Terrible artist," said Sam. "Like Grandma Moses, only not even folksy—just amateurish."

"There were a lot of them about. Here are a couple of other pictures done about the same time. They were jealous of their amateur status, it seems. This one was done in 1833."

"I see what you mean. Still uses the brush like a three-quarter-inch ratchet. But you didn't check these out of the library to do an essay on dreck. What's so special about them?"

Maggie rubbed her hands together. "Well, for one thing, these pictures take you back to the right time and place to start thinking about our ghost. He's been around for a long, long time! Out of the four informal histories of West Point in the nineteenth century, two mention a ghost directly and one makes what I think is a coy reference."

"You know a coy reference when you see one."

Maggie smiled at the prints. "Here in 1876—the year of Custer's downfall—we have John Waverley Upton's whimsical little book on the uncollege and its quaint local legends. On page eighty-six, right after the usual stories of Molly in the supe's kitchen and

whatnot, is a description of a ghost who seems to fill the bill."
Maggie read aloud:

" 'Less amusing than these mischievous apparitions, however,
is the ghost of a soldier in the uniform of a half-century ago who
haunts the area to the south of the superintendent's house. According to a tradition passed on by the former Miss Bridget Hardesty
of Highland Falls, an octogenarian who served for a time as a maid
for the family of an instructor of mathematics in the 1820s, the
spirit is that of Captain Adonijah Proctor, her last employer in
service. According to this venerable lady, whose faculties are scarcely
diminished by her advanced years, Captain Proctor and his family
occupied a dwelling on the old faculty row from about 1822 until
the twelfth of December 1830, at which time the entire edifice
was utterly destroyed by a fire. Among the dead were Captain
Proctor's wife and a young child who was a special favorite of all
who knew the family, including the cadets and Colonel Thayer.' "

Sam put his arm around Maggie's shoulders, but she was absorbed in her discovery. The book was an old, small volume with
the ribbed binding and elegant gilded facings of an earlier age
before the invention of paperbacks and perfect binding. But even
when the book was printed the story of Captain Proctor had scarcely
been remembered except by an ancient Irish servant. Sam also
knew that the old Professors' Row was represented now only by
the old and elegant quarters of the superintendent, extensively
changed over the decades. The superintendent's mansion had once
been occupied by Colonel Sylvanus Thayer, the Father of the
Military Academy, whose tenure marked the establishment of many
of West Point's continuing traditions and of pedagogical philoso-
phies that were then years in advance of their time. Thayer's statue
looks south now from the corner of the parade plain on a line parallel
to the old faculty row. Sam noted also that, if Captain Proctor's
house had been to the south of the superintendent's, it might well
have stood in the area occupied by the present 47th Division of
the old North Barracks area.

"Now, here's a map," said Maggie, "thoughtfully provided
for us by Lieutenant T. B. Brown, Third U.S. Artillery, Class of
1826. The date on it is 1830, and sure enough, here's Proctor's
house right here between professors Douglas and Mansfield. Isn't
this a work of art? He even draws in the kitchen gardens!"

"It looks to be in the right place," Sam admitted. "The Forties should be right about here, judging from the position of Thayer's house."

Maggie turned again to the book. "Here's where it gets good, darling; listen to this.

" 'Captain Proctor survived the fire, but dwelt for the years between the tragic extinction of his beloved family and the Mexican War in smaller quarters closer to Highland Falls or, as it was then called, Buttermilk Falls. At the outbreak of the war, he requested detachment from the faculty and accompanied the invading forces of the Republic. According to his friend Winfield Scott Hancock, hero of the late war who knew him whilst a cadet, Proctor died while detailed to the Sixth Regiment of Infantry at the storming of Chapultepec.

" 'The first reports of mischief appear in statements by a Sergeant Theophilus Roarke, who was serving as Sergeant of the Guard on the second of November 1835. One member of his detail, known only as Corporal O'Hanlon'—"

Sam snorted. "Who cast this drama, the Abbey Theatre? They can't all be Irish."

"Just wait," said Maggie; "we still haven't got to Mrs. Seamus O'Grady. But listen—the smell of the peat fire is all over this story.

" '. . . known only as Corporal O'Hanlon, complained that he was being spied upon and teased by a small child who, on account of the darkness and the trees, could not be descried from his post. When asked to tell what the child was doing, Corporal O'Hanlon replied in a dudgeon that the "wee urchin was laughing" at him. Sergeant Roarke appears to have delivered a tongue-lashing to his guard which included, I should speculate, a summary critique of the battles with John Barleycorn for which the corporal's race is justly famed.' "

Maggie paused to observe that Liam really needed to read this volume, which was filled with slurs on the good name of Saint Patrick's sons.

" 'But when Sergeant Roarke was summoned a second time by the excitable Corporal O'Hanlon, it was for a different kind of disturbance. The child, reported O'Hanlon, was weeping "most pitiful" off in the bushes, and somebody "had better see to 'er, th' wee thing." Corporal O'Hanlon, it seems, had had quite enough of his sergeant's evil opinion for one night and was thus reluctant to leave his post for any reason, however charitable.

31

" 'Sergeant Roarke, however, was not so cautious and, hearing sobs of a small child that appealed to the more sentimental side of his nature—a secret, we might speculate, to his soldiers!—he began, with O'Hanlon's aid, to beat the bushes in search of the miserable imp. When no sign of the waif could be detected after a most diligent search, and this despite the continuation without cease of the childish weeping, first from here and then from there, or so it seemed, O'Hanlon and then Roarke seem to have suddenly lost enthusiasm for the endeavor; both soldiers, in fact, quit O'Hanlon's post in some earnest, for which precipitate flight they received the vigorous reprimand of their officer.' "

"That, I can picture," Sam grinned: " 'By the faith, Cap'n sor, 'twas a most terrible thing, th' wee pitiful *cailin* a-sobbin' and a-carryin' on, and her nary more form than th' moonlight.' "

"Sam, last night you very clearly said that Track's cadet mentioned a child crying."

That brought Sam up short. "Yeah, he did mention something like that. Some cadets heard kids cutting up and then crying in the company study room or something."

"It fits, darling. Look, we have these two worthies crashing around in the bushes looking for a crying child who isn't there in November 1835. Remember, our unhappy friend Adonijah Proctor is *still at West Point*, drowning his sorrows down at the local bar or whatever. Now, listen. Adonijah somehow got word of the incident:

" 'Now, Captain Proctor, who had become something of a lone and tragic figure, questioned the soldiers closely about their adventure; and thereafter the crying child was reported on many occasions near that post, most especially in the late autumn. But the reports, which had some currency in the late 1830s, dwindled to a precious few by the time of the outbreak of the war with Mexico, and Captain Proctor's spirits, which had been umbrous for some years, failed altogether. His request for service in the field was rather unusual due to his advanced age, but someone seems to have interceded on his behalf to gain the assignment that was to cost his life—though, as General Hancock reports, that life may have been extinguished without sorrow, and in the hope, we might imagine, of a reunion deeply longed for.

" 'We find reference to the weeping child again in 1857, under circumstances evocative of Corporal O'Hanlon's encounter. About that time, also, we have the first account of a specter in the antique

32

uniform of years past. The apparition haunts the stretch of land once occupied by Captain Proctor's house. Tradition has it that this new figure is none other than Captain Adonijah Proctor, come to join his lost child. It is comforting to note, however, that the ghost is described by its familiars, including two former cadets with whom I served in the war and who told me much about its ways during the winter encampment of 1864, to be altogether harmless and, in some way they were at a loss to describe, benevolent.' "

Sam lay back on the rug. "When did you say this was written?"

"In 1876," Maggie replied. "The author spent most of his last years at West Point and retired to Cornwall-on-Hudson in 1887. This history of West Point was one of two books he wrote; the other was less history and more memoir. I think it may have been self-published in a very limited edition for his friends. Anyway, there don't seem to be any copies left."

Sam frowned at her in disbelief. "Jesus, Mag—where did you find out all this?"

"Dear old Mrs. Seamus O'Grady."

"You weren't kidding! So who is Mrs. Seamus O'Grady?"

"She works in the library, and apparently has since the Gettysburg campaign. She is the oldest of the old, feeblest of the feeble. Interviewing her was like boxing with an amoeba. But she had the goods, and knew all about old Adonijah."

"Holy shit, Mag, she can't be *that* old!"

"Of course not, silly man. She knew about Adonijah because I wasn't the first to ask about him."

"Aha!"

"In fact, she was asked twice. The first time was in 1947, the last in 1968. The later one was part of the hoopla generated by the ghost incident that year, and was prompted by an inquiry from some colonel, she didn't remember who—"

"That's helpful."

"Actually, that started her off on a long complaint about how stupid it was to start cataloguing books by the Library of Congress system. I had to slap her around a little to get her back on the subject."

"You're hard as woodpecker lips, Mag."

"That's me. Have you ever heard of the Ladies' Reading Club?"

"I confess no knowledge of such a body."

33

"Well, according to Mrs. O'Grady, the Ladies' Reading Club is an informal group composed of the wives of active and retired faculty, dating from the days when wives around here were women of leisure. The group met two afternoons per month, and at each session one or two ladies would present papers on some topic or other. In 1947 one member chose to present a paper on the ghost of Adonijah Proctor."

"Who wrote it?"

"Mrs. O'Grady does not recall. However, she contends that this very book was used by the old bat, whoever she was, to report the ghost; and that in 1947 it was already known as the 'ghost of the Forty-seventh Division.' "

"Eureka."

"You don't sound thrilled, my love."

"Maggie, I am not trying to find a ghost. I am trying to devise hypotheses that *eliminate* the supernatural as a cause for this nonsense."

"You mean to lie there and tell me you don't want to find a ghost?"

"Wrong, dearest lady. I am saying I shall *not* find a ghost. There is none because there are none."

"Beast! I just spent the whole damned day interviewing a senile old librarian who hasn't done anything for the last forty years but step on silverfish, and you sit there and tell me you don't care about Adonijah Proctor?"

"I *care*, I *care*. I just have no expectation of finding him on either side of the grave."

Maggie slammed the book shut, stood up, and headed for the kitchen. "I'm sure Liam will appreciate my efforts."

"I don't doubt it. Track says everything he knows is covered with cobwebs."

"Cobwebs indeed," called Maggie from the kitchen. "If there are no cobwebs in *your* mind, it's because there is no way to force entry through a closed door."

"Ooh!"

A wet Bronx cheer echoed from the kitchen.

"Mag, forgive me and fetch a glass of something."

"Fetch it yourself, Bondurant."

"Okay, Mag. Let's settle out of court. I handle the part of

this horseshit I feel comfortable with—which is to say, anything I can display on an oscilloscope."

"Philistine!"

"Liam looks at the matter on the assumption—"

"Presumption, illiterate sod."

". . . presumption that the ghost is inside the head and not outside, and you, my dearest, may take the road overgrown with weeds and shaded by tangled boughs."

Maggie came in with two beers and a bag of potato chips: " 'And that's the road to fair Elfland, where you can I maun gae.' "

"Sometimes I think that's where you came from, Mag."

"*I Married a Chick from the Fourth Dimension?*"

"I hope you don't think I have only one dimension."

"Of course not, dearest man. You have at least two."

3

*T*rack's cadet arrived promptly at 0930. He looked the part: tall, broad-shouldered, blond, and nervous, and visibly shaken. Sam had expected him to show some effect—a brief telephone call had worried Track, and Track didn't worry for nothing. It occurred to Sam that Tetzel looked like one who has seen a ghost.

Track started the session by certifying that Tetzel was not an airhead. "John has been coming to see Patti and me since he was a young yearling. He's been straight arrow all that time. I also know Stu Broadnax thinks he's a super troop, and the only reason I brought this open can of nightcrawlers to you guys is because I know a lot about this man's integrity and judgment. If John thinks there's something worth looking at, I'm convinced."

Tetzel blushed under his pallor.

Liam, draped again in a chair, stirred and looked benignly at Tetzel. "Why don't you tell us what's going on and why you think it's important enough to come into this chamber of horrors to tell us a ghost story?"

"Sir, I almost didn't say anything at all. But this thing had been on my mind for a week or so, and I told Major D.; and then after Monday night . . ."

"Let's begin at the start," said Sam.

"Yes sir. We—ah—we started hearing some rumors back in September that something was wrong, before I knew anything about the plebes and their problem. It didn't seem like much at the time, and it was a kind of a joke in the company. Back in the middle of September one of the platoon leaders—Andrea Linnell, who's in the Forty-sixth Division—told me some firsties had reported some kids running around the TV room. Not *in* the TV room, they just heard noises while they were watching TV."

"Did they see anything?" asked Sam.

"No sir. Just heard laughing and scuffling, they didn't know where from. That's what they told Andrea. We're close to the gym, and sometimes kids—younger ones, mostly, officers' children— hang around outside after they've been to the pool or something. There are some other kids, real dirtballs, that come in once in a while after taps. They might make a little noise, and we've had a couple of windows broken. Andrea asked if they sounded like they were outside or inside the division, and the firsties said they couldn't tell. The voices were faint, but didn't sound like they were from outside.

"I called Regiment and reported it. I talked to the S1; he thought I was crazy, but he had the guards check late at night for a week or so, and nothing turned up."

Liam inclined his head forward, encouraging the cadet. "Did anybody try to find the source of the noise?"

"Yes sir, every time. Andrea said they looked high and low, in the latrines, up on the stair landings. They kept hearing the noises, but they didn't find anything. Finally Andrea went over there one night while it was going on, and inspected the whole division. She said it was weird—it didn't sound right, somehow, not like real voices."

"What did she mean by that?" asked Sam.

"I asked her that, too. She said she couldn't explain it. It didn't sound like real sounds."

"Real sounds?" said Sam. "How can something not sound like sound?"

"Sir, I don't know. That's just what Miss Linnell said." Tetzel continued in this vein for some minutes, describing the company's jokes about the gremlins, and adding that, jokes or no jokes, the TV room was losing popularity as a place to gather.

"Then, about three weeks ago, the noises changed. The kids weren't laughing anymore. They were kind of whining and some- times crying—not just your everyday crying, but real screams. Then it just stopped. About that time, Andrea came up to me one day at noon formation and said she had a beanhead that needed to see me. I asked her how come, and she said I wouldn't believe her if she told me, and just to talk to the plebe. I told her to have him report right after the evening meal.

"He showed up, all right. I knew him mostly as a minor

spastic—nothing big, just minor stuff. He was a little disorganized. His squad leader was on his case a lot, and I'd heard his roommate didn't like him much, which doesn't help."

Liam wondered if the kid pissed in the sink. His first plebe roommate, a thin, asthenic boy from Pennsylvania, had been so terrified of the hazing that he had hit on this stratagem to avoid hallways and the chance of discovery by upperclassmen—until Liam had caught him in the act and told the poor kid he'd be eating his own balls on a hard roll if he did it again. Liam had pictured the haunted plebe as a clone of this historical victim.

"Was he—is he—having academic problems?" asked Liam.

"No sir, nothing big. A D in Psychology." Sam laughed. "He's not all that bright. A jock, mostly. Hockey puck. Looks like a side of beef with a face."

Liam revised his mental portrait. Such cadets never let mere hazing come between them and the urinal.

"Does he have friends in the company?" asked Track.

"Not many, sir. He's a little belligerent. Doesn't talk a lot, not many laughs. Sort of a BJ attitude."

"Excuse me," said Sam. "A what attitude?"

"BJ attitude, sir. Bold before June. Not respectful, doesn't take the Fourth Class system too seriously."

"Thank you," said Sam. "I'm culturally deprived."

"I thought they stopped using the word after I graduated," said Track.

"Why don't you tell us about the plebe's visit?" said Liam.

"Yes sir. Mister Barstow—that's the beanhead's name—came to see me that night. I was surprised, sir, at how he looked. Usually, he just looks pretty blank. Not rebellious, but sort of imperturbable. That night, though, he looked different. He was tired, and having a lot of trouble getting the words out.

"He started by telling me he had a big problem. He stalled around a lot, and I remember thinking oh, boy, he's just found out he's queer. He said he hoped it was his imagination, or maybe it would go away, but he was losing sleep and losing weight and screwing up in class. So I told him to quit beating around the bush. Then he looked at me and said, 'Sir, my room's haunted.'

"I didn't know what to say. But now he finally loosened up; I guess he'd been waiting to dump all this on somebody, and now he was on a roll. He said he'd been waking up before dawn off and on for a couple of weeks and seeing this thing standing by his bed, and he'd stare at it and it would look at him, and then there would be all these little floating lights and the thing would turn and walk through the wall. He said the room would get cold while it was happening, and he'd really feel it when the thing was gone."

"What was 'the thing'?" asked Sam.

"He said it was a man, a sort of transparent gray man in an old-fashioned uniform with a cloak and one of those baggy visored caps like they wore in the Mexican War."

"Did his roommate see it too?"

"Not at first, sir. His roommate's a guy named Eliot Carson. Pretty straight guy, helps—helped—Barstow along in his courses. At first Barstow kept waking him up, but the thing was always gone, and Carson got disgusted with him and told him to go see a shrink or a spook-chaser or whatever he wanted, but to let him sleep."

"Instead, you come to see one," said Sam. Liam ignored him.

"I guess so, sir. Anyway, one night Carson happened to wake up, and saw it too—he heard Barstow make a noise and looked around the partition into Barstow's alcove. It was there, and just like Barstow had said. That was after midnight Thursday last week. I guess when his roommate saw it too, he figured it was less embarrassing to talk.

"Well, I asked him a whole lot of questions, and he was pretty sure of himself. I asked him if he wanted to move to another room, and he said no, the thing seemed sort of friendly in a way, almost as if it was protecting him."

"From what?" asked Track. "Did it talk to him?"

"I asked him that, sir. He said he didn't know. One thing he did say, though—he had the impression there was something else there, too, something that wasn't so nice. It was just a feeling, he said, and something he saw or thought he saw once or twice out of the corner of his eye. He couldn't describe it, and talking about it seemed to agitate him. So I dismissed him and told him to send Carson to see me.

"Carson came in a few minutes later, and he was in even rougher shape. He said he'd seen the ghost twice—once the way Barstow described and once while Barstow was asleep. The second time was the night before we talked. He said he didn't know anything about 'harmless,' he just knew the thing was no joke. I asked him if Barstow had told him about it, and he said yeah, he'd mentioned it a couple of weeks before, but he—Carson—had tried to kid him out of it.

"His description was the same as Barstow's, plus he told me something Barstow apparently forgot. On the night they saw it together, they found water on the floor after the thing had left; cold water, like melted frost. That scared Carson, because he said it was something he couldn't laugh off. The water was real.

"Then Andrea grabbed me on Sunday morning and told me Barstow had taken off during the night. Carson didn't miss him because it was an optional breakfast and he thought Barstow had gone; then he found Barstow's absence card wasn't marked and his hat was still sitting in his wall locker."

"Had they seen the ghost that night?"

"No sir—at least Carson hadn't. But Carson says he's a sound sleeper, and tends to put in serious rack time on Saturday night. He also said their window was cracked again, and he slept through it, so he must have been doing some formidable z's."

"Window?" asked Sam.

"Yes sir. They have a windowpane that's always getting broken. Andrea was really pissed about it—the engineers have been over three times since August to replace it. They say it's something about temperature changes warping the frame."

Liam stirred. "You said earlier there had been vandalism. Could this have been deliberate?"

"I don't think so, sir. After all, the room is on the second floor, and it's always the same pane. I don't think your average vandal is that fussy or that accurate."

"I got a window that does that," offered Track. "Also a toilet that backs up because the pipes are too narrow and a door lock that cooperates with the key at least three out of five times, unless it's raining, in which case the odds drop to two out of five. Welcome to government housing."

"I talked with Andrea about it, and we decided that if it was bad enough to make Barstow check out, I should go to Major Broadnax."

"Has Barstow called anybody?" asked Sam. "I don't want to get you off track, but has anybody called his home? Any idea where he went?"

"No sir. The CQ said he heard somebody walk past the orderly

41

room at about oh-three-thirty, but figured it was somebody headed for the latrine. Oh, also he said he'd heard the kids—the crying and carrying on. That may be why he didn't check out who was wandering around."

"Was there any reason to believe Barstow might go AWOL before this?" asked Liam. "People don't usually just leave; they usually give some sign of it."

"Yes sir, I know what you mean. Not recently, but he talked about resigning during beast barracks—so my roommate said. That's Mort Hazlett, who was Barstow's platoon leader on beast detail. His squad leader sent him to the counseling center, hoping somebody would give him encouragement . . ."

"To leave or stay?" asked Track.

"He didn't say, sir. But he ended up staying, at least until Saturday night."

"Or Sunday morning," said Liam softly.

"You said you decided to talk to Major Broadnax," prodded Sam.

"Yes sir. But I wanted to try one more thing. I had to be cool. I finally decided to try sleeping in the room and see for myself."

"If you'd mentioned that on Sunday," said Track, "I might have given some contrary advice."

"That's what I figured, sir," said Tetzel. "Anyway, I moved over there after taps Monday night. I slept in Barstow's bunk. I didn't take much of this seriously. I figured it was a case of bad dreams or plebe nerves or some joker in the division amusing himself. It took a little while to drop off to sleep, but sometime after midnight, I guess the rack monsters got me.

"I remember having some bad dreams—I guess this was just before I woke up. Then—you know how it is, sometimes, when you're having a nightmare you start waking up and suddenly you realize it's a dream? That's what I felt. I was just barely awake enough to recognize where I was. Then I felt this kind of sense of being paralyzed. I was groggy, but I tried to move my arm and couldn't.

"Then I somehow sensed there was someone there. I was on my side, facing the wall, and I couldn't see anything, but I knew something was there, I felt it watching me. It was only then I remembered why I was there and made the connection. That really hit me like—well, I don't have a good word. I just felt like all the

42

strength was drained out of me, like I was completely helpless, and whatever it was could do anything to me."

"More about how you knew without seeing it," said Sam. "Did you hear or feel anything?"

"Just a pressure, sort of. I remember thinking about this character in *Catch-22* who was always worried about a cat sleeping on his face and suffocating him . . ."

"Hungry Joe," said Liam.

"Yes sir. It was like that—like a big, soft cat sleeping on me. My mouth was completely dry. I took a deep breath—it was hard to do—and all I could do was sort of croak or hiss. I could barely hear my own voice, but I guess it was loud enough to wake up Carson.

"The noise was also enough to release the pressure a little. I managed to roll half over on my back, and I remember seeing this sort of a gray cloud over the bed. I could barely make it out. It moved a little, then I could feel Carson shaking me awake, saying 'That was it, sir, that was it.' "

"You said Carson was 'shaking you awake,' " said Liam. "But you said before that you were already awake. Which of you was right?"

"I knocked Carson's hand away sir, and told him I was already awake. He said he'd heard me make a noise, and when he looked he saw the ghost and me sitting up on my elbow looking at it. He said he watched me for a long time, and then the thing did its disappearing act through the wall—that's what Carson said—and I just kept staring, so he came and shook me."

"You said earlier," said Sam, "that they had been seeing a gray person, not a cloud. Did you see anything like that?"

"No sir. I don't really remember much of what I saw. I can't picture it now—just sort of a pale blob. And I saw it gradually fade, I think. Barstow and Carson always saw it turn and walk through the wall with a bunch of lights around it, they said. I don't know anything about that."

"Did you notice anything else unusual?" asked Track.

"Yes sir. All of a sudden, just after Carson shook me, I felt cold. It was cold as hell in the room. I put Barstow's green girl around me . . ."

"His *what?*" said Sam

"His extra blanket, sir. We call it a 'green girl.' Carson saw

43

me and said it always got that way. He asked me to come over to the radiator. It was turned on, but you had to put your hand within a half an inch or so to feel any heat. And there was frost on the windows. That was a real kicker, sir—I checked in the morning, and it hadn't got below freezing."

"How do you know?"asked Sam.

"Sir, I looked in the newspaper before breakfast—it was only supposed to be in the high thirties."

They were silent for a while. Track glanced at Liam, who was biting his lip. The cadet seemed embarrassed.

"John," said Liam finally, "you said earlier that you were having some kind of a bad dream. Can you remember what it was about?"

There was a flicker of suspicion on Tetzel's face. "It wasn't about the ghost, sir."

"Fair enough," said Liam, "but I collect dreams. I'd like to hear about it, if it's not embarrassing."

Tetzel laughed. "It's not that kind, sir. I never have those on Mondays." Track snorted.

"I don't remember how it started, sir. I guess I drifted into it from something else. I guess I'm not much on dreams that make sense. I just recall dreaming I was at home on leave. My mother was in it, and my little sister Jeannie. Mom was mad at her about something. I don't remember what it was, but she was talking quietly, really strange—she never talks like that—and Jeannie was real quiet, scared. Then my mom dragged her into a closet in her room, where she keeps her dolls and toys and old half-eaten candy bars and whatever, and locked her in and told her she was going to stay in there until she was right again. I don't remember what she said, exactly—I think it was 'right' or something like that. Until she was 'right' again. I tried to stop her—Jeannie's terrified of the dark, and she was starting to cry and yell and pound on the door. It was about then I started to wake up."

Liam nodded and said, very softly, "How old is Jeannie?"

"She's eighteen, sir. She's in her last year of high school. In the dream, though, she was six or seven, max. That closet full of toys got filled with shoes and dresses and other junk long ago."

"Did such a thing ever happen? Was that a punishment in your family?"

"No sir! We never even got spanked or slapped or anything

44

like that. My mother would try to reason with us like we were adults. That was her philosophy, treat us like adults, then if that didn't work turn us over to Dad. That wasn't his philosophy, I can tell you, but he never locked us in the closet."

Liam leaned forward, alert now. "John, could I impose on you to take a couple of simple tests? Even if they might sound a little silly?"

"Sure, sir. Right now?"

"Right now. Sit up straight in your chair, John, and put your feet flat on the floor. That's right. Now, put your hands on the arm rests. Now look at me. Look at the tip of my finger. No, don't move your head." Liam moved his finger about six inches in front of Tetzel's eyes, which crossed slightly as he stared. "Now, without moving your head, I want you to follow my finger with your eyes. That's right, follow it right up, just like you're looking up at your eyebrows. That's right. Now, keeping your eyes up like that, without moving your eyes, slowly, carefully, lower your eyelids, no just your eyelids, keep the eyes up; a little more, that's right. Okay, relax your eyes." Tetzel blinked hard and looked inquiringly at Track, as if to ask if Liam were to be believed. Track smiled.

"One more test," said Liam. "Remember, I told you they might seem silly. Now, close your eyes. Just relax. Now imagine I've just tied a balloon to your left wrist, a big balloon filled with helium. You can feel the pressure, a slight, steady pressure, pulling up on your arm. If you relax completely, just let the balloon do its work, just relax absolutely and yield to the pull of the bal—" At this point, Tetzel's arm moved slightly, as if pulled up by the imaginary balloon. Liam bit his lip again, then continued hastily: "Yield to the pull of the balloon, that's right, just let your arm move up." When Tetzel's hand was about six inches over the arm of the chair, Liam told him to open his eyes and relax again.

"John, have you got a free period this afternoon?"

"Yes sir. I can come back at fourteen thirty or a little after."

Liam leaned forward again. "Have you ever been hypnotized?"

Tetzel smiled and looked at Track again. "No sir. Why do you want to hypnotize me?"

"I think it might help you remember more carefully what you saw and heard, even if you were only half awake at the time. I'm sure you described what you recall from Monday night as accurately

45

as you could right now, but there are details we might pick out if we take another approach."

"John," said Track, "better check the time."

Tetzel looked at his watch. "Sorry, sir—I have a class in about six minutes. Sure, I'll try whatever you want. Should I come back here?" Liam nodded, thus scheduling Sam's office, to Sam's disgust. Tetzel agreed, and left the office in a panic to reach his class.

Track spoke first. "Well, am I taking bets?"

"Very impressive," said Sam. "This will make Maggie's week."

"What do you think, Liam?"

"Like Sam," said Liam slowly, "I'm impressed."

"Is it a ghost?"

Sam and Liam both shook their heads. "No, Track," answered Liam, "the ghost is in their minds."

"But the two beanheads describe it the same way, and Tetzel saw something, for sure."

"Well," said Liam, "they all describe a gray form. But with the exception of Barstow, who saw it first, they all heard a description of it *before* they saw it. The description is not only suggestive, but also very simple to translate into autosuggestive form, because they have all seen uniforms of that sort in the museum and in the old prints on the library walls, in briefing slides on the history of West Point, in a lot of places. I don't find that too hard to explain."

"How about the cold?"

"Remember, Track, Barstow had told him about the cold, which was suggestive, plus being a supernatural cliché of sorts, like the faithful dog who senses the apparition first. Also, I think there may have been real physical factors. He had been lying on his side after facing away from the ghost, and he said it was a tremendous effort. The arm may have been clumsy for that reason. He may have cut off the circulation to one arm, and that might have been the one he used to push through the ghost; the coldness he felt could have been the sensation starting to return."

"What about not being able to move, Liam?"

"That's very natural. His mood was morbidly suggestive before going to sleep, and he was primed by the nightmare. I suspect the experience started as a waking terror—a *cauchemar*—half in and half out of dream. A state like that is very similar to a hypnoidal state, and there can be effects like the hysterical paralysis. It might have been helped along by the nerve-pinch that made his arm cold, if in fact that happened."

"Didn't any of that get to you, Liam?" asked Track.

"Yes, it did. It all did. There was something I'm still uneasy about—other than the supposition-on-supposition I've used to explain this experience—and that's something I'd rather not talk about right now."

"What about both of them seeing it?" asked Sam.

"*Folie à deux.*"

Sam resisted the temptation to tell them about Maggie's discoveries. His own reaction was much the same as Liam's, but he was less smug because of the points of similarity to the earlier stories. He was not inclined to see a ghost, but worried about a fraud on the part of the plebe, Barstow, that might have sucked in his roommate and company commander. Did Barstow ever check out the Upton book? It should show on the circulation card. Maybe he read it in the library without checking it out. How could Maggie find out?

Track left to meet a class and Sam checked out of the area to visit the laboratory across central area. He spent most of his time on one or two research projects and teaching classes and labs for the cadets who majored in his field. The lab was his pride and joy, built from nothing out of begged money, scrounged equipment, and hard-won grants. Most of the officers in the department had not the slightest idea what Sam was doing two blocks away in his rooms full of silent winking computers, mysterious machines, and racks of caged white rats. Sam couldn't have cared less.

In fact, in recent years Sam had given up trying to explain his trade to strangers, and settled for "army officer" or "college teacher." Maggie tried hard to share his love of technical arcana, but her preferences were literary and esoteric. Sam was just as happy with this arrangement. Maggie was a separate part of his life, and he preferred it that way. For one thing, it was troublesome to try to explain what he was doing to anyone who did not know the words. He could talk to Maggie about her own delights because in her presence his mind would wing to the other pole of imagination charged by the written word and the mysteries of things unguessed and full of secret promise.

At the lab, Sam called a council of war. The lab technician, a dour specialist four named Ortega, had spent most of the morning scrubbing the rat cages in anticipation of a new shipment for the plebe psychology course. The NCOIC, Sergeant Saganian, had spent the morning upstairs in the counseling center trying to make time with Colonel Lane's receptionist, and was still at it when Sam arrived. Ortega took great pleasure in fetching him down again. Captain Salinger, a first-year officer who comprised half of Sam's faculty assets and boasted a background in computer science and quantitative psychology, was extracted from the data processing lab. Sam pulled student desks around in a circle and explained to them briefly that they were going to use the tools of rational science to investigate the ghost of the 47th Division.

"No shit, sir?" said Saganian. "We're gonna find a ghost?"

"Dead wrong, Sarge. We're going to find what people think is a ghost but isn't. We have strong testimony from observers whose honesty is not lightly questioned; we're going to listen to more this afternoon. Now, a lot of this testimony seems to involve things that can be measured—particularly the sound of a child crying, a visible thing that may or may not be 'visible' in the objective sense, and—easiest of all for us to test—an unexplained change in subjective temperature. We have the assets to measure all these things, plus monitoring the physiological changes in any person in the room."

"We setting up in the barracks?" asked Saganian.

"We have to," said Sam. "When the company commander comes back this afternoon I'll arrange a place with him that can be secured when we're not there.

"Now, this is going to require four complete instrumentation packages.

"First, a video system with a remote pan-and-tilt drive and remote focus and zoom, so we can look at any location in the room without going inside, plus one of the video recorders. Also, take the infrared video out of the vision lab and mount it on the drive next to the regular camera so we can see thermal images. Rig a switch so we can record off either video.

"Second, one of the microcomputers with input-output interface and an array of thermocouples to watch the room temperature in a number of locations over time. Figure on eight channels of analog-to-digital input." He looked at Salinger. "Write a program that will average all channels over some fairly short analysis epoch—say ten seconds—and give us a hard copy for each channel separately; after each night's observation, I want a graph of temperature by channel by time. I also want an IF/THEN routine to give an audible alarm if any channel records a drop below some nominal range. Make the trigger point some named variable, and we'll insert a value when we check out the normal room temperature range on site."

"No problem, sir," said Salinger, almost rubbing his hands in glee.

"Excuse me, sir," said Saganian. "I have the feeling this is going to involve a lot of night work."

"You're getting smart, Sarge. You and Ortega can trade off for as long as the project lasts. We'll work out comp time, so you can sack out during the day.

"Now, we'll also need the biocomputer. I want to monitor heart rate and skin conductivity, and maybe respiration from an impedance pneumograph from the occupant. We'll need some shielded cable to stretch from the computer to the subject and a reliable but unobtrusive way of keeping the sensors attached. You guys work that out."

Saganian nodded; he liked this kind of project, sensing independence and the need for a little no-questions-asked ingenuity.

Salinger was puzzled. "Sir, why do we need to measure the physio off the subject? What does that have to do with the ghost?"

"Watch my lips, George: *There is no ghost*. Liam thinks the visible manifestation may be a sort of waking dream. If that's true, then the latency between the onset of strong autonomic indicators—increased heart rate, rapid change in galvanic skin response and so on—should show alarm *before* the ghost is reported visually."

"You mean he should start having a nightmare while he's still not awake and seeing the room, then report the thing after he's 'awake'?"

"That's it. I also want to see if it coincides with rhythmic sleep changes. For that reason, we also have to monitor two channels of electroencephalograph output. We'll filter one channel for alpha waves and one for beta."

Salinger and Saganian nodded.

"Okay," Sam concluded, "get together what you need, and plan on moving the equipment over on Saturday, so we won't disturb the cadets' study time banging stuff around. And get some sleep." He paused, then said to Saganian: "George, I know your cadets will try to pin you down in class about this."

Saganian grinned. "I guess they'll want to know where their computers went."

"Go easy on the subject, and ask them not to spread rumors. I promised Colonel Pretorius to keep a low profile. If we get anything worthwhile out of this nonsense, we can teach it as a case study next year."

"We don't stand a ghost of a chance of keeping it quiet, sir."

Sam laughed. "It's not so grave a problem as all that; just don't accept any interviews from *Newsweek*."

"No sweat, sir," said Saganian, "we're used to dealing with the visible spectrum."

"That's the spirit," said Sam. "Now get all that stuff together and I'll be back tomorrow morning with a whole different set of instructions." He picked up his overcoat and headed for the door. "Oh, by the way, George . . ."

"Sir?"

"We already have a title for the journal article. 'Shades of Gray.' "

4

Tetzel returned promptly after his afternoon class. To Track's surprise, he asked to talk to Liam alone for a few minutes before the meeting continued. Sam and Track left to check mail and finish the ragged ends of the day's business, and Liam shut the door.

"There was something that's been bothering me," said the cadet, "about this morning. It didn't hit me at first, but after lunch I started thinking about it, and it seemed a little strange. I'm not sure why."

"One more strange thing," said Liam, "won't matter much now, will it? Don't be shy about it."

"Well sir, I started worrying about that dream—the nightmare I had right before I woke up."

"I was interested in that, too."

"Really, sir? Well, actually it wasn't the dream most of all, but what I said this morning when I was explaining it. Remember how I said my little sister is scared of the dark?"

"Yes, I do. A pretty upsetting scene."

"Well, I don't know why I said that. Jeannie isn't afraid of anything. I don't remember her ever being scared to have the lights out, even when she was little. It's really weird, sir. I said that this morning because I seemed to think it was true, but right after I left, I started to ask myself why I ever said it. It just seemed like it was right. I'm sorry, sir . . ."

"No," said Liam, "you were right to bring it up. Dreams fool us sometimes. But sometimes, too, they make more sense than what we say or do when we're awake."

"Do we have to tell Major D.? It's kind of embarrassing; I don't want him to think I lied about something."

51

"Oh, it wasn't a lie," said Liam, "not in the way we usually mean it. But I won't mention it. Was there anything else you remember about the dream?"

"Well, there was another thing that happened just before I remember waking up, but it didn't have anything to do with the ghost . . ."

"We don't know that," said Liam. "It might be important. I have to know what your mood was when you woke up: how you felt, how alert you were."

"It was typical Tetzel dream-garbage. I have kind of dizzy dreams sometimes just before I come to—that's what Mort says, by the way, I don't 'wake up,' I 'come to.' "

"Me too," said Liam.

"This time—it was right after the closet thing with Jeannie—there was this other woman or girl saying something and hugging me from behind. It wasn't my mom and it wasn't Jeannie, somebody else."

"Anyone you recognize or remember?"

"No sir. A girl, I think, or a young woman, but she felt really huge—I mean, I had the feeling she was really big."

"Or you were really small," said Liam. "What did she say?"

"She . . . this sounds idiotic, sir . . ."

"Dreams do that."

"She kept saying a name. 'Nora.' She sounded like she was saying 'Nora who? Nora who?' "

"As if she wanted to hear a last name?"

"Yes sir. Then she was singing, kind of softly; I don't remember the song, just that she was singing, and the singing was the last thing I remember before I woke up and saw the ghost."

"Okay," said Liam. "Have you thought about the hypnosis idea?"

"Are you really going to hypnotize me?"

"Only if you want to," said Liam. "I want to help you remember more details and get some other observations from you. It's also very important in establishing what happened to know how suggestible you are."

"Do you think somebody hypnotized me, sir?" Tetzel was clearly unconvinced.

"Not quite. But sometimes we seem to do much the same thing to ourselves, and it's especially easy when the situation is suggestive and we aren't fully alert. It may well cloud how we interpret things."

"Okay, sir. But my vision wasn't clouded. Something was there, and it was there when Carson and I were both awake."

"I've heard of a lot stranger things," said Liam. "Now relax a minute while I summon the other inquisitors."

Liam found Sam and Track sitting on a bench in the hallway, being savaged by Doris Gilmer. Sam saw Liam wave and broke away with a promise to pick up the abuse later. They arranged themselves in Sam's office as in the morning session.

Liam explained that he had conducted a hypnotic suggestibility profile with Tetzel and had his agreement to do a more complete induction. The only topics to be covered were the description of the ghost and other still uncertain aspects of the incident itself.

"Now, please remember," said Liam, leaning forward and emphasizing his quiet manner with an uncharacteristically direct stare into the cadet's eyes, "hypnosis is really not what you've been led to believe. We are going to use the word *trance* to describe what is going to happen, but that's only because we don't have a better word. You are not going to go to sleep, hypnosis is not like sleep; it's more like a very, very alert state, but you will be alert to a much narrower range of things than you normally are. How deep a trance you enter is entirely your own decision. You should also understand that I do not in any way control your responses. It's not like in the movies: you aren't 'in my power.' You will just feel very, very relaxed and alert. If we want to end the trance state, I will just say 'One, two, three, four, five,' just like that, 'One, two, three, four, five,' and I will touch you on the shoulder just like this, and you will come out of the trance state, no matter how deeply you may have chosen to go into your trance state."

Track noted with fascination that as Liam delivered these commonplace instructions, the tone and cadence of his voice gradually changed, the form of his sentences became oddly repetitive and rhythmic. He realized that Liam was already beginning the cadet's induction. Liam began a new line of patter that spoke of a floating sensation, aided by a breathing exercise; Track guessed that the deep breathing was intended to induce a very slight hyperventilation, which would in turn lead to the beginnings of a "floating" sensation the cadet would interpret as the onset of a trance. Using a short series of descriptive images, Liam led the cadet into his trance—to Track and Sam the word seemed very appropriate after all—and finally Tetzel's eyelids closed and he sat immobile in the chair, his head swaying very slightly as he breathed.

"John, how do you feel?" Liam sat back in his chair, too; Track sensed a very subtle tension on his face that belied the soothing voice.

"Fine, sir. Very relaxed."

"All right, John, we're going to talk about the ghost again. I want you to remember everything that happened as clearly as you can."

"Yes sir."

"Now, you will find that it is as if your consciousness is split. One part of you can savor the calmness, the sensation of physical detachment; you won't have to listen very carefully to what I am saying to you because the other part of your consciousness will hear me very clearly. Do you understand?"

Tetzel took a slow breath and said, rather indistinctly, "Yes sir. I'll hear you."

"Sometimes, John, we want the subject to forget what happens during the trance. In this case, I want you to remember everything I say and you say."

"Yes sir."

"John, I also want to tell you that your consciousness will hear only me when I talk to you until I ask you to do otherwise. You will hear me only when I talk to you; you will not hear me when I talk to Colonel Bondurant and Major Dortmunder. Do you understand?"

"Yes sir."

Liam turned to Sam and Track. "Okay. He's somewhere in the Crab Nebula. He's a very strongly suggestible subject, which I expected him to be. Now, I'm going to ask him some questions about things that trouble me, and after we've finished, I'll cue him to attend to your concerns, if you have them." They agreed.

"Okay John. Do you still hear me?"

Tetzel's lips opened with a faint smacking noise. "Yes sir." His words were quiet and faintly slurred. Liam frowned.

"Now, John, I want you to remember what you saw on the night you slept in Barstow's room. Imagine yourself back there. Your ability to remember details will be very much better than it normally is, and you will be able to picture the things that happened with great clarity. What time is it, John?"

"I don't know, sir."

"Are you asleep?"

"No sir."

"Have you been awake long?"

"No sir." He was silent for a long moment. "I am just waking up."

"Have you been dreaming?"

"No sir."

The three officers looked at each other. "Have you dreamed at all tonight?"

"No sir."

"Is it dark in the room?"

"No sir. It's light."

"Are the lights on?"

"No. There is a light outside, shining in through the window."

"Which window?"

"The window opposite the bed."

"Facing the MacArthur Wing?"

"Yes. But there is more light. I can see it as I wake up. I don't know what it is."

"Describe it."

"It's gray, like bright starlight, and it moves a little."

"How does it move?"

"I see the shadows shift, like someone moving a light."

"Is someone moving a light?"

"I don't think so."

"Are the edges of the shadows sharp?"

Tetzel squinted as if peering closely through his closed eyes. "No. The shadows are fuzzy. They only move a little."

"Which way are you looking?"

"Toward the window."

"Are you lying on your side?"

"No, I'm on my back. My head is facing to the side."

"Look up."

Tetzel actually turned his head slightly. They all watched him intently as he looked up to see what they presumed would be the ghost. They saw the skin tighten across the cadet's face and his eyes open slightly; his emotions were hard to judge. There was fear for just a moment, a fear that washed over them all, more compelling fear than this morning when he had recited his simple narrative. But that disappeared and was replaced by something else. Sam thought it was a blank, passive expression of wonder. Track saw the face of a pilgrim at Lourdes. Liam wasn't certain what he saw, but it made him far more uneasy than the momentary terror had. There was something in the cadet's expression that bespoke total vulnerability, dangerous vulnerability.

"What do you see, John?"

"He's there." His voice was flat, matter-of-fact.

"Who's there?"

"The man Barstow saw."

"Is it a man, John?"

"No."

"What is it?"

"I don't know."

"What does he look like?"

"A gray man."

"What does he look like, John?"

"He's gray. He's the light that flickers. A pale light. A sad light."

"A sad light?"

"So far away, like cold stars. Sad to be so far away."

"But he's standing over you?"

"Yes. He's bending over my bed."

"Then why is he far away?"

"I don't know. He's there and far away."

"What is like cold stars?"

"His eyes."

"What about the rest of his face? Can you see the rest of his face?"

"Yes. No. Not clearly. It's dark around the eyes, like he's tired."

"But the eyes are like stars."

"Just the tiny points, like faraway reflections."

"Are they reflections, or lights themselves?"

"They're reflections of the light of heaven."

Startled, Sam and Track looked at Liam, who shrugged, then back at the cadet.

"What do you mean, John?"

But Tetzel didn't answer. The corners of his mouth turned down slightly and his jaw tensed. Suddenly his eyes filled with tears; the eyelids opened and he stared through Liam at something beyond. The tears trickled down his face in a stream. Track and Sam were slightly behind him and could not see his face from the full front; Liam could, and he saw vast and overwhelming grief and unforgiving torment. If these eyes reflected a light, he thought, it wasn't the light of heaven.

"Why are you sad, John?"

His voice trembled. "I don't know."

"What do you see, John?"

"She's afraid."

"Who's afraid, John?"

"She's afraid! She's afraid!" He pressed his arms close to his sides and clenched his fists.

They saw Liam's face go taut with urgency. *"Listen, John. One, two, three, four, five!"* He touched Tetzel on the shoulder. Tetzel did not respond. His face was now pale and completely expressionless. As during the induction, his head swayed slightly with his breathing.

Liam leaned forward and put his hand on Tetzel's shoulder. "Listen to me. You will come out of the trance when I count to five. *One, two three, four, five!*" Liam clapped his hands in front of the cadet's face. There was no sign of a change. Liam sat back and chewed his lip. Track and Sam exchanged uneasy looks.

"Listen, John," Liam began again. But then Tetzel took a sharp breath and mumbled a few words; the three officers leaned forward in unison to listen.

"Torch one two," said Tetzel.

"What, John?" Liam's lips parted slightly, the first sign of real alarm Track had seen in the quiet man's demeanor.

"Torch one two!" said Tetzel, more urgently, *"Torch one two, torch one two!"* His voice was loud now, alarmed; then he sighed and seemed to shake his head.

Liam began again, trying to keep tension out of his voice. "John, I want you to—"

Track jumped as if prodded with a spike. Tetzel's eyes had opened so abruptly the event seemed to be accompanied by an almost audible click, a frightening, mechanical suddenness. He turned his head and looked directly at Liam. There was no more trance. Tetzel was fully alert. There was a look in the cadet's eyes that only Liam could see, and one he would never forget.

Tetzel's arm came up abruptly, as if crudely animated, and he placed it with a rapid, clumsy movement on Liam's shoulder. Then he smiled, a smile made terrible by the unwavering intensity of his gaze, and spoke:

"It's you, buddy. The old duty concept." Sam and Track both started. The voice was strong, certain, not trancelike and, most of all, not Tetzel's. Liam jerked back into his seat, away from the cadet, but Tetzel's grip tightened and his fingers wrapped themselves around Liam's cloth shoulderboards and the stitching of the shoulder loop began to give way. *"Remember?"* Tetzel said in the same voice. *"I asked you then. The old duty concept."*

Liam lunged forward and pushed Tetzel back into his chair, slapped a shoulder with his fist and whispered: *"One, two, three, four, five. Wake up!"* But Tetzel went limp, releasing Liam's shirt, and started to breath heavily; his eyes rolled up under their lids, and he swayed and started to fall over the chair arm.

"Jesus, Liam!" said Track. *"He's hyperventilating!"*

"I know it, God damn it! Help me lay him down on the floor! *One, two, three, four, five!"*

Then Tetzel stopped gasping for air, and his eyes closed. They replaced him in the chair, and gradually he seemed to calm down.

"John," said Liam, "can you hear me?"

"Yes sir." Tetzel's trance voice was back.

"John, are you afraid?"

"No sir."

"Are you alone?"

"Yes sir."

"Do you want to wake up?"

"Yes sir."

"Do you remember how we decided to wake up?"

"Yes sir." Sam noticed that Tetzel's eyes were filling with tears.

"Listen, John: When you wake up, you will remember nothing about what you saw or heard during the trance. Do you understand?"

"Yes sir." Tears streamed down Tetzel's face.

Liam hesitated. "Is she still afraid?"

"She's gone."

"John, one two three four five. Wake up." Tetzel opened his eyes and turned his head back and forth as if his neck were stiff. "How'd I do, sir?"

"You did just fine, John. What do you remember?"

"Everything, sir. Just like you told me."

But Track smelled a rat. Tetzel was cheerful and unaffected; none of the terror and awe and torment that had passed through the man were visible now.

"John," said Liam, "we have a few questions, just to see how well your recollections match what we saw."

"Shoot, sir."

"Why did you come out of the trance?"

Tetzel looked doubtfully at Liam. "You tapped me on the shoulder and counted to five, just like you told me."

"Why did I bring you out of the trance?"

"I don't know, sir."

"What were we talking about?"

"The ghost, sir. You asked me what the face looked like."

"And what did you say?"

"I didn't say anything, sir. You brought me out of it."

"John, do you remember anything about 'reflections of the light of heaven'?"

"Sir?"

" 'Reflections of the light of heaven.' Do you remember anything about it?"

"No sir."

Sam said, "What about . . ." But Liam stopped him with a gesture.

"John, listen. I brought you out because you were having an intense emotional response. You don't remember any of it?"

Tetzel looked at Liam with suspicion, and with something else Liam could not quite decipher. "No sir. I don't remember anything about that."

"John, touch your face."

Tetzel looked at Liam as if he had asked him to stick out his tongue. "Sir?"

"Touch your face, your cheeks."

He did, and he felt the moisture. He looked at his fingers, then wiped his face again. He blushed. "What's all this, sir?"

59

"Tears, John. Don't you remember anything about why they got there?"

"No sir. I just remember you asking me to describe the ghost."

"Okay, John. Now listen: You don't remember all that happened during your experience. This happens. A part of us sometimes splits things away from our normal stream of consciousness and keeps us from confronting them, particularly if they're very unpleasant or sad or frightening."

"Like repression, sir?"

Liam grinned. "You remember Plebe Psych, I see. Yes, one word we use is *repression*, but I prefer *dissociation* when I try to explain it. You have the right idea. Don't stew about it. I think we all have these little hang-ups, and usually they're better left alone, which is why I brought you out."

"I understand, sir."

"If you do, John, you're the only one in the world who does."

"All right," said Track, "what was all that? He really had me going."

"Me too," said Liam. "I never saw a response like that. Never. He was very suggestible, as the eye-roll and arm levitation tests indicated. The quickness of the induction, the slurred voice—you don't see them too often."

"How accurate were his descriptions?" asked Sam. "Was he reporting what he saw?"

"He's reporting what he thinks he saw, and it affected him profoundly. Some of it may be tied to dissociated childhood experiences. Some of it may be—I don't know. I have to think."

"Shit fire," said Track, "I just about jumped out of my skin when he grabbed you and talked in that damn voice! What was that?"

"Are we dealing with a multiple personality?" asked Sam. "I seem to recall that's classified under dissociation disorders."

"It's also very rare," said Liam. "I've never seen one."

"Maybe you have now."

"I just don't know. I doubt it. Cadets are screened before admission. But the dream, the morbid theme of torturing a child, I don't know. Sometimes multiple personality—I say sometimes, but there are so few valid case studies it's hard to point to trends—sometimes it seems to happen with a history of very repressive family life. But I don't see much lack of personal or social adjustment with Tetzel."

"Damn right," said Track. "He's no fruitcake."

"But who the hell is that woman?" Sam persisted. "What was that 'torch' business? Whatever it was, it had his undivided attention. And 'duty concept'?"

"I don't know," said Liam. "I couldn't understand him."

"Sounded like a cadetism," said Track. "They hear a lot about it here, to understate the matter."

"Why did he go for you?" said Sam, intent on Liam's reactions. "He moved like a zombie. Have you ever seen that before?"

"How should I know? No, I haven't seen that before. But I was the operator. I was in front of him, so he grabbed me. It was like a waking dream." Liam grabbed the arms of his chair to conceal the shaking of his hands. "Anyway, I don't think any of that was coherent."

"Coherent my rosy red ass," said Track. "He knew what he was saying."

"Gentlemen," said Sam, "this is a fascinating test of wits and Freudian clues, but it is also fifteen minutes past close of business, and I hear the duty officer locking doors. I propose we continue elsewhere, less formally, and away from walls with ears."

Track looked at his watch. "I got an idea. Let me call Patti and I'll tell her I'll pick up pizzas on the way home. You can meet us at our place at Stony."

"I'll get Maggie," said Sam.

"I'll bring a pillow," said Liam.

"What?" said Maggie. "Out to dinner? After I've been working for hours in the kitchen creating a gourmet meal? Leave a perfectly good home to go eat pizza?"

"Well," said Sam, lamely, "it was a—"

"Great! I'll get my coat!"

Track and Patti lived in majors' quarters on the top of a mountain overlooking West Point, a housing area aptly named Stony Lonesome. It was a ghetto for young families and drivers with

61

nerves of steel who made their daily trip through a gauntlet of small children darting heedlessly out of driveways on tricycles. Stony Lonesome was a disease pool for measles, chicken pox and croup, a commodity exchange for pathogens where days out of school were bought and traded like soybeans and beef futures. The small lawns were trampled into desert waste by the troops of children who ran wild as wolves among the rocks and red brick government duplexes. A few brave families had planted small gardens, but Stony Lonesome was built atop what Track claimed was the world's largest homogeneous chunk of granite, and most of the plantings grew awry in its thinnest of soil, looking desperate as bonsai.

At Track and Patti's, one sat on the floor. Sitting on the furniture involved lifting and hauling stacks of newspapers, toys, and books. Sam and Maggie were ambushed by two children as they came in the door—a surprise, since the lesser Dortmunders were supposed to be visiting next door. The younger one, a disheveled girl of eight named Dana, explained in a rush of incoherence that she had thrown up in the neighbor's family room and that, when they saw Track's car pulling in, the neighbors decided Dana would be better off at home. The older was a surly, loutish boy of twelve, physically a clone of Track. His most expressive utterance this evening was a grunt of indifference. Maggie liked him; he was his own person. But Dana was her favorite.

Sam was Dana's special friend. "Sam, come and see Raymond!"

Sam grinned, disarmed. "How's Raymond doing these days?"

"Come and see him—I just cleaned his cage. I gave him a new toilet paper tube, and he sleeps in it!"

"Dana," said Patti, "why don't you go get Raymond for Colonel Bondurant?" Aside to Sam: "You *don't* want to see her room. . . . OSHA would close us down if they saw it." But Dana was already pounding up the steps. She was wearing sneakers, but she had a way of making them sound like wooden clogs; the neighbors across the firewall counted out the days of their lives by Dana's trips up and down the stairs.

While Dana was on this errand, the men recounted the day's excitement. Maggie watched Liam's face as Track described Tetzel's hypnosis. Track showered Liam with praise for his skill and sensitivity; Liam was obviously uncomfortable, and tried to change the subject. Sam was very quiet, directing his attention to the carpet and occasionally making a neutral comment. She knew he was jealous, and loved it; she pressed Liam for details and ignored Sam until she decided—with great reluctance—that he had suffered enough. Without pausing in her attentions to Liam, she slipped her hand to Sam's knee and squeezed.

"Hey, watch that stuff, Maggie," Track said very seriously. "Sam's a well-known *prev*ert."

"Don't I wish."

Patti extracted two bottles of wine—one red and one white—from the kitchen, and they were busy pouring and resetting onto cushions when Dana reappeared with Raymond. Raymond was a white rat of venerable age, a veteran of the cadet conditioning laboratory. Sam had taken Dana to the vivarium a year ago and let her choose one of the identical red-eyed desperadoes who pressed their quivering pink noses against the cage wires and, one by one, stood inspection. Sam vetoed some candidates after reading the cadets' comments on their cage cards: "Dumb"; "Eats human flesh"; "Goes for the throat." They narrowed the field down to three identical Sprague-Dawley males. Dana held each one and squealed as it struggled or clawed or looked up at her with trusting myopic eyes of watery carmine. The last promptly disgraced itself on her dress and so lost its last chance for life (for, although Sam delicately avoided the subject, the unchosen rats would all be sacrificed after the last cadet lab was over). The final choice was promptly named Raymond, and immediately became the befuddled recipient of more love than a rat can fairly expect in its short, dull life.

Sam took Raymond from the girl's hands and looked into the gentle animal's shiny eyes. He noticed that they were a little pale and milky. Oh shit, he mused, the sorry rat's getting old. I won't envy Track when the little bastard finally kicks up his heels and dies. Then Sam noticed a soft lump behind Raymond's left foreleg. A tumor. It'll get larger, sure as hell. It's probably benign and encapsulated, he thought, but it's going to worry Dana.

"Dana," he said, "have you seen this bulging place on Raymond's side?"

"Yeah," she replied; "Buddy says it's cancer. I told him he was full of shit."

"Dana!"

"Well, he is, Mommy. Isn't he, Sam?"

63

"He sure is, Dana. I don't think it's cancer. It's probably just a simple tumor—rats get them pretty often. Especially these tame white ones."

"Does he hurt?"

"Does he look like he hurts?" The rat sat in Sam's hands twitching its nose contentedly.

Dana smiled. "He looks just fine. How long is he going to live, Sam? Is he old?"

"Well, these are special rats. They're called Sprague-Dawleys, and they don't live as long as the kind you find in a junkyard. Maybe a year or so in a steel cage. But Raymond lives in a nice warm house with wood chips and the best food . . ."

"He eats Milky Ways," said Patti.

"Yeah," added Track. "They're hell on his complexion."

"Oh, Daddy! Rats don't have complexions!"

"I'd go easy on the Milky Ways anyway," said Sam, horrified.

"Let me hold him," said Maggie. In her hand the rat squirmed ineffectually, its naked tail swinging in slow circles. She held it like an infant and it stared up at her with unfocused adoring eyes. "Oh, Sam—he's precious." She grinned ruefully at Patti. "After two years with Sam, even a rat feels cuddly."

"My first impulse," said Patti, "was to shoot him out of his boots. That tail! Go on, Dana, take Raymond back to his lovely tube. Maggie, the damned thing loves to sleep in a toilet paper tube."

"Makes you appreciate the simple pleasures of life," Sam observed.

"Forget the simple pleasures," said Maggie. "I want to hear about the ghost."

2

Maggie

Vain is man's ill-speaking and blame of women,
The twanging of an idle bowstring.

—Euripides

5

*O*kay Liam," said Maggie, "why don't you believe in ghosts?"
"Who says I don't?" Liam replied, settling in again at
the foot of Track's sofa. The wine had been passed around for a
little more than an hour while Sam, Track and—reluctantly—Liam
described the interviews with Tetzel and the hypnotic induction,
and Maggie revealed the results of her research on Adonijah Proctor.

Maggie was not to be deflected. "You give every sign of treat-
ing Adonijah with as much disdain as Sam does. You three sphynxes
must have stared that poor cadet into gelatin."

"Oh, don't misunderstand," said Liam. "I think there *is* a
ghost. I just think it originates in some very powerful subjective
forces in the psyche, not some objective twilit world of the un-
dead."

Maggie's eyelids lowered slightly as she looked at Liam. "Don't
patronize me, FitzDonnell."

"I wouldn't dare," said Liam. "I like my eyeballs in their
sockets. Are you a believer?"

"I don't dismiss things just because they don't fit in my neat
little world of loose nuts and bolts."

Liam smiled his most infuriating smile. "Are you a reader of
supernatural tales, Maggie?"

"Of course. I sometimes write them." Track recognized her
wintry smile and hoped the innocent were out of shrapnel range.

"Who's your favorite?"

"H. P. Lovecraft. Yog-Sothoth was my girlhood hero. I still
remember reading 'The Rats in the Walls' when I was thirteen."

Patti slurped her wine. "Rats in walls? Lovecraft? Sounds like
our quarters at Leavenworth and those awful sex therapy books
Sam used to have."

Liam ignored her. "Lovecraft was a writer of decadent horror stories, a strange reclusive New Englander who spun a horrible private mythology of otherworldly beings. There are strange smells and bestial noises and unspeakable rites howled out on mountaintops in rings of standing stones, backward villages with inhabitants made simpleminded and webfooted by inbreeding, sorcerers and theriomorphic first cousins—"

"Therio what?" asked Patti.

"In the form of a beast," said Maggie. "Like Track at happy hour."

"Anyway," said Liam, "his stories are not for those of uncertain stomach—like Track *after* happy hour . . ."

"Christ on an ever-lovin' crutch," said Track. "I was just *listening* to all this bullshit—when did it get to be open season on *me*?"

"Yeah," said Maggie, refilling her glass, "give Yog a break."

"Why," Liam persisted, "do you read that stuff? Does it make you feel good? Do you laugh? Cry?"

"You tell us," said Maggie.

"Because you aren't satisfied with shopping malls."

"Patti is," said Track. "She hikes to Paramus every weekend."

"Nonsense," Patti retorted. "It takes me all weekend to clean up after you and the kids."

"Shopping malls?" said Maggie.

"Shopping malls," said Liam. "No cathedrals, just shopping malls. No mythology, no gods in the storm clouds, just a credit card and the worship of a plastic Mammon."

"A replacement for a soul that can still wonder," said Maggie.

"I never thought of you as religious, Liam."

"I'm not, Sam. My grandfather was a Catholic who ran a dry-goods store in South Carolina in a town full of Protestants who thought nuns shaved their heads. He had to renounce the faith and join the Masons to get any business. My father was an indifferent high Episcopalian, what we used to call 'bells and smells.' But he used to joke about being in a church based, as he said, not on faith, not on mercy, nor hope nor love, but only the horny impulses of Henry the Eighth. Why sweat it, he figured, if you can change back and forth to make a buck. And his son, two generations from the Knights of Columbus, is an agnostic."

"And not happy," said Maggie.

"Bullshit," said Track. "You're no agnostic. You're a pagan. You worship in the high places. Lord knows what else you do on those long jogs on the Redoubt Trail."

"*I* know what he does," said Maggie. "He stands in the middle of a ring of stones and howls out incantations from the dreaded *Necronomicon* of the mad Arab Abdul Alhazred."

"What in the hell are you talking about," asked Sam, furious at being left out.

"You had to be there," said Maggie. Patti laughed indelicately.

"I still don't get it," Patti said. "What does all this have to do with the ghost?"

Liam sighed. "The part of us that feels happy in the shopping mall is only part of our innate psychological equipment. There is another part, usually back in the shadows. It's the part we could go to church to nurture. We feel it as a need to believe in something transcendent and ultimately unknowable. Not the church here and now, with trendy sermons and refreshments and Sunday school for the kids. I mean the church where the bread becomes the flesh of Christ, the wine—not grape juice—becomes His blood. The church was literally the house of God, a God whose path is dark on the wings of the storm. A living God, and we ate him for Sunday brunch—think about it—and He made His home in our living souls as an unsolvable mystery whose face was hidden by the wings of seraphs and didn't resemble George Burns. And when we deny it exists—it mutters and threatens."

"Then it's a religious need?" asked Patti.

Liam smiled. "No, a psychological one. You—"

"I heard that patient sigh," said Maggie. "You're saying, then, that we need ghost stories because the poor psyche hasn't got dragons and trolls and gods to look up to or down on or whatever and MasterCard can't buy everything. How trite can you get? I have a hard enough time putting up with Sam's insufferable punditry without hearing it from you. I had to wade through Jung and Fraser and Bettelheim to sit here and get talked down to by the Emerald Isle fraud? 'Oh Maggie, you poor benighted bimbo, how sorry I am to have to chew your food for you.' "

"Oh, Maggie," said Sam.

Liam looked at her cautiously. "I stand corrected."

"You don't mean it," she said, "but I love hearing you say it."

Liam looked at her without expression for a moment, then

69

reached for the bottle of wine, which still had a glassful sloshing in the bottom; Maggie held out her glass and Liam poured slowly until it was half full, then poured some into his own. They touched them together with a sound as soft as a wind chime. "You're right, Maggie. You had at least as much to say as I did. I'm sorry."

She took a dainty sip. "No you're not. But you're embarrassed. That's much more satisfying."

Maggie huddled in the front seat with her head against the side window as Sam drove down from Stony Lonesome to their Lee Road quarters. She was thinking about Liam and how utterly unlike Sam he was, yet in some inscrutable way so like him. Like Track, she was a little afraid of him.

It was different with Sam. There were parts of his character over which her wiles had absolutely no influence. They lay at the core of his being, and her most subtle attempts to penetrate were like efforts to camouflage a tank by rubbing vanishing cream into the armor plate. At the center, his dark secret soul was beyond her, and she was convinced it was the part of Sam—perhaps the *only* part—worth having.

What was Liam about? Sam was silent in Liam's presence. No one else had that effect on him. She knew Sam well enough to dismiss any speculation that Sam was overwhelmed. Sam's mind traveled different paths, but he was at least Liam's equal—and Sam was quicker and wielded an instant wit where Liam's humor was quieter and far more philosophical. Sam always seemed to be studying Liam when the "Emerald Isle fraud" was talking (Sam never talked about his trade—he held forth), and Maggie wondered now what he was trying to discover.

"I'm sorry I went for Liam's throat," she said to the chilly glass of the side window. She could see the reflection of Sam's face illuminated by the green glow of the dashboard lights.

"We all deserved it. We get wrapped up in our own erudition so often: 'inebriated by the exuberance of our own verbosity.' "

"You stole that," she said to the reflection, "from Benjamin Disraeli."

"I don't blame you, Maggie. Liam can never seem to remember until it's too late that you're nobody's foil."

"Not Liam's, anyway. I hope."

"You scored on Liam. He'll never forget it."

"That's what I'm afraid of," she laughed. "And please try to find a better way to put it."

"No," said Sam, seriously now, "you just struck Liam for the first time as a force to be reckoned with. You didn't recognize the look on his face. It doesn't appear there very often."

Sam turned into the driveway of their quarters. The sudden shift of direction dislodged Maggie from her position propped against the door, and she clutched suddenly at the dashboard. She felt lightheaded and sleepy from the wine. It was not her custom to drink steadily, but the evening had been a rare one. Shattering the prim façade she maintained for the sake of Sam's standing in the department contributed a feeling of release to her mood; another part of it was a lingering elation at recollection of the look on Liam's face during his flaying. She had become silly and kissed Track when they left; Patti had giggled (she was even farther gone than Maggie), and Sam had guided her out with a tenderness he usually didn't display in public. All in all, she thought, a good night. All it takes is a few chains clanking in the attic, and even Sam loosens up.

He parked and circled around the car to open her door. They stood together and looked out over the Hudson River. The moon was down. In the dark a barge was being moved down the channel by Constitution Island and the running lights of its tug reflected off the water in red and white icicle traces. Maggie breathed out slowly and enjoyed the foggy plumes in the air, turning cold now after the October warm spell that always seemed to precede the glacial end of fall. She enjoyed this part of the year most. Sam took her on long weekend drives, up into the Catskills, across the river into Connecticut and up to New Hampshire or up the coast to Cape Cod (which she hated in the summer out of sheer misanthropy and loved off-season because nobody in his right mind would disturb them). If time was short, they would ride north and west to Otterkill or go for walks in Black Rock Forest; if the whole weekend was before them Sam was likely to drive down country roads that seemed chosen at random, then turn with a sudden spontaneity into some rustic inn (which always seemed to have room for them). They would kick through piles of leaves, eat a long wine-washed dinner by a fireplace, and spend the better part of a Saturday night in

71

joyful, sodden carnality. The wonder of it all was only a little diminished by her accidental discovery that they were not spontaneous flights of fancy; the phony bastard memorized the routes beforehand and always called ahead for reservations. That, she admitted to herself, was Sam in a nutshell.

She looked up at him. He was watching the tug and barge pass under the light on Constitution Island. "Sam?"

"You cold?"

"You know better than that, soldier."

"Let's go in. It's after midnight."

"Let's not," she said. "This may be the last night we can make it to Lee Gate without a team of huskies." Sam took her hand and they cut through the neighbors' yards to the sidewalk along Lee Road. By this time of the night the streetlights were turned off. A light wind had come down from the north, through the gap between Storm King Mountain and Breakneck, and the lights of Newburgh sparkled and danced through the trees. Maggie's wine high was gone now, and the chill revived her. They were alone on Lee Road; no joggers or walkers of dogs would be out to share the world with them. By and large Maggie hated West Point, chafed under the restraint and insularity, hated herself for being an unemployed army wife. But tonight she felt just a fleeting elusive hint of what Sam, Liam, and Track felt for the place. To her, it might be only a terrible gray monastery full of innocent youth playing at warrior-monk, a lonesome pile of Gothic granite rubble in a stony wilderness, but to others it was something far more beautiful. It had a mysterious force of attraction that made ambitious and capable men like Sam and Liam abandon the lives they could have had elsewhere in order to live out the years here.

Then the mood was broken as a squat, dark shape broke from the bushes beside the road and darted into a storm drain. She squealed and grabbed Sam around the waist; he lost his balance and fell heavily on the grass beside the pavement, his gold-braided service cap flying into the street and rolling into the gutter. Maggie fell on top of him and he wrapped his arms around her and she felt him laughing silently. She lay on top of him trying to get her breath back. Her heart was thudding desperately; she wondered in a panic if her bladder had mutinied. Then she recovered herself and pounded on Sam's shoulders. "What the hell are you laughing about?"

"Well, this is a funny place to roll around. There's frost on the grass."

"What *was* it?"

"A raccoon." He kissed her hard; their teeth grated.

She pulled herself away indignantly. "What did you do? Wire ahead? Have it catered?"

"What the hell are you talking about?"

"Never mind. Kiss me again." He did, and then she rolled on her back, heedless of the cold damp grass on her camel's-hair overcoat, and clung desperately to Sam as he teased her with his tongue and breathed the scent of her hair which was now decorated with wet leaves.

"This is scary," he said after their breath came back. "I just had the most terrible feeling."

"What 'terrible feeling,' Bondurant?"

"That I'd wake up in the morning half frozen inside a ring of toadstools and find you gone, my beautiful lady without mercy."

"Leave you here and give up a crack at your pension plan?" she said. "Not a chance."

Then she stiffened; Sam's ears were worthless after the years with tanks, but Maggie heard the jogger and tried to silence Sam. It was too late. In a few footfalls he was passing them. Sam kept his head down and closed his eyes. As the sound of the shoes on pavement faded, they heard the solitary runner call back: "You ought to try that inside!"

Sam clambered to his knees. "Shit. Who in his right mind would go running after midnight?"

"Who in his right mind would roll around in the wet cold grass with his wife beside a public thoroughfare?"

"Somebody who's horny enough to lay a minefield. Let's go home."

"Coward."

"Come on, Maggie. The son of a bitch'll run as far as Lee Gate, then turn around and come back. Let's get out of here."

"Bondurant, if you really had balls you'd make love to me right here in the dews and damps."

"Dews and damps, my ass! Those are ice crystals. And the MP sedan cruises along here after the lamps go out."

"You heard me, Bondurant."

"You win, Maggie. I'll write you a memo for record tomorrow.

73

Sam Bondurant hasn't got balls. Now let's get up and go back to our warm quarters and reopen the bidding."

"Now or never, Sam."

"Maggie, you're batshit out of your mind! How much wine did you drink?"

"Keep a civil tongue, knave. *I* don't need strong drink to get *my* courage up."

"It's not a question of courage, you maniac, it's a question of sweet reason . . ."

The jogger passed them again, returning from Lee Gate. "Stop whispering," he panted. "I can't hear you."

Maggie laughed and then, when she was quite recovered, offered Sam her gloved hands and primly allowed herself to be pulled upright. He found his hat next to the raccoon's storm drain and tried to brush the dirt and fragments of yellow grass from his overcoat and the knees of his green uniform trousers; Maggie picked leaves from her hair. On the ground beneath him, her hair in disarray, she had been a faerie-woman, *la belle dame sans merci*. Now she was Maggie again, and Sam loved her more than she would ever know in her life, because telling her was impossible for Sam. They walked back to their quarters in silence, the faint clouds of their warm breath mingling in the crystal air of the season's first cold, clear night, while Orion and Cassiopeia and the Great Bear danced, heel and toe, in the immense dark vault of the sky.

Maggie was so tired that she could barely bring herself to undress and turn back the sheets. When Sam came out of the shower, she was curled up on the bedspread in naked, innocent oblivion. He covered her with an extra blanket and turned out the light.

About the time Sam and Maggie were rolling in pagan abandon in the grass, John Tetzel woke up in a cold sweat. He sat up in the darkness and looked at the alarm clock, then lay back again and stared at the shadows the lights outside the windows had stretched across his desk. His roommate was snoring softly, and it was a joyful sound, a sound that said it isn't true, it was just a nightmare, none of it ever happened and there was the sound of Mort Hazlett's snores to prove it.

After two nights of dreams, he had come to dread lights out. Each night he told himself they wouldn't come. Each night they did. When he was ten and sometimes had nightmares, he would play a game. After he had been in bed for a while and knew sleep would come, he would clear his mind and wait for the first new thought to enter, at random, into his stream of consciousness. Then he would tell himself that it was that thought that was on his mind, and if he dreamed it would be about that and not something darker. Sometimes it worked, but not always. It was a pleasant idea and a comfortable superstition. But now it was no good. The dream came anyway.

It came in strange ways, sometimes of itself and sometimes out of other, stranger dreams. And it was never quite the same. The first time, it had been his mother locking Jeannie in the closet. Now, more frequently, it was another woman, a slender, beautiful, severe woman, who scolded Jeannie in a quiet, certain voice that was somehow more terrible than shouts or anger might have been. She locked Jeannie in with a curious large black key, and his sister's shouts were muffled behind the door as if the darkness were devouring even the sound of her. Most terrible was the soft, earnest sound of the woman's voice, the frightening distance between the words and her manner of saying them.

And tonight, as only rarely before, he heard another voice— a girl's voice, somewhere behind him. The voice was not his mother's voice. He lay there in the dark barracks room breathing slowly and trying to think calmly, but it was no one he could place. The voice was a friend's voice, a sympathetic voice, but he could not understand one word of it. *Ma noyra hoo*, it seemed to be saying, *ma noyra hoo, a vick*, strange, nonsensical gibberish, yet soft and merciful. Like the chatter of a madwoman. Then soft arms were around him, comforting arms, and he buried his head against her softness, trying to shut out Jeannie's sobs and the pathetic pounding of her small fists. *Vwill hoo tyinn?* said the madwoman's voice full of comfort, *v-will hoo tyinn, ma gry-een?*

Tetzel closed his eyes and thought about tomorrow's partial review in fluid mechanics. The strange, crooning, madwoman's voice went away.

He had come back to his room after the hypnotic session and found dozens of cadets waiting in the hallway; word had spread fast through the corps. He had slipped away without being seen and spent the rest of the afternoon with his friend at brigade staff. When he finally had to go back to the company area the crowd had dispersed.

Mort, his roommate, was thoroughly irritated, though. He had been obliged to fend off the curious most of the afternoon. Even at intramural football, which was a long safe distance away on Buffalo Soldier Field, he had been constantly pestered by cadets who wanted to know about the famous John Tetzel who saw the ghost. By the time he returned to the barracks to shower before dinner he was thoroughly sick and tired of ghosts. He had the satisfaction of finding John in a grim mood as well. Tetzel did not have the slightest intention of discussing his day.

Supper was the first nightmare of the evening. For the moment, Tetzel was the focus of interest in the corps. Last week, he reflected, it had been the afterglow of Linda Ronstadt's concert in Eisenhower Hall. Next week it would be something else. But for now, right at this crucial moment, fame was John Tetzel's; Tetzel and the goddamned ghost were riding high. He could not have known now, in late October, that the ghost would be written into the script for the Hundredth Night Show, the graduating class's musical extravaganza, nor that he would be immortalized by a clever drawing in the *Howitzer*, the cadet yearbook. For now it was enough just to finish dinner and slink back to the barracks and anonymity.

Even this notoriety might not have been altogether unpleasant, but he knew what the other cadets did not—that there was something more than a brief autumnal diversion in this. This was *for real*. He knew it even if that arrogant rat-zapper and his magical friend Mandrake didn't. He had *seen* the damned thing, and it wasn't funny. But the ghost wasn't the worst part. The real dread came from something else—the dreams. They were the source of the true horror, the fear that even the light of day was powerless against.

There were two things he knew about the dreams. He couldn't prove either of them, but he knew they were so.

First, they were not morbid fancy. There was a warning in the dreams, and if he was too deeply frightened to speculate as to what it was, he was at least wary enough to know it was worth fearing.

Second, they were not *his* recollections. The scene was no longer a place he knew. It was no longer his closet. It was still

Jeannie, as she was years ago. It was still his mother, sometimes; but increasingly now it was another, a woman unknown to him. And the gibbering madwoman who comforted him as he cried in fear was not part of his past—yet he knew her in some incomprehensible way. He turned to her and buried his face in her breasts without fear. He knew her, her name was on his lips.

He pictured the hallway as he lay in bed, trying not to think of it. Pale blue-gray hallway, a chair rail, a bare floor, uneven boards. A strange smell, musty smell, and the sharp scent of a woodfire in his nostrils. On the wall he could picture the painting that hung in his father's study, a hunting scene with dogs and a pheasant. He heard his mother's voice, soft and certain and yet strange, edged with some trace of triumph that was somehow discordant, obscene; and beyond it his sister's sobs and her small soft hands pounding again and again on the door. Then, there was the voice again, for him alone, and it said safety, it said warmth, but it said nothing: *Ayshth, a vick, ayshth! Nock ish thoo!*

And the vision suddenly filled him with a sadness that came from nowhere, from somewhere secret, from another time, a sadness that almost stopped his heart and breath. Tears trickled down his cheeks from the corners of eyes marked with a grief known only to those who have looked into the darkness of the Well of the World's End and turned away.

He tore away the sheets and blanket and fell on the floor on his hands and knees. Mort turned over, sat up and stared at him. "What the fuck are you doing on the floor?" he demanded sleepily.

Tetzel didn't answer. He got to his feet somehow and, staggering out of the room in his underwear, he reeled down the hallway to the deserted orderly room and dialed Track's number.

Patti, on the edge of a hangover, fumbled the receiver once before she finally had it firmly against her ear. "Yes?"

Tetzel leaned against the charge-of-quarters' desk; he was shaking, and nearly dropped the phone himself. "Ma'am, I'm sorry. I know it's late. Is Major D. there?"

"Who is this? It's after midnight."

"Ma'am, I'm really sorry. This is John Tetzel. I'm sorry. I have to talk to Major Dortmunder."

She was wide awake now. The urgency in Tetzel's voice was unmistakable; he was in trouble. Track was awake now, too, and looking at her strangely.

77

"What is it?"

"It's John."

"Who? Tetzel? Shit, I thought it was your mother in the hospital again. Gimme the phone. John? What the hell's up, studly? It's awful late."

When he answered, Track understood what had scared Patti. The cadet's voice shook. "Sir, I'm really screwed up. I have to see you tomorrow, you and Colonel FitzDonnell. I'm really screwed up, sir. I need help, bad."

"What's the trouble, John?"

"Sir, I'm sorry to bother you . . . ."

"Can that shit, John. You got a problem you call Major Track. What's going on?"

"Sir, I'm having these freaky dreams, and I think they have something to do with the ghost. I can't shake them; I can't sleep, I'm scared and I don't know why. It was worse tonight, worst yet. It's really scary. No shit, sir, I'm in bad shape. Can I see you tomorrow?"

"Tomorrow, hell," said Track, "I'll come over there right now. Sit tight, I'll call the officer-in-charge . . ."

"Oh, no sir! Don't come over now. I don't want anybody to know about this. It's bad enough now, all kinds of people hanging around, razzing me about the ghost. If this gets out, they'll all think I've gone apeshit."

"You got a free period tomorrow, stud?"

"First period, sir."

"Great. Now listen: You get your young ass over to my cubicle at oh-seven thirty tomorrow. You be there, bright and early."

"Yes sir."

"And John . . ."

"Sir?"

"Where are you?"

"I'm in the CQ's office, sir."

"Ain't you got a phone in your room? You're the company commander."

"Yes sir. I didn't want Mort to hear this."

"Okay, fine. But you use the phone, either one, and you give me a ring right away if you start going off the deep end, you hear?"

"Yes sir. Thanks, sir. I'm sorry I woke you up."

78

"Stud, people waking me up is the story of my life. I'm no virgin to stand-to."

"Apologize to Mrs. D., sir, okay?"

"Shit, John, she's asleep already."

Tetzel went back to his room and collapsed onto the bed. Mort was snoring. The dreams did not return that night.

6

*M*aggie slept until nearly nine o'clock. She was still under the blanket at the foot of the bed, and her first sensation on waking was the roughness of the coarse wool on her skin. She stretched and rearranged the blanket to cover her feet. Mornings with no schedule were always the best for Maggie. She would rise with Sam at six and make a show of preparing breakfast and then, when he was safely out the door, dash up the stairs and leap back into bed. Sam was not deceived, though, and such had been his tolerance that he usually retrieved the *Times* from the yard and placed it on the nightstand before he left for Thayer Hall. Maggie, to her credit, knew that Sam would spend the first half hour of his day reading his own copy of the *Times* in his office; her morning luxury was thus untroubled by so much as a scintilla of guilt.

Her mouth tasted metallic and felt furry, but otherwise she felt only a slight nausea, not the throbbing agony of a wine hangover. In truth, she had not had all that much the night before—her euphoria had been more a product of the moment and the company than of the fruit of the vine—and the squares of blue morning sky beyond the bedroom windows were enough to revive her. The tracery of the oak branches in the front yard was etched sharply against the brightness, and the breeze of the night before was gone. It was cold. She could sense it from the clarity of the sweet fall air and the hissing and moaning of the old steam heating system. This was going to be a day worth getting up for; there was only the hospital appointment at eleven, then the quest for Adonijah Proctor through the Ladies' Reading Club.

Sam had forgotten the paper this morning, or else had decided not to chance waking her, and she was left to soak under the delightful blanket. She had no idea how she had come to be curled up nude at the foot of the bed—her last memory was of combing dirt and grass out of her hair—but she suspected the worst. Her going to bed must have been more like passing out than falling asleep. No wonder Sam had sneaked out! She rolled over on her side and saw more debris from the lawn on the bedspread. She ran her fingers in her hair and more fell out. No bath last night. At least, she thought, I won't have to change the sheets.

She pulled back the blanket and stood, a little shakily, by the night stand. Her vision darkened for an instant, and she sat on the edge of the bed again. She put her head between her knees until the blood returned, then stood again. This time she made it to the bathroom, and threw up neatly in the toilet. Cold water and liberal toothbrushing took away the sour taste, and a hot shower banished the nausea.

She did not dress right away, but stood at the sink and blew her hair dry and combed it carefully. Time for a permanent on Saturday, to soften up Sam. She walked into the hall and opened the linen closet; a full-length mirror was nailed to the inside of the door, and she examined herself for a long moment. She turned sideways and winked at her reflection. "Nice tits, huh? You're a swine, Bondurant, but you've got good taste." Not bad for twenty-nine, she thought, not too bad at all. A lot a girl could still do at twenty-nine, with a little help.

She dressed in her wool suit with the yellow silk blouse Sam had given her for her last birthday. This was the "executive suit" she wore to impress the dizzier wives and to intimidate their husbands. It worked on the typical dull career plodder, who invariably married a woman who represented one of three categories. The first was the toothy, buxom lobotomy with the brain of a gerbil, the metabolism of a pet rock, and an unshakable faith in hubby's genius. Self-propelled bitches made up another category; Maggie could not intimidate this sort of vampire except by dazzling the husband, who was apt to be easily dazzled after years of bondage to a bloodless, ambitious Nosferatu. Category three was the polypropylene Barbie doll. The PBD was intelligent enough to present a flawless exterior and winning smile, but in years of meeting the army's expectations had abandoned whatever viscera she once had for a food processor. After ten to fifteen years of being a perfect wife, the PBD was damaged goods, a capable woman shrunken to the scale of those mindless smiles who inhabit the spotless kitchens of television commercials. Maggie never prodded one of these; there was a hint of a ticking sound in such a woman, the clockwork fuse of a time bomb.

Maggie preferred the men. This did little to enhance her distaff rating. Her only female intimates were Patti Dortmunder, who was as unaffected by the army as Track himself, and Doris Gilmer. She admired Doris because Doris could handle Sam. That was a rare skill, worthy of the respect one gives a geisha who can make Godzilla jump through a hoop.

But today she had to track down Alice Fetterman, reigning president of the Ladies' Reading Club. She opened her office— the house had three bedrooms, two of which served as separate offices for Sam and Maggie—and switched on the computer to check the day's schedule.

Sam had bought her an IBM for Christmas the year before to rescue her from a sagging spirit and to coax her to start writing again. It had worked. She loved that damned thing, and in the last year she had turned out three short stories (two published in a pulp mystery magazine) and a chapter for a collection of commentaries on *Sir Gawain and the Green Knight* assembled by her old dissertation adviser. While the computer warmed up, she found Alice Fetterman in the post telephone directory. She was listed with Colonel Matthew L. Fetterman, Department of English, Mahan Hall, residing in quarters on Wilson Road. She dialed and a musical feminine voice answered. Yes, said Alice Fetterman, I will surely be at home this morning and yes, of course I would be delighted to talk with you about the Ladies' Reading Club. They agreed on eleven thirty.

The computer was warmed up, and there was a message indication. She called it up. Sam had punched it in before leaving at seven:

DIDN'T WANT TO WAKE YOU; YOU LOOKED LIKE A MAENAD WITH A FULL STOMACH AFTER GRUBBING AROUND LAST NIGHT. HOPE YOU FEEL GOOD ENOUGH TO JOIN ME FOR LUNCH AT THE CLUB, 1330.
TRACK CALLED AT 0630—TETZEL IS HAVING PROBLEMS AND WE'RE MEETING AGAIN

THIS MORNING. I'LL BRIEF YOU OVER LUNCH.
I ADORE YOU.

SINCERELY YOURS,
YOG-SOTHOTH

She checked her wallet for her ID and medical card before leaving, then called Sam's office. He was in a meeting, said the secretary, with Colonel FitzDonnell and a cadet. Maggie left a message confirming lunch at one thirty and left for the hospital.

Actually, the cadet had left Sam's office at eight thirty. Sam and Liam stayed shut up in the office for more than an hour after listening to the tape recording of the cadet's statement. Liam had insisted on a verbatim record, and the cadet had readily agreed. In fact, the cadet would have agreed to nearly anything that might let him sleep again—in his room at night, that is, since he was getting plenty of sleep in class.

Tetzel had been in better spirits by the time the sun came up and breakfast was over, and had apologized again to Track. Track shut him off: "Cut the crap," he told the cadet. "It seems like nothing now, but you gotta face another night." Liam was relieved when Track had to leave to meet a class. Tetzel might, paradoxically, be less constrained in talking to strangers.

In fact, Tetzel was a chatterbox. Sam attributed this new garrulousness to a reaction against fatigue. Whatever the cause, both Liam and Sam were glad of the recorder; Tetzel rambled and digressed and repeated himself, determined to empty his memory and exorcise its shadowy contents. He revealed that the dream had first come on the night he spent in the haunted room, and in the two nights since had kept him awake until dawn. It came again and again, whenever he drifted to sleep, changing subtly with repetition and evolving into a grotesque ritual that was most frightening because, though some of the characters were familiar, it was definitely (in his words) someone else's dream.

"Why do you think that, John?" asked Liam's voice on the tape as they replayed the conversation after Tetzel was gone.

"It's hard to say, sir. The things I recognized at first—my room, Jeannie, my mother—started changing. When I saw them in the dream the first time, I knew they were mine. But the new stuff, the changes, they don't feel right. It's like somebody in me knows the place, the people, and I feel the familiar things, but part of me is a stranger."

Sam hit the pause key. "I don't like this. The sense of alienation, a trace of pathological thought processes. He needs to go to the counseling center."

"Nonsense," said Liam. "He's in touch with reality. He's having nightmares, nightmares connected with his experience in the room. There's no need to turn him over to Ward Lane."

Sam looked at Liam suspiciously. "Since when are you so laid back? Start the tape again."

The cadet described the hallway in the latest form of the dream. He was most distracted by the unevenness of the boards on the floor and the smell of the fire.

"What's so strange about the floor?" Sam had asked.

"Sir, it isn't like the floor in a modern house. It looks more like what you see in an old house, like at Williamsburg. It looks old—not old, but old-fashioned. And the smell was scary, too."

"Why was it scary?"

"It was like a wood fire in a fireplace; but the fireplace wasn't drawing too well."

"Why did that scare you?" Sam had asked.

"Sir, I think whoever the ghost is had something to do with that house a long time ago. I know it sounds flaky, but I think when I'm dreaming that dream, I'm somehow getting sucked into whatever place the ghost is. I don't like it."

"I think I'd be a little scared, too," Liam had reassured him. "But don't worry—you're not the first person who ever had dreams that seemed significant or morbid or 'too real to be dreams.' The dreams are important, John, but they aren't pulling you into an alien dimension. They're revealing another dimension of your own mind."

But Tetzel had not been convinced, and as the tape played on, they listened to the cadet arguing about the fine points of the dreams. It was obvious that establishing the existence of the ghost—or of some other outside agency—was important to him. A ghost was preferable to some undetermined loose screw in his own head.

Finally Liam had intervened. "Tell us again about the crazy girl, John."

"I never saw her, sir. She was down the hall, then behind me, holding me like I was a little kid."

"Was she your mother?" Liam had asked. "As you remember her from years ago, perhaps?"

"No sir. My mother—only she wasn't my mother anymore, she was the cruel-sounding woman—had walked off down the hall, leaving Jeannie locked up, crying. The girl had a different voice."

Liam: "How different?"

"Higher-pitched. But it was strange, kind of musical. The words, if they were words, didn't sound right. Her tongue didn't seem to be working right. Some of her sounds—like the *k*s—were a little slurred, like she was drunk or making babbling sounds."

Liam had pressed him. "Do you remember anything she said?"

"No sir. She wasn't speaking English. Not any language I know of."

"Think about it. Do you remember any specific sounds?"

There was a long silence on the tape. Sam remembered the cadet had closed his eyes, reconstructing the mad gibbering. "Yes sir," he said finally. "I remember something like '*ma noyra hoo.*' And she sometimes said something like '*a vick.*' "

Liam had sat back in his chair and gnawed his lip. "John, when did she say '*a vick*'?"

"What do you mean, sir?"

"Did she begin a sentence with it? End a sentence?"

"Well sir," the cadet said thoughtfully, "I can't say, really. It's hard to remember. I'm not sure what was a sentence and what wasn't."

Another long silence as the tape ran. Then Liam's voice again: "John, do you want to try hypnosis again?" Sam had been quietly aghast. Liam's scare on Tuesday had seemed a near thing, and Sam was surprised to see Liam so ready to court disaster.

Tetzel, however, had shared none of Sam's fears. "Great, sir. Same procedure?"

"Not quite," Liam had said. "This time, I'm going to instruct you *not* to remember. Any objections to that?"

The cadet had been a little uneasy. He had suspected, Sam imagined, that Liam was planning to open a large can of worms

86

and didn't want to have to replace them after the trance. But he had agreed when Liam promised to reverse the amnesia suggestion if nothing too frightening emerged.

The induction had been quicker this time. In a few minutes Tetzel had been in the same deep trance as before. Liam had brought him into the dream quickly and led his recollections to the mysterious babbling girl.

"What is she saying?"

"She's saying nonsense."

"What nonsense? Can you hear the sounds?"

"I can hear them. I can't say them."

"Why can't you say them?" Liam had asked.

"The sounds are strange. Some of them are strange. I can't say them." The cadet's speech was slurred again.

They heard Liam take a breath, then say firmly: "Try. Try to say what the girl is saying."

More silence. Then, hesitantly: " *'Ma naw-re hoo, ma nawre hoo, a vick.'* And something like *'v-will hoo t-yinn.'* I can't say it right. It's like *'chin,'* the last word is, but not quite."

"That's very good, John," Liam had said. Sam had sensed something new in Liam's voice and demeanor. "Now, where is the girl?"

"She is behind me. Her arms are around me. Now she's humming to me."

"Humming or singing, John?"

"Humming."

"Can you hear the tune?"

"I can hear it."

"Do you recognize it?"

Silence. Then: "No sir. I've never heard it."

"Can you hum it for me, John?"

More silence. Tetzel had tilted his head as if listening to the pipes of Pan; he had smiled and, lost in the music, he let his lips part. As the tape ran on silently, Sam recollected the cadet's appearance. It dawned on Sam that, for this brief moment, John Tetzel had no longer been a stranger in a strange land; he belonged there, listening to the mysterious girl humming. This, Sam guessed, was the key to the frightening end of the session.

Then the cadet's voice began again; not words, but the tune, crudely rendered *(La da da, da dum . . .)*. Sam looked at Liam.

The psychologist was as intent as when Tetzel had actually been approximating the tune. Sam had never heard it before, but it seemed a lullaby of sorts, one with a queer, amorphous phrasing. The strain seemed to wander on randomly and then, after an impossibly long time, repeated itself. At first, Sam thought the cadet's performance was a sort of tonal wool-gathering, but as the melody went on a pattern became apparent. It was uncannily sweet, a faerie-song. Now, as when the cadet had first started to hum, Sam felt his skin crawl. This was *for real*. No computer input-output hardware could possibly address the effect this eerie tune had on the two officers. Sam's impression was compelling: The melody was not Tetzel's, it was something else, something from another time, yet familiar.

Then Liam stopped the tape and ran it back to the beginning of the tune. There was silence, then the cadet's humming. To Sam's astonishment, Liam hummed along, then began to sing softly, confidently, in unintelligible phrases. Then Sam remembered.

"I've heard that. It's a folk song, from back in the folk music craze in the sixties. Some weird thing with a gobbledegook refrain." Liam smiled.

The cadet's humming finished, and they heard Liam's voice: "All right, John. That's fine. Can you remember any words?"

Tetzel had frowned. "It starts *'Shule, shule, shule aroon'*; then *'Shule* something something something *shule go coon'* . . ." The cadet had gone on, remembering a word here and there. "Then 'Something something *ma vorneen shlawn*,' or something like that."

Liam: "All right, John. That's fine. Now on 'five' you will come out of the trance. One, two, three, four, five." Silence on the tape, masking what had been Liam's discomfort at seeing, again, no response. "One, two, three, four, five." Nothing. Liam had sworn softly and tried twice more to call the cadet back.

Sam's voice on the tape. "What now?"

Liam: "I don't know. It's the same response he had last time, only longer. I was afraid of this. He'll come out of it on his own after a while, but I don't want him to have to explain why he was late to class."

They had watched Tetzel silently for a few minutes. The cadet appeared to be asleep. Then Liam had smiled and touched the cadet on the shoulder. Tetzel's eyes opened at once.

The tape: "Ready, sir?"

Liam: "*Cead mile failte rumhat abhaile.* You're already finished. You did great, John."

Tetzel: "Really, sir? You haven't started yet."

Liam had backed up the tape to the beginning of the song. "Ever hear that tune before, John?"

Tetzel had looked suspiciously at Liam. "What's that, sir?" The cadet had looked at the tape recorder, then at Liam, then Sam. For just a moment, Sam had thought he saw a flicker of recognition; then it had disappeared, and there had been a barely perceptible hint of hostility. Sam thought now: He recognized it, and he didn't want to. Why? Was it part of his dream, or part of something else? There's something about that tune that gets to him, something he doesn't want to think about, and the sound of his humming on the tape makes it hard to forget, hard to explain away.

Liam: "That's you. Ever heard it?"

Silence, as the cadet listened. "No sir. Sounds weird. Is that really me humming that? Is it a real song?"

Liam: "I think I've heard it before. John, where's your home?"

Tetzel: "Bakersfield, California, sir."

Liam: "What was your mother's maiden name?"

Tetzel: "Sir?"

Liam: "I said, 'What was your mother's maiden name?' "

Tetzel: "Shapiro, sir."

Liam: "*Fall-che ron-gat ow-all-ye, a vick-o.*" (Or so it sounded to Sam.)

Tetzel: "Sir?"

Liam: "You don't recognize it?"

Tetzel: "It sounds like what the girl was saying in my dream."

Liam: "John, do you speak any languages? Other than English, I mean?"

Tetzel: "German, sir. I had two semesters in high school and picked it up for another two years here."

Liam: "Nothing else?"

Tetzel: "No sir."

Liam: "Does anyone in your family speak another language?"

Tetzel: "My mother speaks a little French, sir."

Liam: "You remembered that the girl in the dream said something like *'ma naw-re hoo a vick.'* Does that ring any bells?"

Tetzel: "That sounds like what I heard in the dream, sir, now that you mention it. I don't know what it means."

Liam: "How about *'v-will hoo t-yinn'*?"

Tetzel had not recognized this phrase, either. By that time the cadet had been in danger once more of missing class. He had been confused and angry that Liam offered no further explanation.

"All right, you goddamned druid," Sam said now. "What the hell was all that about?"

"Sam, we have a whole new range of possibilities. We *have* to know whether Tetzel has ever had any access to that old book Maggie found. We also have to search every possible source and find out if he could have read the story anywhere else, *anywhere*."

"I agree, but that's going to take a bit of research. What about books that are out of print? Upton's history was. I guess there's a chance we can find all the histories of West Point—most of them must be in the library—but what about other sources, informal ones? Anyway, why is it so important now? It was a natural step before."

"Remember Maggie's story from Upton's book? What was Upton's source for the original story of Adonijah Proctor?"

Sam thought a bit. "A family servant, years after the fire."

"A family servant. What was her name?"

"Hell, I don't remember."

"I do. It was Bridget Hardesty."

"Okay, Bridget Hardesty, fresh from the auld sod. Faith and begorrah. So what?"

" *'Mo naire thu,'* the dream-girl said, not 'Nora who.' It's Irish, Sam, colloquial Gaelic: 'Shame on you.' Then she said *'Bhfuil tu tinn, a mhic.'* I think the first part means 'Are you sick?' The last words—the *'a vick'* he talks about—clearly mean 'my son.' "

"Cowabunga." Sam sat back and exhaled through pursed lips.

"The song, Sam. You were right—it's an American folk song, and when you heard it back in the sixties it *did* have a nonsense refrain. But it wasn't always nonsense:

Shule, shule, shule aroon,
Shule go sucir, agus shule go ciuin,
Shule go deen durras, agus aylin l'yum,
Is go de tu a vourneen slan.

The nonsense refrain is worn-down Gaelic—*Siúil a rún*. He was sing-ing the Irish words, not the nonsense. This will make Maggie's day."

"It hasn't made mine," said Sam. "How can we deal with this? Where could he have picked up Gaelic?"

"That's a good question," said Liam in his druidical manner. "Any ideas?"

"As a working hypothesis, I would surmise that he once heard it spoken and somehow it went into very long term memory. Under hypnosis, and with a small prod from autosuggestion, it surfaced. The phrases aren't all that specific to the situation. They could be just random snatches of conversation." He raised his eyebrows at Liam. "Of course, the other possibility is he looked up some phrases and he's lying in his teeth."

"That has always been a possibility."

"But not a likely one."

"No," Liam admitted, "not a likely one."

"So, where does that leave us? I can't verify gibbering Irish ghosts with thermocouple readings."

Liam was unsympathetic. "I never saw much in that to begin with."

"Prithee, why?"

"Because you don't have hypotheses. What are you expecting to find? Eerie electrical discharges?"

"For the last time," said Sam, finally fed up with Liam, "I expect to find nothing. No cold spots, no auras, no strange vibra-tions, no nothing. But that's a precondition to dismissing the bullshit and concentrating on your favored loose-screw theories."

Liam grinned one of his rarest grins, a mannerism so unex-pected it gave his face a startling youthfulness. "Don't worry, Sam. I'll let you handle the screwdriver."

Alice Fetterman proved to be a veritable gold mine of lore on the Ladies' Reading Club, having inherited the chairmanship in 1962. They chatted for over an hour by a cheerful fire in the Fettermans' great empty quarters on Wilson Road. These vaguely Tudor struc-tures with wood paneling and unexpected rooms were reputed to have been the fruit of Stanford White's architectural whimsy; Alice

91

Fetterman confided to Maggie that Mr. White got just what he deserved.

Maggie explained the circumstances of the ghost investigation. "I really need a lead on somebody who might have heard the paper read in 1947. Mrs. O'Grady at the cadet Library—"

"Oh, dear," said Alice, "did she give you that song and dance about the Library of Congress catalog system?"

"She certainly did. She was most adamant."

"I know." She shook her head. "The poor thing's mind is slipping like a wet avalanche. I ran afoul of her last about three years ago when I did a paper for the club on the Warner sisters. It took me the better part of an hour, the longest of my life, to get her on the subject. But when she finally finished her critique of the catalog system, she helped me dig out everything I could ever have possibly wanted to know about Susan and Anna Warner. She knows the library's holdings like no one else, but she stands guard over them like the mummy's curse."

"Was she right about the paper delivered in 1947?"

"Oh, heavens, Maggie! Do I look like I was around then? I shall have to consult the club's archives." She set her tea down on a marble-topped table and walked to a polished mahogany Queen Anne desk by the fireplace. The sun was streaming in through the glass, and Maggie detected a thin layer of dust on the upper surfaces. Alice Fetterman, she thought, I love you!

The older woman shuffled through the center drawer and at length produced a cardboard accordion file. She brought it back to her chair by the window. "I don't have much call to pull this thing out. Bernice Gort gave me this when she turned over all the files about ten years ago. She was the last president; served for God knows how long. I think she took office while Max Taylor was superintendent. She would have been a member in 'forty-seven, because Hob Gort—his name was Hobart, he's dead now—was head of Engineering all during Korea and didn't retire until 'sixty-one." She thumbed patiently through the sheaves of paper.

"Here it is! 'The Spirits of the Corps,' September 1947. Mrs. O'Grady's memory is flawless. Oh my!"

"Yes?"

"Well, it was presented by Bernice Gort! You are in luck today, Maggie."

Maggie smiled. You have no idea. "Is she still alive?"

"Oh, yes! She doesn't usually come to meetings, though. She had a stroke a few years ago and can't drive. She lives in a perfectly lovely house up on Storm King, along the road to Cornwall. God-forsaken spot, they never plow the snow in the winter. But simply exquisite view. Huge rooms, fireplaces so huge you could make sacrifice to Moloch, abomination of the Midianites! She can't keep the place up, living alone."

"How can I get hold of her?"

"Not easily, dear. She has a hearing aid she keeps turned off most of the time. She can't hear the telephone. Let me try to call her anyway." She abandoned jasmine tea once again and retreated to another room. Maggie heard her a few minutes later, shouting into the telephone. Hearing aid not working? Will I have to bring my own megaphone?

After a good many muffled shouts, Mrs. Fetterman returned. "Bernice, as you may have guessed, is not a lover of telephones. But she will be pleased to receive you."

"When can I see her?"

"Dear, when you're Bernice's age any time between dawn and dusk is just fine. I recommend late morning or early afternoon; she sags a notch or two as the day wears on. She's by no means senile— her wits are still sharp and she has a keen sense of humor—but her racquetball days are long over."

"Do you think she'd mind if I just barged in a bit after lunch?"

"I know she'd be thrilled, Maggie. Oh, by the way . . ."

"Yes, Mrs. Fetterman?"

"Bernice is a lovely person, just lovely. But she has a dog that is the terror of Orange County. Don't wear your good clothes."

Maggie looked down at her wool suit. "Good advice. I'll put on my lcdcrhoscn and hiking boots."

Alice saw her to the door. "No need for that, Maggie. Just don't turn your back on him."

Maggie rushed into the Officers' Club at forty minutes after one and stood in the entrance of the main dining room, searching for Sam. Finally she saw Track at a crowded round table near the rear corner, and caught sight of the back of Sam's head. Track saw her as she crossed the room and waved, and all the officers except Doris Gilmer stood when she approached. They were all members of the department, and discussion had been dominated by Saturday's football game against Boston College. Sam had not a glimmer of interest in football, and had been sawing away gamely at the daily special, rumored to be veal. As soon as he saw Maggie, he sensed something extraordinary about her—a brightness of countenance, a just discernible change in carriage. Track noticed it as well, and looked at her suspiciously.

She greeted the officers cheerily and kissed Sam on the cheek; he blushed and looked uncomfortable. When they were seated again—Maggie found a chair between Doris and Liam—Track said: "Don't worry, Maggie. He's just shy."

Maggie beamed. "How little you know. This man spent his evening embracing me passionately on the cold ground beside Lee Road last night."

"Maggie!"

"Oh, be a sport," said Doris. "You *are* married. We all suspect you touch each other when nobody's looking."

"I'm not so sure," said Herb Fischer, who taught counseling. "Sam never misses a chance to lecture."

"Don't feel too bad," said Doris. "He calibrates those biocomputers on his own body—I've seen him do it—so he *must* have a heartbeat."

"Wrong," said Sam. "I have a centrifugal pump set at seventy revolutions per minute. That's how I calibrate. Maggie, what trouble did you get into this morning?"

Maggie told him about Alice Fetterman and her plans to visit Bernice Gort on Storm King after lunch. Although Sam, Liam, and Track had been uncharacteristically taciturn on the subject, the rest of the diners had heard of the ghost project. They had used up most of their superficial jokes and turned to more important concerns. With Maggie's revelations, their interest returned. Sam briefly described the session with Tetzel (omitting any reference to the hypnosis).

Maggie shook her head. "Liam, where did you learn Gaelic? And why?"

"No mystery," Liam said. "I did a paper during my first year in grad school on legends of filicide and their interpretation in

Freudian theory. One of the legends was from an old Irish fragment from the *Tain* . . ."

"The what?" asked Herb.

"The *Táin bó Cúailgne*," said Maggie. "*The Cattle Raid of Cooley.* It's part of a narrative tradition called the Red Branch Cycle."

Liam noticed that Maggie had pronounced the Irish correctly. "Anyway," he went on, "in one story, 'The Slaying of Aoife's One Son,' a hero named Cú Chulainn has occasion to kill his only son in combat. There was only one translation in the library, and some idiot had checked it out in 1971 and then disappeared with it. All that was left were some annotated books from Sweden with the damned thing *in the original Irish.* I had to find a grammar and lexicon—they had *those* anyway—and translate part of it."

"Jesus," said Herb.

"What did you conclude?" asked Maggie.

"When fathers write myths, the sons get killed. Laios is revenged by Cú Chulainn, Hildebrandt and Rustum."

"What the hell are you talking about?" Doris asked.

"Several good reasons for family planning," said Sam.

Maggie smiled. Track sipped his coffee. He did not join in the Liam-baiting. He thought about countering with the example of Telemachos and Odysseus, but decided he had a reputation to protect.

"By the way," said Sam, "George Salinger called just before lunch. He has all the equipment ready to move over to the Forty-seventh Division. We'll do it Saturday morning. Want to help?"

"Great! When are you going to see the room?"

"Right after lunch; Liam and I are going over to meet Stu Broadnax at two."

"Rats!" said Maggie, "I'll be chitty-chatting with old Mrs. Gort."

"Don't worry," said Liam, "I suspect we're going to be there for a while."

"Are you going to help move the gear over?" asked Track.

"No, I have to beg off. I'm leaving for the weekend."

"Uh-oh," said Track. "Going to Boston again?"

Liam nodded.

"Liam," said Maggie, "this is ridiculous. I'm beginning to doubt this woman's existence. When do we get to see her?"

"As soon as I find a way to muzzle Doris and Track."

"Aha!" said Track, "a hothouse flower?"

"Hardly. Maybe I'll coax her up here for the Halloween party next Friday."

"Great!" said Maggie. "I've been looking forward to that party for weeks! I may even get old Smilin' Sam into a costume this year."

Liam's expression showed a measure of doubt.

"What costume would be just right for—what's her name?" asked Doris.

"Anna Perugino," said Liam drily. "I'll ask her to come, but I wouldn't bet on it. She's not wild about stirring from Boston for my amusement."

"We wait," said Maggie, "with bated breath. Meanwhile, how shall we array Sam?"

"He'd make a dandy Darth Vader," suggested Doris.

"Not a bad idea," said Maggie. "Basic black and heavy breathing are always appropriate."

Sam rose from the table. "Come on, gentlemen, we have an appointment with Stu Broadnax in fifteen minutes." He rested his hand on Maggie's shoulder for just an instant and their eyes met. "See you at home. Be merciful to old Mrs. Gort."

"What are you talking about? I'm going with you to see the room first."

"Yeah, Sam," said Track. "Surely you can't deny her that."

"Maybe," suggested Doris, "he *wants* to sleep on the front porch for a week. There's no accounting for taste."

"This is an official meeting," said Sam. "We—"

"Nonsense," said Maggie. "Don't be a pill. How can you get all bureaucratic over a haunted room? There aren't any rules to cover *that*, are there?"

"Let her go," said Track. "Who'll care?"

Sam sighed. He could think of two or three dozen rules that scowled with stern disapproval, and six or seven rather important hostile people who would do more than scowl, but there was no helping it. "Okay; just a peek. You have your trip to the Gort mansion."

Maggie patted his hand and smiled. Sam hustled away with Liam, but Track stayed behind for a moment. When the last witness was gone, he leaned down and kissed Maggie on the forehead. "Congratulations, gorgeous."

"For what?" Then she smiled and winked. "Thanks, Track. Who trained *you*, the Amazing Kreskin? I wish Sam noticed."

"Don't worry about old Smilin' Sam. You just have to get his attention."

"Pray, how?"

"Want to borrow a ball-peen hammer, gorgeous? A good tap between the eyes helps."

"Don't be too hard on him, Yog—he loosens up on the rare and precious moment."

"I already figured *that* out, Mag; parthenogenesis seems a tad farfetched. I just hate to see that sad smile when you tell people he loosens up sometimes. He's just like the rest of us—a product of faulty toilet training."

Maggie laughed. "Well, I pity poor Adonijah Proctor. Nobody can freeze a room like our Sam."

7

Sam, Liam, and Maggie met Major Stu Broadnax at the Central Guard Room shortly after two o'clock. They left immediately for the Forties, since the classes that began at ten after one would be released at any moment, and an officer who tried to cross Central Area on foot between classes was obliged to return the salutes of hundreds of delighted cadets. It was one of the few opportunities available to cadets for mild revenge. It was almost as though the groups of cadets were in silent communication on a strategy of harassment, and somehow agreed on a precise timing of movement from group to group as the officer passed, in order to elicit the maximum possible number of salutes. Sam had never been amused, and soon picked up the habit of simply saluting rhythmically as he walked against the stream, ignoring individuals and repeating an endless litany of greeting. Liam responded in his own way by checking the clock before leaving Thayer Hall and making no appointments that obliged him to swim against the gray tide between classes.

"John Tetzel has a class next hour," said Broadnax as they walked briskly in front of Washington Hall and turned into the sally port toward the Forties. "Andrea Linnell is waiting for us in front of the building."

"She's the platoon leader who lives in the division?" asked Sam.

"Yep. Damned fine cadet officer," said Broadnax, "a real flamer. Weighs about forty pounds dripping wet, but she rose right to the top even as a plebe in Beast. She isn't wild about the ghost flap, though."

"Why not?" asked Maggie.

"Well, I'd have to guess it violates her sense of good order and discipline. And she's famous for looking out for her bean-heads—God help one that goes deficient in anything, he'll find himself surrounded by academic sergeants and dragged in chains to some professor for additional instruction. Do you know, Liam, she hasn't had a single plebe quit or go deficient since she took over? They call her Mother Superior."

Andrea Linnell was standing beside the steps that led into the 47th Division when they arrived. She saluted them crisply. Broadnax introduced Liam and Sam, and explained Maggie. The cadet nodded and shook hands with each of them in turn. She was short and wiry, with pale blond hair and freckles, and chilly blue-gray eyes. Sam guessed she was capable of being pretty, but for that she needed to be wearing something other than a uniform and more than a dusting of makeup. Now the effect was the quintessence of tomboy: GI soap and no bath oil. But Liam knew she was the first woman in her class to be engaged.

Liam and Sam were both lieutenant colonels, and thus out-ranked Broadnax, but she addressed herself to the tactical officer. Maggie did not, strictly speaking, exist, though she guessed this was a courtesy rendered on the presumption that since she was not really authorized to be in the barracks, she wasn't, strictly speaking, there. "Sir, Cadet Carson is in the room. Cadet Barstow is still gone."

"Anything heard from him?" asked Liam.

"No sir. I talked to his father this morning; he hasn't reported in there, or called." This observation delighted Maggie, who tried hard to imagine a college freshman "reporting in" to his mommy and daddy.

"Lead on," said Broadnax. Cadet Linnell led on.

The newer cadet barracks—Eisenhower and MacArthur wings on Central Area and the New South Barracks named for Lee and Sherman (no doubt to their shades' consternation) were arranged as dormitories, with long rows of rooms opening on common hall-ways. These were administratively more practical than the older barracks, since the cadet chain of command could reach many cadets at once via the hallways, and inspections could be conducted swiftly and with a minimum of detour. The oldest barracks still in operation, however, were arranged in divisions, or clusters of rooms arranged vertically around stairwells. The divisions were de-monstrably old, their wood trim rubbed and scratched by the rifles of generations of cadets returning from parade. No coat of paint could make them look new.

But there were compensations. This old arrangement of rooms was more intimate than the newer ones; it fostered a sense of community among its residents. The division was a home, something the new barracks could never be. All basis for community was lost in their sterile open corridors, in the monotonous sameness of their rows of rooms.

The three officers and Maggie followed Andrea Linnell up the narrow steps to the first landing. She knocked sharply on the door nearest the head of the steps; they could see the nametags of Barstow and Carson. There was a moment's pause, then she opened the door and entered ahead of the officers. A male cadet in an athletic uniform stood at attention beside the window, and reported to Linnell. She told him to be at ease. "Sir," she said to the visitors, "this is Cadet Carson."

"Good afternoon, Mr. Carson," said Liam. "Understand you have an extra roommate."

"Afternoon, sir. I guess so." The levity was lost on the cadet, who was now standing uneasily with his hands behind his back.

"We're going to have to sort of wire up your room," said Sam. "We don't want it to bother you, and we'll keep it out of your way. I don't expect this business to last for more than a week or so, if that long."

"That's okay, sir," said Carson. "Mr. Tetzel told us what you wanted to do. I'm all for it, sir."

"Do you think we're going to find anything?" Liam asked.

"Yes sir."

Liam looked closely at the cadet. "Why are you so positive?"

"Because I saw it, sir. If I can see it and Mr. Barstow and Mr. Tetzel can see it, it's there."

"Has Mr. Tetzel talked to you about it?"

"No sir. He hasn't been back since the night he . . . since the beginning of the week. But it's all over the corps, sir, what he saw."

"Any idea why your roommate went over the hill?" asked Sam.

Carson looked at Broadnax, then, uncomfortably, back at Sam. "Sir, I think he got scared. By something he saw. I think he panicked and took off."

"Why do you imagine he might do that?" asked Liam.

"We talked about it the afternoon before he left, sir. About how he was afraid something was about to happen, there was some change. He wouldn't talk much; that was after he'd seen Mr. Tetzel."

"Did he actually say anything about leaving?"

"No sir. I just came back from breakfast and it dawned on me he was gone."

"Did he take anything with him? Anything at all?"

"I couldn't find anything missing, sir; but there may be some personal items gone; he was real private about his personal stuff."

"No pictures, letters, anything like that?"

Carson thought a moment about that one. "Not that I know of, sir."

"His wallet, driver's license, credit cards?"

"He kept all those in his lock box, sir."

"We opened it after he was reported AWOL," said Broadnax. "There were two letters from his father, a high school class ring. No money, no wallet, nothing like that."

"Sir," said Carson, "that reminds me—he cashed a check on Friday, I remember him putting the cash in his lock box."

Broadnax looked at Liam and shrugged. "Maybe he meant to do it as early as last week. We won't know until he calls in or turns up somewhere."

While Liam questioned the cadet, Sam looked around the room. It was small, with a sort of ordered clutter. There was a partition between the cadets' beds—he remembered from Tetzel's report that Carson had stepped around it to see the ghost, when it was with Barstow, and again when Tetzel had confronted the thing. There was a space of bare wall over the bunk he took to be Barstow's, bracketed by a clothes locker and the rear wall; this, he noted, must be the place through which the ghost leaned to spy on the occupant of the bed. It had to be that bed, he reasoned, because the window was not, owing to the partition, visible from the other bed. The wall must also be the place through which the form had departed, if Tetzel's description had been accurate.

"Mr. Carson," said Liam, "are you afraid of it?"

"No sir."

"Why not?"

"Sir, it's hard to say. I was scared at first, just like Mr. Barstow.

102

But he told me it didn't want to hurt anybody. He said he could just tell. When I saw it, I remembered what he said, and pretty soon I could see what he meant. It was like I could feel what it was feeling."

"Like telepathy?" asked Liam.

"Not really, sir. No words came to my mind. I could just sort of feel how he was feeling, and it didn't scare me."

"What do you think he was feeling?"

"I can't say, sir. It was nothing really specific. I just felt like he knew about—I don't know, sir, like he knew about being sad and afraid. I don't know why, sir."

"Did the feeling last after he was gone?"

"Yes sir—a long time. I still feel it, sort of."

"When was the last time the ghost came?"

"Last night, sir."

Broadnax, who had been idly checking the desks and the tops of the clothes presses for dust, looked sharply at Carson. "What! Again last night?"

Carson went uncertainly to attention again. "Yes sir. He comes about every night now."

"Why didn't you tell somebody?" the tactical officer asked.

"I already did, sir. Mr. Tetzel knew, and we didn't see any reason to bring it up again as long as—"

"Miss Linnell, I want to know *every time* anybody sees anything."

The platoon leader agreed to render a daily report; Sam wondered what Broadnax proposed to do with that piece of information. Perhaps it would become just another recurring report like the number of socks lost in the laundry and the number of cadets, by company and class, on sick call.

Liam told the cadet to relax; he went back to "at ease" with a sidelong glance at the tac.

"Mr. Carson, have you been having any unusual dreams?"

"Not me, sir—at least I don't remember any. Mr. Barstow had nightmares."

"Any idea what about?"

"Not really, sir. He's told me afterward it's about being locked up, something about a 'real bitch of a woman' locking him in a closet—no, somebody else being locked up—and setting a fire

103

outside. He wakes up talking to himself sometimes, and I've heard him talking in his sleep. Sometimes he wakes up still talking; if it's really bad I wake him up myself."

"Do you ever hear what he says?"

"Not really, sir. He's sort of indistinct, hard to understand. Once I think I heard him say 'Papa' or something like that. He won't talk about it anymore."

Liam turned to Broadnax. "I need to talk to Barstow, as soon as he surfaces. Let me know right away if you hear anything at all."

"You bet, sir. I hope he shows up soon. His folks are fit to be tied."

"Okay," said Sam, "where can I set up my ghost-hunting machinery?"

"How big is it?" asked Broadnax.

"Oh, a large polygraph, about two by two by six feet high, two microcomputers and peripherals, sitting on two tables about the size of classroom desks, a printer on its own table. Just about fit on the narrower wall of one of these rooms. And," he added with a rueful smile, "I have to set them up on the other side of one of the walls of this room."

"Why?" asked the tac. "Why not set them up in the room?"

"We have to instrument unobtrusively."

"Are you afraid of scaring the ghost away?"

"No," said Sam, "that's Liam's department. I just want to affect the physical setting as little as possible. At the same time, though, I can't set up the stuff too far away. I'll have very-low-voltage signals traveling over wire. Even with shielded cable and sixty-hertz filters, I'll have interference, and the longer the cable is the more noise I'll pick up. It has to be next door to keep them as short as possible."

Broadnax looked at Andrea. "What do you want to do?"

"Sir, the next room has only one cadet—his roommate is at Walter Reed for the rest of the term. Hartman, sir, the back injury."

"What about the cadet who's still there?"

"That's Tate, sir. I can move him up one level for a week with Willis and Puryear. We can shove the wall lockers and bunks toward the door, and they can move the equipment in right against the common wall."

After some technical questions by Sam, who was disturbed by

the small number of grounded wall sockets, they looked at the room where the instruments would be set up. They agreed to haul the gear over in a pickup the next morning while the company was at the parade and finish installation while the football game was in progress and most of the cadets were at the stadium.

Liam stayed behind in the room. He tried to remember what it had looked like so many years before, when he had come to visit and stayed for hours of bull sessions. It had been repainted since then, at least once. Eighteen years is a long time. Corey had been dead nearly that long. God, Corey. This room doesn't need any more ghosts, he thought. He closed his eyes and touched the wall gently with the tips of his fingers; it was cool—not cold as they said the ghost had made it, but cool as the black granite slabs that stood mute witness to another ghost, to a vast wall of ghosts. The army of the dead, Robert Service had called them: *They are coming— it's the Army of the Dead.*" But another army, other lonely graves; not Magersfontein, not Spion Kop, but An Loc and Binh Dinh and Hue—God, Hue—and the A Shau and the Ba Long. He opened his eyes. The paint is new, he thought, but it never really covers. They're still here, the army of the dead. Then he felt a real chill. *"Torch one two. Torch one two. It's you, buddy—the old duty concept."*

"What did you say?"

"Nothing, Maggie. Just thinking aloud. I had a friend once who lived here." They were alone.

"What? In here? Ye gods! Were there ghosts then?"

Liam smiled his slow, maddening smile. "Not then. Our kind of ghost never shows itself until we're old enough to know it for what it is."

"You sound like Ebenezer Scrooge reborn." Maggie peered around the corner of the partition into Barstow's empty alcove. "Looks too clean to be haunted. Don't ghosts need cobwebs or something?" As soon as the words were out, she regretted them; Liam deserved better than a flippant, lame joke, whatever had prompted his reverie. But Liam laughed gently.

"Since you mention it," he said, "dust balls—the kind you find under beds—are known in cadet jargon as 'ghost turds.' "

It did not hear their shared jest; it could not hear, in the accepted sense, nor see. It dimly sensed them in a way neither would have understood. The one was dark, shadow of a shadow, and it sensed his pain, drawn to it, feeding from it. The other almost glowed in the field of its diffuse knowledge, glowed with life within life, afire with the power it hated and desired. It launched itself through the air, and not a mote of dust trembled at its flight. It spread and encircled them and raged beyond their senses, mad with rage and alight with the fury of impotence, like a beast of the forest in winter, drawn by the campers' fire, hungry, yet daunted by the light.

Maggie frowned. "It's cold. Did Sam or somebody open a window?"

Liam looked at the window frame. "Here's one pane broken; here, feel—cold air's coming in." Maggie did, and shuddered.

When they came outside into the light again, it was after three and the cadets were starting to trickle back from their classes. Maggie thanked Broadnax and Andrea Linnell and left for her visit to Bernice Gort. Liam was anxious to get away. Stu Broadnax saluted and started back to Washington Hall and his office, but the general exodus was disrupted by the arrival, in high dudgeon, of Lieutenant Colonel Lane of the counseling center. He did not waste time on preliminaries. "What in the hell is this goddamned nonsense you're pulling with these cadets, FitzDonnell? I'm supposed to be dealing with these people, not you!"

Lane was out of breath from a fast walk; he had seen Tetzel shortly after lunch and, upon discovering that the cadet had been not only interviewed and counseled, but actually hypnotized *twice*, he had raised an alarming furor at the counseling center. He had then called Liam's department and terrorized the secretary who answered the telephone. Since the department head was out (and generally avoided answering Lane's calls when he was in), the executive officer had absorbed the force of his rage, holding the receiver away from his face as if it were a venomous snake grasped behind the head. Blessed with the gift of gab, this officer deflected the clinician's wrath by informing him politely that Lieutenant Colonel FitzDonnell probably had all the answers, and was at present, to the best of the executive officer's knowledge, with Lieutenant Colonel Bondurant and Major Broadnax at the cadet's room—whereupon the receiver at Lane's end had been slammed down with prodigious force.

"You've talked to Mr. Tetzel?" asked Liam.

"You're damned right I have! What the hell business do you have hypnotizing cadets? This is damned irregular, and as soon as I can get hold of that gas-bag department head of yours, we'll damned well get it straightened out. In the meantime, you and Bondurant get your asses out of the cadet area!"

Sam finally spoke up, having calmly measured Lane for a folding chair. "Now, Ward. Let's go talk about this like gentlemen." He put his hand on Lane's arm.

"There's nothing to talk about. You people are nosing in where you're not supposed to be. It's that damned simple. It's clear to me you two haven't got enough responsibility to be messing around with any of this, and the best thing you can do is get the hell out right now."

"Come on, Ward. Let's just go talk. I know you have a point, but there's no reason to get all that worked up. We don't intend to make a big thing out of this . . ." Lane allowed himself to be dragged away by Sam until the two officers were out of earshot. Broadnax was pale; he did not answer to Lane, but Lane was one of the commandant's men, and so was Broadnax. Sam and Liam were not. Andrea had stood at attention, stunned by the spectacle of officers speaking abusively—a weakness that she had imagined vanished with the affixing of gold bars on one's shoulders. Sam and Lane stood close together across a stretch of pavement. Liam stood, arms crossed, watching with amusement as Sam talked, his gesture a pantomime of politeness and sincerity. Lane stood facing him, arms akimbo, his neck turning from second-degree pink to full-blooded red to angry maroon.

"Listen, you asshole," Sam said, smiling and marshaling the posture and honeyed tones of sweet reason, "Liam and I are over here because the deputy commandant, on instructions from your boss General Harrington, told us to come over here. Be very, very alert, because I'm going to tell you in great detail and perfect sincerity what is and is not going to happen. But I'm only going to do it once.

"First, we are going to bring all our equipment over here from the laboratory on Saturday morning. We are going to spend Saturday setting it up and calibrating it. Then, starting Saturday night, we are going to begin measurements. We are going to stay here until we have collected the data we need, which should take about a week. We are going to have the complete cooperation of the commandant—who asked us to do all this good stuff—the regimental tactical officer, the company tactical officer, and the cadet chain of command. And, Ward, we are going to have your own smiling and polite assistance.

"We are going to have your assistance because, although you are a complete, gaping asshole, a swollen bag of flatus—which means a bag of fart, you might add that to your vocabulary, thus increasing it to about two hundred words—although you are an indifferent psychologist . . . despite all these shortcomings, Ward, you are a passing imitation of a hominid, albeit primitive, with at the very least a rudimentary instinct for self-preservation, or so I infer, since despite your having farina for brains and BBs for balls, you still hang on to your commission. Being so gifted by God against His better judgment, you will understand after the briefest reflection that no one, especially no one of your modest faculties, will want his boss to know that he blew his cool by verbally assaulting two officers of equal grade, using foul and profane language in spite of the superintendent's condemnation of such behavior at the last officers' call. You will not want your boss to know that you made an ass of yourself in front of an innocent cadet—look at her, Ward: look hard—and in front of Major Broadnax, who is a witness who, like you, works for the commandant. Got that, Ward? Now, I hate to offer advice that has not been specifically solicited, such advice being most frequently ignored. But I'll make an exception in your case, if only because I have an ROTC commission and don't know any better. Here is my soundest, most considered advice. Get lost, Ward. I won't ask you to apologize in front of Stu and the cadet, because I know from long experience that army officers with very loud voices often have very small gonads, and that small gonads and big fucking egos also travel in pairs. But your absence will be welcomed by everyone here, including you when you have time to reconsider."

The spectators, of course, heard not a word of this. They merely observed that Sam had fallen silent and was looking mildly at Lane, who turned abruptly away and stode off in the direction of Washington Hall.

Sam rejoined them. "Miss Linnell, Colonel Lane regrets his intemperate remarks and hopes you weren't offended. We all have our limits, and he was past his own. Don't judge him too harshly until you've found yours."

"Yes sir."

There was an uncomfortable moment, then the cadet asked Broadnax if she might retire to take care of company business. As she walked away, Broadnax said, "Jesus, Sam—I was afraid he was going to have a stroke. What did you tell him?"

"I just gave him a different perspective, Stu. He's a reasonable man, just like all of us. See you on Saturday."

Bernice Gort's house was a solid, two-story farmhouse built when ugly was in fashion. Once it had been a study in green, but years of gentle neglect had improved its impact on the eye, softening it to a dignified gray. It was barely visible from the road through a wall of cedars and a carelessly tended boxwood hedge.

Maggie guided the car up a narrow gravel drive. Her impression of the place improved when the drive curved alongside the front porch. The house was perched on the edge of a steep slope, with the river and the roofs of Cornwall stretched out below it. It was a place of retirement and contemplation, and Maggie felt an inexplicable sensation of contentment and sadness, a feeling that spoke at once of happy memories and things lost. She shut off the car engine beside the concrete steps that led up to a short stretch of leaf-covered turf in front of the door and looked out over the valley to the ruined fortress on Bannerman's Island and Breakneck Mountain on the far shore. Is this how Sam and I will end up? she wondered. Is this how *I* will end up, remembering Sam and raking leaves until I'm too old to lift a rake?

She climbed the steps and tried to find a doorbell or a knocker.

There was neither. She tapped on the frame of the screen door. A long silence followed. Oh, drat, she thought, Old Bernice has her damned hearing aid turned off. She opened the screen and tapped on the solid wood door inside; more silence. She tried the door knob. It was unlocked, and she opened it a crack.

Things happened fast. A low-slung, sable form wormed its way through the opening and surged out past Maggie, pausing for only an instant to appraise her with a baleful black eye. Uninspired by her potential as prey or sport, the huge, curly, unclipped poodle scrambled off the porch and tore off down the gravel drive in the general direction of Albany. Right behind the dog came an incredibly tiny woman whose face was creased with exquisite wrinkles like a dried-apple doll's. Her voice was not the voice of a small woman, though, and it echoed down the road to Cornwall: *"Satan! You son of a bitch! Come back here!"*

"Oh, I'm sorry!" said Maggie. "It was my fault. I let him out. It was an accident."

"Oh, don't worry about it, young lady. Satan always comes back. Sometimes it's days, but he always comes back. I pray a lot, but he still comes back." The old woman smirked. Then she said, "You must be Mrs. Bondurant. Come inside and we'll talk over old times."

Mrs. Gort made coffee for them. "Wrong time of day," she apologized, "but I can't stand tea; puckers my gums. And you haven't suffered, young lady, until you have felt your gums pucker." She served in a sort of library at the rear of the house. The windows were tall and narrow and looked out on a small patio bordered by dark fir trees. Leaves from the surrounding woods were tumbling across the yellowing grass and gathering in drifts against a stone boundary wall. Wrought-iron lawn furniture equipped with faded, dirty cushions was still on the brick patio. Maggie guessed that Mrs. Gort did not use the patio these days, and wondered who would volunteer to carry the heavy metal furniture away to winter storage.

I'm here to ask her about ghosts, thought Maggie, but there are enough ghosts here to hold a square dance. The library was filled with bookcases (for this was a real library) and, in the spaces between them, framed photographs and memories. The life of Brigadier General Hobart G. Gort was chronicled there: Cadet Gort, Class of 1927; Lieutenant Gort and his company lined up on the steps of stucco barracks, Gort himself kneeling in front with the guidon, Schofield Barracks, Hawaii, 1932; Captain Gort, Fort Benning, 1936. The whole maturing and mellowing of that youthful, angular face was there for inspection. There was Colonel Gort, professor and head of the Department of Military Art and Engineering. Another photo put him with Bernice and a group of what Maggie presumed were children and grandchildren in that wretched little backyard: Brigadier General Gort, retired. But in that picture it was high summer, and the patio was dappled with sun; Bernice held his arm, and the smallest child, a girl of about four, leaned shyly against her skirts; the general had been laughing about something when the shutter clicked.

In contrast, the library was dark now, even in midafternoon, because the sun was already behind the summit of Storm King. Bernice had turned on a table lamp, but the walls seemed to absorb its weak yellow glow.

"Alice said you wanted to ask me about the ghost paper," Bernice said happily after apologies for the quality of the coffee ("Decaffeinated—hate the sludge, but that effete doctor at West Point took me off the real stuff"). "Nobody has asked me about that foolish thing for years and years. What brings you to it?"

Maggie told her about the ghost investigation, but did not mention her own research on Adonijah Proctor. Anticipating Liam's lofty critique and Sam's mania for objectivity, she wanted to hear Bernice's recollections first and without prompting.

"Well, I can't say I'm surprised," said Bernice. "They turned that room into a trunk room and just forgot about it. Very shortsighted, but just what you'd expect of that crew in the commandant's office. I told them it would just happen again."

"Well," said Maggie, "you were right. Apparently they opened it again in the sixties, and there was another haunting incident. Then, of course, they made it a supply room again, and forgot. This year, my husband says they needed space and opened it. Presto!"

"Not surprised a bit. They're like the ancien régime: learn nothing and forget nothing. It comes from pumping one career-mad general after another through the place; they know nothing, but they *have* to change things because leaders change things just to see the trouble it causes. Oh, I hope I didn't misunderstand Alice—your husband *is* permanent?"

Maggie admitted as much, to Bernice's evident relief. "I get more garrulous every year. Sign of age; nobody but that pea-brained Satan to talk to. I was sure I'd offended you. Hob always used to give me hell for my indiscretions. What department is your husband in?"

"BS and L."

"BS and *what*? Is this some new bureaucratic creation, slouching off to Bethlehem to be born?" Bernice's distaste for bureaucratic creations was clearly of long tenure.

Maggie smiled. "Behavioral Sciences and Leadership, Mrs. Gort. Sam's a psychologist."

"Oh," she said with relief, "just a name change! They used to be Military Psychology and Leadership, and then the Office of Military Leadership. Dear friend of mine, Red Shipley, used to be head. What a smoothie! That weasel could grin a jabberwock to death. Hob thought he walked on water—he was one of Omar Bradley's protégés. Dear man. Died in 'sixty-two, down in Arizona. On the golf course, Hob said, so I expect he died with a smile on his face."

She refilled Maggie's cup with coffee (decaffeinated) and looked out the window at the parade of leaves. Maggie sipped in silence. The old woman was elsewhere, perhaps where the summer sun speckled the patio and there was the laughter of children.

Finally she returned. "I'm sorry, Mrs. Bondurant. You don't have all afternoon, even if I do. I still have the paper—I dug it out after Alice called, along with some notes I took when I was writing it. Most of what you'll need is in there."

"If I may ask, what conclusion did you draw about the haunting?"

Bernice suddenly laughed, a sound as light and elusive as the dry leaves. "How does one 'draw a conclusion' about a haunted room? If one does, my dear, one never admits it."

"No speculations about who the ghost was?"

"Oh, I'll *speculate* if you want, but it wasn't *a* ghost. It was two: sad old Captain Proctor and his unfortunate little Annabelle."

"Ah, a familiar name!" said Maggie. "Where did you find out about old Adonijah?"

"There was an old, old book in the library . . ."

"Upton's *West Point on the Hudson*?"

112

"The same. I take it you braved the cadet library. Is Betty O'Grady still there?"

"Good Lord," said Maggie, "she was there in 1947?"

"Indeed she was. Her husband was Master Sergeant Seamus O'Grady—only she called him 'Hamish' or something equally outlandish—who worked for the Master of the Sword for years and years. I used to see her all the time. I was a great scholar in those days, Mrs. Bondurant. Not just the Ladies' Reading Club, either. You know, I majored in mathematics at Wellesley. I was getting my MA when Hob swept me off my feet in 'thirty-two."

"I know the feeling," said Maggie.

"If I may ask, Mrs. Bondurant, why are you involved in this quest?"

"Please call me Maggie, ma'am. Because I'm bored."

"Aha! The professor neglects you?"

"No, not at all. It's just that he has this grisly dedication to his work, and we don't have that to talk about. We're actually *sharing* this project. I'm doing the background research . . ."

Bernice laughed. "You know you're getting old, Maggie, when you become a part of the 'background research.'"

Maggie changed the subject to Bernice's sources for the 1947 ghost paper.

"Well," she replied after a brief reflection, "mostly I used Upton's *West Point on the Hudson*. There was also a brief reference to the ghost in Schofield's memoirs. The most interesting, but less usable, of course, was Upton's other book, the memoir."

"Memoir?"

"Oh, yes! He wrote an autobiographical collection of sketches on life at West Point. It was self-published, of course. An odd book, not at all like his informal history. Didn't Betty O'Grady mention it?"

"She did," said Maggie, "but she said it didn't exist any more."

"Oh, nonsense! If they haven't thrown it out—and they never throw anything out!—it's still there. She must be losing her wits."

"I had the impression from what she said that she had never seen a copy."

"Then she *is* batty. She found the thing for me in 'forty-seven. It was an old book, binding was loose. And the pages were rather

113

badly stuck together at the end—never found out how the plot came out."

"How much was in this book about the ghost?"

"Quite a bit, as I recall—and, if memory serves, part of it contradicted the story in his history. In fact, he flitted back to it once or twice, seemingly quite out of context. I think he was fascinated by the business."

"Do you think he was just obsessed by the supernatural?" Maggie asked.

"I don't think so. My, it's been so many years! Oh, yes! Now I remember! You know, Maggie, I have a phenomenal memory. I think it comes of turning off my hearing aid and talking to no one except Satan. Anyway, Upton, you know, was a friend of General Hancock—I think Hancock was three years ahead of Upton at the Point—and Hancock had known Proctor himself during his cadet years, when Proctor was professor of ordnance or something. I can never keep the old departments straight. Hob was furious when they dismembered Art and Engineering and created those other bureaucratic upstarts. It was his last battle, poor man." Bernice lowered her voice out of deference to General Gort's picture. "You know, Maggie, Hob was a terrible engineer. I loved and trusted that man and we were happy for fifty-two years of marriage. But I'd never live below any dam he built. But God! That man was a bureaucratic infighter! He should have been the dean, but he was too old when the old dean finally retired. I thought they'd just mummify him—the dean, not Hob—and varnish him and leave him there in that great chair in the conference room. Matter of fact, given that man's level of activity I don't think anybody'd have *noticed* . . ."

She was clearly prepared to make the most of her captive audience, but help arrived just in time with a terrifying crash as Satan, having shoved aside the front door, entered the library at a gallop. The moment his feet hit the wood floor, they skidded in the four cardinal directions, and a look of manic desperation lit his eyes as he slid into a small oriental rug. The rug slipped and folded under one paw, and the other three legs went skyward. He hit the floor with a heavy thud and struggled there for a moment in a whirling tangle of black legs, curly hair, and glistening saliva. Maggie sat watching with amusement, but Bernice was paralyzed with the knowledge that a real disaster was only moments away and there was nothing she could do to head it off.

"Watch out for the cup, Maggie," said the widow, "it's antique Limoges."

Satan arched his back, did a sort of reverse Immelmann on the bare floor, and landed on all four feet. After pausing there for just an instant, momentarily surprised at being upright again, he launched himself at Maggie. The rear paws hit the fold in the rug, and the whole thing shot out behind him in a blur, coming to rest against the wall. Maggie held up the cup and saucer and locked her knees together (her father had once owned a golden retriever, and she knew something of dogs' ways—which were similar, she reflected as her life flashed before her, to those of men). The huge poodle brushed aside a mahogany butler's table with a silver service sitting on it and, coming heavily to rest with his front paws on her lap, began to lick Maggie's face with single-minded lasciviousness.

"Maggie, I'm so sorry," said Bernice after dragging Satan, his toenails skidding wildly on the floor, into the pantry and bolting the door. "Satan was not Hob's idea, he was mine—to keep me company after Hob passed on. I am told by old friends that I am a passably intelligent woman, but that dog is living proof that I am capable of quite creative stupidity when left to my own devices."

Maggie had rearranged herself and wiped the damp patches where the poodle had slobbered on her dress. "No problem, Mrs. Gort. I dated someone like that once in my wild undergraduate days."

"Satan will be pleased. What were we talking about before the interruption?"

"You were telling me about General Hancock . . ."

"Was I? Oh yes. As I was saying, Hancock—quite a hero of the Civil War, a corps commander—was a student of Proctor's as a cadet; it must have been just before Proctor's quixotic end in Mexico. He—Hancock, that is—apparently thought the world of old Adonijah, and they got to know one another quite well. Now, all this fell together when Upton, who graduated, I guess, right before the Civil War, got to know Hancock. I don't remember much of *that* story, but I think Upton was on his staff from early on, and later commanded a brigade under him. Then, after Appomattox, Upton went back to the Point to languish as a professor, much like Proctor. It would be a big help if you could prevail upon Betty O'Grady to get off her silverfish and find that book."

"Actually," said Maggie, "when I grilled her before, she changed the subject to the new catalog system. I almost never got her back on the topic."

"Oh, she was a whiner even as a young woman. You know she came from Highland Falls, don't you? I think she was third or fourth generation. But I don't want you to have to get *me* back on the topic, do I? I vaguely remember that Upton heard the story of the ghosts from Hancock, and a lot more besides. He also makes some references to a letter from Hancock in the history, doesn't he?"

"Yes," said Maggie, "I remember the passage. I had the feeling it was full of information, but he said it was 'no longer extant.' "

"Really. Well, you need that book. Lean on old Betty. There were some comments that were not in the spirit of the other book, if you'll pardon the expression, and they may be worth your attention." She extracted an old manila envelope from a stack of magazines on the butler's table. "This is the report I read to the club all those years ago. I read it over again before you got here, and I'm embarrassed—it seems shallow and superficial now, but remember I was a much younger woman then. Ignore the cute commentary."

Maggie accepted the envelope; it was satisfyingly heavy. "Thank you so much; I'll return it as soon as I can."

"Why bother, dear? I'm not going to use it. I don't even use this library anymore, except to receive the occasional guest. Why don't you just invite me to the club when you read your own work?"

"Oh, I'm not a member of the Reading Club—I'm just helping Sam, as I . . ."

"Well, why not? You're obviously an educated woman, Mrs. Bondurant. I'm sure Alice Fetterman would be happy to sponsor you in."

"Oh, actually I was hoping to find a job. Alice said the club meets during the day, and I don't see how I . . ."

"Oh, nonsense. You just don't want to be identified with what you consider a coven of middle-aged sherry-sippers."

Bernice's accuracy alarmed Maggie. "Not at all, Mrs. Gort. I didn't mean to suggest—"

"I know you didn't. Please understand, Maggie, the Reading

Club began in the days when there was absolutely nothing else for ladies—that's what we were, by the way, not women. The club was a genteel way for educated women to keep from going stark raving mad. It worked, or at least I flatter myself it did. If you think the Point is isolated now, you should have seen it in the forties. We might as well have been living behind the stockade at Fort Laramie. So, we made do. Maggie, the club has been around here for a very, very long time. So many things have been here for so long. West Point is a strange place"—Maggie nodded—"and it does strange things to people. The big trouble is, people come to love it. Not just the graduates, not just the faculty—I mean even the people in town who have worked there for years and years. If there are ghosts, Maggie, I think this is the kind of place they gather. Did you ever hear of a haunted drugstore? Or a haunted car wash?"

Maggie admitted she had not.

"It's where people love, Maggie—or, I suppose, where they hate. If there really are ghosts, that's the place to find them. And the deeper the love or the hate, the longer they stay. West Point is full of ghosts. We nurture them, like country people who leave a dish of milk out for the elves. West Point, like it or not, absorbs your life, and sometimes it sucks you dry of life, as it did Hob . . ."

"Surely," said Maggie, "it isn't as bad as all that."

"Oh, but sometimes it is. After Hob retired, there was nothing left for him. Oh, he went to the department functions for a while, but after a few years nobody knew him, and finally he stopped trying. He wrote an article or two for *Assembly*, but his heart wasn't in it. You know, Maggie, he died three years after he retired, and I think he died, as they say, because he didn't know what else to do with himself."

Maggie asked her why he couldn't enjoy his children and grandchildren.

"I beg your pardon?" said Bernice. "Oh, the picture on the wall. Those aren't our children, Maggie; those are the children of cadets we sponsored over the years. The year Hob retired, I invited some of them who were stationed on the East Coast to come to the ceremony. Do you know, Maggie, four of them did, and brought their families? We had one son, but he didn't make the reunion. I'm afraid he was killed in 'sixty-six. He would have been fifty-seven this year, but all we have of him is a silver star in a plush

117

box, which isn't much to show for all those years. He was Class of 'forty-eight. His wife stayed with us when she came to visit before he graduated, a week before they were married."

"Do you still see her?"

"No, Maggie. She remarried years ago. I don't think she can stand to think about West Point, much less visit me. I don't blame her, never did." Bernice's eyes suddenly welled up with tears. "We collect ghosts, Maggie. I'm sorry . . ."

"Oh no, Mrs. Gort . . ."

"And I live by myself in a haunted house." She drew herself up in her chair, still a tiny, aged woman but with a dignity that touched Maggie. "When you're as old as I am, Mrs. Bondurant, it takes more than a splash of holy water to make them go away. And if they did—what then?" The two women looked at each other in silence: Maggie proud and full of joy and ambition; Bernice Gort sitting erect and composed in her chair, balancing a cup and saucer and taking solace in the invisible host of the past that swirled about her in the darkening library.

They stood at the door. Maggie held the envelope with Bernice's paper and Mrs. Gort held her arm affectionately. From the pantry came the soft scratching and muffled barks of Satan, furious to be let out. It was after five o'clock, and the sun was well down behind Storm King. It was turning cold and the wind was lessening as if cowed by the shadows.

"Listen, Maggie, you find a life for yourself, if you can do it without losing what you need in your husband, or what he really needs from you." Bernice drew Maggie's face down to her and kissed her on the cheek.

As Maggie slid into the car, the last she heard of Bernice Gort was a shout of *"Shut up, Satan, or I'll strangle you!"*

118

3
Liam

chill of winter
a slowly failing fire
faltering desire

Darkness of Darkness
we meet on our way
in loneliness

8

*L*iam shut down his office at three o'clock on Friday, changed into a civilian suit, hastily packed a folding bag, and left West Point. The drive to La Guardia was always a trial; the United States Military Academy is scarcely an hour's trip from New York City, but its utter isolation is apparent as soon as the traveler passes the Thayer Gate. And now Liam was in an impatient mood. He was only fifteen minutes into the trip and already pounding the steering wheel. Calm reserve was for company; now he was alone, on the way to Anna, and frustrated at every delay.

His last trip had been in late September—it had been almost a month now, and the old malaise was there again. The cave-dwellers in his spleen yawned and stretched, and he felt their gnawing. The irony was not lost on him. Indeed, since meeting Anna Perugino, irony had been his constant companion on what he modestly considered the road to ruin. As on all his other happy trips to Boston and this woman he loved, his spirits would ride an implacable sine curve, agony to giddiness to a different kind of agony. It was therapy for hubris.

He had met Anna six years before, amid the wreckage of a divorce and the custody rout when Linda had told him after his third transfer in five years that she no longer wished to participate in this game, that she was selling Boardwalk and Park Place, picking up her little piece, and moving back to Durham. Great, Liam had said, orders to Fort Benning in hand, go back to Durham. Sniff tobacco leaves and marry somebody named Jim Bob who owns a pickup truck with a sixteen-gauge goddamned shotgun on a rack in the cab and raises kudzu for fun and profit. But the kids were gone, in her sole custody for reasons Liam was unable to fathom. And she hadn't married anybody named Jim Bob who raised kudzu;

121

she had married a professor of journalism in Chapel Hill and his children called this man Daddy. No problem, he thought as he passed the exit that he knew led to the Rockland County Psychiatric Center, I lost my children but, by gum, I got Anna.

Anna worked for a computer firm in Dedham, Massachusetts, called Analog and, having had no more success at marriage than Liam, sublimated her own frustrations through an ambition which, if not exactly blind, was at least deaf to Liam's entreaties. Anna was rising at Analog as she had at her previous two jobs, by cool manipulation and, Liam suspected, by occasional resort to the lay-away plan. A trail of blood marked her climb. She wore her femininity like a lace nightie over a spiked breastplate, and impaled incautious men on it without a second thought. Liam had written a poem about her once for her amusement, and in part it offered these sentiments:

> *Emotions, she would always say,*
> *And penis envy are inconsistent,*
> *So I'll just plunder, gorge and prey*
> *And hold my love forever distant.*

> *SING: Husbands, lovers, millionaires,*
> *If I can't have one, I'll cut off theirs—*
> *Woman, lady, kitten, bitch,*
> *I'll save myself for someone rich.*

But such was her pride she framed the poem and hung it in her office. One day, this gesture announced to Liam, I'll have *your* family jewels up there, tanned and stuffed and mounted on a mahogany plaque with a brass name plate. I guess she may yet, he thought, and she'll pay the taxidermist with a little kiss.

She had come to Fort Benning to brief the commanding general of the Infantry Center on an improved fire-control computer for mortar-fire direction. She brought a long-haired flunky in a corduroy suit to carry the hardware, and directed the man this way and that as with an invisible prod. But the general got all silly when she briefed, her clear, crisp monologue and the austere but stylishly understated wool suit complementing huge ingenue's eyes. Liam was taken at once by her diminutive feet. Had they been bound? Raised by missionaries in China, he had thought, kidnapped and held by the bloodthirsty warlord Wu Fu-Yu, and so coveted by his rivals that . . . then he saw the eyes. They were enormous, deep brown and accented by a judicious brush, eyes to topple a warlord. But he looked again, and blinked. He had the overwhelming impression that there was nothing behind them; no, there was something there, but peering out as if through a one-way mirror. I look in this girl's eyes, he thought, and I see the reflection of my own folly. The general made some witty comment and she laughed, a loud, unfeminine laugh. But it had to be robust; nothing less would pass through the looking glass of those eyes.

She had stayed behind after the briefing and he had suggested a tour of evening culture in Columbus, Georgia, which he reckoned would kill at least thirty minutes; he found himself talking about his divorce and his children and his frustrations. He thought her curiously shallow and self-centered, somehow like an adolescent in a stylish adult's suit. But she was oddly disarming as well, and he found himself ensnared.

She was gone the next day, and Liam went back to work as usual. But Anna was on his mind; he pictured her ingenuous movements and the strange eyes, and he heard the artless music of her laugh. For the next few days his paperwork—all but the assessment of the Analog fire-control computer—went begging, and even the secretaries snickered. Finally the chief of staff, a bald-headed redneck from Arkansas, took Liam aside and suggested that he had better take a week's leave or swallow a couple of forkfuls of saltpeter or find another career. Liam opted for the leave, called Analog and tracked down Anna, then celebrated his success by telling her his first lie: that he was going on temporary duty to the Boston area. Did she know any good restaurants thereabouts? Well yes, she allowed as how she did; quite a few, in fact, with a wide range of price and cuisine. "What kind do you like?" she asked.

He took a chance. "French?"

"Great! I'll send you a list."

"I can get a list from the Chamber of Commerce," he replied. "How about company?" And she had agreed. He had never been entirely free from her from that moment, and never content.

He turned off the Palisades Parkway for the George Washington Bridge and paid the toll. The traffic was picking up a little, Friday afternoon traffic, but most of it headed the other way. He turned onto the Deegan Expressway on the far side of the Harlem

River and by the time he passed Yankee Stadium the little demons were dining with unseemly relish. He took his mind off the traffic and rehearsed his first words to Anna.

"Holy shit!" Liam stood and gaped at her, his overcoat dangling over his arm, the belt touching the dirty carpet of the concourse. "What have you done?"

"Thanks a lot! I like it. Everybody likes it."

"Jesus, you're a natural brunette. Your skin color, your eyes. How could you do it?"

"Don't be provincial, Liam. Everybody knows I'm a brunette. They're not supposed to think I'm a natural blonde."

"What are they supposed to think? That you polish your hair with brasso?"

"Welcome to Boston." She looked slightly away from him, avoiding his eyes, her delicate mouth compressed just enough to show a cool, impersonal hurt. He knew the gesture well, but familiarity had not armed him with sufficient contempt to resist it. He gave in with a mental shrug and decided that, if they had to be on Anna's head, then blond highlights were just dandy. He put down the suitcase he had carried on the shuttle and kissed her lightly on the cheek. "You're beautiful."

She smiled and lifted her chin ever so slightly, eyelids just closed. It was another gesture he knew only too well; it meant *Gotcha, sucker.*

"This is all I brought," he said. "Let's get out of here. I'm tired of terminals. I need a drink. I need food."

"You've come to the right place," Anna said with the jaunty air of a millionaire yachtsman. "Follow me." They walked quickly through the terminal, past glum knots of passengers waiting for luggage to appear. Anna was in the lead, and she ignored their stares with studied placidity. She was not dressed for a two-bill dinner this time, Liam noted with a mixed relief and disappointment. *I get off cheap; but so does she, if I know my Anna. This is a routine night out*—soft beige wool sweater, dark wool skirt, slit in front and disclosing smooth knees and slender calves. *Who is she tonight? The old battered purse is there. She must be the no-nonsense woman on the way up. Heaven help the working girl.*

124

That night it was North Italian: veal in wine sauce with artichoke hearts and a white wine in honor of the pale and delicate flesh. The restaurant was a hole-in-the-wall. It was Anna's favorite, and she attacked the veal like a lion feeding on fresh zebra. Liam chewed slowly and watched her in the candlelight. The eyes had not changed in all the years he had known her, and were set off tonight by careful brushwork. In the soft and uncertain luminance the effect was of a Byzantine empress—probably Theodora, Liam proposed in private dark glee. What *anekdota*, sad and breathless, hide behind the eyes of my sphynx? As opaque as they are beautiful, he thought, the eyes that never quite look at me, that never quite reveal.

She was on the offensive tonight. "Why do you still put up with this army crap after all these years?" She had polished off medallions of veal and an antipasto and was ready for action.

"Fun, travel, adventure," Liam said. "A chance to kill people and break things. Terrific food. What more could a real man want?"

"Decent pay."

"I do all right, Anna. When you toss in the quarters and the commissary and PX and medical care, there's a lot left over for the occasional dinner in Boston."

She shook her head. "Okay, forget the pay. Wallow in altruism. I still say you should be in a university doing real work, dealing with grad students and real professors. You have what it takes to do what you're doing elsewhere. Sure, you'd make less, but you could spend your leisure moments making some wide-eyed innocent coed or graduate assistant gasp and sigh for a lot less than it takes to feed me and wish I were somebody else."

"You seem to think you have me pegged with great precision."

"Somebody has to, Liam. You don't know who you are from day to day."

"Yeah, well, I take my ID card out and check every hour on the hour so I know what name to scribble on memos." He regarded her with absurdly studied gravity.

She ignored him. "I have one thing that means something to me: my job. I'm going to knock the industry dead. And there are all sorts of men around ready to help me enjoy myself while I do it. You don't have any real objective; you just drift along, examining yourself and fighting yourself to a standstill. What do you want, really?"

"Let's go back to you. You're building your life on nothing, nothing at all. What will you do with yourself when you're not young and dazzling anymore, when you've reached the plateau in your career? Your philosophy is like Keynesian economics: built on infinite growth and finite resources. Who's going to pay the deficit?"

"Not me, Liam. Nobody will. I'm not leaving anybody behind to mourn, and I'm not growing old. I refuse to outlive my useful and happy life. And I won't drag anybody with me."

Liam dropped the subject and went back to his veal. Anna scared him at moments like this. There was a hardness about her, a crystal cocoon that protected whatever was inside and kept him from touching her.

That is the problem, he thought later, just before dawn. He was always awake early; since cadet days the hour before reveille was his own time, and nothing could intrude. Anna was still sound asleep, her knees drawn up and her back to him. He could see the sheet rise and fall with her slow breathing. There is something inside that crystal shell. There has to be. I love this bitch-goddess. I bear the scars of her in secret places, but I have never touched her, never. I see my own reflection in her eyes, sensing only dimly what hides on the other side. If I could just find what touches her, what frightens her, what (if anything) hurts her. *Vain is man's ill-speaking and blame of women*, Euripides wrote, *the twanging of an idle bowstring; and I shall prove it. Their covenants have no witness.* But she is right. If I were really what I claim to be, I would never quote Euripides.

He rolled toward her and molded himself against her back; when his feet touched hers he recoiled from their coldness. A heart that small can't carry blood *everywhere*, he thought. But her shoulders were warm and he could smell what was left of last night's perfume; he breathed it in slowly and then kissed her gently on the back of her head. There was no movement. His hand slipped around her and found her breast and he traced the nipple softly with a fingertip. Anna stirred slightly at this, but then moved her shoulder forward, rejecting him. The stirrings of an erection deserted him. Oh well, it was an idea. Her passion for him was such that their lovemaking was roughly as frequent as the Winter Olympics and half as warm. He kissed her again and settled in passively against her back. He whispered "I love you," something he seldom did in recent years. Anna did not stir.

Now he could see the beginning of light coming through her window. She would sleep until nine or ten after a late night. He would be asleep again, too, once his predawn prayer was over. Dearest my love, he thought, my precious lady, my bitch-goddess, sparkling and chiseled like a Waterford crystal decanter. I can just glimpse the wine through the glass, but I never taste it. Sweet, I imagine, but laced with belladonna; beautiful lady, deadly nightshade.

Dawn came without a sound. Liam slept through it.

Sergeant Saganian and Specialist Ortega picked up a ton-and-a-quarter truck from the transportation motor pool at 0730, while Liam was sound asleep in Boston. Sam and Captain Salinger met them at the lab with a hand truck, and they all killed half an hour drinking coffee before facing the job of moving nearly half a ton of equipment to the 47th Division. The toughest challenge was a huge ten-channel polygraph, about two hundred unwieldy pounds and nearly six feet tall, topheavy with a seventeen-inch multi-channel oscilloscope. Saganian's predecessor, a diminutive staff sergeant, had tried to manhandle the thing down two steps and trapped himself in a corner behind it, in which humiliating state he had remained for nearly two hours before Salinger found him. This time they were obliged to move it up two steep and narrow flights of steps into the room next to the ghost. The balance of the equipment could be broken down into smaller loads, but it would still take most of the morning just to move the equipment in, much less set up, test, and calibrate the instruments.

By the time Saganian drove the truck through the sally port and up to the division, Andrea Linnell had cleared the room where the equipment would be installed and shifted most of the cadets to other areas in preparation for an inspection and the parade that would entertain the crowds before the football game. It was just as well, Sam observed; once they started moving the polygraph up the steps no one could move up or down, and the safety hazards involved in shifting heavy loads made it the better part of valor to have the cadets away. However low they might seem in the general pecking order of the army, woe betide the unshriven soul who let one be gratuitously injured or inconvenienced.

Sam's nightmares came true. Halfway up the first flight the tall contraption began to sway. Salinger and Sam were on the bottom, lifting; Saganian and Ortega (Saganian holding on to the back of the oscilloscope for dear life while Ortega stood behind him contributing worry and hand wringing) stood above. The polygraph tipped toward the officers. "Hold on to the son of a bitch!" Salinger yelled. Pulling for all he was worth, Saganian tilted the machine backward. The sergeant was forced back onto the steps by the weight of the thing, and then the casters on the bottom slipped off their step. The polygraph bounced down onto the next step with a sickening lurch and drove, edge on, into Salinger's foot, prompting a squeak of pain, and a stream of profanity from Saganian. This critique was directed at Ortega, whose contribution to the disaster was no more than an incidental sin of omission.

"God damn it," Sam shouted, "leave Ortega alone and help me get this fucking catafalque off Salinger's foot!" With eyes popping out and mouth set in a grimmace of agony, Salinger gurgled agreement. After endless moments of grunting and an occasional moan, set against Saganian's aria of curses, the cabinet finally tilted up. With a neigh of relief, the injured lab officer jerked his foot from under the edge and fell backward, to the bottom of the steps. He sat at the bottom of the flight, trying to remove his shoe and see if the foot was broken, but Sam was now trapped behind the polygraph. If he went to help Salinger, there was no way Saganian could hold it, and it would roll down the steps and probably kill them. On the other hand, Sam alone was not strong enough to push the cabinet up the stairs, and Saganian and Ortega could not get a firm enough grip to pull it. Sam cursed under his breath; it was at least thirty minutes before the cadets would be back from inspection, and the barracks area was deserted. Salinger finally got the shoe off and observed, after a brief inspection, that he appeared to have a broken foot.

"That's just marvelous," said Sam, "just fucking marvelous. We are now officially screwed. How long can you hold, Sarge?"

"I don't know, sir," Saganian grunted. "I can't get my fingers on anything back here without screwing up the wiring."

"So screw up the wiring," said Sam. "This is a matter of life and death."

"Sir, this stuff is obsolete and we ain't got any fucking schematics; if I rip this wiring out, we'll never get the son of a bitch working again."

Oh my polygraph, oh my ducats, thought Sam. "Any suggestions?"

"Yes sir," Saganian replied. "Scream for help."

They screamed for help. There was no answer.

"Ghost, where are you now?" said Sam. "Okay, Sarge—we're going to roll this thing back down the steps. One step at a time. If I start to go and can't hold it, I have to depend on you two to keep me from getting killed. Remember: I'm signed for four hundred thousand dollars' worth of lab property, and if I die you'll stay here for the next ten years getting it inventoried."

"Roger that, sir," said Saganian. "We'll hold it or die trying." They nearly did. After ten minutes of straining and grunting to the accompaniment of Saganian's low running commentary, they had managed two steps. A mere fourteen remained.

"You guys having trouble?" It was Major Broadnax, standing in the entrance in front of Salinger, who was still reclining and massaging his foot.

"No, asshole, we're just having a coffee break," Sam hissed. "Will you get up here and help me with the son of a bitch?"

"Gee, I don't know," said Broadnax, "this is my best set of perma-press greens. They snag real easy." He stepped daintily over Salinger. He shoved in beside Sam and helped him lift. "Jesus, sir—what's this thing made out of, depleted uranium?"

"Mostly steel," said Sam, "and a lot of vacuum tubes. Now shove, God damn it."

"Right," said Broadnax. With a grunt and a mighty heave, they brought it over the last step. Sam sat on the landing while Saganian ran to call for an ambulance. The hospital responded promptly, and the driver, a cheerful specialist five, examined the foot and solemnly pronounced it broken. Sam thanked him for his trouble and for the diagnosis. Salinger moaned.

After the injured lab officer was safely gone, Sam said: "I'm glad I'm not a superstitious man."

"Not to worry, sir," said Broadnax. "Everything from this point on has to be downhill."

129

"I'm sorry you said that," said Sam, leaning back against the wall with his eyes closed, sweat streaking his face. "We still have to move the damned thing downstairs when the project's over."

"Here's to a long project," said Broadnax.

"What I really regret," said Sam maliciously, "is that Liam missed it all. He should really have been a part of this."

Broadnax laughed. "I could make his day. I really came over to tell you about my interview with Colonel Street this morning." Street was the regimental tactical officer.

"Was the colonel in a rare mood?" asked Sam. Street was famous for his dislike of the touchie-feelie wimps and faggots in BS and L.

"Rare," Broadnax affirmed. "Pretorius called him last night after Lane complained about your disagreement Thursday afternoon. Apparently Brother Lane did not take your advice. Pretorius argued him out of a general court-martial or a keelhauling or whatever Lane had in mind, but I guess he decided he had to give the bastard something to keep him from having a stroke, seeing as how he's the com's man and you and Liam work for the dean. Anyway, he told Street to pass on to you that Liam is under no, repeat no, circumstances, to interview any more cadets who may be considered for counseling center referral, that Liam will not, repeat not, hypnotize any more cadets. And finally, Pretorius asks that, if you speak to Lane again, you chew him out in words of three syllables or more so Lane won't figure out he's been offended."

"Pretorius's very words, or just words to that effect?"

"Pretorius's very words, edited by Street, further edited by me."

"Well, that's great. So much for the interviews we needed— or Liam needed, anyway. I guess all we have left is the high-technology solution. Hot dog, neighbors. It's amateur hour."

Shortly after this exchange, Saganian and Ortega returned with the truck and the rest of the equipment. Captain Salinger was in the emergency room; his foot was in fact broken, and he would be kept in the hospital overnight, largely because his state of mind was likely to lead to murder if he were allowed to limp about the streets unsupervised.

The rest of the instruments were stacked in the test room next to the haunted cubicle in fifteen minutes. Broadnax stayed to watch the hookups and checks, and Saganian, proud of his knowledge of technical arcana, explained each apparatus. Two microcomputers were placed against the common wall that divided the haunted area from the instrumentation room.

"These here are thermocouples," said Saganian. "They measure temperature. We're going to string them all round the room next door. They'll give us real-time data on temperature change."

"What good is that?"

Sam answered. "All the witnesses report a subjective drop in temperature. We don't know yet if it's real or just some sort of hysteria."

"Hysteria? I didn't think the cadets were that agitated."

"I don't mean they were hysterical, the way we usually mean it," said Sam. "I mean it in the sense Freud did—a physical sensation or other effect that has psychological and not physiological origins."

"Oh, of course."

"Liam thinks the reports of cold are just subjective. That's why we want true readings," said Sam with a shrug.

"Do you agree?"

"I don't know," Sam mumbled, worrying a loose toggle switch. "That's really not my field. I just make lights flash and buzzers buzz."

"I got it hooked up, sir," said Saganian. "We'd better test it before we go any further."

"Fine," said Sam. "Crank it up." Saganian turned on the computer. It was mounted in a slot in a steel rack with the keyboard projecting out. The disk drives hummed and clicked, and after about a half a minute the prompt message came up on a tiny television screen in another rack position. Broadnax was impressed. It looked professional. For the first time, he started believing in the project and concluded that Colonel Pretorius had chosen the right people to do the work.

At that moment the display screen went blank. Saganian listed the character flaws of cathode ray tubes in general and, for their benefit, summarized the ancestry of this particular one as he tinkered in the dark rear of the rack. Presently the screen was working again. Broadnax applauded politely.

"Just a loose BNC connector," said Saganian. "Try her again now." Sam entered a few commands and the disk drives came alive again. The screen filled with columns of numbers.

"This is the thermocouple routine," said Sam. "The numbers in each column represent the temperature at a given five-second interval."

Broadnax nodded. He had a weakness for gadgets. "But where do the thermocouples go?"

"Next door in the haunted room."

"How are you going to get the cables to the computer?"

"Through the hole."

"What hole?"

"The hole we're going to have to knock in the wall, of course," said Sam with a smile and tilt of the head.

"Now, wait a minute, sir! You mean you're going to screw around with the wall—put a hole in the wall?"

"I don't know how else to do it. I suppose we could use some of our infrared systems and dispense with the wires."

"That sounds a lot better."

"Great," said Sam. "Then you won't mind the window."

"*What* goddam window?" The tactical officer felt his feet go numb. So this, he thought wildly, is hysteria.

Sam shrugged impatiently. "The window we'll have to put in the wall to let the infrared beams through so we can dispense with the hole in the wall to let the shielded cables through."

"How big would the window have to be?"

Sam regarded the wall thoughtfully and scratched his head. "Well, let's see. We need full room coverage from three or four angles, both walls that lie along Barstow's alcove. I'd say—conservatively, of course—about two by three."

"Inches?" Broadnax asked hopefully.

"Feet. Of course, that's a conservative estimate, as I say. We might have to . . ."

"Shit," said Broadnax, "I can't punch a two-by-three-foot hole in the wall!"

"Guess we'd better go with the cable then," said Sam, shaking his head sadly.

"Damn right."

The cadets came back from the parade and left again shortly after for Michie Stadium and the football game. Broadnax stayed behind to watch Sam and the technicians and to make certain that the hole in the wall was as small as possible. By two o'clock the array of instruments was in place and the sensors and the television camera on the pan-and-tilt drive mounted in the haunted room. The electrodes and sensors for physiological measurement were arranged over Barstow's bunk. The electroencephalograph electrodes were plugged into a junction box above the pillow, and the thin wires and cold cup sensors dangled down to the level of the blankets. Saganian turned on the main power switch, and the roomful of magic came alive like a Disney exhibit, with purrs, clicks, and finally the warm colorful glow of display screens and indicator lights. Finally, he turned on the TV camera and panned it around the cadets' room.

"Well damn," said Broadnax. "That's amazing. Now, will it really catch a ghost?"

"If he's there," said Saganian, "we'll sure as hell catch him, sir."

Broadnax looked at the displays. He recognized the temperature indicators, eight spidery green lines crawling across the screen. They fluctuated slightly. Whenever the lines reached the far side, the computer beeped softly and a five-digit number appeared at the bottom of the screen, then the printer buzzed briefly. "What's it doing?"

"It gives us a real-time display of the temperature on each of eight channels," said Saganian, "sampled five hundred times a second. Then, when it's sampled enough to fill up the screen, it averages the temperature and prints it out. That gives us about one hard average sample every three seconds. Temperature isn't going to change so fast that the sample rate'll miss it, and it saves paper and disk space."

"Great," said Broadnax. "Now what's this?" He indicated a narrow box fitted neatly into the rack; it had a small display screen with a line of short red bars that pulsed up and down along the bottom of a graph.

"That's the audio microcomputer," said Ortega, who had once worked for a recording studio and knew about such devices. "We're using it as a real-time sound analyzer. It measures thirty-two frequency channels at the same time—that's those little bars that jump up and down. The fluctuations you see there are the ambient noise in the barracks. Here, sir, I'll show you." He stepped out of the instrumentation room and into the ghost room, then recited "Mary Had a Little Lamb." The bars formed shifting peaks and valleys as he talked.

"That's fascinating," said Broadnax as Ortega came back into the test room. "Now, what the hell do all these wires do?" He indicated a bundle of multicolored thin wires that disappeared into the back of the polygraph that had broken Salinger's foot.

"Those are the inputs from the EEG sensors in the next room, sir," said Saganian. "They'll display brain waves on that big TV screen."

"You say there's not supposed to be anything coming through them now?" asked Broadnax.

"Nothing, sir. We have them going through shielded cable and we filter out the sixty-hertz range so we won't have to watch the AC current think."

Broadnax pointed at the oscilloscope screen at the top of the polygraph cabinet. "Then what's making those yellow lines wiggle?"

9

They stared at the display tube. Eight glowing amber lines snaked across the screen on even parallel tracks and then, on reaching the end, started over from the beginning. Broadnax was right. The lines were not straight; they surged up and down in unison, following an irregular, jagged course. All the lines were alike in their pattern of excursions, with no apparent coherence.

"I give up," said Sam. "What is it?"

Saganian squinted at the screen. "Beats me, sir. I guess the cable—no, the cable's shielded—the electrode wires it must be, the electrode wires. They must be picking up some kind of signal. I don't know what it could be, though. They look like EEG."

"So does any random complex noise," said Sam. "We have some noise in the system somewhere."

"But where, sir?" Saganian asked. "And what? It sure as hell isn't any normal power source. The system's filtered for sixty hertz. And look—there's a slow wave at about five or six hertz. What could cause a form like that?"

"No idea," said Sam. "Maybe it's a beat, summed from higher frequencies. But we sure as hell have to find out. I can't make valid measurements with all that garbage in the background."

Broadnax didn't want to be left out. "What are you talking about, sir?"

"We're not sure. The fluctuations we're getting have to be from the EEG sensors—that's electroencephalograph, brain-wave sensors—on the other side of the wall. They're long thin wires with little gold-plated cups on the ends. We attach them to the subject's scalp and ear lobe—that's for ground—and measure tiny changes in potential between two electrodes. The changes represent the algebraic sum of millions of tiny potentials on the cortex in the vicinity of the measuring electrodes."

"So that's a mumble of brain cells up there on the TV?"

"Oh, no—there's no subject over in the other room, no brain. The electrodes are just dangling there, hanging from the junction box we just finished nailing into the wall over Barstow's bunk. What's happening is, there's some kind of electrical noise and the electrode wires are acting sort of like an antenna, picking it up."

"Is that unusual?"

"Well, yes and no. We expect to have sixty cycles per second in the background because of the AC current. But our machine's got a filter that blanks out the sixty-hertz band. And anyway, the noise is certainly not sixty hertz—at the speed those traces sweep across the screen, sixty cycles per second would sort of paint a blur across the phosphor. Also, I'm not certain why we're picking up anything with the wires just dangling. Any spurious signal I'm used to would be pretty weak. Whatever that junk is, it isn't weak."

Broadnax grinned. "Anything ghostly about it?"

"That's as good a guess as any," Sam laughed. "It *does* look like a human EEG. I mean, the general selection of frequencies looks like the sum of the frequencies you find in the cortex. I'm not sure why a ghost would have nerve potentials, though."

"Do brain waves project around the room?"

"Absolutely not! They're confined to the surface of the brain."

"Look at that," said Saganian. The traces quivered briefly in a regular, dramatic burst of activity.

"See, Stu," said Sam, "that looked like a human alpha burst. That's a peculiar waveform with high frequency and high amplitude, around eight to fourteen hertz. We see it when the section of the brain we're measuring is relaxed."

"Then the ghost is asleep?"

"No, alpha only occurs in some isolated stages of sleep. It's more common when—damn it, you have me saying it! Listen, there is no ghost thinking. There's some unexpected kind of electrical noise in . . ."

"What's that, sir?" asked Saganian.

The form of the waves had changed. The random pattern of excursions had been replaced by a repeating series of rounded humps followed by sudden, short spikes.

"It looks like an EKG backward, sort of," said Ortega.

136

"That's a measure of electrical impulses in the heart, Stu," said Sam. "But the spike is too short. And, as Ortega says, it's backward."

"Ever seen anything like it?" asked Saganian.

"Yes," said Sam, "I think I have. But I can't remember where, or what it was. I'll think of it eventually, and then maybe we can fix it."

"It sure doesn't look like anything *I* ever saw," said the NCO. "I wouldn't know where to start looking for a source."

"Well," said Sam, "how about in the room? Go around and see if the stereo's on or something."

"I promise you," said the tactical officer, "there ain't no stereo in there."

"I'll see what he has that might be doing it," said Saganian, and disappeared through the door into the hallway. They heard the door open and the *clump-clump* of Saganian's booted feet.

"Sir," said Ortega, "look at it now." The dome-and-spike pattern was gone, replaced by a random pattern of rapid small changes.

"Well," said Sam, "our noisy friend has come alive again. That's similar to beta waves—it really looks like conscious, awake human brain activity." As they watched, the magnitude of the excursions slowly increased. Within a few seconds, the spikes of each line almost touched those of the adjacent traces.

"Damn," said Ortega. "That's some signal." He raised his voice. "Hey Sarge, what're you doing over there?"

They heard his voice faintly: "Turn on the RTA, sir. Turn on the tape. Hurry!" Sam adjusted the microcomputer that performed audio frequency real-time analysis for a very high gain. The yellow bars shifted and peaked, pulsing and bouncing across the screen. Ortega started the audio tape recorder.

"Got 'em on, Sarge!" Ortega shouted.

"Colonel Bondurant," Saganian squeaked from the plebes' room, "come over here, carefully! Quick!" Sam looked at Broadnax and shrugged, then stepped out into the hallway. He saw Saganian back out of the room, eyes wide. "Listen, sir—listen real close. Do you hear it?"

Sam listened. He heard nothing. "Sarge, I'm damned near deaf. Stu! Come here, quick!"

Broadnax scurried around the corner of the door.

"Do you hear it?"

The officer closed his eyes and tilted his head up, concentrating. Then his eyes popped open and his head bobbed assent. "Christ almighty! I do hear it."

"Both of you shut up!" said Sam. They looked at him in amazement. "Don't talk about it—it's important. Just listen." Although puzzled by his vehemence, the listeners complied. Sam strained to hear, but there was nothing but the insistent, dogged ringing that followed him everywhere. He walked, almost on tiptoe, back into the instrumentation room.

"Ortega," he whispered, "turn on the thermocouple channels." The lab technician typed a few commands into the computer and the orange lines scrolled across the video display. They were much less jagged than the "EEG" signals on the polygraph's display and were scarcely moving. Nothing there, no change in temperature.

"Sir," Ortega hissed, "look at the polygraph." The EEG-like signal was fading. In a few seconds it was gone. Sam signaled Ortega to be quiet and waited for a response from Saganian and Broadnax.

It came almost instantly. "I don't hear it anymore," he heard Saganian say. "Me either," answered Broadnax. "It's gone. Boy, oh boy. I don't believe it. I truly don't believe it."

"No!" said Sam. "Don't talk about it. Hang on a second." Picking up the end of the recording paper from the polygraph, he tore off a section, then ripped that piece in half. "Gimme your pen, Ortega." He took the lab technician's marking pen and the chart paper into the hallway.

"Here, Stu. Write down what you heard on this part of the paper, then give the pen to Saganian."

"Never mind, sir," said the NCO, "I have my own pen." He took the other piece of chart paper and scribbled on it. Sam collected their notes.

Broadnax had written: *A child crying.* Saganian's note read: *A little girl crying.* He showed the papers to them. Broadnax shook his head in amazement. Saganian leaned back against the door and whispered: "I'll be a son of a bitch."

"Did you hear it too, Sam?" asked Broadnax.

"No, I didn't. But that doesn't mean anything. I have a bad hearing loss in the high frequencies—occupational hazard for tankers. Was it faint, or could you hear it clearly?"

"It was clear, sir," said Saganian, "but it was strange. It didn't sound real."

"What do you mean, 'didn't sound real'?"

"I don't know, sir. Sort of—"

"Wait! Paper again!" He handed the sheets and pens back to them, and they scribbled dutifully. Saganian wrote: *Hollow, tinny, like it was ringing in my head.* Broadnax's impression: *Distant—like an old Victrola. Heard from far away.*

"Well," said Broadnax, "that was what I call quick results. First time you turned your stuff on, eureka!"

"No eurekas yet, please," Sam said with a good-natured grimace. "All we have so far is spurious signals and two auditory hallucinations."

"Hallucinations, sir?" said Saganian. "We both heard the crying."

"You were both primed to hear it," Sam pointed out doggedly. "We've discussed the cadet reports before. That might have been enough to do it."

"What about the tape?" asked Ortega.

"Good point," said Sam. "What *about* the tape? Did you have the gain set up high enough, Ortega?"

"Shit, sir—I had it cranked way up. You could see the bars jiggle on the RTA. You could hear a field mouse fart."

"But what if the crying was . . . well, if it wasn't a real sound?" asked Broadnax, a little reluctantly.

"You mean, what if it was some sort of telepathy?" said Sam. "Would the tape record it if it were just in your head? No, it wouldn't. It wouldn't respond to stray bits of 'psi energy' or whatever mysterious spoon-bending forces we have to imagine to make telepathy come true. But even if the instrument didn't record any real sound, that only raises another question."

"What's that?" asked Broadnax.

"Why didn't I hear it? I have high-frequency hearing loss, but telepathic transmission sort of presumes nonauditory reception. If so, I should have been able to hear it as well as you, since it would logically bypass or ignore damage to my inner-ear structures. So— let's run the tape."

The result evoked an explicit obscenity from Saganian. When Ortega played back the magnetic tape, they heard only a confused hiss of random noise. Over the static, they could hear the voices in the hallway (the microphone had been above Barstow's bunk) and Sam's sharp commands to curtail discussion. These were loud enough to make them flinch—Ortega had indeed turned the gain up, but any subtle passing of gas by the odd field mouse would have been effectively masked by the noise.

"Kiss my ass," said Ortega, "there's something wrong with the head, or maybe the tape's fucked up. We lost it."

"Maybe not," said Sam. "Run it back through the RTA." Ortega rerouted the wires to play back the recording through the audio computer for frequency analysis.

The results were unencouraging. The bars on the display covered the audible spectrum. "Look at that," snapped Ortega, "It looks like fucking white noise."

"See, Stu," said Sam, "it's worthless. The noise in the system is over a whole lot of frequencies, so we can't just filter it out. We'd be sure to filter out any of the crying along with the noise."

"You mean," said Broadnax, "there's nothing we can do."

"Probably not. Let me think on it. This will be the only certifiable weird event, the way our luck is running. If there's a way to extract our sobbing child, we'll find it. I'm in a hurry to get this project over with."

"Why the hurry, sir?" asked Broadnax.

Sam grinned maliciously. "I can't wait to move that polygraph *down* the steps. This time," he said, with a significant look toward Saganian and Ortega, "I'm going to be on the top looking down."

Betty O'Grady had the misfortune to be working in the basement of the library when Maggie entered the building on Saturday morning. Betty was methodically cataloging new acquisitions, barricaded at her desk behind piles of books with fresh, crackling bindings and untouched pages. She took great pleasure in handling new books. The old ones bothered her no end—the weak bindings and easily turned leaves with the hint of human touch about them revolted her. Had she the authority to forbid, cadets would never be granted access to the stacks, since this would preserve the precious volumes for some undefined and comfortably remote posterity.

She cringed when she heard Maggie's voice in the hallway, asking directions from one of those empty-headed girls the librarian seemed to hire every week. These girls appeared to have the useful life span of mayflies, departing before they had accumulated enough time to know microfiche from gefilte fish. To those girls Betty O'Grady was widely known as the troll who guarded the bridge between great books and mere readers. On this Saturday she would gladly have validated her reputation for the sheer joy of making someone suffer for the fact that she was obliged to be in the office on Saturday.

She remembered Maggie clearly from her visit early in the week. This was a woman to be reckoned with, Betty thought grimly, one of those damned bossy officers' wives. And she wanted to know about Upton's books, of all things. That was another matter, a real caution. I never thought anyone would come after that one again, she thought, not after it hadn't been asked for in nearly twenty years. Some things just never quite die.

Maggie appeared in the door, and Betty O'Grady peered at the tall and imposing young woman over her parapet of books like a rifleman over a stone wall. To Betty O'Grady, Maggie looked like the Winged Victory of Samothrace with a head.

"Well," said Maggie, "Mrs. O'Grady herself. And how are you this fine morning?"

"I'm really not supposed to be in here at all," Mrs. O'Grady whined, "Saturday is my day off, and—"

"But how lucky I found you in," Maggie exulted. "If you hadn't just happened to be in, I'd have had to wait until Monday!"

"I really haven't time to talk, Mrs. . . . ahhh . . ."

"Bondurant, Mrs. O'Grady, Margaret Bondurant. I came in early in the week looking for sources on ghosts at West Point. Remember?"

"Oh, yes. You found quite a bit, as I recall. Was the material of any help?"

"Oh, it was just marvelous. I particularly enjoyed John Waverley Upton's *West Point on the Hudson.* Do you remember our discussions on that little book?"

The older woman felt a twinge of apprehension. "Why, yes. I'm glad you found . . ."

"We also talked about a companion volume, Mrs. O'Grady. A self-published memoir by Upton, called—oh, what was it called?"

"I really don't—"

"Oh, of course. *My Years at West Point.* Saw print first, they say, in 1881. Do you remember? I asked you about it. You said the West Point Library didn't have a copy, never had."

"Yes, that's right. The book was self-published in a *very* limited edition. We have no copy of it here, and I doubt seriously if—"

"But of course," said Maggie, "you have charge of a very large number of titles, and it's easy to forget one or two."

"Mrs. Bonaventure," said Betty icily, "I . . ."

"*Bondurant.*"

". . . never forget something like that. There is no such book in our collection."

"Please punch it up."

"If you insist, but . . ."

"Please punch it up." Mrs. O'Grady sullenly switched on her computer terminal and let it warm up. She drummed her old fingers on the edge of the keyboard. When the prompt appeared she entered the title and author. Almost immediately, the reply came: TITLE NOT FOUND. CHECK SPELLING.

"There, Mrs. Bondurant. I'm sorry. We just don't have it."

"But you did. What happened to it?"

"Mrs. Bondurant," said the woman, rising from her swivel chair and pressing her advantage—had she been born a hamadryas baboon, the hair on her back would have stood erect—"we have no such volume, we never had, and I am very, very busy. Now, if you'd like to take this matter up with Mr.—"

"Mrs. O'Grady, Bernice Gort assures me that she has not only seen but checked out and read the book. She did so in 1947, and quotes from it in her paper on the subject of ghosts at West Point. I might add she also acknowledges the kind assistance of Mrs. Elizabeth Cleary O'Grady. Now, I'm certain you know as well as I do that Bernice Gort never had a lapse of memory in her life"— Maggie was guessing about this—"and I suspect you yourself have had very very few. I have some experience with librarians, Mrs. O'Grady. They never forget. Never. I also took the liberty of talking to your supervisor a few minutes ago, and he assures me that there is a file of volumes lost or stolen or destroyed. Be a dear, Mrs. O'Grady, and consult that file."

Betty O'Grady knew it when she saw it. Maggie was one of those who had at some point in her life learned about librarians. She surmised that Maggie had once been a graduate student and in order to survive had developed the knack for battering down the static defenses that the guardians of the card catalog orchestrated with the skill of field marshals. But Betty O'Grady was no ordinary librarian. She was the cream of the cream; she was the best. She had perfected the mobile defense as well, and recognized Maggie as a worthy opponent. She hadn't had a challenge like this since 1966, when she had held off the dean of the Academic Board for three weeks on the establishment of that instrument of the devil, the reserve shelf. Old General Bracken, God rest his soul, he was a tough customer. But this Maggie Bondurant was another. And she had an advantage she hadn't guessed, couldn't know: Betty O'Grady was afraid of her, because of the book, the one book that had made her violate the sacred trust of the librarian.

"Well, Mrs. Bondurant, I'm afraid the list is not on the computer system. In fact, most of it is made up of hand entries; only the last six or seven years are on the tapes. I'll have to look in the old binders. Could I call you when I have the information? I'm afraid my memory isn't what it used to be. If Mrs. Gort remembers it, of course it was there, but . . ."

"Why don't you start by checking the last six or seven years, if they're on the computer? Who knows when the book disappeared?"

Almost had me, Betty thought. "Well, of course. I'll do that little thing right now." She punched up the missing volume list, secure in the knowledge that the book would not be listed. "There," she said with a note of sympathy for Maggie. "It isn't there. Now, searching the binders is another matter. That will take—"

"Oh, Mrs. O'Grady," Maggie said, "I wouldn't think of making you do all that just because I'm curious about a book. Just show me where the binders are, and—"

She raised her hands in horror. "Oh, my goodness! I can't just let people go rummaging through all my files! Lord knows *what* might happen! You'll just have to wait until next week or so, when I can get around to it."

"Oh, I won't damage your binders. It's no trouble at all for me, Mrs. O'Grady, and you have such a busy schedule it seems a shame to let you waste time on this silly notion."

"Mrs. Bondurant, it's contrary to library policy. I'm sorry. It's not my decision."

"Oh well," said Maggie, "if it isn't your decision, it isn't. I wouldn't ask you to violate a library policy."

"Thank you. I'll get to it when—"

"I'll just ask Mr. Pennington upstairs for permission. I'm sure he has the authority to let me do it, and you wouldn't risk getting into trouble." Maggie paused and smiled, hoping Betty O'Grady would capitulate and save her the trouble of convincing Pennington, whose name she knew only from the library directory in the lobby. She misjudged her quarry. Betty stood her ground.

Pennington stood his ground as well. He was enormously fat and had, Maggie soon learned, no eye for a well-turned ankle. Cleopatra had met her Octavian. No, he insisted, only library personnel were allowed access to the circulation department's archives, but yes, he allowed, he would ask Mrs. O'Grady to get to the project as soon as possible. Here lies a fool, thought Maggie, who tried to hustle the East.

She took the trouble to go back to the stacks, and checked the shelves around *West Point on the Hudson*'s location, on the off chance the memoir was shelved but somehow unrecorded. There was no trace, and she felt her hands start to swell from her dust allergy. She thought of joining Sam at the barracks site, but decided not to enter the cadets' Central Area unescorted. Her resulting mood as she reached the door of her quarters was not improved by the sound of the telephone ringing inside while she fumbled for the keys. In a mad dash up the kitchen steps to answer it in time, she tripped and mangled her shin on the corner of the refrigerator.

It was Alice Fetterman. "Oh, Maggie," she said, "I'm so glad I caught you at home—I've been calling since breakfast."

"You just about missed me again," said Maggie, massaging her leg, which was skinned and starting to bleed. "I just got back from the library."

"That's just why I was calling. Did you find the book?"

"What? You mean the Upton memoir? No, I'm afraid not." Maggie frowned into the receiver. Her talk with Alice had been short; she could not recall having mentioned the book.

"Bernice called me last night, Maggie. She told me about your conversation Thursday, and something else occurred to her that she forgot to mention. She asked me to pass it on to you, for what it's worth."

"Whatever it is," said Maggie, "I'll take it! Betty O'Grady and the library have me stymied."

"Well, Bernice told me she had the feeling when you left that there was something else. She thought about it all yesterday, I guess, and finally it came to her. She said she remembered another problem with that book about twenty years ago, when the ghost was last rattling its chains and the superintendent ordered an investigation. I haven't read Bernice's paper, of course—have you had a chance to look at it?—but she says the haunting's particulars were pretty much the same as when she wrote the paper in 'forty-seven. Anyhow, the last time the ghost turned up, an investigator from the History Department was looking into the traditional background, and *he* found the memoir right there in the library stacks, where it was supposed to be. Bernice remembers it because Betty O'Grady mentioned it and because the History Department officer sent Hob a thank-you note for Bernice's old Reading Club notes. Bernice is really embarrassed beyond words, she says, for not remembering it when you visited."

Maggie bared her teeth and shook a fist at an imaginary Mrs. O'Grady. "Alice, please tell Mrs. Gort I owe her one. The plot begins to thicken. Do you know I talked to that O'Grady critter this morning, and she claimed the library never had a copy?"

"Did they lose it?"

"According to the venerable lady, it never graced their stacks. But Bernice not only cited it in her paper—which I *have* read, by the way—but also acknowledged Betty O'Grady's assistance. The old dragon denied it stubbornly."

"Well that's not all," said Alice. "Do you know I've *seen* the thing somewhere?"

"You're kidding! Where?"

"Well, that's the problem. I can't remember." Maggie made a frightful face at the receiver. "I just recall picking up an old book," Alice continued, "and being vaguely surprised to see that it was a memoir about West Point. I'm pretty certain it was the one you're looking for. But it was some time ago, a few years, and I can't remember where I was. I do know I wasn't in the library. It was at a flea market or a yard sale or something like that. I remember I almost bought it, but it was in bad condition, so I put it back."

"Oh, no," said Maggie. "I wish you'd bought it! Who knows where it is now?"

"Well, of course, I had no idea it was of any use except as a decoration. I'd have picked it up for a bookshelf relic, except that the back pages were gummed up. It looked like a total—"

"What about the back pages?"

"Oh, they were sort of stuck together—looked like somebody had spilled a little syrup on them and given the book up for lost."

"Alice, that's the book from the library! Bernice said the back pages were stuck together! Anyway, how many copies could there be floating around? It has to be the missing library copy."

Alice didn't answer for a long moment. "You must be right. But I know I didn't see it in the library. Why would a library book be anywhere else?"

"How much is an old book like that worth?" asked Maggie.

"Not much, I should think—especially not damaged."

"Maybe Betty O'Grady snitched it and sold it. Maybe she's covering up a theft."

"I don't think so," said Alice. "It would hardly be worth it."

"I guess not," said Maggie, "but it seems pretty strange that she would deny the book was ever there when it obviously was."

"I wish I could remember where I saw it," said Alice, "but it was a long time ago. I'm not pinning my hopes on finding it, even if I remember where it was—not after a lot of years."

"O'Grady might know. I'll try squeezing it out of her on Monday. Maybe the new evidence will make her crack. Anyway," Maggie gloated, "I'll enjoy the look on her face when I confront her. She's a guilty gal, Alice, and I don't know why."

On Saturday night the ghost incident claimed its first certain victim. The story had spread through the Corps of Cadets like chicken pox in a day-care center, and almost eclipsed talk of the upcoming Army-Navy game. The diversion of interest worried the commandant enough to cause him to publish a cautionary message through the chain of command, a terse reminder that this sort of nonsense can get out of hand, and that more serious business faced the corps than adolescent high jinks. This announcement, of course, did not produce its intended calming effect. The first casualty was Lumpy

Dilworth, a huge varsity linebacker from Florida who was known to have a fear of the dark. Prior enlisted service, including nine weeks in Ranger School, had not banished Lumpy's instinctive dislike of owls, bats, and the dead of night. The story of his panic one night during plebe year when a group of his classmates had induced him to try a shortcut through the cemetery had provided one day's merriment, and was not forgotten now that Lumpy was only months away from graduation.

Memories of this three-year-old joke tempted a cadet named Fred Comar to array himself in a sheet and hide in Lumpy's clothes press. When Lumpy returned from a racquetball game in the gym at ten thirty-five (recorded with precision—2235 hours—by the officer-in-charge who sorted the matter out), Fred Comar emerged from the locker, shrouded in linen and only dimly seen in the darkness of the room, and moaned horribly for Lumpy's entertainment. Lumpy was not entertained. Neighing in terror, he tried to leave the room in great haste. Sad to say, he had partly closed the door on entering, and crashed full tilt into the edge of the obstacle, breaking his nose and, owing to his considerable size, wrenching the top hinge from the door jamb.

The second casualty of the ghost incident was Fred Comar. Lumpy broke a racquetball racket over Fred's head. Since Lumpy was a football starter, and the Navy game was coming up, there was talk in the Association of Graduates of a lynching as well, with Fred's neck filling the noose. Calmer heads prevailed. On the whole, Fred profited by the incident. Previously a rank unknown in the corps, he would emerge as something of a folk hero, especially since Lumpy forgave Fred and went on to glory, pulpy nose and all, against the Navy line.

They had slept in on Sunday—Anna was an early riser on weekdays, and celebrated the weekends with late nights and late mornings. She shared the Sunday paper with Liam, and by ten o'clock the pages were spread untidily over the bed and their bodies were smudged with ink. Liam read the book reviews; the leisure section was Anna's.

"By the way," he said after discarding the book supplement, "I want you to come down to West Point next Friday."

147

She knew Liam well enough to be wary. "Any special reason?"

"A once-in-a-lifetime opportunity. The department's Halloween party."

"A costume party?"

"Yes, a costume party. You wouldn't want to miss it. How many costume parties do they have at Analog?"

"Are you joking?" she said. "It's a costume party every day around there! Computer people have no taste. My boss still wears double-knit sport coats."

"Well," said Liam, "are you game?"

She bit her lip. Going to West Point meant entering Liam's territory. She liked Liam where he was, on her turf. Here in Boston he was controllable; in West Point, she was less certain. Despite the advantage she held over him—a very simple one, yet the most powerful weapon in any arsenal, being loved without the burden of loving—she was never sure what went on behind Liam's deadpan façade. She sensed in him a black intensity that was held closely in check. Once, when she first had known him, it had found release in his frenzied and altogether bewildering love for her, and it had frightened her; she had drawn back instinctively, deflecting him, and her evasions had hurt him. Now he was easier to be with, reserved and cautious, a troubled circumspection replacing the unguarded disclosure that had once been his manner with her. He was still generous and attentive and deferred to her moods, but his letters, once full of endearments, were now rare and at once polished and oddly terse. It occurred to her now, though it never had before, that she was less comfortable with the distance she herself had ordained than with his old extravagance. Anna was intelligent, confident, attractive and clever. But she also knew her one great weakness. Her courage was a fraud, created by the deference of others who stood in awe of her. Disarmed by her beauty and aglow with plans of conquest, the men she confronted in her work were deaf to the subtle whisper of steel as they were laid open from ear to ear. But Anna was not made for an open slugfest at any level, and she knew that Liam was. She also knew—although Liam did not—that he was capable of hurting her if he took it into his head to do so.

But Anna was also capable of great folly when an attractive offer presented itself. The idea of a costume party touched her

148

where she was still a woman with the ancient frailty of the gender. On the rare moment, she was capable of indulging that frailty. There was a dress an admirer had bought her last spring, one she had not had occasion to wear since then. It had no back at all and very little front, and her itch to make the local peasantry stand agape had been thwarted by a stolid succession of patient escorts who would have fainted dead away if she had worn it. It was this caprice and nothing else that made her smile at Liam and agree to the trip.

"What are you wearing?" she demanded as she sorted through her dresser for a slip.

"I really hadn't thought about it," he replied, watching her sway around the room with the childish carelessness that never failed to move him. "Maybe I'll just wear a gold chain attached to a ring in my nose and give you the running end."

"Better wear more than that."

"I'll think about it. Have any ideas for yourself?"

"Not really," she said into the bathroom mirror. "I'll have to consider it."

"I hope you're coming. I'm not sure people up there really believe you exist."

She laughed; the sound echoed in the bathroom. "Oh, they'll remember me, don't worry."

Liam felt a premonitory chill.

Anna drove him to the airport. The traffic was unusually heavy, and they missed the five-o'clock shuttle; this left Liam an unexpected forty minutes before the next departure to La Guardia. They strolled through the terminal. These were uncomfortable moments for both of them, faced as they were with twin truths that could not be evaded at such a moment: Liam could not ask the important questions and Anna could not supply the answers. The questions hung between them in a space of dead calm air. They chatted about the shortcomings of economy flights, and Liam told her a story about a memorable stewardess on a charter flight from Travis to Saigon years before. She responded with a happy laugh, and then they both fell silent as they always did.

149

"Look," he said, "it's late, there's no reason for you to hang around. Call me when you have your arrival scheduled for next week."

"Great! I'll call you." He looked at her and there was an awkward moment when he almost told Anna he loved her; she sensed it and suspended breathing for the event, tensed herself to evade his words. But he only kissed her lightly and said: "I'll try to prepare West Point for La Perugino. It'll take some planning and coordination. There are evacuation plans to update, medical supplies to requisition, disclaimers to print and distribute . . ."

She laughed aloud, and passersby looked at them and smiled at a couple who seemed so absorbed in one another that they could bring themselves to laugh in a shuttle terminal.

10

They met again on Monday at Track's quarters. Sam was sore all over from the polygraph struggle, and Maggie was in a surly mood from a morning battle with Betty O'Grady. Track and Patti tried their best to set a lighter note, but it was soon apparent to them that they were trying to kid Orestes and Electra out of a Mother's Day funk.

Liam was in a slow burn because of Colonel Pretorius's prohibition against further cadet interviews, which he considered a sellout. He believed that the commonality of dream themes among cadets with firsthand experience of the apparition was a key to understanding the visits in the 47th Division. The ban on cadet interviews had been extended to all cadets, not just those somehow considered ripe for counseling. A Monday-morning request for clarification from Colonel Pretorius had been deflected, and it was clear from the colonel's testy reply that a reclama would be as the buzzing of small insects in the commandant's ear. Liam's department head refused to intervene or request assistance from the dean, on the reasonable grounds that the investigation had been requested in the first place by the commandant, and the commandant could therefore establish the rules.

In Sam's opinion, the key to keeping the investigation from foundering lay in finding a way to improve the quality of the tapes. He recognized a decline in enthusiasm for the project at the commandant's office. The flap with Lane and the disruption of a company area, made worse by Colonel Street's pique over the hole Sam's team drilled in the wall, had caused second thoughts. A success early on—the sort that a clear recording of the weeping child might have provided—would have been a godsend in securing continued official sanction. Sam did not share Maggie's awe of the

151

supernatural, but he was stubbornly committed to finishing the project that had cost buckets of sweat and a broken foot. Sam was obliged to teach Salinger's classes until the injured instructor could walk again.

Maggie had confronted Betty O'Grady with Mrs. Gort's recollections. The wily librarian had used the weekend break well, however, and was again composed and imperturbable. Whatever had been the former status of the book, she insisted, it was no longer part of the library's collection. As to the likelihood that the volume described by Mrs. Fetterman had been the library's—well, that was patent nonsense, as no book would ever be reshelved with the back pages stuck together. It was far more likely, she insisted, that Bernice had secured the book from some other source and merely suffered a lapse of memory. In any case, the book was certainly not in the library, and she could find no mention of its loss in any of the manual files. Maggie decided there was no point in bothering Pennington again since there was really no answer to Betty's argument. Maggie knew the woman was lying and, though she would not cavil at such violent means as bamboo splinters and mustard enemas to prove it, she bridled her passions for the sake of Sam's reputation. Instead, she pointed out that the present excitement had fallen perilously close to Halloween.

"It's Wednesday—two nights from now! Of course, the provost marshal won't let the kids trick-or-treat until Friday night, and even then they have to be back in before dark. Before dark! Can you imagine?"

"Shit," said Track, "when I was a kid we didn't even *start* trick-or-treat until it was too dark for anybody to identify us. Back before dark, my ass."

"You're right," Maggie said. "That's what's ruined Halloween. Next thing you know, they'll be letting the kids out of school."

"What has that got to do with it?" asked Sam.

"That's what always made Halloween special," she said, suddenly enthusiastic. "It wasn't an establishment holiday. Since you didn't get out of school, it was unofficial; you sort of had the impression that the authorities would have stopped Halloween from coming, but since they couldn't do that, they could sure as hell wash their hands of it."

"But Maggie," said Patti, "we always spent two or three weeks in school getting ready for it—posters, pin-up decorations, reams of orange and black construction paper, and that awful-smelling library paste."

"It wasn't awful-smelling," said Maggie. "It was nice. I used to eat it when I was in the third grade. But that arts-and-crafts dodge was only a clever trick. They wanted us to think it was their idea, to hide the fact that it was really that day of the year when the dark side of childhood brandishes a bloody axe over civilization."

"Jesus," said Track, "remind me never to go trick-or-treating with you."

"She's right," said Liam. "Tolkien suggested in a lecture once that children, who are innocent, prefer justice. Adults, who know sin, prefer mercy. Look at the original, pre-Disney fairy-tales. They're grisly enough to warrant a George Romero treatment. The queen in *Snow White* didn't just suffer defeat at the hands of seven short people and a handsome prince; her husband had her feet clamped into red-hot shoes and she danced herself to death. That's what always happens in the *real* children's tales—children's stories that were put together for children by people who understood children. It's a point we deliberately overlook," said Liam. "We don't see it from the child's viewpoint."

"You see a lot of knees that way," said Track.

"Exactly!" said Liam. "The child is surrounded by giants, and they aren't benign giants. They're all-powerful and—here's the terrifying part—they're capricious and unpredictable, because their logic is different. The child is constantly at their mercy. When the kid is an infant, they toss him around. When he starts to walk, they tell him when to go to the bathroom. Freud noted some peculiar things about kids—"

"Yeah," said Track, "we know."

"Other than that," said Liam. "But this is less talked about; you don't run into it until Freud is going hot and heavy about the Oedipal situation. One reason the little boy is so terrified about the stirrings of Oedipal lust and the aggression toward his father is that *he thinks adults, who are omnipotent, are also omniscient.* They can read his mind, they know what he's thinking, and Daddy is going to punish him. Now I'm not a Freudian, as I've said on more than one occasion, but the point is well taken. Children have a deep—and practical—fear of adults. When they're very small, they are at gravest risk from adults."

"Is that where the grimmer stories come from?" asked Patti.

"Quite a few of them," said Liam. "I did a paper on that once . . ."

"Oh, shit," said Track.

". . . and read a good deal about the darker themes in myth and folklore that address this early fear. *Snow White*, *The Sleeping Beauty*, and *Hansel and Gretel* are really tame essays in the craft. The worst is a very ancient story that recurs from culture to culture and time to time, and never gets any more appetizing. I encountered it as 'The Rose-Tree' in a book on English folklore by Joseph Jacobs. A little girl—everychild—fails three times to perform an errand properly, for reasons quite beyond her control, to the satisfaction of her stepmother. The stepmother cuts off her head by trickery, and cooks and serves up the liver and heart to her husband, who is none the wiser, though he comments on the taste. But the girl's half-brother, who has some sympathy for the deceased, secretly buries the balance of his friend in a box beneath a rose-tree. When the rose-tree finally flowers, a white bird sits in the top of it among the blossoms, and sings:

> *My wicked mother slew me,*
> *My dear father ate me.*
> *My little brother whom I love,*
> *Sits below and I sing above,*
> *Stick, stock, stone dead."*

"Oh, yuk," said Patti.

"In the Grimms' shop of horrors, it's called 'The Juniper Tree,' and the cheerful ditty appears in Goethe's *Faust*. There's a version in Hungary as well, and God knows where else."

"What happens to the 'wicked mother'?" asked Maggie.

"In the English version," said Liam, "she's crushed by a millstone."

"What use can all this have?" asked Sam, by now thoroughly disgusted with Liam's success at hogging the audience.

At this moment, Dana came in to say good night. She was wearing a green nightgown with Kermit the Frog stenciled on the front.

"Dana," said Patti, "you get up there and feed Raymond before you go to bed. You know that's your job."

"Yes, Mommy, I didn't forget." She kissed Patti and Track and scurried up the stairs.

"So, what are we going to do now?" Track asked. "Just hope we get something good this week on the night shift?"

"I guess so," Sam said. "The tape is crap. I fiddled around most of Sunday and today in the lab trying to squeeze something out of it. I had no luck at all. That static is too thick. I'm sorry, troops—that wasn't a real run, we were just setting up and I was demonstrating it for Stu. There was no time to test it out and calibrate it. If the little bastard cries for us again we'll be ready, but meanwhile all we have is 67.4 seconds of garbage."

"Let me hear the tape of the cadet's song again," said Maggie. Sam rewound the cassette to the sequence of Tetzel humming the faerie-song from his trance. They sat quietly, listening to the simple, haunting tune.

"What did you say this one's called?" asked Patti.

" 'Siúil a rún.' The words are in Irish. It's the lament of a maiden or a young wife whose man is 'gone for a soldier.' It's an old theme; thousands of Irish men in the centuries after Cromwell became mercenaries—the 'wild geese'—fighting for every cause but their own."

"Yeah," said Sam. "And every one with an even number of arms and legs and less than two centimeters of webbing between his fingers emigrated."

Maggie's tongue flicked briefly at Sam, snakelike. "Including the famous Bridget Hardesty, whose ghost is obviously still beside that same billabong."

"Give me a break," said Sam.

"Speaking of which," said Maggie, turning once again toward Liam, "is the mysterious lady coming or not?"

"She'll be there," said Liam, "if I have to drag her by the ankles down an interstate highway. Anyway, she warmed to the idea when I told her it was a costume party."

"Ah! It appealed to her sense of the dramatic entrance? And what, may we ask, is this vulpine creature going to disguise herself as?"

Liam cast a sidelong glance at Maggie. This, he mused, is going to be a duel of titans. "We are not," he replied, "at liberty to reveal Madame's pretty conceit. I suspect, however, that it will cause many hard-ons and much gossip."

"Can't wait," said Sam. "Shall we have a photographer from the *Pointer View* on site?"

"I don't recommend it. You can all have a laugh, but I have to go home with her and, not having John Milton's fertile imagination, prefer to go through the balance of my life with my eyes in their sockets."

A small, uncertain voice said: "Mommy."

"Dana," said Patti, "I told you ages ago to . . . *oh, no!*" Dana stood at the foot of the stairs cradling a small, pallid form. "Oh, honey, is he sick?"

"He's dead, Mommy."

"Oh, honey, show him to Colonel Bondurant."

She walked silently over to Sam and solemnly handed him the rat. Sure enough, Sam thought to himself, old Raymond is definitely dead. "Well, Dana, he *is* dead." *Ding, dong, the rat is dead*, sang the Munchkins, *ding dong Dana's rat is dead.* And here I sit, a forty-one-year-old experimental psychologist, cradling a dead rat while my small circle of friends and this stricken child stare at me on hopeful tenterhooks, while time stands still and the Boston Symphony plays *Deutsches Requiem* and I am supposed either to raise this rat from the dead or teach Dana Dortmunder to face death philosophically. But I am neither God almighty nor E. B. White, just Sam Bondurant clutching a dead rat. Kiss my ass, Oh Great Script Writer, kiss my ass or give me some good lines.

"Dana," Sam finally said, "how long did you have Raymond?"

"A year," she said in a tiny voice.

"Was he happy living here?"

"Yes." There was a tiny catch in her inhalation; only Sam caught it.

Sam tried another tack. "Dana, do you know what a mayfly is?" She wiped her nose and shook her head.

"Sure you do, honey," said Track. "Mayflies are those bugs that hatch out and bring the trout to the surface over at Moodna Creek when Daddy goes fishing."

"That's right, Dana," Sam continued. "But mayflies hatch and live and mate and lay their eggs and die, all in the space of a few hours. That's not a long time to live, is it?"

"No-o-o." Her voice quavered.

"Well, it's enough for a mayfly. Just long enough. I don't hear the mayflies complaining. They don't know enough to be jealous

156

of us. Rats don't live very long either, compared to us, but what time they have is just enough to have all the life a rat is supposed to have. I don't think Raymond is jealous of us; I think he's just very, very happy he had a family to love him."

That really did the trick. Dana burst into tears, sobbed loud enough to wake the dead—or just short of it, since Raymond did not stir. She stood in front of Sam, her arms straight down at her sides, making no appeal for comfort. "Oh, Punkin," said Track, "Sam's right."

Finally, Patti held out her arms and Dana allowed herself to be comforted. When she composed herself, she said: "Mommy, can we bury him?"

"Sure, honey. We can put him in the backyard in the morning."

"Ah, I'd recommend something more timely," said Sam delicately. "I—ah—think Raymond passed on several hours ago, and time is of the essence, since there may be another essence by morning, if you catch my drift."

"Can't we just put him in a sandwich bag and tie off the top with a wire twisty?" asked Patti.

"Patti," said Sam, "have you ever seen those old films of the *Hindenburg* landing at Lakehurst?"

"Gotcha. Honey, why don't you go get a coat on and some slippers; we'll bury Raymond in the backyard."

"I want to bury him where we buried Blitzkrieg," said Dana. "Out by the playground."

"Blitzkrieg?" Sam asked.

"Blitz was her brother's hamster," Patti explained. "He expired two summers ago."

"Punkin, that's a long way away," said Track.

She looked at him with fine reproach. "Raymond's dead forever."

"I'll get my coat."

They moved in solemn procession out of Track's quarters, Dana leading the way with a flashlight in one hand and Raymond, shrouded in a plastic bag, in the other, as they walked Indian-file down a dirt footpath that intersected the Redoubt trail. The post engineers had cleared a space in the woods years before and installed a small playground. Blitzkrieg's forgotten sepulcher was on the edge of this forlorn clearing, a sad place at the best of times and not improved by the darkness or the task at hand.

Track had brought a spade. He did his work with agonizing slowness—the soil was rocky and hard to dig. Finally there was space for Raymond. After Dana placed him, baggie and all, in the shallow hole, they stood in a circle, silent and pensive. Maggie was chilly. "Stick, stock, stone dead," said Sam in a faint whisper. She elbowed him.

"We have to say something," said Dana. "Like when they buried Major Koenig." Walt Koenig had been killed in a helicopter crash in Honduras that summer, and had been buried in the West Point cemetery. He was an old friend of Track's, and the family had attended as a group. Dana had been impressed.

They all looked at Sam. You're on a roll. Speak.

"Well," he said, "we all knew Raymond. It seems a small thing, the passing of so tiny a soul, but a soul's worth is measured by the love that follows it to the grave and beyond. By that measure, Raymond's loss is felt with a keenness far out of proportion to the length of his life or the limits of his intellect." Sam turned to Dana. "Dana, of what faith was Raymond? Do you have any idea what his preferences might have been, had he been a person?"

Dana shook her head.

Sam sighed, then held his hand over the tiny grave. "*Yisgadal v'yiskadash*," he intoned, "*sh'may rabo. Requiescat in pacem*, Brother Raymond. Amen."

Dana hugged him.

"Folks," said Liam, "I have to go now. It's bedtime in the corps, and I have the ghost duty tonight. Wish me luck."

"Sam," said Maggie, "that was beautiful."

"What was beautiful?"

"The way you handled Dana when she found Raymond dead. I always knew you had a soft side." They had driven straight home after the funeral. Sam was attaching a name plate and shoulder boards to his uniform shirt for Tuesday while Maggie folded laundry on the bed.

"*I* didn't think it was all that masterful. All I did was make her scream and holler."

She left the laundry to go over and kiss Sam on the cheek. "You tried, dear one. There wasn't a lot anyone could say. I almost cried when you talked about Raymond dying happy because he had a family to love him. I always knew you weren't such a terror about kids."

"Well, I can tell you, I had about run out of comforting rationale. When I think of all the damned rats I sacrificed in grad school while I was doing research with Fritz, I could blush. Hypocrisy, thy name is Bondurant."

"Hypocrisy, my foot. No hypocrite could have handled it the way you did. You're a natural. You might even make a good father, with careful training."

"Don't get carried away, Mrs. Bondurant. The best thing about Dana is her age. Three years ago she was throwing food. In another five she'll have orange and blue hair and a dose of genital herpes. She's just at a fortunate point in her childhood, not cute enough to be sickening and not old enough to be charged with felonies."

"Sam," she said, shaking out a pillow case, "give yourself credit."

"I do. I headed off a maudlin display and planted a rat. Anyway, I got one good result out of all that passion. Dana solved my weeping ghost problem, maybe."

"What?" Maggie's smile disappeared.

"When she started crying, I switched on the recorder. If I run that through the real-time analyzer, I can get a fix on the formants associated with a child crying, then concentrate on those frequencies and—"

Sam never saw it until it was too late. Maggie's fist caught him by the right eye, full force; she had wound up and swung from far left field, and she was not a small woman. His glasses flew off and out the hall door with one ear piece separated, and he staggered into the open closet. He saved himself from falling to the floor only by grabbing at a tie rack.

"You bastard!" she hissed at him. "You goddamned freak! You didn't care anything about that child!"

His nose was bleeding and the side of his face had been deeply scratched by the glasses. He looked at her in a sluggish astonish-

159

ment, not entirely certain what had happened. "What—what are you doing?"

"I'm seriously thinking about leaving you, you bloody, heartless son of a bitch! I was nearly in tears when you comforted that girl. I was ready to believe you were human for a change! Congratulations, Sam. You fooled me. I think you've always fooled me."

"What are you talking about? I cared about Dana. I even cared about Raymond. I helped her pick him out, remember?"

"I don't believe you, you bastard! You've always been nothing but a façade. Most of the time you don't even bother with the façade."

"Look, it was a target of opportunity! I wasn't taking advantage of a crying kid, for Christ's sake! You're the one who's so keen to find a ghost . . ."

She came at him again, this time with her nails, but Sam was ready, and his reflexes were not entirely lost after the years of schoolmastering. He caught Maggie's wrists and held her against the wall. She tried to kick him in the groin, but he parried her with his knee and pinned her tightly with his body. "Calm down, damn it, Maggie! Can't we talk about this?"

She spit on him. "There isn't a whole hell of a lot to say, you bastard. You've already said it all."

"What's the matter with you? I didn't do it to hurt Dana— she didn't even know what I was doing. Nobody did, until I told you."

"I'm glad you did." Her voice was reptilian. "Now at least I know what we're up against."

"We're not up against anything right now," said Sam, "except aggravated assault."

"So sue me! Let me go and I'll do it again!"

"One more time, Maggie: What in the hell is the problem with you?"

"I'm pregnant, you bastard."

He did let her go then, but she didn't attack. She slid down the wall and came to rest sitting on the floor, then started sobbing out of control. Sam sat beside her, his back against the wall. "How did that happen?"

"I don't know! I guess somebody's been s-screwing me!"

"I mean, I thought you were doing something."

She took a deep breath; she was choking with every few breaths, but managed to say: "I was . . . I was, but I . . . guess it wasn't fool . . . foolproof."

"Well, I'll be damned."

"Could be. You . . . you just got a good . . . start on it."

"Are you going to have it?"

"I don't know," she said, her voice a dead monotone. "Am I?"

"Do you want to have it? I mean, we never talked about it. Aren't you a little old?"

"You always know just what to say."

"Oh shit, Maggie! I mean, I want to have it if it isn't dangerous for you!"

"You're forty-one, Sam. But you're not having it. I am. I'm your little child bride."

"Then let's have it."

"Oh, great. Yes, since I'm young enough let's have it."

"Shit, Maggie. Give me a minute to get used to it."

"Let me know when you're used to it. I—I don't want to press you."

He wiped blood from his face. "I still don't know why you hit me."

She snuffled for a minute without answering him. "I . . . I was ready to tell you when you hit me with that marvelous news about your damned computer. M-my blabber about how nice you were with Dana and her damned dead rat was just to soften you up." Her voice rose in volume and became shrill. "I just thought I'd seen you caring enough about something besides yourself to deserve to have a baby, to have my baby. You never show me anything but tolerance and you never show me you love me, all you ever do that's intimate is screw me, and that doesn't go very damn far to make you a good father, and when you told me you detached yourself from that poor girl's grief and recorded her damned voice for your damned real-time analyzer while she was crying her guts out, I wished I'd never gotten pregnant, and I wanted to make you hurt for it. I really did."

"You must have. Christ, you hit like Rocky Balboa."

She looked at his face for the first time. He was going to have a black eye that would make a raccoon proud, and a trickle of blood was running from his nose down into the corner of his mouth. She

161

saw for the first time that he was crying, too. She had never seen him display any more emotion than the granite gargoyles on the clock tower of Pershing Barracks. He leaned his head back against the wall and closed his eyes. She leaned against him and pressed her face against his shoulder. "We've really got to stop hitting each other."

"Yeah," he said. "I read in *Reader's Digest* some years back that giving your husband a concussion is one of the five danger signals of a failing relationship."

"Get flippant, Bondurant, and you'll look like the Lone Ranger tomorrow, not just like Moishe Dayan. Oh, Sam. I wanted this to be a lot different. We can tell him when he's old enough to understand that I tried to murder you to celebrate the blessed event. How will he like having a hysterical mother?"

"Her real problem may be a one-eyed flippant father."

She inspected his eye. "Oh, Sam—we've got to get you to the emergency room. I really nailed you."

"It's all right," he said. "I've looked worse."

She laughed and kissed him, very gently, on the unturned cheek. "I'm sorry, dear one. I've not hit anybody recently. I'll try not to make it a habit."

"I hope to hell not. I don't know what it was like where you come from, but they frown on murder in New York."

"Well, at least I'll get you cleaned up." They went into the bathroom and she wiped the blood from his face with warm water and hydrogen peroxide. It did not help a great deal, sad to say. His face was already swelling and the eye was ringed with traces of purple. They stood together at the sink and looked at themselves in the mirror. Sam grinned and said, "Yo, Adrienne!"

"Oh, you don't look that bad. Well, I guess you do. Actually, it looks sort of cute. Your face asymmetrical, I mean."

"Now I'm two-faced."

She turned on the shower and unbuttoned his shirt. "Get yourself ready for bed. I'll get some aspirin and a bandage for your cheek."

"Get me some tape for my glasses while you're at it. I can teach classes looking like a nerd tomorrow, thanks to Maggie Ali."

"Don't get wise, Bondurant."

He held up his hands. "Don't hit me!"

When he came out of the shower his eye was swollen nearly

shut. Meanwhile, Maggie had taken a bottle of champagne from a special camouflaged corner of the refrigerator, and two glasses from the cupboard, and still had time to clear away the last of the laundry and change into her emergency-summit-meeting nightgown. After making short work of the wine, they concluded a welcome entente.

Finally Maggie was satisfied that life could resume. She kissed his puffy dark eye. "I like it," she said. "It'll go with my dark suit."

Sam went to sleep, finally, in Maggie's repentant embrace. At three thirty-five in the morning the telephone exploded. She awoke with a start and leaned over Sam to pick up the receiver, dragging her elbow across Sam's swollen eye. This elicited his attention as well as a yelp of agony.

Maggie was always terrified by late-night telephone calls; such a message had once heralded her father's death. "Yes?" Liam heard her distant, distracted tone and instantly regretted calling.

"Maggie, this is Liam. I'm sorry to get you up. Is Sam there? I'm over at the barracks."

"Of course he's here, Liam. Did you expect him to be outside, hanging upside down in a church steeple? What on earth do you want?"

"Maggie, we have something going on in the ghost room, and I need to talk to Sam. I'm sorry—duty calls him."

"Okay." She shook Sam gently. "Come on, Sam. Liam's on the phone."

"I'm already awake. Didn't you hear me scream? You got my eye again. Who was your family doctor, Josef Mengele? Here, give me the damned phone. Liam? What's up?"

"Sam, we're getting a strange signal on the EEG from Carson. He's been asleep for about two hours. Maybe fifteen minutes ago we started getting a rhythmic pattern on both EEG channels. I can't imagine it's coming from his brain, so it must be a spurious source from somewhere."

Sam propped up his pillow and touched his wounded eye tenderly. "What does it look like?"

"It completely obliterates the EEG patterns. He was in strong beta, possibly REM, until about fifteen minutes ago, then this thing came along. Ortega's with me. He checked out the amplifiers, filters, all this incomprehensible garbage you set up over here, and he can't find anything wrong."

Sam sighed. He was fully awake now. "What does it *look* like, Liam?"

"Slow potential, positive, domelike, pretty high amplitude, followed by a rapid, short-duration spike, about three or four times a second."

"Roger that. We saw that on Saturday morning when we were getting set up. You're right—it isn't from Carson's brain. I think it's a malfunction in the room's lighting system. It came in before with the EEG sensors dangling in thin air. There's a noise source of some kind. I remember thinking that I'd seen the pattern before, but I sure as hell couldn't place it. I imagine an electrode has slipped off Carson's head. Don't wake him up. No point until we find that noise source. What does his heart rate look like?"

"Kind of low. Looks like about . . . oh, wow."

" 'Oh, wow'? Can we be more descriptive?"

"Sam, his pulse rate is up from the last time I checked. He's up around seventy-six."

"You said he was in beta before you lost the EEG and got the garbage. He's probably dreaming about pussy or something. No, he's a West Pointer. He's dreaming about jogging."

"Thanks, Sam. You're a big help. I'll call you if we get anything else unusual."

"Please hesitate to call me, Liam. Good morning."

"Sleep tight, Sam."

Sam blew a kiss and replaced the receiver. "What a night," he said, leaning back against his upright pillow.

Maggie was sitting up, massaging her eyes. "Was it anything interesting?"

"Oh, I don't think so. Liam saw an artifact on the brain wave recording. We saw it on Saturday, too. Some kind of a weird electrical source in the barracks area. No big thing. A little bothersome. I have a feeling I know what it is, but I just can't place it."

"You awake?"

"No, Maggie. This conversation has been an essay in somnambulism."

"I mean, are you *really* awake?"

164

"What? Really awake? *Now* what? Did you forget to turn something off?"

"No," she said, touching him gently, "I was thinking about turning something on."

"Hey, watch it! That's private property, Mrs. Bondurant. At least be kind enough to be gentle with me, this time."

"No," said Maggie thoughtfully after a thorough assay of the matter, "you're not awake yet."

"If I know you, you'll make a big thing of it." He stroked her hair and rolled toward her.

"I don't know if it's worth it, Bondurant. We're a bit on the petite side this morning. Overwork, I guess."

"Don't go off half-cocked, dear lady. You have a hard task before you, but I'll go to any length to help out." He drew her toward him and kissed her cheek, then tickled the edge of her ear playfully with his tongue. " 'Petite'? We'll see about . . . *Oh my God!*"

Maggie jerked so hard she nearly fell off the edge of the bed. "What? What did I damage this time?"

Sam lunged for the telephone and cursed when he could not find the dial numbers in the darkness. He turned over the night stand lamp trying to grab the chain pull, then growled and jumped out of bed. He switched on the wall light and dialed the telephone. Maggie watched, terrified, as he drummed his fingers on the table and cursed under his breath. "Liam? Sam. Listen, go in there and check Carson right away. Right now! Don't hang up! I'll hold the phone while you check on him. Wake him up!"

"Jesus, Sam. What is it?"

"That damned dome-and-spike pattern isn't an artifact, Liam, it's a fucking petit mal seizure, an epileptic seizure. Go check him, right now. He won't be twitching, it won't be a tonic-clonic fit, it's like a blackout! Hurry up!"

There was a long silence. The telephone was in another cadet room, and Sam could not hear any noise in the background. Maggie moved to sit beside Sam on the edge of the bed and put her hand on his. "Is it the cadet?"

"Yeah."

"Is he all right?"

"Probably," he said impatiently. "I don't know yet."

"Is that kind of a seizure dangerous?"

165

"It's not like a grand mal fall-down-and-twitch. Petit mal is usually sort of like a momentary blackout, but it has a distinct EEG pattern during ictus . . ."

"During *what?*"

"The seizure. Preictal, ictal, postictal, interictal, tweedle-dictal, whatever. By the way, congratulations. I love you. I forgot about both of you until just now."

"So did I. I love you too."

"What the hell is he doing? Come on, are you writing a first endorsement? Oh, brother. Why didn't I recognize that damned dome-and-spike for what it was? And why did we get it on Saturday? That *must* have been an artifact. Hello? Liam?"

"Yeah, it's me, Sam. Sorry I took so long. I had to gather my wits."

"Is he all right?"

"Yeah, Sam. Carson's fine. I'm not."

"What's the matter? You sound strange."

"I feel strange. Hang on, Sam. There. I just sat down on the floor. I thought I was going to pass out."

"What in the hell is the matter?"

"I think I just saw a ghost, Sam."

Liam and Ortega had been staring at the oscilloscope traces when Sam called. The top two lines were EEG, or were supposed to be, the next was a pulse from a pickup crystal taped to Carson's left index finger, and the rest were not attached and the glowing lines were flat. The EEG lines were displaying the strange periodic hump-and-peak formation that had replaced the busy normal brain activity. "Beats me, sir," said Ortega. "I got no ideas. We ought to get the electricians in here tomorrow or something."

"Yeah, maybe. I guess it's like Colonel Bondurant said. The electrodes must have disconnected. Maybe he rolled over. I can't tell on the TV monitor. There just isn't enough contrast." The telephone rang in the next room. "Now what?"

Liam stomped down the hall and picked up the telephone. Ortega listened. There was a short silence, then Liam said: "Jesus, Sam. What is it?" Another silence, then Liam ran down the hall. "Come on, Ortega, the cadet's having a seizure." Ortega bounded

166

up and followed Liam to the door of the plebes' room. Liam turned the knob, pushed the door open abruptly, and took half a step in, then backed out again as if he had been roughly shoved. He stood there in the doorway, staring into the darkness. Ortega was very quick to guess what had happened, and looked past Liam into the room. He saw nothing but the dim shapes of bunks, desks and a partition between the cadets' alcoves.

Liam had been poised on entry to turn sharply right, toward Carson's bunk. While trying to get a visual fix on the far alcove to make certain he did not go careening into unseen obstacles at a dead run, he had seen something that was now ineradicably etched in his memory.

Ortega tried to look around Liam into the darkness of the room, but recoiled violently back into the hallway as he felt something unseen rush out of the door and surge past him. He felt nothing but a chilly movement of air; but he knew without really seeing that something had come that way. He later claimed that some people have more than one set of eyes, and his spare set was formally opened at that moment.

Liam felt it as well, but his attention was directed at the shadows near Carson's alcove. He recognized it in an instant. It was a subtle, indistinct, faintly luminous form. But something lay unused inside Liam FitzDonnell as well, hidden perhaps in centuries of ancestral memory and awakened abruptly in him by the sudden and unsought confrontation with a force that flaunted its contempt for rational thought and gathered about it the Host of the Air, the tattered, gray-shaded phantoms of unreason. There was no doubt, no hesitation; the somber demon of his hidden soul recognized it for what it was, and he felt the physical cold travel over his body.

It was standing at the foot of Carson's bed, but it had turned and was looking at Liam with a dark intensity. He could see the eyes clearly, eyes that looked at him from the next world, eyes that said You know, you must know, you dare not look away. They were sad eyes, eyes that refracted the light of grief and loss from an infinite remoteness; they were crystalline lenses that subtly reflected the pure light of God, blended the rainbow of creation into pure white crystal shining specks of stars, glistening foci of all the losses of a sorrowing world.

It was not, after all, a tall figure, but its cloak made it look

167

like a hovering presence that ruled the darkness. The cloak sparkled on its shoulders as if wet with dew; it seemed to hang open in front, but its edges were not clear enough to discern.

Its head was turned toward Liam, and he knew he was somehow dimly perceived by the thing. For no reason he thought of it peering at him through a smoked glass, faintly sensing Liam's substance. The eyes knew him, and there was something in them that Liam feared, that he had feared from the start: an entreaty, perhaps; a call to arms.

Liam saw a darker shape beyond this figure, partly blocked by the alcove wall. He was prepared for the more terrible presence he had abstracted from the cadets' dreams, but it was not so; the darker presence waited patiently while the other eyes held Liam in thrall.

The figure stepped back from the cadet's bunk and turned away from Liam, then walked slowly toward the wall. It moved clumsily, almost like a cartoon crudely animated. As it moved away, the hidden shape moved into its place, and Liam reached out with his hands; but the shape turned away and vanished.

Then, as Liam backed out of the doorway, the room was filled with dancing points of light, and the points circled faster and faster, scurrying flakes of pale luminescence, whirling around a center where there glowed a tiny light, the light of distant stars, the reflection of the light of heaven. The whirling fragments, as if summoned by a cry beyond the limits of mere human sense, spun away through the circling vortex and, one by one, streamed through the wall over the bed. And the room was cold.

11

A rumor spread through the corps by midmorning on Tuesday that the BS and L team had seen a ghost. No one could imagine where the rumor began; neither Liam nor Specialist Ortega had discussed the matter, and Carson had readily agreed to keep quiet. Many months after the fact, wiser heads were inclined to believe that the rumor had spread on its own without real substance, and its appearance at the same time as the actual event was no more than coincidence. Whatever the case, by noon meal formation the mood of the brigade was not altogether reserved, nor was the approach of the Army-Navy football classic being accorded the seriousness it was officially reputed to warrant.

Colonel Pretorius, anxious lest the whole affair acquire more than its share of notoriety, instructed the cadet first captain, a handsome but humorless young man from Vermont, to make some cautionary remarks at the noon meal. The results were not what Colonel Pretorius intended.

The portraits of past superintendents stared down at the first captain from the walls: MacArthur, in a dramatic pose with short overcoat and riding boots; Maxwell Taylor with his disarming hair parted in the center; William Westmoreland posed stiff and self-conscious; Robert E. Lee appearing oddly uncomfortable in a blue uniform. They all looked at the First Captain. Not a one smiled except MacArthur, who was probably thinking about his flapper sweetheart over in Tuxedo Park.

At another time, it might well have been the first captain's finest hour. Two circumstances intervened. First, the week was one full of midterm examinations and stress, and the corps was edgy and high-strung. Second, fate had decreed that fried chicken be the day's entree.

The first captain's words were brief and direct, but mostly brief. He was interrupted first by a cheer for Lumpy Dilworth, and then—at midpoint of a dramatic sentence—by a drumstick that struck him on the chest. Long after the fact, many witnesses agreed that the choice of fried chicken at that particular meal was the necessary and sufficient catalyst for the disgraceful episode that followed. In the next few moments, the giant mess hall was filled, from stone floor to vaulted ceiling, with a blizzard of chicken breasts, thighs, and wings.

So legends are born. Two yearlings on guard by the main entrance swore they saw Robert E. Lee's eyes close for a long, terrifying moment.

"We have a problem," said Sam. "Pretorius just called me. They had some kind of a riot in the mess hall at lunch."

"Yeah," said Track, grinning broadly. "I heard. Food fight. Fried chicken. Nailed the first captain, too, right in the kisser they say. Wish I'd have been there."

"Well," said Sam, "you should thank your lucky stars you weren't. The whole area is ankle-deep in chicken carcasses and cooking oil. The com is eating cockleburrs. Training aids has just received a big order for crucifixes. And we are right in the middle of it."

"How?" asked Liam. "We've been here in the department since eleven-thirty."

"Because," Sam explained with a savage smile, "the first captain was talking about ghosts. We are associated with ghosts. In the absence of a good, healthy sequitur, we can always fall back on old, reliable illogic. In addition, some moron hung a balloon covered with a shroud in front of the poopdeck—right in the first captain's face—and then the riot broke out. The com blames the ghost project."

"What are we supposed to do?" asked Liam.

"We're supposed to brief Pretorius, Street, and the com at sixteen hundred this afternoon—that's three hours from now—on what we have accomplished. I have the impression it had better look good."

"What am I supposed to say?" asked Liam. "I really needed a few days to get myself ready to testify about last night. I'm still not quite sure I believe it."

"We have hard data to back up your hallucinations."

"Once," said Liam with a faint smile, "I'd have gotten pretty mad at a stupid, arrogant, know-nothing statement like that from a low-life like you. Today, though, it doesn't bother me a bit."

"Glad to hear it," said Track, " 'cause you're gonna need all the headspace you can get when we try to pass all this off on that happy-go-lucky trio. All we need is to have Lane there too."

"What a coincidence," said Sam, "his name was also mentioned as being on the guest list."

"Marvelous. Just fucking marvelous."

"Liam," said Sam, "how are you going to tell them about the incident last night? This is going to be tricky."

"Sam, I don't know. I hope I can be convincing. I probably don't look convincing."

"Shit," said Track, "that's putting it mildly. You look like somebody who just saw a statue bleed. Whatever it was you saw in that room, it must have been a pisser."

"I don't want to see it again. It *looked* at me. I'll never forget it."

"By the way," said Sam, "you said something about how it 'walked funny.' So did Tetzel. What did you mean?"

"I don't really know. I can't picture it very well. There was just something—something unnatural about it."

"Like it was an animated cartoon, you said?"

"In a way. It was like poor animation. It didn't look natural. There was something wrong with the way it walked."

"Did it look fake?" asked Track.

"No. Not contrived, if that's what you mean. It was no hoax. And it was sentient. It looked at me, and I sensed very strongly that it knew it was looking at me. I'm not going to lay that on the com just yet, because I can't pin down what I mean."

"Liam," said Sam, looking sharply at him. "Sure as hell, one of those plug-uglies is going to ask us, each one of us, if we believe it's a ghost. What are you going to say?"

"Sam, I don't know."

"Track?"

"Don't ask me, I just teach leadership."

"Well," said Sam, "we'll at least present a uniform impression of indecision. This is going to be an interesting meeting."

"Without the word 'interesting,' " said Liam, "we'd all perish for want of euphemism."

"Not me," said Track. "I never use 'em."

"It isn't our purpose to hinder your investigation," said Colonel Pretorius. "After all, we asked you to conduct it. Whatever you people across the street in the Dean's bailiwick might think, we don't enjoy looking foolish. But General Harrington does have some concerns."

"That's an understatement," said the commandant. "I appreciate the original motive behind this project, but I don't think any of us had the slightest idea at the start what it would turn into. Essentially," the commandant said, tap-tapping his pipe into a polished ashtray made from a 105-millimeter shell case, "by conducting the investigation at all, we are giving the impression to the cadets—and worse, to the media—that we consider the possibility of a bona fide supernatural event. I don't think that's really in our best interests."

"We don't have a media problem yet, sir," said Pretorius.

"We will," said the general. "I don't share your optimism about keeping this thing in-house. My observation has been that anything you want to keep in-house inevitably ends up in the outhouse, and the more embarrassing it is, the quicker it breaks loose. I'd bet an assignment to Fort Bliss some happy reporter is doing a quiet job on us right this moment. And we're going to have to deal with that when it comes." He turned to Sam, Liam, and Track. "But that's our problem, gentlemen, not yours. As long as you don't start granting interviews to some tabloid and end up on page one next to a candid shot of Ronald Reagan looking down the front of Liz Taylor's dress." They all smiled politely.

"What we need to know," he continued, "is whether you have enough right now to put an end to the investigation and let things get back to normal."

"No more damned food fights," said Lane.

"Don't worry about food fights," said the commandant. "Food fights are my problem." Lane shut up.

"Well, sir," said Sam, "we've only had one night to work. We were set up over the weekend—Saturday morning, with Captain Broadnax's help, we got the instrument suite installed—"

"Knocking a hole in the wall to do it," Colonel Street volunteered. The general waved him off.

"And we cranked up last night for the first full test. The equipment is very sensitive and was configured to cover about as many parameters as seemed profitable to measure. Lieutenant Colonel FitzDonnell had the duty last night, along with my lab tech. They opened up the measurement at midnight and kept it going until about oh-three forty-five."

"Why so late?" asked the general.

"The background interviews suggested that things never started to happen until after midnight; most activity was around two-thirty in the morning until dawn."

"You said the experiment lasted until only a quarter before four. Did the equipment break down?"

"Well, sir," said Sam, "first, it really isn't an experiment. We don't have hypotheses, we don't have real criteria for deciding whether we find anything. With this kind of a nonparadigm, you just have to hope something hits you between the eyes. At about three-thirty, something hit us between the eyes."

The commandant frowned and relit his pipe. He leaned back in his leather chair and looked around the room. Lane shook his head slowly.

"Sir," said Sam, "it's probably better if we go back to the start, to Saturday afternoon. In retrospect, I'd have to say that's when we had the first indication of activity, though we didn't recognize it at the time."

"Take your time, Sam. You have a reputation for extemporaneous oratory. Use it."

Sam described the experimental setup in detail. The commandant listened carefully. He held a master's degree in electrical engineering, and Sam and Liam were relieved to hear him ask sensible questions. They were also delighted to observe Lane's consternation.

The general was particularly alert to the problem of temper-

173

ature change—he recognized this as the most convincing single dimension, since it could be easily measured.

"It's worthwhile to mention," said Liam, "that subjective cold can be induced hypnotically. Autosuggestion was one of our first hypotheses."

"Yeah," said Lane. "We know about your masterful hypnotic tricks." The commandant waved Lane off again.

Sam then described the sound-analyzing system.

"Why," Pretorius asked, "did you want to measure sound?"

"Because of reports of noise made by apparently nonexistent children. It was part of the picture in the Forty-seventh Division haunting."

"But," Pretorius insisted, "is it worth all that? Couldn't it just be kids prowling? Real ones, I mean?"

"Of course, sir. But the sound of a crying child has been associated with the Forty-seventh Division ghost since the late 1820s."

"What?" said the commandant. "You mean the barracks have always been haunted? But the buildings were built in this century."

"Sir, that's true. But before the Forties were built, the ghosts were associated with that stretch of ground. My wife found a number of references dating back to Colonel Thayer's superinten-dency." Sam explained Maggie's discoveries.

"So, the sound equipment is to catch the sound of the crying."

"Or any other changes in sound associated with the ghost appearances."

The pipe went out and had to be relit. "Do ghosts generally emit characteristic sounds?"

"I have no idea, sir. It just seemed worth a try. Anyway, third, we measure physiological parameters of the person sleeping in the bed. We chose EEG—that's electroencephalography, brain-wave measurement—and heart rate. The brain waves were to give us some objective measure of alertness and the heart rate is a measure of arousal. Both are processed by a third special computer." Sam happily recited his EEG lecture.

"Why are these important?"

"Because, first of all, I wanted to know when the subject woke up with respect to any activity. In addition, there is a tendency—reported first in 1947 by a member of the Ladies' Reading Club as part of a report on the incident that year, and echoed in interviews with the cadets last week—for the sightings to follow a period of nightmares. We can get some fix on this by measuring heart rate and brain-wave patterns."

"Thank you. Is that all you measure?"

"Well, we tried a remote video camera mounted on a drive platform that pans and tilts to look around the room. Unfortunately, it's hard to get enough light. The images are so washed out as to be virtually useless."

"And what have you found so far?"

Sam told him about the odd signals on the EEG and the dome-and-spike pattern. "We presumed they were just spurious electrical noise from some unknown source. Any number of things could have produced such a complex of frequencies. The regular patterns were more puzzling, though. I had the feeling I'd seen them some-where." Then he explained the report by Saganian and Broadnax of the child crying, and the common report of an unusual, unnatural tinniness to the noise.

"Did your tape system work?" the general asked.

"We got nothing but static," said Sam. "There was a problem with the tape head. But I'll say more about that later."

"Go ahead, then." The general relit his pipe again and puffed determinedly.

"On Monday, we started the regular watch schedule. Liam had the first night, so I'll let him carry it from here."

Liam spoke slowly and deliberately, aware that his testimony would be hard for the men in the room to accept. He was having a hell of a time with it himself.

"We—that is, Specialist Ortega and I—waited until Cadet Carson was ready to quit studying and go to sleep. We put the sensors on him, and half an hour later he was snoring away.

"The heart rate and temperature channels were set to give an alarm if the measurements went outside fixed normal intervals. Of course, every time the plebe shifted in the bunk, there was a spike and we'd get a beep. After a while we got used to it. This went on until about oh-three fifteen.

"At that point, Ortega noticed a new pattern on one of the EEG channels; then it spread to the other channels. The subject had been asleep for several hours, and shortly after three his brain waves were mostly theta—that's a high-frequency, low-amplitude busy and irregular activity associated with conscious awareness and what we call REM or paradoxical sleep."

"That's rapid eye movement?" the commandant said.

"Yes sir. At the same time, his heart rate elevated. We presumed he was dreaming."

"Was there a change in temperature?"

"Very slightly depressed, from sixty-eight degrees to about sixty-four in ten minutes. This is unusual, but not impossible. Then, at about a quarter after three, the EEG anomaly started, as I said. We watched it for a while, and Ortega tried to find something wrong with the machines. He had no luck, and I started to get uneasy, so I called Sam."

"Was he happy to hear from you at three-thirty?" asked the general, turning to Sam. "You look like you had a bad night. How many rounds did you last?"

They all laughed, including—for the first time—Colonel Lane. Sam had endured a full ration of merriment because of the black eye. "I had an accident last night, sir. And no, I wasn't in a good mood when Liam called."

"He described the brain-wave problem to you?"

"Yes sir. I presumed it was the same spurious signal we saw on Saturday. I told him to ignore it, that we'd fix it in the morning."

"Which is what I did," said Liam. "But then Sam called back in a few minutes."

"I remembered where I'd seen the pattern before, in a book on neuropathology. The odd dome-and-spike pattern is associated with a peculiar kind of seizure disorder or event called petit mal. Grand mal involves what we call tonic-clonic seizures, classical motor events we usually associate with epileptic 'fits.' Petit mal is not as dramatic—it's more like a temporary blackout. But I was afraid this was happening to the subject—Cadet Carson—and told Liam to check on him. I still hoped it was a case of external noise or a glitch in the polygraph."

"I ran down the hallway to wake up Carson," said Liam. "The first thing I did was throw open the door. At the time I noticed that the doorknob was extremely cold, but I didn't reflect on that for too long. I don't know much about epileptic seizures, it isn't my field. I knew Sam was upset, and I was afraid for the plebe. I stepped inside and tried to find the light switch before I went blundering around in the dark.''

Liam fell silent again and leaned forward in his chair, staring at the floor. The room was still. Lane had folded his arms and was staring at Liam with a smirk on his face. The commandant squinted at some point on the far wall past Liam's head. The only sound was a tiny sucking noise as he puffed away at his pipe.

"I want to say this very carefully," Liam said at last. "Everything I'm going to describe now flies in the face of all the principles of logic and proof I know and accept. I want you to know why I'm going to take the position I am. It's a total reversal of all my prior assumptions about this phenomenon, and I don't want to discredit everybody on the team by sounding like a fruitcake." The commandant nodded without taking the pipe out of his mouth. He looked mildly at Liam and waited.

"When we start trying to tackle problems that really lie well outside our training—or, in this case, damned near anybody's training and experience—we start discarding our accustomed methods and paradigms and start relying on the principle of parsimony. As you know, parsimony simply tells us that, all other things being equal, we're generally better off using the simplest explanation that fits all the facts. Sometimes, though, parsimony turns on us and makes us draw conclusions we don't care for."

"And this is one of those times," said the commandant, "when Occam's razor draws blood."

"Yes sir. When I opened that door I saw a ghost. That's the only explanation I know of that fits all the facts of the matter. I don't like it. But the alternatives—at least the ones I can think of—are so outlandish, a ghost seems conservative."

"Whatever you saw," said the general, "impressed you."

Liam smiled and looked at the floor for a moment. "Yes sir. I was impressed."

"Why don't you let us in on the secret?" said Lane.

Liam took a deep breath, then leaned back again in the chair. "I saw a transparent figure standing over the bed. It was pale and luminous, like a ghost in a movie. It was wearing a cloak of some kind, long and with a shoulder cape like the cadets' full dress overcoats. I thought there was a high, open-front stock collar exposed by the open cloak. It was wearing a baggy visored cap like the ones in the Mexican War. The face was indistinct, but from a change in posture I knew it had turned to look at me."

Liam had their complete attention. He described the figure in as much detail as he could recollect, but made no mention of the other, dimly sensed shape. The commandant listened quietly, interjecting only to query Liam about the ghost's eyes; then he returned to his pipe. After the account was complete there was another pause.

"You had all this equipment up there," said Lane. "Did you get anything besides your unimpeachable eyewitness account?"

"As a matter of fact," said Sam, "we were in luck. We have the EEG anomaly on tape. We also show a drop in temperature over the three or four minutes between my second conversation with Liam—when I told him to check the cadet for possible seizure activity—and the point when the image disappeared through the wall. The wall dropped seventeen degrees, from fifty-eight to forty-one degrees. That's only three degrees warmer than the outside temperature. The baseline sensor on the floor dropped six degrees at the lowest point. The wall temperature, of course, is the average of the seven sensors in the array. There were differences. The center sensor, for instance, read seventeen degrees at its coldest point, much colder than the outside. Liam and Specialist Ortega inspected the wall—along with Carson, who was awake by now, as you might imagine. There was a circular area of frost on the wall at the apparent point of exit. As the cadets had reported earlier, there was also melted frost—at least, cold water—on the floor. This became important later."

"Did anything register on the video camera?" the commandant asked.

"Not on the main camera. There was insufficient light. But one extra thing I did against that possibility was add a camera mounted next to the regular video that produces images in infrared; it gives us a thermal picture. It doesn't display on the monitor, but I record the images on a videotape unit.

"I had high hopes; but when I played them back, I saw only very indistinct images. Carson was visible in his bunk as a hot spot, and when I reversed the image to dark-hot mode so anything colder than the surround would be picked out as a bright area, it was hard to make anything out. There seemed to be something there, but it was hard to tell its shape.

"So this morning I recorded a few single frames and digitized them, then did an image enhancement to pick out edges. I used a system that is sensitive to 256 gray levels per pixel with a resolution of 680 by 400 . . ."

"You just lost me," said Pretorius. "What are 'gray levels?' "

"The computer reads a picture as a matrix of fine points, called picture elements or pixels. The more pixels, the finer the resolution. This one is 680 by 400. Each pixel is coded to a level of brightness or shade of gray, with 256 possible values. Of course, we lose color when we do this, but since the human eye can only differentiate about fifty or sixty shades of gray, it gives us precision, which is what is really important. I wanted to enhance edges, and there is a mathematical routine that does this for us.

"I used the CRT camera to make some Polaroid shots of the results. Here's the first one; this was derived from a frame after the apparent seizure activity." He handed it to the general.

"Okay. Now, what is this dark, horizontal pattern?"

"Sir, that's Carson's body heat standing out against the cold room. Remember, dark is hot, light is cold."

"And this thing is the ghost? This blurry, conical thing over on the left?"

"I wouldn't go that far, sir," said Sam. "It is an area of the environment that is colder than the surround by about five or six degrees."

"Why is it blurred?"

"Unknown, again. Possibly it has no sharp edges to enhance. Possibly it was moving."

"On the floor, this mixture of dark and light stuff . . ."

"Look at it closely, sir." The general extracted a magnifying glass from a desk drawer and examined the photograph for a long minute.

"Well, I'm not sure, but it sure as hell looks like tracks. The ghost didn't wipe his feet."

"Sir, the cameras were mounted in tandem on the pan and tilt, and they were moved here and there during the evening. We had a lucky break. They're controlled by a joystick, and it's supposed to have an automatic lock—when you let go of the control, the thing is supposed to stop. It doesn't. In this case, when Ortega ran out of the room it kept drifting down, and in passing got us a dandy shot of the floor. Here's the unenhanced shot."

A pass of the magnifying glass, and the commandant smiled. "Clear as day! They're tracks."

Sam handed him the last photograph. "Here's that same frame, edge-enhanced." This time the general looked for a very long, quiet time. Lane twisted in his chair. "Yes," the general said, finally, "they're tracks. But I notice two other things."

Sam nodded.

"There are two sets, one large and with broad, cleated soles. The other set is just streaks, I think, less distinct; but it's separate, because I can see where the cleated tracks have been overlaid. They're both lighter than the surrounding floor, so—if I was listening earlier—colder. Right?" Sam nodded again.

"Now also," the commandant continued, "there is other stuff on the floor, irregularly distributed in spots and smears. In a few places it covers parts of the tracks; in others, the tracks have apparently smeared it. What does that suggest?"

Street chimed in. "Both deposited together?"

"Apparently. Also, the other stuff is dark, almost as dark as the cadet in the bunk. Hence warmer than the tracks." He glanced at Sam and raised his eyebrows. "Right?"

"That was my impression, sir."

"So, two critters of some kind, one with big cleated boots, one with no clear trace, stomping around in cold water which is still on the floor after the room is open, and also in some kind of ectoplasm or something that's warm. Was there anything like that on the floor?"

"No sir," said Liam. "When Carson and Ortega and I looked, there was just cold water. But the second set of tracks—the cleated ones—are no mystery. Ortega went into the room about an hour before the incident to replace a ground electrode that had slipped off Carson's ear lobe; Ortega was wearing boots, which accounts for the overlying tracks."

"Let's put that aside for now. Liam, you mentioned bad dreams. Did the plebe in question—Carson?" Liam nodded. "Did Carson report bad dreams?"

"No sir," Liam replied. His voice was soft, and Lane strained to hear. "We understand that Barstow did, before his disappearance; and Tetzel is still having them. The Barstow and Tetzel dreams are similar in content." Liam was startled. It was obvious the general had listened very carefully to his pitch as well as Sam's, and was homing in on a key element.

"You'd better explain," said the commandant. Liam described the elements. "So," the general pressed, "you find a common thread? Some sort of child abuse?"

"A bit more than that, sir. The dreams have a quality of blending the dreamer's personal experiences with the anomalous theme of a child being restrained or locked in a room."

"And the senseless speech?"

"That was reported by Tetzel. I never had a chance to interview Barstow, of course; and Carson apparently doesn't have nightmares."

Ward Lane was looking troubled. "Sir, I can shed a little light here. I interviewed Mister Barstow at the counseling center about two weeks ago."

All eyes were on Lane. Liam's lips, Track noticed, formed the soundless expression of a kennel metaphor.

"The session was in a clinical evaluation, and most of it is confidential, whether Mister Barstow is here or not. I think I can safely say that Barstow reported one female personality who speaks in an unknown language, and one who threatens. I'm no linguist. Anyway, my guess is a sort of *folie à deux*, a shared disorder."

"I see," said the general, "sort of. So there are characters in the dreams who are unknown to the dreamer?"

"We have no way of knowing for certain," said Liam. "Tetzel reports at least two: an adult female who began as his mother and finally evolved after repetitions into quite a different woman, and a girl, not seen, who offered comfort and sang a song in an unfamiliar language. I recognize some of the phrases as probably being Irish. The girl calls the dreamer 'my son' several times—the Irish *an mhic*—and hums a tune that appears to be a very old Irish song. It isn't a song frequently found on Irish music albums. The usual folk groups don't perform it because the words are Gaelic and the tune isn't very appealing unless you have the Irish ear."

"By this," said Pretorius, "you are suggesting to us that it would be hard for the cadet to lie with any authenticity."

Liam tilted his head quizzically. "I long ago discarded any theories about deliberate lying, sir. Too many people have experienced too many things."

181

"I agree," said the general. "Now, is there anything else we need to know?"

"Yes sir," said Sam. "I do have something that may give us some solid support for continuing the project." He opened his briefcase and extracted a cassette recorder.

"I mentioned earlier how we ended up with garbage from the tape system on Saturday, how the crying child's voice was indistinguishable. I worked with Sergeant Saganian all Sunday trying to pry something out of the tape, but no luck. There was random noise all over the audible range of frequencies. As I said, there was a problem with the recording head. We fixed it, but it was too late to help.

"The problem is, the noise buries the signal. What I mean is, the 'signal' is the meaningful information, the child crying. It's nonrandom. The noise is random, and acts to camouflage the signal. It's a basic problem in psychophysics. I could have tried to reduce the noise by some means if I knew where to look in the spectrum. But I didn't."

"I'm an engineer," said the commandant, "not a biologist or whatever you are. But I suspect you're about to tell me that any complex combination of periodic wave forms can be analyzed by use of the Fourier series."

"Yes sir. That's what our microcomputer does when we use the real-time analysis routine. A sound has peaks where the power of certain frequencies is high while others are low. By looking at a plot—a power spectrum, which the computer gives us—we can identify the principle Fourier components. These are related to changes in the speaker's vocal tract as he speaks—the peaks shift."

"And," said the general, "the Fourier components for a child are found higher in the spectrum than, for example, yours."

"Yes sir," Sam replied. I have him in the bag, he thought. It's no longer an administrative pain in the ass or a disciplinary problem. It's a technical demonstration. "The trouble was, I needed a comparison signal."

"As a reference spectrum," suggested the commandant.

"Exactly, sir. As it happens, I managed to get a recording of a child crying last night. It was pure luck, if you can call it that, and not under the happiest circumstances. It also had some unfortunate results for me, but I won't bore you with them. Suffice to say, the recording could be analyzed by the computer and give

182

us a feel for how to tease out the other more elusive noises, since we now had frequency ranges. We had to hope our model—Major Dortmunder's daughter, who suffered a sad loss—cried in the same general way as Annabelle."

"Annabelle?" said Lane, squinting at Sam as if he had just brayed like a jackass.

"Annabelle Charlotte Proctor. Maggie's researches identify one ghost in this case as the seven-year-old daughter of Captain Adonijah Proctor, a professor of drawing from 1822 to 1847."

"Thank you," said Lane with polite irony.

"Then there are two ghosts?" asked Pretorius.

"By tradition," said Sam. "The one Liam reports seeing would be Captain Proctor himself."

As if by mutual consent, they all shifted in their seats. The commandant's pipe had gone out again, but he sucked absently on the stem and made no attempt to relight it.

"Let's go over the traditions later," said the commandant. "I want to hear about your computer trick."

Sam described his technique to the commandant in some detail, while Lane and Pretorius squirmed. Track was lost, but enjoyed watching the discomfort of the counselor.

"We couldn't really resurrect the original sound in its full range, but by enhancing the peculiar modulations in what we knew were the frequency ranges of a small child, we could do a fair job of reconstructing the timing and tone."

"And?" asked Pretorius.

Sam rewound the cassette and pushed the play switch. There was a rushing noise. "That's the original recording from Saturday. In a few seconds the scrubbed signal starts." They all stared at the recorder as if the sound could be seen as well as heard. In a few moments the rushing stopped. They could barely hear a sort of tinkling sound. Sam turned up the volume.

The general looked at Pretorius and sucked his pipe. He was neither a superstitious man nor a fatuous one. His career had consisted largely of one assignment after another with airborne infantry units. He held a master's degree in mechanical engineering from Georgia Tech, and he had been appointed commandant of cadets at a time when the intellectual quality of commandants had seen bad days. His missions, articulated rather bluntly by the Chief of Staff of the army, were to patch up long-standing petty animosities between the office of the commandant and the office of the dean of the Academic Board, and to improve the performance of army football. Ghost-hunting was not his mandate. But he was an astute man, and his reputation as a killjoy was largely a carefully managed ploy to meet the expectations of a community that could compare him to many commandants whose tenure was long over. He had consented to this meeting at the strong recommendation of Colonel Pretorius, who in turn was responding to Ward Lane's fulminations. The food fight only hours before had caused ripples on the placid surface of West Point, but he was not worried overmuch by the breach of discipline. He had been no stranger to excess as a cadet, and as a squadron commander in the 11th Armored Cavalry Regiment in Vietnam he had accepted the fact that men needed to relieve stress from time to time, and the degree of relief needed bore an exponential relationship to the degree of stress.

He had only half listened to the first part of the briefing, his mind being engaged elsewhere. At length he had recognized that there was something extraordinary in the intensity with which these officers viewed the happenings in the old barracks. What he had first viewed as a curiosity he now took seriously.

The sound from the tape was difficult to describe. It was far from high fidelity and obviously artificial—a computer voice. But there was a curious quality about it nonetheless, and it was also obvious to everyone who listened that it was no mistake, no wishful thinking, to call it what it was. Under the machine approximation was a real human feeling. It was not a child weeping for a skinned knee or a scolding. It was a child in mortal terror.

They listened without comment through the tape sequence. The commandant extended their project through Sunday.

4

The Rose-Tree

What are the roots that clutch, what branches grow
Out of this stony rubbish?

—T. S. Eliot
The Waste Land

12

*C*orey Fletcher, seventeenth in the Class of 1966. Silver Star for heroism in ground action against a hostile force in the Republic of Viet Nam, 22 February 1968; and a Purple Heart for the sniper's bullet that tore away half his head and stopped his life. Old Corey. Liam felt tears in his eyes. Jesus, Corey. Yes, Corey, looking fit and full of life, for a dead man.

Liam was breathless, late for chem lab; he found his place at the lab bench beside Corey at the last moment, before the class was called to attention. The acrid smell of the reagents brought back a poignant sense of things lost forever. "Made it, huh?" Corey said with a wink. "Old Leemy, late for everything."

Corey, Liam said, but no more words came, just tears.

Torch one two, torch one two, this is torch two three, torch two three. We got automatic weapons fire from the right, in the ruined ville. I'm up to my ass in alligators, Leemy, and no time to drain the fucking swamp . . . wait . . . holy shit, we got incoming, they got a mortar. Wait, out . . .

It was hot, and Liam could smell the sharp odor of charcoal smoke from village fires and the sharper odor of burning grass. The throaty, crunching sound of the mortar rounds landing near the flank platoon, the crackle and terrifying rushing urgency of the 7.62 machine-gun bullets. He could judge the direction—front and right, mostly from the right near second platoon.

Torch two three, torch one two, over.

One two, this is two three romeo, two three's down, say again two three's down. We're taking heavy fire from the right, better get the hell over here. I say again—

This is one two, shouted Liam. Say again: Is two three hit? Is two three hit?

Affirmative, two three's bought it. Two three's bought it. You better get your asses over here or we're all buyin' the fucking worm farm; say again . . .

A dust-streaked sky, heat. God, the heat. Liam stared up at the sky and the dust that swirled and danced in the prop wash. He felt tired, unspeakably tired, but there was little pain now, just a sleepiness that beckoned him to float passive and willing into the darkness at the center of his vision, the darkness that would spread to blacken the zenith of the sky.

Don't you do it, said Corey. *There's no rest there. You keep your eyes open, stay on your toes, Leemy.*

He felt the bounce again as the litter-bearers carried him to the dustoff, looked up into the crew chief's face and heard the medic shout at the platoon sergeant. But the words were almost beyond comprehension. The blackness was spreading. "Shit, man," said the medic, black and wide-eyed and sympathetic, "them motherfuckers do you a J.O.B., nail you for the big ass. You got stitched right up the side. No sweat, man, we fix you right up, a little fuckin' tape here, a few staples there man, you on the motherfuckin' bird home. No body bag for you, man. We know our shit. You tell 'em I said hi back in Oakland, man. Hey, man, we got him loaded, let's get the fuck out of this place."

And the blackness spread and Liam found himself drawn into the center of it. On the other side was light, first seen as a distant point of glowing yellow, then sunlight and trees with leaves red and gold. It was a scene in miniature at first, as if seen through a telescope backwards; then it expanded and he was drawn into it and his pain and terror vanished.

It was cool even in the bright sunlight, the grass dappled with yellow oak leaves and more falling in graceful spirals. There was Bridey and her corporal, refilling platters of food, apples and berries and sliced meats, and Ethan, a glass in his hand, eyes gazing down

188

the row of trees toward the Academy building; the colonel, erect and graceful and impossibly young, no man ever more fit to wear the epaulet, talking to Mansfield beside the great maple that stood before their house. The golden child laughed and clapped as Bridey's boy tried clumsily to roll a hoop along the patch of hard earth by the road.

The Antique, oldest of his class, bowed a courtly bow and handed the golden child a flower from the roadside. The girl imitated his bow, and he addressed her softly in French, which always delighted her. The Antique smiled his shy smile, kept in reserve like Hannibal's African levies for only the most excruciating tactical necessity moments, and his normally reserved countenance was transformed. His hair was damp from playing with the children, the heavy pewter-gray wool of his uniform a torment in the autumn sun.

Liam looked, and she was at the door again; he saw her face and knew she had passed through another of her spells. The edges of her delicate mouth were turned down in stern disapproval, and there were patches of angry lividness on her cheeks. She called the girl, and the Antique bent and whispered to her and she smiled as he launched her gently to Eliza.

Liam looked at Bridey, still serving the outdoor table, as she called to her boy. Her man, the corporal, took him playfully by the ear and led him away. Liam sighed and closed his eyes. The breeze came up again, and the chill reminded him that he had begun to sweat.

Liam looked at the lawn again, and the scene was frozen in immobility: Bridey turned to watch her husband and the boy as they walked up the road, the colonel and Ethan in mid-speech, Eliza and the girl gone inside and the door closed. Then the door grew smaller and smaller and the darkness came in from the sides and swallowed him. But on the other side of the blackness was white sunlight, not the gold of autumn, and a vast stony waste that stretched in all directions, and a dead, dry, white-barked tree.

Yes, said the Old Man, *it is a beauty. Best of the lot.* Liam looked at him and laughed. He was old, careworn, all wrinkles and a scraggly,

189

yellow-white beard that grew in all directions. His face was burned nut-brown by the sun, by years of labor in the sun, and when he smiled he showed sparse yellow teeth. A century old he could be, and frail with hands knotted and stained by labor in the earth. He leaned on a crooked garden rake nearly as tall as he, and he was dressed only in a dirty khaki shirt and baggy khaki trousers with worn, stained knees; his feet were bare, dirty and callused. But then he smiled at Liam, and his eyes, startling blue, flashed with a merriment that scorned wit in favor of joy. He tilted his head at Liam and grinned, a grin of yellow teeth and old gums and spar-kling, joyful eyes.

Look here, boy, said the Old Man, *you can't see the roots, but they go deep, deeper than this stony ground. This was once a garden, as you saw yourself. The roots go deep, boy. They entwine themselves about the bones of him that was first, and on the branches was him who was and is to come. Look now, boy, look at what a grand tree you planted.*

And Liam looked at the branch nearest him, and on it were long, sharp thorns, sharp and shiny as if cast in bronze; and on the tips of the thorns there was blood. He looked beyond the near branch and saw that there was blood on all the thorns, on all the branches.

Here now, said the Old Man, *do you think I am beautiful?*

No, Liam admitted, not beautiful.

Well, said the Old Man a trifle huffily, *you ain't so pretty yourself. Now kiss me, boy.*

Liam kissed the Old Man. He expected the Old Man's breath to be foul. But it was not. It smelled like any old man's. Just old.

Well, said the Old Man, *just look at what you done, boy.* And Liam saw that the tree was alive, it had great dark green glossy leaves. Then, as he watched, great blossoms burst open all over the tree, great snow-white flowers; and on each he could see a glistening moisture.

Where does the dew come from in this desert? asked Liam.

Now you're getting smart, boy. Those are her tears.

I did all this?

Don't be proud, boy. This is only one little tree, and there's still a big desert to water with a few tears. And look up there. And in the top of the tree, Liam saw a flutter among the blossoms, and there was a bird, pure white and without a mark but its two bright silver eyes, and he heard its song. And, though he could not say why at first, its song made him feel cold and afraid, suddenly terrified that he might find himself alone in the stony waste.

Come here, now, said the Old Man. *Come and touch me.* And he held up his hands as if to gather rain drops, but instead the white bird in a flutter of spotless snow-white feathers alit in the Old Man's twisted hands. *Here you are, my child, come and warm yourself.* And he held the bird, suddenly tame, against his old dusty khaki work-shirt. The song ceased and the bird's silver shining eyes closed.

See boy? She rests with me. Don't you worry about her, no spot to burden her little wings. There are others I could mention not so fortunate, of course; mercy is without limit, but wisdom is in short supply. Here now, little sister, you fly back. He held up his hands again, palms to the sky, and the white bird took flight again to the top of the tree, covered now in flowers.

What have we here? said the Old Man with a soft merry laugh, looking down at his feet. *You're still here, are you? Helped this boy find me?* And there was Raymond by the Old Man's feet, content-edly grooming himself. The Old Man picked the rat up gently, and its watery ruby eyes gazed at the Old Man while its muzzle twitched excitedly. As the gnarled fingers stroked Raymond's head, the ruby eyes closed. The Old Man gazed around slyly, and winked at Liam to seal a conspiracy. *I'm not supposed to,* he said in a whisper, *but I let 'em in anyway. Who's to know?* He put Raymond down gently at the foot of the tree and wiped his hands fastidiously on the old khaki workshirt. *I love them all, the little ones,* the Old Man said, *but a rat's a rat and the fellows never miss a chance to piss on you.* Liam smiled and the Old Man shook his head in good-natured weariness.

Well, boy. What more would you know?

Will the tree always bloom, Father?

Only if you water it. Are you deliberately obtuse, boy, or just proud?

Liam lowered his head, mortified. When he looked up, the Old Man and the tree were gone and the stony waste was now a hallway, low-ceilinged, with pale painted walls and a floor of sea-soned boards. The woman stood at the head of the hall, erect and proud. She had gray, pale eyes, with dark hair pulled severely back from a high, porcelain-white brow. Her austere dark gray dress touched the floor and rose tight about her neck in a spray of white lace. She is beautiful, Liam thought, a queen in exile whose last

191

crown jewel is pride. But her hands were locked in front of her, bony and tense, as if clasped by her cameo ring; they were white and thin, starveling hands, and they gripped each other with grim strength. And now Liam saw her eyes again, and he saw they were mad eyes, staring at him in bottomless hate and revulsion.

I know you, she said, *I know you well enough, and I know what you've done, husband. Did it give you pleasure? What are whores for, but pleasure?*

No, said Liam, it wasn't that at all.

Out! Get her out, gibbering filthy foreign monkey, chattering whore! Get them both out, the Irish brat too!

Then she was quiet, and Liam felt the chill of her affliction, as her eyes rolled back under their lids and she was there but not there, as if her own soul had fled from her rage.

Liam turned and the hallway was gone. It was snowing, and the snow on the ground was lit by the vivid, terrible light of a fire, and the falling snow danced in the yellow light like fireflies. The fire burned hot, drawing the air into the window, and the flakes spun in a circle on the wind and vanished into the blaze like moths drawn to the light of a lamp. Around and around they flew in a demon-circle and into the fire.

Anna stood at the stone table in the stony desolation, her great dark ingenue's eyes painted with kohl and a diadem on her head like a crescent moon. Before her on the stone was a bronze tripod and in its bowl a flame, oily smoke that rose to the dust-streaked blue sky.

Anna held a slim knife in one hand and in the other was a white bird, calm and resting without a struggle in her grasp, its eyes of gleaming silver fixed on Liam. Anna looked at Liam with pity in her eyes painted dark and huge against the pale face. *I can't help you,* said Anna, *you have to do it yourself.* She brought the point of the knife down in the center of the white bird's spotless breast and pressed down until at once the blood came in a single crimson spot. She placed the still-white form with its single tear of bright red on the fire, and the smoke turned white and rose to the sky.

Liam turned away, and at the edge of the darkening woods he saw the eyes, twin points of luminance that reflected the light of heaven, sad and infinitely remote. Then the twin points paled and became many, suddenly fixed on the clockface on the bedside

192

table. It was three-thirty in the morning, Wednesday, the thirty-first of October, All Hallows Eve.

"Sir," said Sergeant Saganian, "I'm going to be very, very glad when this project is over."

"What's the matter," said Sam. "losing too much sleep?"

"Not that, so much. It's just all this sitting around in the dead of night. Like having permanent charge-of-quarters duty. I'm not a night person."

"Then you're in luck," said Sam. "It's tomorrow already. Oh-three thirty. And you get a break. Me, I have to meet class at oh-eight forty and a two-hour lab starting at ten after one. While you're snoring away on compensatory time, I'll be slaving over lecture notes and dragging comatose cadets through the mysteries of—of whatever I'm teaching today. I can't remember."

"Hell, sir, it can't be all that bad. All you have to do is shoot the breeze and tell jokes for an hour at a time."

"You ought to try keeping cadets awake after lunch. It's like delivering a eulogy at a pet cemetery. How we looking?"

Saganian checked the instrument displays one by one. The EEG traces showed deep sleep. Heart rate sixty-two. The room temperature hovered at fifty-one (Carson had wanted the window open tonight). The audio display showed only a row of short, flickering columns across the audible range. The video, as usual, showed very little. There was a very dim light shape that was the exposed top of the sheet on Carson's bed. The luminous dial of his alarm clock was brighter. Sam panned the camera right and left with the joystick. Nothing but fog. Without light there could never be enough contrast. The video was a waste of time unless they found some reason to turn on the room lights. Or unless something bright chose to enter.

"I'm gonna be pissed," said Saganian, "if we never see anything at all after all this grief. Ortega'll never let me forget it. What can we do to stir something up?"

"Not a thing, Sarge. Cheer up, though. It's the witching hour. All the activity has been around this time."

"You're right, sir. Son of a bitch, look." He pointed to the oscilloscope and the EEG tracks. There were bursts of unsynchronized high-frequency, low-amplitude activity. More theta. They laughed. Since he had dropped off to sleep at eleven fifty-two, Carson had gone into such activity repeatedly, only to drift again into deeper sleep. Once he had tossed and turned and even moaned. Saganian had felt his heart race as the EEG traces went wild. But Carson had merely detached the ground electrode from his ear lobe; Sam had crept in without lights and replaced it.

Now Carson was either awake or in paradoxical sleep. His EEG was that of conscious alertness, irregular tiny spikes replacing the gentler waves and sleep spindles.

"I should have had a myograph channel," said Sam, "and taped it to an eyelid. I could verify REMs. Shit. I always think of this stuff too late."

"No sir," said Saganian. "You thought of it already. You told Captain Salinger to rig it when you first briefed us last week."

"Oh really? So, what happened?"

"There were insurmountable technical difficulties, sir."

"Forgot it, huh?"

"Completely. Oh, crap." Saganian closed his eyes in despair. "The damned video's out from the computer." He was right. The tiny five-inch screen on the computer rack was blank. Saganian was furious; it had failed three times since Saturday. There was now no way to observe the line graphs that showed temperature changes from the thermistors.

"No problem, Sarge," said Sam. "Just turn on the paper drive at the slowest rate and we'll record that way. I'm going to close down at four-thirty anyway. Chart paper's no more expensive than anything else these days. But tomorrow, without fail, replace that video unit."

Saganian turned on the polygraph pen drives and the paper drive. The power light glowed blue in the dim room.

"Sir, we got noises." Saganian pointed at the RTA. There were local spikes in three places, shifting up and down the scale at irregular intervals, surging upward and then subsiding.

"Not very loud," said Sam. "What? Less than ten decibels? Let's give her a listen." Sam put on the ear phones. Nothing. No, perhaps a faint, impossibly indistinct sound like a flute. "What am I doing? I can't hear this shit. You try it." He handed the headset to Saganian.

His eyes opened wide. "That's it, sir! That's her! Swear to Christ, sir, it's her!"

"Okay, Sarge. Keep it quiet. Start the tape."

Saganian quietly shifted his chair to face the left-hand bank of instruments and turned on the audio tape drive. Sam glanced at the temperature traces on the chart paper; they were perfectly flat. No change. EEG showed strong beta, heart rate was up now to sixty-eight. He panned the video back to Carson, then zoomed back to take in more of the room. There was still haze. He could see the white oblong of the sheet, nothing more.

"Still crying, sir," Saganian whispered.

"Yeah," said Sam. "Pulse elevated slightly, no change in temperature. No EEG change." The absurdity of his chatter suddenly struck Sam. Saganian was wearing the headphones and was blissfully unaware of Sam's mutterings. Now, he thought, now let's see those famous dome-and-spike patterns. Where are you when we need you? He looked again at the lines of red ink on the chart paper that showed temperature variations. The lines were still flat for all eight thermocouples. He looked at the RTA display in front of Saganian: still the flickering dance of bars, the mute phosphorescent testimony to a nameless presence in the next room.

Carson's pulse was now seventy beats per minute.

Saganian touched Sam's arm. "Look at the video, sir." Sure enough, the small black and white screen that shared a rack position with the blank computer display showed movement. It was formless, indistinct, but it was brighter than the image of the white sheet folded over Carson's blanket. It moved randomly, like an aurora in a winter sky.

Sam looked again at the EEG traces on the oscilloscope. There they were, the slow potentials followed by a sharp, brief spike. They registered on two channels strongly, less so on the other two. The strongest were on frontal and fronto-parietal, weak on temporal and temporal-parietal.

"What the hell do we do now?" Sam asked himself quietly. "Is the kid having a petit mal seizure? Is it garbage? What in the pluperfect hell is going on, and how do I handle it?" He looked at the temperature traces. They were still perfectly flat.

He tapped Saganian on the shoulder and signaled to him to take off the ear phones. "Just monitor the noise on the RTA screen, Sarge. Listen, we have everything breaking loose but the temper-

195

ature. Carson's pulse is up like he's been running in place, we have that screwy seizure pattern, we have the crying, and we have something visual going on. I may hate myself for this, but let's let it go full cycle and see what happens."

"He isn't in danger, sir?"

"I doubt it. It can't really be a seizure. A real one would never have lasted this long, I think. I don't know for sure. As far as I can tell, he's still dreaming, and that screwball petit mal pattern is something out of left field. Let it go a little while and we'll see what develops."

"Okay, sir. I'm not exactly wild about going in there, anyway."

Sam grinned excitedly. "What's the matter, Sarge? You look like you've seen a ghost."

"Shit, sir. You should have got a look at Ortega after that goat-rope last night. He said something came roaring past him outa that room, and whatever it was, it was pissed. He didn't even want to talk about it. We may have to tie him to the chair tomorrow."

"I'm not breathing real slow myself," said Sam. "When I looked at that movement on the video tape, I . . . Hel-lo, now what?" There was still the auroral shimmer on the video display, but now there was a bright point of light that hovered in the upper edge of the field. Sam tilted the drive upward and centered the spot. He guessed it was about four or five feet above the floor, over Carson's head, but he had no visible reference point he could use to place it exactly.

"Sarge, I want to look at this through the thermal. Switch the cables. Quietly—that's right, the BNC connector hanging next to the rack, just switch it for the one on the video input. Yeah. Okay . . . Cowabunga!"

"What's the matter, sir?"

"Look, there's the spot. It has a strong thermal signature, like a lighted cigarette. Damn, that's a real hot spot." Then Sam was silent for a moment, and Saganian was surprised to see him do a double take.

"What's up, sir? Does he smoke?"

Sam didn't answer, but tripped a toggle switch on the thermal imager control. Instantly the picture was reversed, as if from positive to negative. The spot was now dark against a pale background divided horizontally by a brighter, irregular streak.

"Look," he said, "and remember this in case the tape gets ruined. That light streak is Carson's body heat from the bunk. When we looked at the spot first, I had the imager set on 'black-hot.' Now, lighter colors are hotter on the image."

"You mean the spot's cold?"

"You got it," said Sam absently, "scientific proof positive of a witch's tit." They watched the display for a silent minute.

"Was it there before?"

"I don't know, Sarge. I don't remember seeing it. I don't know what it could be." He switched back to dark-hot.

"Did it just move?"

"Maybe. Watch." Sam pulled a fiber-tip pen out of his pocket and made a tiny mark in the center of the glowing point. They saw the spot move in a short horizontal arc first to the left and then to the right of the ink mark.

"What do you think, sir? Do we go in?"

"Wait." The spot moved a little farther, almost rhythmically, just perceptibly back and forth.

"Maybe the pan-and-tilt drive's vibrating."

"Negative," said Sam. "The motor stays off until I trip the relay with the joystick. I wish to hell I had a reference."

"The clock, sir."

"Right you are." Sam moved the video camera's center of field down to the clock face on Carson's desk and placed the ink dot on the twelve. They watched it for four or five seconds. There was no discernible movement.

"Whatever that other thing is," said Sam, "it's moving by itself." He turned the camera back to the glowing spot. Once again, he saw the slow rhythmic movement.

"Let's see what else there is." He started moving the video camera in a careful series of rectangular excursions from the central spot. Then for no apparent reason it jammed. "Now what the hell?"

"It does that sometimes," said Saganian. "Jiggle the joystick around and it'll break loose, sir."

Sam tried it, and to his relief the drive whirred and clicked in the next room and the mechanism broke free from whatever gremlin had bound it. But Sam's feeling of relief was short-lived. At that same moment the spot suddenly divided into two points of light, the original moving slightly to the right and a second coming into view abruptly to the left. His breath stopped and he felt his skin crawl; his hair quite literally stood on end. He heard Saganian whisper something unintelligible.

The human visual system is exquisitely sensitive to very subtle things, and the most impoverished information can be very accurately classified at a glance as lawful or unlawful for any natural class of event. The human brain is clever and quick on the uptake, and if Sam's body reacted with a visceral uproar, it was because Sam knew as clearly as he could know anything that those two points of light were the eyes of a moving, sentient form, and those eyes had, in response to the noise of the pan-and-tilt drive, turned and looked at the video camera—and, through the cable to the screen, at Sam.

Sam and Saganian were paralyzed. The eye-points tilted slightly as if in curiosity, then slowly blurred and spread, seeming to merge. The luminance gradually lessened, then flashed for an instant and broke up into a thousand dancing fragments.

"Now!" said Sam, and before he could disengage himself from the chair, Saganian was up and out the door. Sam was after him in an instant, and by the time he turned outside the instrumentation room Saganian was reaching for the doorknob of the plebes' room. He turned it and Sam expected to see him push the door open. Instead Saganian's eyes grew wide and he stared at his hand. "Oh, no. Christ, sir, help! Get me off!" Saganian looked at Sam in helpless panic.

Sam looked at the sergeant's hand. The fingers were clutching the brass doorknob, and Sam saw what he first thought was smoke curling between them; but then he saw the thick frost on the metal. "Sir, God damn it, I can't get it off! It's burning me!"

But Sam knew that Saganian's hand was frozen to the metal. It would be useless to pull it off by force; the skin on the sergeant's palms would stay on the doorknob. "Stay put," Sam said. "I'll go get some hot water."

Saganian laughed desperately, his face wet with tears of physical agony and fear. "I ain't going anywhere, sir. Hurry up! Hurry up!"

Sam dashed down the flight of stairs to the latrine and spun the hot water tap all the way open. It spattered over his uniform, but it was cold. Seconds passed, and the warmth stubbornly refused to come.

"What's the matter, sir?" A cadet from the room next to the latrine was standing in the doorway in his gray robe and shower clogs, staring at Sam as if he were quite mad.

"Get something to hold water! A can, a coffee pot, anything! Hurry up!" The cadet disappeared. Upstairs Sam could hear Saganian moaning in fear.

The water was finally getting warm. Sam heard a commotion in the next room; they must be tearing the room apart for a pot of some kind. Now there was steam, and Sam allowed a little cool water into the mixture.

The cadet reappeared with his roommate. "This wastebasket's all we got, sir. Is it okay?"

"Hell yes," said Sam. "Here, fill it with water and come upstairs." Dashing out of the room, Sam ran up the stairs two at a time. Saganian was leaning forward, his face turned sideways and resting against the door, his hand still frozen to the doorknob. His eyes were closed.

"Please hurry, sir. Please. Hurry up. I can't feel my hand anymore. I don't want to lose my hand. Hurry up. Something's on the other side of the door, I can feel it. Please hurry." Sam looked down the stairs. The two cadets had filled the wastebasket with steaming water and, side by side, were lugging it up the steps, steaming drops splashing out with every step. Behind them, other cadets were coming out of their rooms, and two more were looking down from the next level. "One of you," said Sam to the group on the next landing down, "call Mister Tetzel and tell him we have an injury. Then call the hospital and get an ambulance. Then call Central Guard Room and tell the officer-in-charge we have an incident in this division."

The water bucket arrived. "Okay, Sarge. I'm going to start pouring hot water on the doorknob. It's going to trickle on your hand. It's not scalding hot. It'll thaw your fingers." He motioned to the cadets, and they started carefully pouring the water. "Try moving your fingers."

"I can't sir. I can't move my hand."

As the water flowed around Saganian's paralyzed grip, Sam tried tentatively to pry his fingers loose. He felt the touch of the metal; cold, cold as hell, but no longer cold enough to stick to the skin. The thumb detached itself, then the ring finger, and then, as Saganian lunged back with a terrified movement, the rest came

199

loose. He lost his balance and fell against the wall behind him.

Sam pulled one of the water-carrier cadets next to him and grabbed the bottom hem of his bath robe, wrapping it around his hand to hold the doorknob. At this point the door opened and Carson looked out sleepily from the dark room. "What's going on, sir?"

Sam stared at him in disbelief. Carson looked around at the cadets standing in the hallway and then at Saganian, crumpled against the wall on the far side of the hallway, staring at his bleeding hand. "What happened, sir? Somebody have an accident?"

Sam shook his head. "Just wake up?"

"Yes sir. I just heard a bunch of noise out in the hallway."

"Having dreams?"

Carson looked back into the darkness. "I don't know, sir. I don't remember. Yeah, now that I think about it: it was—I was walking in the snow. I think I was walking in the snow."

"He must have been, sir," said one of the cadets in the hall. "He must have melted it on the floor." The light from the hall had illuminated sparkles of moisture on the bare board floor near the entrance to Barstow's empty alcove. Sam bent down and touched it with his fingers. It was cold.

The officer-in-charge arrived five minutes later, and shortly after that an ambulance flashed its way through the sally port and pulled up to the 47th Division. Saganian had collected his wits, but his final wrenching away from the door had torn off three patches of skin from the palm of his right hand. He left with the ambulance, and Sam had to wonder what effect the morning's fiasco would have on official enthusiasm for the project.

The OC, a short, powerful infantry major from the 2nd Regiment, knew about the ghost investigation—there was a new annex, as a matter of fact, in the OC instructions that described the nature and location of the project, listed the responsible officers and their telephone numbers, and removed the 47th Division (very temporarily, but to the delight of its cadets) from the list of areas for late-night inspections.

"I'm not sure how to write this," said the OC. "I've pulled

this miserable duty a million times, but I never had anything happen quite like this."

"Tell me about it," said Sam. "I'm beginning to wish I'd stayed with armored cavalry. It's safer and more predictable."

"What do you think it was, sir? Am I supposed to put down in my report that a ghost chilled the room?"

"That," said Sam, "is your business. I recommend you be very, very conservative. That's what I'm going to be, believe me. But since you walked all the way over, look at this." Sam rewound the videotape and played it for the OC. They watched the auroral shimmer, then the stationary spot.

"What the hell is that?" asked the OC.

"Watch," said Sam. And presently the dots did their dance.

"Damn," the OC said. "Eyes."

"That's when Sergeant Saganian ran out and tried to open the door."

"How cold was it in there?"

"Good question," said Sam. "The TV screen where we usually monitor the temperature was on the blink, so we couldn't watch it while it was happening. We'll look at it tomorrow in the lab, it's all on disk. But look, we were recording it on chart paper as a backup." Sam picked up a pile of folded paper with spidery red lines. "Now here, maybe a half hour ago, you see all these lines go down very quickly, not more than fifteen or twenty seconds for this steep slope. Neither of us was watching, so we missed it."

"But they stop going down," said the OC.

"I screwed up," said Sam. "Actually, the pens just couldn't move any farther. These pens have a fixed excursion; they're only a few inches from pivot to tip, and they peg out against mechanical stops so they won't get tangled with each other. What happened was, it got so cold so fast they all pegged, and it was over so quickly we didn't see it. We watched straight lines, but didn't realize why they were straight."

"But the beanhead didn't freeze," the OC pointed out. "And that doorknob had to be incredibly cold for your NCO's hand to freeze to it. Was it just cold at the door?"

"No," said Sam, "those readings on the chart paper are from eight thermocouples, seven on the wall and one in the middle of the floor, and they all pegged out. I don't know why the plebe didn't notice it. Maybe we'll know more when I get a look at the data on disk tomorrow."

"What are you going to do now?"

"Close up shop until tomorrow night. Enough is enough."

It was after five o'clock when Sam arrived home in Lee Area and undressed and showered in the hall bathroom to keep from waking Maggie. Exhausted and elated, he stood under the hot water, letting it run down his face and over his shoulders. So much for the last conservative hypothesis. All that graduate training wasted. All of it dissolved in a shimmering phosphorescence. Maggie was right after all.

Those eyes, he thought. I didn't see any of that sadness Liam and the cadets saw. Just points of light. Maybe something was lost in the video. Eyes they were, but I saw no grief, no malevolence, nothing but passionless sight. Was it the video? Was it me? What would Maggie have seen?

He dried himself off and put on his old terry-cloth bathrobe. Maggie was still asleep. He slipped carefully into bed. By constitution and experience soldiers are partial to warm sheets after a long night of wakefulness. Because of his seniority, Sam did not have to stand duty as he had years before, and there is little night duty to stand at West Point in any case. The officer-in-charge was from the commandant's pool of lucky selectees and Sam, of course, worked for the dean. Even the academy duty officer stood only a telephone watch at his quarters after six o'clock. But earlier in Sam's career there had been many all-nighters: hour after boring hour at a duty officer's gray steel desk with a loose-leaf binder full of instructions, telephone numbers, and standing operating procedures slipped into clear plastic covers, and the inevitable drawer full of pulpy erotica for the OD's reading pleasure, and a beard that grew as you sat there, and your body feeling as if it were covered with slime for want of a shower. But the all-nighters were justified when he could finally slip into bed or under a poncho liner, even in the years before Maggie. She had missed all that. Sam had been a senior major before he ever met Maggie, and she had never had to wake him up for duty. Nor, for that matter, had she ever had to kiss him good-bye at Travis or Oakland before the eighteen-hour flight to Tan Son Nhut or Bien Hoa or Cam Ranh. Their baby would never have to get used to the father who was a stranger with a new, frightening face. Maggie would never have to feel fear at the ring of a telephone, never face a chaplain and a survivor assistance officer, never receive a package from overseas, pitiful remnants of a life—letters, clothes, a paycheck endorsed by a summary courts officer half a world away. Not much to regret after all.

Maggie stirred. Sam touched her hair and she sighed. "Back already?"

"Just a nap before I start the day. Sleep well, Mom?"

"Mmmm. Any ghosts?"

Sam said nothing. Maggie opened her eyes, barely. "Sam, don't mess with me. I get violent, remember?"

"Yes, dear lady. Old Adonijah favored us with his presence."

"Wonderful," said Maggie. "Tell me later." She closed her eyes and was asleep again.

13

*T*here's no point in getting so riled," said Alice Fetterman as she turned the car out of Washington Gate and down the Old Storm King Highway toward Cornwall. "she's just a bureaucrat. You can't fight *them*, Lord knows. They're hydra-headed. Lop off one and there are ten more, each one as inert as the first."

"I don't want to lop her head off," said Maggie. "I just want to find that confounded book. *Then* I'll cut Betty O'Grady's heart out." They were on their way to Bernice Gort's mountain home for tea and a strategy session.

"I admire your restraint, Maggie. Is Sam like you?"

"No, thank God. It would be like Jiggs and Maggie."

"Has he decided to believe in ghosts yet?"

"He won't admit it. But the scare last night made him a believer, I think, at some level. He was exhausted this morning, and apparently Liam was in bad shape as well. Sam called me just before you pulled up and said they were taking a day's break from the exorcism."

"I can understand Sam being worn out," said Alice, "but why Liam? I thought you said yesterday he'd had a day to rest up."

"Well, he was up late last night and then apparently he had trouble sleeping. Sam didn't know much about it."

"Matt said General Harrington took well to Sam at the briefing yesterday."

"Well, he extended the great ghost hunt until Sunday. Sam was afraid the thing would be abandoned. He was worried when he left for work this morning that his lab technician's injury would cause an uproar. But Colonel Pretorius called him this morning and said not to worry, the deal was still good."

They came to the start of the two-lane cliff road cut into the

205

sides of Crow's Nest and Storm King mountains. There was a sheer drop to the right down to the river. It was a beautiful drive, but Maggie had a morbid fear of meeting a drunk driver or a truck out of control. The bare stone to the left of the road was defaced with initials and the occasional obscenity or high school motto sprayed in pink or orange or black, but there was very little puny men could do to change the overwhelming impression of wildness that reduced both road and graffiti to insignificance. The Hudson River School of landscape painting had begun here, and its theme of a majestic New World Arcadia was nowhere more compelling than on the narrow pavement of Route 218 between Lee Gate and Cornwall-on-Hudson. It was a Washington Irving wilderness, where one might easily imagine a bearded, mossy Rip Van Winkle slumbering beneath a layer of leaves. The hardwood trees were showing their autumnal full dress and Maggie, for all her qualms at Alice's heedless Monte Carlo driving style, was elated.

Sam had seemed genuinely happy on Tuesday, despite the wounded eye, proud of Maggie and, if Maggie had known it, proud of himself for drinking the waters of the fountain of youth, once removed. His head teemed with plans for their child. True, her joke about sending the poor unborn thing to West Point was not well received, but last night Sam had put his arm around her *in front of other people*, an act roughly equivalent to Ebenezer Scrooge trying out a Hula Hoop. And he did it with about as much grace. But, be reasonable Maggie, she thought. If you've taught a jackass to read don't complain because he can't fly.

"You look positively pale," said Alice, "are you all right?"

Maggie had been leaning against the door, lost in thought and staring out the window at Breakneck Mountain on the far shore. She suddenly realized she felt cold, the strange aura of cold she knew from recent experience was the herald of morning sickness. Oh, no. Not in Alice's car, not on a fine day like this.

"Since you mention it, I'm sick. I'm afraid I'm not going to make it all the way to Bernice's without throwing up. I'm sorry, Alice; as you love your upholstery, please stop somewhere."

"As soon as I can, dear, but there's a cliff going up on one side and cliff going down on the other. I'll step on it, though—there are places in Cornwall where . . ."

"Yes! Do it!"

And Alice stepped on it. The road was downhill now all the

way to Cornwall, but it was still two-lane with no shoulder, and as they left the cliffs behind and entered the trees on the outskirts of the village, Alice was being a little arbitrary about lanes. Just past the first house, they ran a police car off the road. Alice ignored him, and so saved Maggie's dignity, since the irate policeman was obliged to kill a bit of time in turning around to give chase. By the time he found Alice's Mercedes parked brazenly near the center of Cornwall, Maggie was in the sanctuary of a rest room in an Italian restaurant.

When Maggie saw sunlight again, feeling much better, Alice was chatting amiably with the trooper. A breathless and innocently graphic description of Maggie's mutinous tummy, no doubt made more touchy than usual by her delicate condition, had turned away wrath. And the sight of Maggie in her kelly green pullover had been enough to transform what remained of the full vengeance of the law into a gentle and tactful suggestion that Alice hesitate before running police cars off the road, give baby carriages a wide berth, and have a nice day.

"Feeling up to the rest of the trip?" Alice asked when the limb of the law was gone.

"Oh, yes. I'm a new woman. Thank God it's only nine o'clock—if they'd been cooking tomato sauce in there it would have been the end of me."

Alice did a well-mannered turn around the wide intersection and headed back toward the mountain. In the rush to get Maggie to a place of private relief they had passed the road to Bernice's. She drove with slow, stately progress past the small houses and shops, an eye cocked to the rearview mirror.

"We were lucky, Maggie. If I'd gotten a ticket from that cop or, heaven forbid, scratched Matt's pwecious widdul car, out would have come the buggy whip."

"That bad?"

"Oh, Maggie," said Alice with an eye-roll that signaled high hypnotic suggestibility, "Matt is a man of dark moods. He is also something of a granny behind the wheel. He drives me absolutely *nuts*. We sit at four-way stop signs for *so* long, and he . . . *oh, my!*" Alice slammed on the brakes; had Maggie's seat belt not been firmly attached, she would have been hurled against the dashboard.

Alice shifted into reverse and lurched backward at a frightening pace. Her control was bad, and Maggie was afraid for her life yet

207

again. But in a virtuoso display of guts and coordination Alice pulled into a narrow space between a battered Volvo and a pickup truck.

"Alice, what on . . ."

"We're in luck, Maggie, I can't believe it! Look!" Alice pointed out the window on Maggie's side. They were in front of a modest antique store with windows full of dusty Victoriana; beside the door was an enormous iron greyhound sitting on rusty haunches, sentinel, thought Maggie, of La Blech Epoque. "This is it, Maggie! I remembered when I saw the dog!"

"Wonderful, Alice. What is it?"

"It's where I saw the book, Maggie!"

"What b— Oh, you mean the Upton memoir?"

"Yes! It was sitting on an old secretary shelf for decoration! It must have been two, three years ago. I don't generally come here, it's mostly dreck and dust, but I was looking for a gift for Matt's sister, and at the time I thought it might be fun to give her that grotesque dog, but of course I didn't—oh, come on Maggie! Maybe it's still here!" Alice charged out of the car and Maggie followed, a little shakily.

The store was closed. Alice was undeterred. There was an upstairs apartment, and she guessed the owners lived on the premises. If she had been up long enough to risk a traffic ticket, she presumed that the owners were awake as well. She rang the bell—not a pushbutton doorbell, but a real bell on a wrought iron fixture with a bell pull—and tapped insistently on the door glass. "Hello! Hello! Anybody there? Hello!"

Store owners, if they are to survive in a commercial backwater like Cornwall-on-Hudson, must develop a fine sense of the customer's character. The owner in this case, a venerable gentleman named Guido Squillace, realized in a flash that whoever was downstairs meant business. By the third "Hello!" he was waddling down the stairs to find out what the loud-mouthed bitch wanted at this hour of the morning.

"We're closed," he whimpered through the glass.

"We need to look for a book," said Alice, voice firm and polite.

"We open at ten," said Squillace. "I ain't had breakfast yet." His only weapon was the whine, and it was, even Alice admitted, a formidable one. It was a whine worthy of a man whose tax returns for the last five years are under audit. But Alice was an old hand herself, and after a brief exchange of sentiments, he reluctantly slipped the latch and let them in.

Having capitulated, he was full of salespower. "What can I show you ladies?"

"I was in here a couple of years ago," said Alice, "and I remember picking up some old dusty books. They were sitting on the shelf of a secretary, in the back there, I think, where you have the screen and the table with that godawful stuffed pheasant now. Where are they now?"

"What? The secretary? I sold that last . . ."

"No, of course not. The books."

"Books? You came here to look at books?"

"Just those books. They are very important to us."

Squillace pursed his chubby lips and stared at the pheasant. "Hm. I ain't seen 'em since I sold the secretary. They gotta be around here somewhere. Remember offhand what they were about?"

"Only one," said Alice. "It was called *My Years at West Point*, by John Waverly Upton. I think it was brown. It had marbled endpapers, and the title was gilt. It was old, printed around, oh . . ."

"Eighteen eighty-one," said Maggie.

"Lemme think," Squillace said. He thrust his fat hands into his pockets and looked around the store. It was packed with treasures: a squad of terrorists could have hidden in ambush almost anywhere without risk of detection. He looked at two battered bookcases and a breakfront that lived up to its name. He pulled open drawers. He looked behind the screen and in the cabinet under the stuffed pheasant. Finally he gave up and called up the stairs: *"Ma?"*

A thin, crabby voice answered him. *"Yeah?"*

"Ma, where are those old books Hamish sold us years ago?" Maggie and Alice looked at each other.

"They're in the cedar chest, honeybunch. Who's there? We're not open yet."

"Thanks, Ma." Guido shuffled in triumph to a cracked cedar chest behind the counter and the cash register. He blew dust off the top. *"Here* they are! I knew they were still around." He fished a stack of books out of the old box and handed them to Alice.

"We'll just look at them," she said. "If we want to buy we'll ask."

"By the way," said Maggie, "how did you happen to get these?"

"Oh, a friend of ours was hard up for cash some years ago—he's deceased now, I'm afraid—and he sold us a bunch of old books for a few dollars. We just use them to have something to put on the shelves. They look so empty if we don't."

"They're very nice. Do you recall the name of the person who sold them to you?"

"Of course. Like I said, he was a friend of ours. Hamish O'Grady. He worked at the academy for a long time. A nice man, too, but hard up for cash sometimes after he retired from the army. He taught riding to cadets, and then worked in the gym after they stopped teaching about horses back in the forties. Not much call for military riding teachers, he said, so he just retired. His wife's a nice lady, by the way; works in the library still, I hear, but Ma and I never knew her very well. Not as well as Hamish. She was a Cleary, born and raised in Highland Falls—Clearys have been around there since Christ was a corporal, and they don't talk to just anybody. We knew her brother better, that was John Cleary that was killed at Anzio in 'forty-four. Hamish was a little younger than Betty, and everybody was floored when they got married. He was from somewhere upstate, and moved here way back. Of course, that was before my time. *Ma!*"

Once again, the thin voice from upstairs, even crabbier now. *"Yeah?"*

"Ma, when did Hamish move to West Point?"

"Who?" said the voice. *"Hamish Burke over in Goshen?"*

"No, Ma—Hamish O'Grady in Highland Falls. She don't track as well as she used to," said Guido to the ladies. "She's in her eighties now; never comes down much anymore."

"He came here back in 'thirty-two or 'thirty-three, honeybunch. He was on his first enlistment."

"Thanks, Ma. She has a terrific memory," Guido observed with filial admiration. "Never forgets anything. Except what happened yesterday or when the bills got paid. I do all that now."

"Any idea where he got the books?"

"Oh, there were a lot of books in her family." Guido glanced up the stairs and lowered his voice. "Confidentially, ladies, as Hamish got on in years he drank a little more than he should. And Betty had him on an allowance—what money they had was hers—

210

and the allowance didn't leave him much for recreation, if you know what I mean. So, when Hamish brought these books around to sell—well, Ma felt sorry for him, poor man. Betty had thrown 'em away, he said, but he fished 'em out of the trash. Ma bought 'em for a few dollars, we could use 'em, as I say, for decoration. And he didn't have a whole lot of time to live by then."

Well, thought Maggie, old Betty O'Grady and her stern silence undone completely by old Guido's big mouth. I wonder what he'd reveal under a little torture?

Alice touched Maggie on the arm. "Here it is, dear—*My Years at West Point*, by John Waverley Upton. And look here, the back pages are stuck together. And look at this." She peeled back the rear cover. Inside it was the scar where a library card pocket had been torn away.

"My goodness," said Guido, "what's the matter?"

"This book was sto— . . . came from the West Point library."

"Hey! I never thought it was stolen. How do you know?"

"We've been looking for this very book," said Maggie, "and we knew the back pages were gummed up. And here's the place where the card pocket was torn away."

"I'll be damned!" said Guido. "Hamish was such a nice man!"

"I don't think Hamish knew," said Maggie. "But don't worry about it. Would you consider selling it to us?"

"Hey, ladies; if it's stolen I couldn't accept money for it. Why don't you just take it back?"

"No need," said Alice. "You aren't at fault, and we need it ourselves. How much do you think it's worth?"

Guido, relieved of pangs of conscience, did not hesitate. "Fifteen dollars. It's a very old book, in excellent condition."

"It's worth about fifty cents," said Alice.

"We'll take it," said Maggie. "Will you take a check? I live at West Point."

"A check will be fine, young lady. I also take all major credit cards." Then Guido's mind clicked. "Hey—you don't know Betty O'Grady, do you?"

"Only slightly; we met last week while I was trying to find this book."

"Maggie," said Alice, "look at this! Old Hamish was really hard up! He sold them the family Bible!"

"Hey," said Guido, "maybe I should give it back to Betty."

211

"Why don't you let us do it?" Maggie said reassuringly. "I have to visit her tomorrow anyway. I'd be happy to."

Guido peered at her with narrow reptilian eyes between rolls of fat. "Maybe it would be better for me to do it. We know her."

"Oh, nonsense," said Maggie sweetly. "I'll have to see her tomorrow anyway, and you'll have nothing to explain that way."

Maggie had him and he knew it. He smiled and said, "Will there be anything else I can show you?"

"Oh, no," said Maggie. "We've taken enough of your time as it is. You've been *so* helpful. Here, let me write you a check." Fifteen dollars was a small price to pay for the bonanza (Guido threw in the Cleary family Bible for free), and while Maggie wrote the check Alice admired the iron greyhound. As Maggie left, she heard Mother Squillace call down from the upstairs apartment: *"Honeybunch! Where's my breakfast? It's late!"*

"Keep your shirt on, Mother. I'm doing the best I can, for Christ's sake!"

Maggie and Alice giggled hysterically as soon as the car doors were shut. Luckily, the local trooper was drinking coffee in a diner and was spared the sight of the red Mercedes hurtling away from Cornwall Antiques with a spray of gravel and a cloud of dust.

They sat in the library again, Hob Gort's mahogany mausoleum, while from the pantry they could hear Satan's muffled barks and the distant fury of his body hurling itself again and again at the locked door. After a while Maggie and Alice became inured to the noise; Bernice simply turned her hearing aid down a notch. Maggie read them the passages on Adonijah Proctor from the Upton book, but Alice only half listened, being absorbed with the inscriptions in the Cleary Bible.

"The point is," said Maggie, "Upton did his own research on the ghost back as early as the 1870s. He cites a letter from a General Winfield Scott Hancock, Department of Dakota, in the summer of 1871 in the prefacing notes. That's several times this guy's name has come up."

"I looked him up after our last talk," said Bernice, "because he seemed to have known something about Proctor. I have the notes here somewhere . . ."

"He says in the preface," Maggie went on, " 'I am especially indebted to my friend General Winfield Scott Hancock, on whose staff I served in the late war, for his help in compiling my observations on the celebrated specter of Adonijah Proctor. He kindled my interest in the matter many years ago by ruminations on that singular topic the night before Longstreet's famous assault at Gettysburg, and I had the chance to meet two other former cadets during the Petersburg campaign who had some knowledge of the affair. General Hancock was kind enough to take time from his difficult command on the Department of Dakota—in the midst, I might add, of serious troubles in the Black Hills and the impending uprising of the Sioux Nation that was soon to prove so vexing to the army in the West. But, since he was a friend of Captain Proctor—one of the few who could be considered a confidant of the old man—his assistance was the key to my own considerations of the strange story.' "

"Here they are," said Bernice. "Winfield Scott Hancock, born February 14—Saint Valentine's Day, how romantic!—in 1824, died in 1886. He graduated from West Point in 1844, served in the Mexican War with the Sixth Infantry. In the Civil War he rose to command the Second Corps of the Army of the Potomac, and his great moment was the defense of the center of the Federal position on Cemetery Ridge against Pickett's division on July 3, 1863. He was noted for cutting a handsome figure, though later in life he inclined to stoutness, and for always wearing a clean uniform, no matter how trying the circumstances. He commanded the Department of Dakota in 1870 to 1872, and ran unsuccessfully for president."

"Squares with Upton's comments," said Maggie. "Now, we find out what he said." Maggie flipped through the book for some time. It was a prose narrative with uninformative chapter titles and no index. Finally, she caught the names of Proctor and Hancock and turned to the beginning of a chapter called "An Indomitable Spirit."

She quickly surveyed the text. "Okay, girls—paydirt! Listen to this:

" 'The most typical of the many legends of haunted places in the West Point vicinity—and quite as ancient as the tales of Molly the cook and Patty Murphy in the superintendent's great house—is that of Captain Adonijah Proctor, instructor of drawing under

213

the celebrated Professor Robert W. Weir and his predecessors, from 1819 to 1846. This is in many ways the very quintessence of the ghost story and one with which I have some familiarity due to my long friendship with General Winfield Scott Hancock, hero of the late war, who was himself an acquaintance of Captain Proctor during his cadet years. This is the story he related to me on the long night before the terrible third day at Gettysburg.' "

Alice put down the Bible and listened to Maggie. Even Satan ceased his mindless protest.

" 'Adonijah Proctor,' " Maggie continued, " 'was the son of an old Massachusetts family, born in 1790 at Braintree and educated at Harvard. He served in the Army in the War of 1812 and distinguished himself at the Battle of Tohopeka, at which General Jackson's forces finally crushed the power of the belligerent Creeks. Ensign Proctor was gravely wounded in the final assault on the breastworks and was not expected to live, but he survived a long and comfortless journey back to Boston and confounded the opinions of the medical profession by daring to survive and prosper, though he ever afterward walked with a noticeable limp.

" 'In 1819 he returned to active service at the request of Colonel Thayer to assume a position as an instructor at the Military Academy, which post he occupied until the outbreak of the Mexican War. He was a skilled cartographer and gifted instructor, and was largely responsible for the excellence of the tutelage in that art which was to prove so valuable in the exploration of the new western territories of the Republic.

" 'In 1822, he married Eliza Wharton of Boston, a woman of excellent family some years younger than Proctor. Her father was the late Doctor Elihu Wharton, a noted theologian whose powerful sermons and lengthy monographs on the moral laxity of the times were well known and whose philanthropy was responsible for much of the flowering of arts and education in the city at the dawn of our century. Eliza, in her turn, was known for her beauty and especially her modesty, and for her devotion to her father. It was also said at the time that her decision to accept Captain Proctor's proposal of matrimony was at first bitterly opposed by her father, who capitulated only when he was convinced that Captain Proctor's modest prospects were balanced by his impeccable reputation and the recommendations of Colonel Thayer, one of the finest educators of that or any other day, and acquainted with Proctor's family.

" 'In honor of the increase in his household, Captain Proctor moved from a small dwelling in Buttermilk Falls into more substantial quarters on the old faculty row. Captain Proctor's fortunes were crowned in 1824 with the birth of their only child, a daughter named Annabelle Charlotte. She was a splendid child with striking golden hair and a sweet temperament that endeared her to the small community of the military academy, and she was a great favorite in particular with the cadets (who numbered many fewer than the present corps). She was known as Annabelle to the young admirers who visited the Proctor house during her few short years of life.

" 'Those years were scarce short of idyllic for Captain Proctor, who was free to practice his chosen profession to the fullest of his faculties, admired by his superiors, students, and peers, and to live a comfortable if modest private life which centered around the golden child and a small circle of other instructors and selected students. Two or three cadets were regular guests of the Proctor home, among them the brightest and most promising of Proctor's students.

" 'Little Annabelle's life was blessed with not only the adult admirers, but the constant company of the children of the faculty and servants, including the small son of the Proctor maid, Bridget Hardesty, who had married Corporal James Cleary—' "

"Bingo," said Alice. "The plot thickens. Have we now discovered the patriarch of the famous Clan Cleary of Highland Falls?"

"Dare we hope?" said Maggie. "Anyway: '. . . who had married Corporal James Cleary, a soldier of her same race then posted to the garrison of West Point. The boy was a year younger than Annabelle, and the two were inseparable playmates, despite the difference in their respective stations. Indeed, Proctor himself treated the young Cleary with almost fatherly affection.

" 'Tragedy struck too soon. As early as 1827, Captain Proctor seemed to be a pilgrim at the Slough of Despond for reasons unknown to his friends, though during this time Eliza seemed to have fallen victim to some unspecified affliction that sorely affected her temperament. As far as their friends could tell, however, Proctor's household conformed to the very model of Christian family life, with its loveliest feature being the charming Annabelle, who prospered and who, by her fourth birthday, was the veritable toast of West Point.

215

" 'On the night of the twelfth of December 1830, while Captain Proctor was on an errand in the town of Buttermilk Falls, a fire struck the Proctor home, consuming it totally in a very short space, and the coldness of the weather and consequent short supply of available water hampered the few efforts to halt the blaze, and by the time Captain Proctor returned, the edifice was afire beyond redemption. As it happened, the doors were stoutly locked and had to be broken down, which further hampered efforts at rescue. Only Bridget Cleary and her son John escaped by leaping from an upstairs window.

" 'The loss of Mrs. Proctor and especially of Annabelle fell hard on West Point. Captain Proctor himself was nearly undone by the disaster, and took a leave of absence for the balance of the year. The cluster of cadets who had been particular friends of the Proctors and admirers of the golden Annabelle was hard hit, and one especially, a promising cadet and excellent student and one of the most gifted of his classmates, thereafter increasingly displayed a morbid side of his nature which ultimately led him to resign.'

"Now here," Maggie continued, "Upton goes into a description of Corporal O'Hanlon's experience in 1835 with the crying child. Let's see—it looks like about the same story as in the other book. Yes, I think some of the text is the same, even. Sure, here he talks about the 'vigorous reprimand of their officer' that tickled Sam so much. I'm afraid old J. W. Upton was not above plagiarizing himself."

"Is that possible?" said Bernice.

"Beats me," said Maggie, "but he sure did it. Now, here we go again. Attention, ladies! Fresh material! 'In the days before the assault on Petersburg, I had unaccustomed leisure to talk with two officers of the class of 1860, engineers of the Army of the Republic, who as cadets had occasion to confront the ghost. Both reported an apparition of the same sort as that described by the doughty Corporal O'Hanlon, and one—who presently serves at West Point— heard the sound of the crying child in that same area. Both, however, reported that the specter of "Captain Proctor," far from exciting terror, evoked rather a profound feeling of sadness, plus the strong impression that the spirit's attitude was one of benevolence rather than menace.

" 'But one sinister sequel to this event . . .' Holy cow," said Maggie, "here we go: '. . . one sinister sequel to this event was

216

the recurrence of troubling dreams; dreams so ghastly as to belie the apparently harmless intent of the ghost. Both men described their nocturnal terrors to me in considerable detail. Due to the indelicacy of theme, I shall refrain from a recounting of their particulars. Suffice to say, the fantasies were suggestive of even unhappier circumstances surrounding the deaths of Eliza and Annabelle Proctor than were generally supposed at the time. Out of consideration to those still living, my own conclusions are and shall remain under the rose. This is small comfort to those who must face the hours of repose, for, to my knowledge, at least one of the men who shared these secrets with me under canvas so many years ago is still plagued by these grim disturbances of slumber.' "

"Sounds bad for our cadets," said Alice.

"God, you don't suppose they're going to carry those dreams to the . . . oh, my!" Bernice's hands reflexively crossed over her heart. "I must choose my words with care!"

"I wonder about Liam," Maggie said. "Maybe that was the excitement last night. God, I hope not. He's so moody at the best of times, I can't imagine what would happen if he had to put up with years of nightmares. Jesus—they'd have to install a raven over his door."

Sam and Maggie enjoyed a night's break from ghost duty. She heated her favorite meal in the microwave and they uncorked a bottle of wine for the occasion. But Sam munched dinner in such oblivion that it might as well have been hot C-rations. He was completely absorbed in the book. Maggie fussed over the Bible. Their evening alone crept on without significant conversation as Sam muttered to himself and Maggie made notes on a legal pad.

"Sam," she said finally, "I have a theory. It's a beaut."

"He looked up from the Upton memoir. "Sweep me off my feet."

"No challenge, Bondurant. None at all. But look here, dear Mrs. O'Grady has been incautious; she has allowed the incriminating evidence of the Cleary family Bible to fall into Maggie's vindictive clutches."

"A bad mistake. What is it? A collection of liturgical notes for the black mass?"

"No, dearest—just a pretty standard old Bible, printed in 1855. But the custom of the Cleary clan of Highland Falls was to record births, deaths, and marriages inside the cover. And so they have, with the last entry dated 1932. Things that happened before 1855 are there too, written in the same hand as the first events after the purchase of the Bible (if that was in 1855 or thereabouts). Whoever it was must have written the earlier stuff down from memory or from an older Bible."

"Sounds reasonable. Get to the bottom line."

"Don't be impatient, dearest man. I'm enjoying myself thoroughly. Now we find that dear old dippy Mrs. O'Grady, who it seems is not nearly so dippy as your precious Maggie first thought, is indeed the living descendant of Miss Bridget Hardesty, born July 1807 in County Fermanagh, Ireland. She is shown to have wed Corporal James Cleary, who was born somewhere in August 1795 and died in May 1838 at West Point. Bridey herself survived until December twelfth—oh, right on Bridget! That was the anniversary of the fire!—until December twelfth, 1889. Her extraordinary life span allowed her to be interviewed by John Waverley Upton. Remember the history? He reports that she was in full possession of her faculties. I'll bet she was! Our Betty O'Grady is certain to be a throwback to this gal from the Old Sod."

"So what?" said Sam. "Are you driving at something, or just enjoying an unfair peek at your blood enemy's family secrets?"

"We still haven't got to the secrets. Now, they had one son, John Cleary, born February 1825, who died in 1877. *He* married Rachel Mahan of Tompkins Cove, and they had four children, of whom only one, John, Jr., survived childhood. John was born in 1854 and died in 1912. He married Elizabeth Ward of Peekskill; they had two children, both born very late in life—John's life, anyway—Miss Ward was much younger. You know about that, don't you? Their son John III was born in 1901 and died in 1944; he's listed as 'Master Sergeant, U.S. Army,' so old Guido's mom was right. He must have been the one killed at Anzio."

"Who in the hell is Guido?"

"Later, dearest. The daughter, Elizabeth, was born in 1907 and is, according to most reports, alive and well and living in the bowels of the cadet library. *Ta-taaaa!*"

"I hate to sound like a scratchy record, but so what?"

"Check the dates, sweet man. According to Upton, our Bridey

left her part-time job in Fermanagh selling cockles and mussels or whatever and arrived on the golden shores of this land of opportunity in time to hire out to the new Proctor family while she was still no more than a budding sixteenish. That would be in 1824, as soon as the Proctors move in. The golden Annabelle arrives less than a year after the housewarming—the *first* one, that is . . .''

"Maggie, I know what this is leading up to."

". . . and a year after along comes young John, son of Bridget Hardesty, to be sure, but of James Cleary as well? Too good to be true. The blushing bride embraced what I suspect was an equally blushing groom. In Upton's memoirs—and I suspect he got the information from an aging Bridget Cleary—he has the bouncing baby boy first seeing light of day in January 1825. But here in the Cleary Bible, the little fellow first squalls in rage on the fifth of November 1824."

"How embarrassing."

"You bet! The ancient and honorable Clan Cleary has a bar sinister on its shield! She didn't marry James Cleary until June fifteenth, 1824, says the Bible. They put God's truth in God's book, up to a point—but old Bridget forgot to fudge when she talked to Upton sixty years later, or maybe she didn't care anymore."

"Do we?"

"Oh, I don't think it helps the ghost hunt. But I can carry the book back to dear old dippy Mrs. O'Grady in triumph. Then she and I will know that I know what she didn't want anybody to know! Plus, I can smile at her tolerantly, knowing she knows I know she discarded a book that was property of the United States government."

"How do you know that?"

Maggie told Sam about Guido Squillace and the unpleasant weakness of Hamish O'Grady. "By the way, I need to call Liam."

"He's probably asleep. Give him a break."

"This will just take a second." Maggie bounced into the kitchen and dialed Liam's BOQ room. There was a long wait, then: "Oh, hi! Maggie. Did I wake you up? I didn't think so. I have a vital question, which only you can answer. How do you pronounce S-E-A-M-U-S? Yes, the Irish name . . . I thought so. But why? How do they get 'Hamish' out of that?" There was a long pause. "Oh. That's what I thought. Thanks, Liam, you're a genius. Bye-bye."

"What in the pluperfect hell was that all about?" asked Sam when she came back to the table.

"One last mystery. Betty's late hubby is listed in the Bible as Seamus O'Grady. I figured that was the same as Hamish, and Liam confirmed it."

"So what was the long silence about?"

"Oh, you know Liam. I made the mistake of asking him how they get Hamish out of Seamus, and he gave me this long dissertation on broad and slender vowels and aspirated consonants in Irish Gaelic—by the way, dearest, I am informed it's pronounced 'Gallic,' not 'gay-lick.' Anyway, that's the last piece."

"The hell it is, Maggie. You don't have enough evidence to accuse Betty of being part of a bastard limb of the Cleary tree. Anyway, why would she throw away the books? Who the hell would ever take the trouble to compare them? Or even look at them?"

"Anyone interested in the ghost, Sam. I think she pitched them in 'sixty-seven or 'sixty-eight when the ghost issue heated up again. It could be that Bernice Gort was close to the truth—or at least Betty thought she was—in 'forty-seven when she read both of the Upton books for her Reading Club paper. When somebody started nosing around the next time, she took radical measures. Somebody might have done a real in-depth project on the ghost, and found out about the wanton young Bridget in the process."

"Who the hell would go to that much trouble?"

"Don't be obtuse, my sweet man. I just did."

"Good point." Sam refilled her wineglass, though the chill was gone from the bottle. "Here's to the Clearys, stalwart sons of Hibernia and skeletal pillars of local lore and legend."

"I'll drink to that," said Maggie gaily, and they clinked glasses.

And Sam said: "And here's to Maggie Marple, child bride, young mother-to-be, and sleuth beyond compare, who slew the troll of the card catalog."

"I'll drink to that, too." They drained their glasses. "You know," said Maggie, "you look kind of cute with that black eye—sort of like a clever, endearing puppy with a spot over his eye. Doing anything tonight?"

"Since you asked, I find my social calendar empty."

"How about a quickie in honor of—in honor of Jamey Cleary and his blushing bride?" Maggie leaned forward on her elbows and kissed Sam. "We share something to blush about."

Liam had in fact been awake when Maggie called, and had been no more than bemused by the topic. He had tried to sleep, but he was in the depths of an emotional slide, and too many things came to mind unbidden to let him rest. He gave up and sat at the Chinese desk again, bolt upright in the hideous uncomfortable carved chair. This is not the time, he told himself, but in the background was the shrill chorus of the demons, louder than ever. *You're wasting time. Cast the runes, coward, let them fall where they may.*

And finally he drew the bag from its hiding place and drew a stone and placed it on the desk top. It was *nyd,*

the rune of constraint. Where I am now, he told himself. Where you've been for years, howled the demons. And he drew another stone, and placed it beside the first. It was *beorc,*

the rune of growth. What other path is there? He drew a final stone, and it was *thorn,*

the gateway. *We knew it,* chanted the demons, *we told you, we told you, there is no other path than the path of the gateway.* Liam placed the stones back in their bag one by one and went back to bed. Now that he had interpreted the runes, the demons let him sleep.

14

*L*iam found a note from Sam shortly before noon on Thursday. It asked him to drop by the human factors laboratory at his earliest convenience. This proved to be after two o'clock, and when Liam arrived at the lab office he found Sam huddled with George Salinger (whose foot was in a cast), Saganian, and Ortega. There was a large television monitor at one end of the room mounted on a rollaway table.

Sam pulled up a chair for Liam in front of the TV. "Here you go, Sigmund—a front-row seat. All we ask is that you watch the screen and give us your impressions."

"I'll do my best," said Liam. "Just don't get too technical. Dare I hope for a videotape of *Citizen Kane?*"

"No. Just watch." Ortega turned off the room lights and the lab, which was light-sealed, turned pitch-black. Sam started a videotape. After a few seconds, a cluster of pale dots appeared on the screen. "Okay," Sam said, "what's that?"

"A bunch of dots."

"Okay, now watch." In a few seconds, the dots began to move from left to right in irregular surges.

"That's somebody walking," said Liam, "or a very good cartoon."

"Right," said Sam. "Actually, it's Ortega in a black coverall with a black bag over his head and reflectors taped to his joints—shoulders, elbows, wrists, hips, knees, feet. We recorded him walking in front of the camera, then turned the brightness down and the contrast way up so all you can see are the reflectors."

"Fascinating."

"You haven't begun to be fascinated, my moonstruck friend.

Watch this." A second sequence started: a similar cluster of lights, stationary, then moving to the right.

"Somebody else walking," said Liam.

"Same person?"

"I guess so. Was I supposed to see a difference?"

"I'll rerun it. This time pull your head out of your ass and pay attention." The picture broke up as Sam rewound the tape: then the sequences played again, in the same order.

"Okay," said Liam, "I'd venture to guess the second subject was female."

"How do you know?"

"Do I have to tell you? I suppose the second body had a different center of gravity. *Vive la différence.*"

"Very, very good. Actually, it was Maggie in black panty-hose and leotard, plus the black bag and the reflectors."

"I'm impressed. Maggie has a future in burlesque. Can I go now?"

"No. Watch this sequence."

"I'll try to restrain my excitement." Another cluster of lights; this time, though, they moved clumsily, their choreography not quite human.

"I guess it was another subject with lights. Did you rent Quasimodo? It didn't look like a normal person."

"Okay," said Sam, "here's one more. Watch carefully." A similar sequence, run once in each direction. Liam was quiet after the run. "So what did it look like?" Sam prompted him.

"Run it again."

"Aha! We have his curiosity. Here you go . . ."

"All right," said Liam after seeing it again, "you're a genius. That's the ghost—the way he walked, I mean."

Salinger and Ortega cheered. Sam was delighted. "That's right, Liam—you're in the presence of real genius. Tetzel was over here right after lunch and said the same thing. The ghost 'walks funny,' all right, and now we know why."

"Fine," said Liam. "Include me in the secret."

"Simple—rigorous experimental psychology triumphs again. This little trick with the lights was demonstrated by Gunnar Johansson in Sweden in 1950. He found that humans are extraordinarily sensitive to the relative motions of parts of an event, like a human walking; that there is a sort of biomechanical invariant we're

224

naturally attuned to. Certain subtle characteristics of these motions can even tell us the sex of the person walking. And we also know if something's wrong. The scrambled figure was Maggie again, but the reflectors were taken off the pivot points and re-taped at other places. I really didn't need to use that demonstration, but I enjoyed moving the reflectors around."

"You sly fox."

"Anyway, I had a hunch—actually, Maggie did after hearing about the 'walks funny' reports, and this was an elegant way of testing it. All I did was move the ankle reflectors up to mid-calf and run the tape again. Both you and Tetzel instantly—and independently—recognized the ghost's 'funny' walk."

"Right. So what did the shift in the reflector prove?"

"It created the same pattern of relative motion an observer might perceive if a hazy, indistinct human figure were walking with the lower leg occluded, as if in a shallow stream."

"The ghost was walking through a stream?"

"Of course not," said Sam. "He just wasn't walking on the floor—not the floor of the cadet room, anyway. He was walking on a floor in *his* space-time reference. Maybe the floor of the old house that was once where the Forty-seventh Division now stands. That—like much of this—is conjecture. Maggie thought of it immediately, and sure enough we demonstrate that it's a plausible solution, at least if we allow the lunatic premise."

"I was going to mention that," said Liam. "You seem to be going overboard on the ghost idea. If I recall correctly, Sam, you were until recently a confirmed skeptic. Have you been carried away by all that clever rhetoric you used to convince the commandant to extend your lease?"

"I'm not carried away by anything but the evidence we have at hand. Anyway, I seem to recall your telling that very same general you had either seen a ghost or flipped your fine Irish lid."

"I'm just getting my licks in where I can," said Liam, smiling his slow, infuriating smile. "You conquered with that tape, you and that sorceress of yours. I'm still waiting to make my contribution to this circus."

"You're the one who's seen the thing," said Sam. "Maggie wants to be in that room so bad she's ready to get a whitewall haircut and dress in fatigues. In fact, I promised her I'd bring her over on Saturday night for the final act. I have the duty then,

225

anyway, and with Saganian's hands screwed up I'll need help."

"Don't let her go into that room, Sam," said Liam with surprising earnestness.

"Well, I'm not contemplating letting her *sleep* in there, of course. She'll stay in the equipment room."

"Listen Sam—I want you to promise me you won't let her go into that damned room. I'm very, very fucking serious." Sam stared at him uneasily. "Listen carefully. I don't know everything about that room and the things that happen there, but I'll tell you something right now: whatever's in there is—well, it's *inimical* to certain things. The demon in that room is legion, Sam. It has at least two faces, or maybe it's two different, distinct personalities. When I saw that thing, and when all my impressions were fixed by the dream—and that dream was no random event, no memory consolidation, no nocturnal sensation—I discovered some very unpleasant things I haven't really sorted out. But if Maggie enters that zone, and I'm serious Sam, *if she enters that zone your child will be in jeopardy.*"

"Cowabunga," said Sam. "You sound like a B movie."

"Don't ask me to explain why, Sam. I can't explain much, and I won't go into what I do suspect until I know more. Which will probably be never. You keep a close eye on her, Sam. You can't keep her away, but to the extent you love her, keep her away from the room. I know in my bones, if Maggie sees the ghost the very least she'll have is dreams."

"Liam, do your theories about this business—what you just said—have any historical context?"

"What do you mean? Am I talking about an actual past that gave rise to the haunting? Yes, of course. I got just a tiny glimpse of it in the dream. So did the cadets, but they only experienced what they were prepared to experience."

"Huh?" Sam raised his eyebrows quizzically.

"I mean," said Liam, "that we all have the same basic furniture in the mind, the same general potentials. But some people have more adequate bridges from the deepest mechanisms to the conscious reality. The cadets are young, not exceptionally self-examined; they lack the symbolic bridges. I'm convinced that whatever happens in there appeals to or somehow evokes things already in the mind of the person who experiences it; if the connections to the deeper things are there, the results are richer and more explicit. The cadets dreamed about things they already knew at a conscious level, their own memories somehow distorted by the force of this new experience. When I dreamed, it went closer to the roots of these mysteries, and it was much closer to the original complex of fears and loves and hates that dance around that room now. Maggie's the same way. I'm afraid of what would happen if the thing or things in there constructed their story out of her unconscious."

Salinger and Ortega had been watching this conversation like spectators at a table-tennis match, looking first at Sam, then at Liam, then back again. Sam noticed them gawking. "Why don't you two take the afternoon off or whatever you want to do? Colonel Fitz and I want to trade creepy stories."

Salinger grinned. "Roger that, sir. Have a nice day." They closed the door behind them, leaving Sam and Liam in the black room under red blackout lights.

"Liam, I asked you that for a reason. Remember when Maggie called you last night?"

"Yeah, just barely. I gave her a mini-lecture on Gaelic morphology."

"Well, she'd found the book she was looking for and some other stuff besides, and now we know a little bit more about Adonijah Proctor and his buddies. We know, for instance, that cadets who saw or heard the ghost over a century ago were troubled by dreams, and the dreams stayed on. There's also a hint of something really unpleasant." Sam explained the "sub rosa" allusion by Upton, described the case of the cadet who drank and sank into morose introspection, and told of the former cadets who had spoken to the chronicler of their horrible dreams. "Does that match any of your trivial, unwholesome ruminations?"

"Well," said Liam, "the world is full of schizoids. Yeah, there are some parallels, but I can't discuss them. I'd like to see the book, of course."

"Good luck prying it away from Maggie; you'd think she had found King Solomon's lost mines. Apparently old Mrs. O'Grady at the library tried to get rid of it, but her boozing Irish husband foiled her."

"What are you talking about?"

Sam recounted the recovery of the book and the Cleary family Bible.

"So, why was the Bible such a find?" Liam asked.

Sam explained the genealogy and the embarrassing dates of birth and wedlock. "So the old troll was doubtless trying to cover up her great-grandmother's tumble with lusty young Corporal Cleary."

Liam didn't answer for a long moment. "I need to see both books," he said finally, "and talk to Maggie. I think I'm starting to understand a little more."

"What?" asked Sam, "did I tickle your unconscious?"

"Yes, but it was pure accident. You wouldn't know an archetype if it bit you on the ass."

"I will *not* wear it."

"Oh, yes you will," said Maggie mildly.

"I won't wear it. I'd look ridiculous."

"If you don't wear it, you'll *feel* ridiculous, the only grouchy old goat in Lee Area with a gorgeous, horny young wife who makes him sleep downstairs."

"Maggie, I appreciate all the work you put into this thing, but—"

"Sam, my precious, you can't *possibly* imagine the trouble I went to making this costume. Nor can you possibly imagine, not being much with needle and thread, what great pains I took constructing my own costume, carefully coordinated with yours and hence useless if you don't wear it . . ."

"No."

". . . and you cannot *possibly* imagine the pains I took to conceal this labor of love . . ."

"No!"

". . . from your prying eyes, carefully dragging all the stuff up the attic stairs every afternoon before you came home . . ."

"*No!*"

". . . and with me frail and in a delicate condition for which, I might remind you, you almost certainly deserve at least partial credit—"

"What do you mean '*almost* certainly'?"

"You'll look dashing and handsome and . . ."

"I'll look absurd."

". . . you'll look like what you *are*, what you insist on being—a crusader for academic excellence."

"Maggie, have a heart."

"I am not the one," said Maggie with sweet reasonableness, "who is rumored to have a bionic cardiovascular system. I am in no danger of being thought selfish and puffed up with false pride—which I think is a venial sin, isn't it? Or is it mortal?"

"Maggie, can't we just—"

"Yes, mortal. I'm almost certain it's mortal. It should be. I don't know what God has in store for those of false pride, but here on Maggie's earth the outlook is starvation, cold stares, and quiescence of sexual favors unparalleled since the Cretaceous bioextinction."

"How do I get it on?" Sam asked.

Maggie had assembled a fair replica of the habit of a Knight of the Temple, with hauberk (a creation from lace that bore a resemblance to chain mail when sprayed with silver paint) and a snow-white tunic with a blood-red cross. The hauberk, adapted by Maggie from illustrations at least as old as the Bayeux tapestry, gave them some trouble.

"It can't go like this," Sam complained. The mail shirt was over his head, pulled down over upraised arms. It would move no farther.

"Well, don't blame me, dearest. I just followed the drawings."

"Well, I can't begin life anew like this."

Maggie giggled. "You could go as a compass."

"It's not funny, Maggie. I can't move my arms."

But Maggie had no immediate answer, and her consideration of the matter was interrupted, to Sam's exquisite discomfort, by the doorbell. Liam had arrived to borrow the book. Maggie enjoyed herself hugely in conversation with Liam, who politely refused to acknowledge Sam's inert presence, as if he had been transmuted into a floor lamp. Finally Maggie allowed Liam to leave for ghost watch.

"Maggie, get me out of this goddamned thing. I quit. Now I know what it's like to be a dangerous lunatic."

"But . . . you . . . you looked . . . so . . . so . . . Oh, Sam!" She broke up again.

He let her laugh until her stomach muscles ached. "O-*kay*,

now that we've had our widdul snicker, perhaps milady would care to get me out of this thing."

Maggie examined Sam's predicament carefully. She took a deep breath. "Okay, Sam. Brace yourself."

"Brace myself? Maggie, what are . . . *Augh!*" She had grabbed the bottom edge of the hauberk and jerked it down hard; the bind at Sam's shoulders released suddenly and the mail coat fell magically into place, as in an animated cartoon. Maggie stepped back and looked at it proudly.

"Damn. That's just dandy, Mag. Now how am I going to get it off? The costume party isn't until tomorrow night, and I have a lab and a colloquium tomorrow, which I am not going to attend in a suit of chain mail."

"Oh, stop worrying. I'll cut a larger neck opening. Here's your shield." It was heavy cardboard, sprayed with yellow enamel; there was a black diagonal stripe and a horse's head in the upper corner, also in black. It was, for Sam's benefit, a replica of the patch of the 1st Cavalry Division, Sam's first and favorite assignment. He had explained the patch to Maggie when she saw it on an old set of fatigues.

He admired himself in the mirror, then frowned. "It's backward, Maggie. The bar runs the wrong way."

"I know," she said. "I painted it that way in honor of the Clearys. Stay here a minute." Maggie dashed up the stairs; he heard her bustling around the bedroom.

"Now turn around," said Maggie from the top of the stairs. "Milady makes her grand entrance." She descended and slipped quietly beside him. They examined themselves as a pair in the mirror. Maggie had made for herself a long medieval gown from a dark green and gold brocade material selected on the same day she found Sam's chain mail. The hem that dragged on the floor was trimmed with fake fur; it was cut low in front and the sleeves widened sharply at the wrists.

"Cowabunga," said Sam. "That's a heart-stopper."

"This," she said proudly, "is the illegitimate offspring of three totally unrelated Simplicity patterns from the PX. I should have an honorary degree in topology for making all the pieces fit together. I *started* this thing on the third of September and didn't finish until yesterday morning. Like it?"

"Is Luther a Protestant? I just wish I could go as a Templar masquerading as a guy in a wool shirt and slacks. Anyway," he persisted, "why the Templars? Why not just a clinking grunt from the retinue of Bohemund, Slumlord of Slopsville?"

"Oh, just a pretty gesture from my days in the English Department. Some traditions identify the Knights of the Temple with the guardianship of the Holy Grail."

"And you?"

"Well, the Grail maiden, of course."

"Aha! I presume you plan to borrow a mule from the vet clinic and ride up to the party."

"I'm flattered," said Maggie. "You still remember!"

"Hell, Maggie, that's no feat of memory. I spent more than a week proofreading your dissertation. Large chunks are committed to rote. I still associate our courtship with that labor, sitting around in my apartment checking out fifty thousand *op. cit.*s and a zillion *ibid.*s."

"You had more than a few breaks," said Maggie, "and were amply rewarded. Don't complain."

"Just one understanding before we crank this up, sir," said Saganian. "This time, *you* can open the door. It's an officer's privilege." His hands were still wrapped in gauze, and his enthusiasm for the Great Ghost Hunt had dwindled somewhat since Tuesday night's disaster.

"Don't worry," said Liam, "I'll do all the door opening, and I'll use my foot." Sam had instructed Saganian to attach one of the seven wall-array thermistors to Carson to ensure that the cadet's body temperature did not fall below safe levels. Sam and Saganian had been mystified by the cadet's apparent insensitivity to the sudden temperature drop. Liam had speculated that whatever was present in the room somehow drew energy from the environment, and so somehow sucked heat from inanimate sources. Sam had added that the EEG abnormalities suggested some mechanism, whether resident in the cadet or effected through the cadet, that selected the energy sources from places that did not threaten the life of the human "tool." Having said that, they had agreed that they were pissing up a rope, though Sam offered Liam fifty dollars to show his courage by presenting their speculations at the annual

231

convention of the American Psychological Association. Liam had replied that no one needed fifty dollars that bad, though, given the decline of the APA, he figured there would be a crowd of some size to hear him speak.

Now Saganian patiently turned on all the instruments and began the thankless task of recalibrating. The video display for the computer that recorded the thermocouple inputs had been replaced, and George had added a subroutine in the program that produced a beeping alarm if the temperature changed more than a few degrees in a sixty-second period. And Ortega had installed a night light in the plebes' room with a switch in the instrument room that provided just enough illumination to allow details to be seen through the video. Finally, they had a camera in the cadet room focused on Barstow's empty alcove with high-speed film and a slow shutter setting, and a remote switch beside Saganian's chair. Sam was determined to be prepared for anything in the three nights that remained.

"Looks okay, sir," said Saganian. "I'd really like to get through one whole night without having to repair something. Are we really shutting down after Saturday night?"

"I guess we will," said Liam. "I'm not sure what else we can hope to find. We have EEG records, temperature records, we have recordings of the crying, and we have the videotape, even if it doesn't look like much."

"I don't know about that, sir," said Saganian. "I still think about those eyes."

"Yeah, they gave me the creeps too," said Liam, "but I'm not sure how I'd go about demonstrating they're eyes."

"There's no doubt in my military mind. I guess you had to be there."

"You don't have to convince me," Liam said. "I saw those eyes on Monday night. I'm not looking forward to the experience again."

"Think we'll get another visit tonight, sir?"

"Yeah, I guess so. We've had a visit every night so far, like clockwork."

"Honest now, sir—what do you think it is?"

"I'm reserving comment. Maybe I'll find out tonight."

"How, sir? Gonna ask him when he comes?"

Liam smiled and watched the orange lines of the thermocouple graph scroll across the computer screen. "Yeah, something like that."

"Is Colonel Bondurant visiting tonight?"

"I doubt it. Last time I saw him he looked like he was going to be busy tonight. Meanwhile, what's this big spike on the EEG?"

"Oh, that's an artifact, sir. That happens every time he rolls over and pinches an electrode. Don't worry, though—nothing starts until two or three in the morning. We got a long wait." Saganian ran through the audio computer routines, then tested the paper drive on the polygraph. He was getting defensive about the machines. The machines knew it at some level and tormented him. So far the instrument suite had not performed flawlessly on any night, and he was almost obsessed with the desire to rack up a perfect score.

Liam was thinking hard about another goal, and his own success depended on the cooperation of Adonijah Proctor far more than on the vagaries of the integrated circuit.

In the next few hours they watched with increasing exasperation as Carson's EEG's showed him slipping in and out of sleep stages. Each time the REM phase started, they would observe an elevation in heart rate, but after two repetitions of this routine, they had seen none of the characteristic petit mal waveforms that had previously heralded the onset of Proctor's visits. After a third period of deeper sleep that lasted until just after three in the morning, they watched the theta wave form on the lines of the oscilloscope and saw the heart rate increase to seventy-four beats per minute.

"This might be it," said Liam. "It's the witching hour."

"Could be, sir. We're showing a very slight temperature drop, maybe a half a degree in the last few minutes."

"I'm not going to hyperventilate over a half a degree," said Liam. "Let's see Sam's famous petit mal formation." But the EEG traces were obdurately normal, jagged beta waves. His heart rate was increasing, however, and soon it peaked at nearly eighty.

"Well," said Saganian, "he's dreaming to beat the band. Shit! There it went!" Indeed, the display screen showed that the EEG signal had been interrupted, degenerating into unpatterned garbage. "He must have knocked the ground sensor loose—it's screwed up all the channels. We can either wake him up or kiss the whole EEG record good-bye for tonight."

233

Liam nodded and watched the trace of the temperature inputs, then resumed his stare at the foggy video image.

"What do you want to do, sir?"

"Huh? Do about what?" Liam was distracted from his trancelike fascination with the instruments.

"Do you want to wake him up, sir? His ground electrode's loose. We can't monitor brain activity unless we wake him up and restick the sensor on his ear lobe."

"No," said Liam, "let him sleep. The temperature and video should be enough warning. I don't want to interrupt the dream, in case it's the precursor of something else."

"Roger that, sir," said Saganian, his voice lowered now to an expectant whisper. "We're down a degree, now."

"Got it. Keep a watch. Any noise?"

"Nothing to speak of, sir. I don't see any spikes in the crying ranges—no, son of a bitch! There they are! Just like last time!"

"I see them. Go ahead and put on the headset and get another tape. I'll tap you on the shoulder if I need your attention."

"Okay, sir. But remember—I'm not keen about going in there."

"I hear you, Sarge. That's my job. Now get that tape going." Liam turned the instrument room light off and they sat silently in the dim glow of the displays. The only noise Liam could hear was the audio tape drive and the soft hum of the blower motors in the instrument racks. He turned down the brightness of the video from the cadets' room to adjust for the darkness, and elevated the video's angle to a point above the luminous clock face. Liam could see only the dim edge of the light wall over Barstow's bunk and the darker vertical partition that divided his alcove from Carson's. Panning right and left, then up and down, Liam searched for Sam's famous glowing eyes, but there was only darkness.

Saganian looked at Liam and gave a thumbs-up sign. "Got her, sir—it's our town crier! Faint, but I can hear her. Want to listen?"

Liam accepted the earphones and closed his eyes when the soft padded microphones were snug over his head. There was nothing discernible at first, but then he heard the thin, tinkling sound that subtly became the terrified sobs of a child. He felt his skin crawl—I'm getting a good idea where a lot of these figures of speech come from, he told himself grimly—and he suddenly wished there could be silence, a merciful cessation of the terrible challenge he knew he was obliged to face. He did not want to do it tonight, it was that simple. Anna was coming tomorrow. He had to be at his best. Not tonight, not tonight, Father, I'm weak tonight. I'll dare the gateway, but not tonight.

"Sir," said Saganian, "we're getting a lot of spikes on the EEG channels, even with the ground gone. He must be tossing and turning pretty bad. His pulse is up to eighty-three. He must be having a hell of a dream. And usually he's perfectly still when the dreams start."

Liam nodded and tilted the video camera down to the bed. There was not enough light, so he carefully adjusted the new dimmer switch that controlled the light source—no more than a night light, really, installed after Sam's frustration with the video on Tuesday—until the untidy lumps of sheet and blanket that outlined Carson's form were visible. There was no movement for a moment, then he saw the sleeping cadet shift just a few inches. The EEG's impotent sweeping lines spiked. He turned the light down again.

"Now we need the ghost," said Saganian. "The evening ain't complete without a visit from Old Nije."

"Who?" said Liam.

"Adonijah, sir. That's what Ortega and me call him."

"Cute." And then Liam saw the faint auroral display, and Saganian, happily relieved of bursting-in-on-ghosts duty, pointed at the video and grinned, then gave another thumbs-up.

"We're in luck, sir. Don't pan too much, sir—it makes noise, and it pissed him off last time."

"Okay, I'm just going to try to find the eyes. Are we getting this on videotape?"

"Affirmative, sir. We've been rolling."

Liam increased the contrast of the video set and tilted the camera up with the joystick. The screen showed only an eerie, shifting, misty pattern of luminance. Turn around and look at me, dumb-ass, he thought; then he laughed softly at the absurdity of the situation.

"What is it, sir?" asked Saganian. He looked sidelong at Liam, wondering what there was to laugh about. His freeze-burned hands were itching.

Liam waved him off, serious again. "I can't find the eyes. Maybe I'm looking at his back. How do we get his attention?"

"Take a picture, sir. We have the camera—"

"Right, I forgot. Do it, Sarge." And Saganian, who was closer to the finger switch, took a picture. They heard a faint click (it was much louder for Saganian, wearing the earphones again), and suddenly the video turned a brighter shade and the furniture in the room stood out in clear contrast.

Saganian cursed. *"Screw it!* I forgot to disconnect the flash!"

"You mean we just popped a flash in there?"

"Yes sir! That got his attention, I bet!"

"I don't see anything but furniture!" Liam panned right and left, but the camera did not seem to move. "The drive's broken!"

"No sir, the flash just etched that last image on the tube. It'll be a minute before we get any new picture."

Liam turned the dimmer up. He could start to see the room behind the afterimage of the flash. There was a dark shape now, off to the right, huge and threatening; but then he saw it was Carson, standing beside the end of the alcove and looking at the wall above Barstow's bed.

"That's it, Sarge! Get ready to pull the plug!" Saganian had no idea what Liam meant by "pull the plug," but he was out of his chair and out the door at a run. He glanced back at the video long enough to see Carson on the video and hear him say, in a conversational tone, "Yes." Then there was a flood of light in the room as Liam entered, and the video went white and cloudy; the picture vanished.

Saganian was suddenly scared. "All right, sir?" There was silence. He left the room again and slipped down the hallway to the door. Liam and Carson were sitting on the edge of the bed; Liam had his arm around the cadet's shoulder. Saganian looked at the video camera. It was covered with white frost, and as he watched a flake detached itself and fell from the lens to the floor.

"It's okay," said Liam, "it's okay. Don't worry about it. We're closing the room, we'll move you out. You'll never have to do it again."

"Yes sir," said Carson. "I can't make it through that again, not the bloody man. But it's not me he wants."

"I know," said Liam. "I know. We'll have to deal with this ourselves. You have to pass all your courses and have enough energy left over to be a good plebe. It's time for you to start sleeping again."

236

"I'll vote for that, sir," said Carson. "I'm sorry—I wasn't lying to you, I just didn't remember the dreams until I woke up tonight. I don't know why. I just thought I hadn't had dreams. I couldn't remember."

"Don't worry," said Liam. "They'll go away when . . . when they're not needed anymore. Now tell me everything that happened."

And Carson described his long, confused dream, starting with anxieties over calculus and blending into the terrible scene with a stern, fearsome woman. "It was worse tonight, sir. Really awful. She—the woman—she was standing there telling me how I was 'conceived in sin' and how nothing like that could ever find 're-demption.' That's the word she used. She called me a rapist, I think—I'm not sure. She was incoherent . . ."

"How about 'papist'?" said Liam.

Carson looked at him, a little afraid. "Yes sir. I think you're right. Then she pointed at me and sort of stood there, and then her arm dropped and she sort of swayed like she was dizzy, and her eyes rolled back in her head for a minute. Then she started again like nothing had happened, and started yelling a bunch of crazy religious stuff about hell, and she said I was 'beyond re-demption' again. I don't remember all of it. Then she had that sort of limp fit again, and I ran out of the room and down a hall, and the lady who babbles caught me again from behind, and I was scared because I didn't expect her. She startled the shit out of me and I screamed. She was huge, just like the other woman. She started saying crazy nonsense."

"*Bhfuil tu tinn, a mhic?*" said Liam quietly. "*Bhfuil tu tinn?*"

Carson looked at him with frightened eyes. "Yes sir, that's it. Then I smelled the smoke again, worse than ever, and I heard the woman saying something, I don't know what—"

"The woman," asked Liam, "or the girl who babbled?"

"The woman, sir; she was back down the hallway, and I could hear her talking, kind of quiet, and the little girl in the room was screaming."

"What did the woman look like?"

"She was older, but good-looking. She had on an old-fashioned dark blue or gray long dress with a lace collar. She looked crazy, sort of, but I don't know why."

"I do," said Liam. "So what happened then?"

"It was hot. There was more smoke, and the girl, the one who babbles, the stuff you knew, she picked me up. I don't know how, she must have been strong as hell. She picked me up, and then I remember being in the snow. It was snowing, and I was cold, and I was crying, real loud, and she was talking to me again, something like *'knock is tu.'* "

" 'Hush, now,' " said Liam.

"But I could see fire in a window close to me, and she dragged me back into the snow. The snow was lit by the fire, and the snowflakes were whirling in circles, and they started rushing into the window where the fire was. It scared me, I don't remember when I was ever so scared."

"Did anyone else come?" asked Liam.

"I woke up then, sir. And he was there, the ghost was there, just like with Barstow. He was standing over me, looking at me. And there was the other, too, the bloody man . . ."

"The bloody man?" said Liam softly. Saganian looked at him wide-eyed. The idea of a bloody man didn't seem to charm him in the least.

"That was the worst. Steve Barstow said there was something else that really scared him. I guess so. He was there, beside the ghost. He was covered with blood, and it looked like half his face was shot away. I could see the bone, and most of his jaw was gone."

Saganian watched Liam. Incredibly, he smiled. "How was he dressed? The bloody man."

"It was dark, sir. I think he had on fatigues, baggy fatigues with patch pockets. He had on a pistol belt and suspenders, and his sleeves were rolled up. There was something taped onto the shoulder of his suspender . . ."

"A hunting knife," suggested Liam.

"Maybe so, sir; it was too dark. What was worst was, when he talked I could see what was left of his teeth on one side. That's when I tried to yell."

"I heard you say 'Yes,' " said Saganian, "before Colonel Fitz came in."

"Yes sir. He asked me if I heard him."

"Heard him? Did he say something?"

"Yes sir, but I don't know how with his face shot off. He said 'Tell Leemie the gate is open'—I think that was it, 'Leemie' or something like that. 'Tell Leemie I'll leave the gate open.' "

Liam sat on the edge of the bed in silence. Saganian and the cadet watched him as he stared at the video cameras on their platform. The frost on the lenses was slowly melting, and fell as water, drop by drop, onto the floor of the room; a narrow trickle was running into the larger complex of ice water, smeared by careless feet. Saganian looked at the clock on Carson's desk. It was 0339, Friday morning.

15

*O*n Friday morning Liam announced his recommendation that the cadets be removed from the room in the 47th Division as soon as possible, and the room converted back to nonresidential uses. Sam concurred. Sam was less enthusiastic, however, concerning Liam's next suggestion.

"That's crazy. You can't sleep in there."

"Sam, over the years I have cultivated the ability to sleep *anywhere*. Anyway, we don't have all the information we need about the ghost, and we haven't really solved the com's problem. That was our charter, remember?"

"It's still a perfectly idiotic idea. If it was dangerous for the cadets . . ."

Liam shook his head patiently. "I never said it was dangerous, Sam. I just said it was interrupting their sleep and study during the first semester of plebe year, which nobody needs, and disturbing the tranquillity of the barracks. The ghost wasn't about to gobble them up."

"No," said Sam, "but we have a staff sergeant with bandaged hands and a ruined camera lens. Things are going on in there that we can't explain or predict. Anything strong enough to lower room temperature seventeen degrees inside of a minute—did you look at that printout?—is stronger than all of us put together."

"Don't go into a panic. There'll be you and a bunch of other people on the other side of that wall monitoring everything that happens. Whenever it looks like it's getting out of hand, you can stop it."

"I still don't like it."

"What can possibly happen?"

Sam gnawed his lip.

"I said, What can happen?"

"You can go off the wall, Liam. It's not only the cold and the crazy EEG patterns and the galloping ghosts. It's the dreams. They scare me more than anything. You've had them . . ."

"I've had one."

". . . Tetzel's had them, Barstow had them, and now Carson. I don't like it. I agree with your assessment—the spookier the mind, the more dangerous the morbid fantasies."

"You draw the wrong conclusion, Sam. I'm most prepared to handle the dreams because I'm best equipped to understand them."

"Bull. You know more than you're telling me, Liam, which just reinforces my worries. I don't trust you to watch yourself."

"What gives you the right to judge my mental state?"

"I think I'm better able to do it than you. You're looking for things the rest of us aren't. And you've been systematically with-holding a few key facts—"

"Hold it a minute—"

"No, you hold it," said Sam. "Here, look at this." He pulled a photograph out of a pile of notes. "Here's that thermal photograph of the tracks. The one with the boot marks you said were made by Ortega. Only Ortega went in there an hour before the temper-ature started to drop in that room, so there was no water on the floor for him to step in, and . . ."

"How the hell do we know that?" said Liam.

". . . and he wears standard-issue combat boots—I checked— and I compared them with the computer-enhanced tracks, and they weren't made by standard boots."

"Come on, Sam, your pictures aren't that good—"

"They're good enough to recognize that tread, Liam. You knew what they were as soon as I showed them to you. You know nobody around here wears those old Panama-sole jungle boots. I dug mine out of the attic this morning and checked them against the computer image. There's no doubt. Besides, if the ghost is walking on a lower level, how would—"

"That was your idea, Sam. Not mine."

"Listen, it's gotten out of hand. There are too many things flitting around that room. Too many ghosts. And *one* of us is rat-fucking with something dangerous and dealing the rest of us out."

Liam crossed his arms and stared at Sam. Then, finally, he shook his head. "We don't have enough data. Results with one

242

cadet aren't enough. You're always harping on the one-shot case study and how naive it is to infer all kinds of underlying motives and mechanisms on the basis of a couple of interviews. That's the weakness of our results so far."

"It's not all that weak," said Sam. "We have repeated observations backed up with hard measurements."

"That's not the point. The whole question right now revolves around the EEG abnormality. Now, that isn't my strong point, it's yours. And you know that's a key. We have to know whether it's an artifact or something systematic and related to the ghost. Anyway, we've gone this far. We can't quit until we know . . ."

"The hell we can't."

"Last night," said Sam, "it came again. What did Carson see? What happened? Saganian's off this morning, and I didn't have a chance to find out."

Liam shrugged. "The typical pattern, same thing we've seen all along. This time, Carson had the dream. There was temperature fluctuation, like before."

They stared at each other. Sam bit his lip.

"Listen, Sam. We don't have any choice. Somebody's got to sleep in there to find out if it's Carson."

"Carson?"

"Carson's been in there for every incident. Every one. He's the only one who could be a cause, deliberate or not. We need to eliminate the possibility that he's a causal factor. Suppose he isn't? What have we got? Cold water, filmy images, temperature fluctuations in a room with a windowpane that keeps breaking during a cold spell, and the researches of the Ladies' Reading Club. Want to take *that* to the APA convention?"

"I don't go to APA," said Sam. "And I'm not proposing to publish this garbage anywhere but in a report to the com. In fact, nothing would make me happier than anonymity after this fiasco is over."

"Sam, we don't have any choice. Somebody's got to sleep in there."

"Okay. Let me do it."

"I got my bid in first," said Liam.

"All right, but you're going to be wired up just like Carson."

"Now, wait a minute! You have all the data . . ."

"No I don't," said Sam with a malicious smirk. "I have to

243

know whether the EEG patterns appear with anybody but Carson. You said yourself that the—"

"Okay, okay, let's compromise. One channel, that's all you need. Just EEG."

"Four," said Sam, "just like Carson."

They heard the telephone. Ortega called from the lab office. "It's for Colonel FitzDonnell!"

"Two," said Liam, edging toward the door. "I toss and turn a lot."

"Two plus pulse."

"It's a deal."

The call was from Major Broadnax.

Anna arrived at two-thirty from Boston. She had brought two suitcases and a hanging bag, which Liam wrestled up the stairs of the BOQ and placed carefully at the foot of his bed.

Anna went right away to the window. "I can't believe this view! And rent-free! I can see why you love it here."

"That's a slender reason for loving. And if you knew what miserable meals I make myself, you'd gag. Our dinners in Boston are the only decent feeds I have."

"Really? I thought I was the attraction."

"Vanity, thy name is Perugino. Now you know the truth."

"So, what's the schedule?" She sat on the edge of the bed and pried off her shoes, then wiggled her toes gratefully.

"Well, I have a class to meet at fourteen hundred—two o'clock, Anna. So why don't you go ahead and take a shower and get a nap. You should be fresh before you meet all these new people."

"What have you told them about me?" asked Anna, her eyes a little less opaque than usual, showing a tiny spark of humor. She lay back on the bed with her legs dangling over the edge, closed her eyes, and smiled a private smile.

"Nothing," said Liam, "that could possibly prepare them for the actuality."

"How is the local community going to react to this strange woman sharing your room? The sign at the gate advised me to turn my watch back a hundred years."

"I'll worry about that. This building has seen stranger things under the light of day, and even worse by dark of night. I think I'll be forgiven. The ducking stool is reserved these days for chronic parking violators."

"But, your friends know you're bringing me?"

"Of course. It's the talk of the town. FitzDonnell's dark lady finally makes her appearance. My stock is about to go way up." Liam sat on the bed beside her. "It's about time."

"Shit," said Anna, "don't you date around here?"

"Of course not. You're the woman I care about."

She looked at him uneasily. "That's not fair. I mean, why bother being faithful to me? I don't reciprocate, Liam."

"I know it. I'm me. You're Anna. I was raised believing in one set of rules, and I stick to them. It makes life simpler."

She closed her eyes again. "No, it doesn't. I was raised on the same rules, and all they do is provide an institutional framework for hurting people."

"Where do you pick up this way with words? You sound like an exam for an MBA."

"Well, I *have* an MBA. But that's beside the point. The rules are no good. What good does it do for me to say all kinds of lovely things I don't mean and make all kinds of promises I can't deliver? That's stupid. You just end up having them thrown back in your face."

Liam cursed himself silently. It had come to this point, as it always did, and poor Anna had only been here for fifteen minutes. "All right," he said, bending down and kissing her gently, "enough of that. You rest up and I'll be back in about two hours. Make yourself at home and plan how you'll wow the husbands and earn the hatred of the wives."

She did not answer, but as he left the room he saw her lying on the bed with her eyes again closed; she was smiling again, that private, rigid, wintry smile.

"Hold still!" said Maggie. "If you keep jerking around I'm bound to stab you with the needle."

"You tickled me. And I can't hit back in this straitjacket. Just watch it."

Maggie jerked the open seams of the "mail" hauberk back from Sam's shoulders and safety-pinned the top together. "Look, Bondurant, if you want this thing to split apart at the critical moment, just let me know. I have to get this alteration done or you won't be able to move or dance or sit down without tearing it. We have thirty minutes to get to this party."

"Relax, Mag. We can be late. You still have to dress."

"No we can't. I don't want to miss the grand entrance of Liam's light of love."

"Somehow," said Sam, "I think she'll take her own good time getting there. Ouch! God damn it, be careful!"

"I warned you. Now shut up and be still."

"Can I help you dress?"

"No. We only have half an hour."

"Why do you get to have all the fun?" Sam whined. "I always end up being the fool and getting needled. It isn't fair."

"Stop bitching, Bondurant. You'll look great. Just don't catch those spurs on anything or trip over the long toes."

"I still haven't figured out how I'm going to go to the bathroom in this thing."

"You'll need two lackeys to help you get on and off your horse," she said. "There! Now you can move like a fully articulated biomechanical simulation."

"Speaking of biomechanical, Liam liked your performance. He said you have a great future in burlesque."

Maggie laughed. "I guess I would have been a gifted performer. Did he recognize me from the lights?"

"He recognized it as a female—after two tries, I might add."

"Is he really serious about sleeping in the room?"

"Deadly serious," he replied. "I guess I could find a better way to put it, though."

"You're worried."

"You're right. It's Liam's old argument about ghost stories come back to haunt us, in a way."

"You're getting glib in your old age, sweet. How does it apply? No, hold still and talk. I have to get this thing laced up the back."

"Well, he talked about the big scare in those stories being the idea of the natural rules suddenly thrown out the window; when the laws of nature are gone, so are the laws of God, in a way. That makes the world infinitely more dangerous and man more help-less."

"That's how you feel now?" asked Maggie through teeth clamped on a needle.

"Damn right. That room is no joke. Inside that door all the bets are off. We don't have the foggiest idea what's really going on in there or what to do about it. No, I take that back. What really scares me is, I *think* Liam knows more than he admits. He's hipped on that false petit mal pattern, and . . ."

"It's not a false pattern," said Maggie through the needle, "it's a signature."

"Huh?"

She extracted the needle. "It's a signature. It's the real phys-ical presence."

"What are you talking about?"

"It's Eliza's signature, dummy. Haven't you thought about these descriptions of her in the dreams? The eyes rolling up? The little 'absences'?" Sam's eyebrows arched at her. "Sam, I looked it up in your damn Sears and Roebuck catalogue of loose nuts and bolts . . ."

"*DSM* III."

"Yes, the book of mental disorders. And I read a chapter on epilepsy, both grand and petit. She had a seizure disorder, Sam; the symptoms, the unpredictable outbursts, the little blackouts. That's her signature in the room, the sign she's still there."

"But that's silly; the ghost people see is . . ."

"Yes, darling, I know—the gray shape of Adonijah Proctor. But they also hear little Annabelle and Bridey Cleary. And the cadets, Sam—Tetzel's dream, on the tape. They're seeing what-ever it is from the viewpoint of little five-year-old John Cleary. Maybe they're all there. But there or not, it's Eliza who's the real force.

"Listen, Sam—the cadets said there's another presence, someone filled with rage. There *is*. I felt it myself, when I was in the room. It didn't occur to me until today that it wasn't just morbid heebie-jeebies. When I was in the room with Liam, I felt something in there that was very, very cold and mad as hell. And Sam," she said after a slight hesitation, "she saw me, too. She was mad at me, not just pissed in general."

247

"Marvelous. How did you know that?"

"I don't know. I sensed it."

"Your sixth sense? Your seventh?"

"Don't get wise with me, Bondurant, just because you aren't running on all five yourself." She resumed her needlework on a particularly troublesome spot near the seat of Sam's hauberk.

"Since you mention it," said Sam, "Liam agrees. He made me promise to keep you away from there. So at least . . . *Ow!*"

"Sorry, dearest, I slipped. Flattered as I am that Liam backs up my instincts, do not even *toy* with the idea of excluding me from the final act of this drama."

"You're not going into that room."

"Well, that can be negotiated. But I'm going to be there when the clan gathers for the climactic night." She snipped a loose thread. "There, that's it. You're ready to storm Acre."

"I don't even like the idea of Liam sleeping in there. I've seen enough of this project. But he's bound and determined to do it."

"I admit he goes off the deep end."

"That's putting it mildly. I hesitate to guess at his motives, knowing Liam. No, I hesitate because I *don't* know Liam. Maybe you have some insight."

"And why, prithee, should *I* have insight?"

"You're a whole lot like Liam, Mag. You're interested in the same things. Maybe you know what he's looking for."

"Oh, that's easy; but it's also the big difference between me and Liam, other than he's nuts and I'm not. I have something to anchor my life on. Liam doesn't. Every card he draws is the drowned man."

"Say *what?*"

"Oh, Sam—he lost his family, he's lost his profession, really, when he decided to become a psychologist. All his roots were in the army; now he's not sure whether he's in the army anymore. He's neither one nor the other. He sits alone in that BOQ room surrounded by gloom and that awful furniture and casts runes."

"He *what?*"

"Yes, really! He explained it to me. He draws runestones at random and projects meanings on them as a sort of depth psychology. He says he could use the random numbers in the daily stock quotations just as easily, but the runes help get him in the mood. I mean, *really*—a man who bases his decisions on a Norse alphabet is not ready for self-government."

"Well, ready or not, he sle in there. And you, my sweet, are the real ghost-hunter, so it's fitting you should be there."

"I'm so flattered I could just burst with pride. Won't my friends in the Ladies' Reading Club be *green* with envy?"

"Instead of bursting with pride, why don't you get dressed? I can finish here."

"No," said Maggie. "It won't take me a minute. I want to see you in this getup." She lifted the white tunic off the back of the sofa and draped it over his head.

"Make a move for the camera," said Sam, "and I'll break your fingers."

Track, a devoted fan of the poet Robert Service, arrived at the party dressed as Dangerous Dan McGrew; this obliged Patti to dress in a sort of abbreviated Victorian miniskirt with net stockings and elastic garters. Her red hair was arranged in a fair approximation of a saloon girl's. All in all, a passable Lady that's known as Lou. There had been far less contention in the Dortmunder household than in the Bondurants'. Patti had learned long ago to put up with most of Track's notions without murmur, and to fall on her sword only when her sensibilities were forced to the wall. The only point of disagreement had been Track's face. He had skipped his morning shave and left work after his eleven o'clock class; since Track's beard grew impossibly fast, by evening Patti thought he looked like Lon Chaney, Jr., in *The Wolf Man*. Track thought it looked just fine.

They followed Herb Fisher, who drove up the steps of the clubhouse on his Harley, his wife clinging desperately to his back; he wore leather, chains, and a motorcycle cap. The smell of gasoline stayed in the building for days.

Doris Gilmer teamed up with Walter Orthwein and J.D.Gordon, two leadership instructors, the latter two in drag, as the Supremes. The collective judgment of the Department of Behavioral Sciences and Leadership after the party was strongly for putting that part of the event out of the collective memory.

No less than three celebrants dressed, of course, as the ghost of the 47th Division. What they lacked in originality they made up in determination. Ned Baumgartner, one of the rare bachelors, got the best of it. He was able to demonstrate by wearing his cadet full-dress coat that he had not gained a pound since graduation; a liberal dusting of white makeup completed the ensemble.

Maggie literally dragged Sam up the steps of the clubhouse. All the way across the parking lot he had fussed about the long mailed toes, but by the time they made their entrance he had developed a sort of aggressive hobble that kept him from tripping over the points of his feet. In the process Maggie gained a new appreciation for sumptuary laws.

"Hey, Sam!" Track called from the bar. "Where's Dorothy and Toto?"

Sam casually brushed imaginary lint from his snow-white Templar's tunic with his middle finger. Track received the message and grinned. Sam took Maggie's coat and stacked it in a back room; when he came out, she was being courted eagerly by Dangerous Dan McGrew, a samurai warrior, and a Supreme. Maggie was aglow, and Sam decided to visit with George Salinger. George was still in his cast; for lack of a better idea he had dressed as a pirate with a crutch (aluminum) and an absurd paper parrot.

"How's the foot?" asked Sam. "You're our first casualty. Don't feel too bad. What with you and Saganian, the ambulance drivers have had a workout."

"Hell, sir—I'm lucky it was my foot. Saganian was bitching this afternoon about how it even hurts to pick his nose. I'm sorry I missed the excitement."

"Well, I guess you can come tomorrow night for the jack-acid test."

"Is it true Colonel Fitz is going to sleep in there?"

"I guess so. It was a toss-up, according to Maggie. I could sleep in there and freeze the ghost out, or Liam could sleep in there and exorcise him with a lecture on libido theory. Liam won the toss."

"I'm not sure who won, sir. I doubt that anyone around here is cool enough to drop off to sleep in that place after all the hoopla this week."

"Don't worry," said Sam; "Colonel FitzDonnell can sleep anywhere. And anyway . . . good God almighty, grant us mercy."

"Sir?"

"Speak of the devil . . . it's Liam and his legendary sweetie from Boston."

There was a brief pause in a dozen conversations as Liam led Anna through the doors of the golf clubhouse. Few of the officers or their wives had any idea who Anna was, and only the few who were Liam's friends expected her.

Liam had assembled an outfit to match his personality and avoid taxing his mastery of home economics: a monk's robe, plain and black, with a cord tied at the waist and leather sandals (borrowed from a neighbor at the BOQ and still full of last summer's beach sand). Liam looked like a monk at the best of times—one, perhaps, with a lot to confess, and certainly not of an order bound by a vow of silence, but nonetheless a monk.

Anna, too, had chosen basic black—a dress that reached comfortably from her waist to the floor, but less comfortably in the other direction. The top was attached in two places in the front and passed around the back of her neck, covering her front as long as she refrained from picking up loose change from the floor. Above her waist in the back, of course, there was nothing at all.

Charming though its main attractions were, Anna's outfit did not seem much of a costume. Its only additional details seemed to be a pale foundation of makeup, with more than the usual attention to outlining the eyes. Sam wondered at first if Liam had forgotten to tell her about the theme of the party. But at that moment Track approached her and Anna smiled. Then Sam saw the plastic vampire teeth.

So did George. "Damn! A natural! Who in the hell is *that*?"

"Liam's lady. I've never seen her myself. It does look real."

"I guess," said George. "Who does her clothes? Edward Gorey?"

"They're quite a pair, though," said Sam thoughtfully. "Mink and monk."

George snorted. "Look at Track, standing there with that thin trickle of saliva at the corner of his mouth."

"Yeah," said Sam. "He's dressed in character, too. Patti's going to be there in about five seconds and strangle him with that garter on his sleeve. Farewell, George—I see Maggie signaling me."

Maggie met him halfway across the room. "Come on," she said in a stage whisper, "I want to meet Morticia face to face."

251

"Had your shots?"

"Be nice, Bondurant! Liam adores her, so she must be a lovely woman despite the teeth."

"Nice bod."

"Shut up, swine. Be cultivated or I'll break your arm."

They joined Track in front of the lovely couple. "Anna," said Liam, "I'd like you to meet Sam Bondurant, of whom you have heard much . . ."

"Lies," said Sam, "all lies and base canards, vicious slanders and gratuitous libels."

". . . and this is Maggie, also known to you."

Anna smiled at Sam—the effect with the teeth was chilling— and then at Maggie. "Well," she said with bouncy goodwill, "I finally get to meet you!"

"It's nice to—ah—see you, too," said Maggie with a glance at the bifurcated superstructure of the black gown. "Liam's told us very little about you—"

"He's apparently been generous with intelligence about us," said Sam.

Anna took the teeth out of her mouth. "Sorry—mind if I give it a break, now that everyone's seen them?"

Track thought of a reply, but Patti was beside him now. There was a moment's silence for the others as well, as they rehearsed and abandoned clever comments.

"You'd better," said Liam, "you've been hard to understand with those teeth clenched in there. Now that you're defanged, can I get you a drink? There's beer and wine punch . . ."

"Wine. You're Maggie? Liam says you have a Ph.D. in . . . what?"

"Medieval literature," said Maggie, bracing herself.

"Oh, yes. What on earth do you do with a degree in medieval literature?" Her great ingenue's eyes blinked slowly. Track thought of a serpent.

"Oh, write stories for magazines, poke around dusty libraries, write chapters for books—stuff like that." Maggie tilted her head and smiled back at Anna. Track pictured a mongoose. This, he thought to himself, is going to be worth the price of admission.

"Really?" said Anna. "I thought it was tough to find jobs in that field." Track thought: Now the hood spreads, the pretty thing hisses a warning.

"Oh, I don't work regularly," said Maggie; "I free-lance, mostly.

Having a husband takes up a lot of time. But of course, you have a lot of time to devote to your job." So she dodges, light on her feet, as her opponent sways and awaits a clear chance to strike.

"Don't you miss the satisfaction of having an independent existence?" asked Anna. (Sway, hiss.) "My ex-husbands couldn't stand to compete with me, it just drove them up the wall when I made more money. Of course," Anna added, "you don't have that problem." (Strike!)

"No," Maggie answered agreeably, "I've just had Sam to deal with; I understand you've had more varied experience. But of course, I'm not all that greedy for a paycheck; I like the recognition." (Dodge! Nip!)

"What?" asked Anna. "You mean for your stories? Well, I guess we all work for what we need most. Here comes Liam with my wine punch." Track awarded them equal points; a few spots of blood, a little spilled venom, but no mortal injuries. They chatted for a few minutes, sipping punch, but the main event was over. Anna wanted to know about the ghost adventure, and Sam told her about his experience on the night of Saganian's discomfiture.

"The doorknob was really cold enough to stick to his hand? That's hard to believe." Her eyes were wide, pupils dark and dilated. Track coolly admired her nipples, suddenly upright against the black fabric. Patti pinched his arm discreetly, leaving a bruise that would linger for days. He turned his attention to Anna's earrings, austere gold cubes.

"I had to believe it," said Sam. "I saw the fog and the flakes of ice, and when he broke loose he left skin on the metal."

"Ooooh. I guess the cadet in the room must have been miserable."

"Actually," said Sam, "he wasn't. The cold seems to leave organic substances alone. I have no idea why. Whatever the reason, the effect seems to be able to pick and choose its targets. Maggie thinks it can distinguish living from nonliving, and draws its energy from the latter. I'm a little unmoved by that idea. I have no idea what sort of mechanism could allow 'it' to differentiate."

"And of course," said Maggie, "if Sam can't understand it, it isn't possible. Sam is hard to convince."

"I'm a lot less hard to convince after this week," said Sam with an affectionate look at his wife. "A look at those eyes makes a believer out of you."

"Eyes?" said Anna. "You didn't mention the eyes. This is exciting!"

Sam explained, to Anna's obvious delight—and Track's. Patti pinched his arm again, and he reconsidered her earrings.

"But could he see?" asked Anna. "I assume he's—what? Incorporeal? Can something like that see you?"

"I can't say much about incorporeality," said Sam. "All I know is that it was certainly checking out the camera. But Liam saw the thing for real."

Anna turned on Liam. "You didn't tell me! You really saw it?"

"I guess so. I saw something." He described his glimpse on the first night. "It seemed to be looking at me; I had that strong feeling, anyway. Since the eyes were indistinct, it was hard to judge the direction of gaze."

"What do you think it was feeling?"

"I don't know." Liam was suddenly uncomfortable. He had no desire to discuss what he had seen in those eyes, not here in the golf clubhouse. He knew what he had seen, far more certainly than anything he had ever seen in Anna's eyes, but what he saw was for him alone. "It's hard to say."

"But, was it hostile?" Anna persisted. "Did it look threatening? Curious? Frightened?"

"More curious," said Liam. "Did you have an impression, Sam?"

"No. Just dots on a TV screen. But the mere fact that they were obviously eyes scared me into a month's supply of Ex-Lax."

"Sam!" Maggie looked at him in mock horror.

"Don't shock her, dumb-ass," said Track. "Her condition's delicate."

"Oh, not that delicate," said Maggie. "And I've long since ceased to be shocked by any of you."

"Yeah," said Track, "you got adopted into a Cro-Magnon tribe, for sure. But she had a good influence on us," Track added for Anna's benefit. "She taught us about bathing and forks."

Anna laughed her loud unfeminine laugh. "And all the time I thought Liam was a sophisticate."

"Oh, he is," said Track. "We still gross him out. But Liam lives on a different, an astral plane. He reads *The New York Times*.

254

And pitches out the sports page. A real limp-wristed type. I even caught him looking at a *book* the other day. And just last week I saw him sitting around in his office, staring at the wall, and I'd give even odds he was *thinking*! Imagine!"

"Mercy," said Maggie. "Don't humiliate Liam in front of Anna."

"Yeah," said Liam, "she prefers to do it herself."

Anna looked at them all a little uneasily, but managed to laugh anyway. She was an outsider, keenly aware that she was off her own accustomed turf, and unsettled by this varied crew: stuffy, wry Sam, who looked up at Maggie and down on everyone else; Track, whose bluffness she immediately recognized as a smoke screen; and Liam himself, suddenly a different person, still reserved and reflective, but without the cryptic quality he presented to her. This was a cast of characters she was unprepared to find at West Point. It was not like the faculty she had faced in her own student experience; these people were so . . . so *earthbound*. But their presentation was too lively to support her smug estimate that Liam was a misfit in a legion of dullards. She sensed after this brief encounter the singular truth that is the most carefully guarded secret of the army: To be accounted good in this trade, one had to be strikingly good; and these were the best the army could muster. She searched her mind for an excecutive at Analog who could compete with these men. It was a null set; they were a mixture of narrow, ambitious pinheads who managed by methods endorsed by Darwin and shy, personally incapable monomaniac software experts. Not a one could have engaged in a conversation with this circle of professional soldiers and held his own. She understood Liam a little better now. Once she had wondered how a man with obviously superior intellect and sensitivity could have found himself in a profession that specializes, after all, in killing people and breaking things. She decided over her wine punch that this was criminal waste of human potential: if she could staff Analog with them, IBM would be a memory. The stereotype of the uncouth killer bureaucrat flickered and went dim.

"Well," said Maggie when she was a private distance away with Track, "what do you think of her?"

255

Track sipped his beer and looked at Anna, who was across the room listening with apparent disbelief to some statement by Doris Gilmer, Supreme. "What do you I think of whom?"

"Liam's *amour*, of course—the Bride of Dracula."

"Nice pair of teeth."

"Teeth, indeed. I saw where you were looking."

"Yeah? I thought I was being suitably heavy-lidded."

"Indeed, you were not. If you had Superman's X-ray vision, that poor woman would have absorbed enough rems to make her hair fall out. But what did you think of her?"

Track thought a minute, searching for a delicate turn of phrase. "A 220-volt AC cordless cunt."

"Ye gods, give the poor thing a break! She's bright and pretty and—"

"Yeah, yeah, I know. She has big beautiful eyes and shapely jahoobies and slender arms and so on, and so on. But she's still dangerous. I listened to that *dans macabre* you two performed there in the ring. I was waiting for the fingernails."

Maggie blinked her eyes demurely. "We're allowed to parry and thrust a little. I don't have a worthy opponent that often. The wives don't draw their swords, Liam's too old-fashioned to cross his with a woman, Sam gets hurt too easily, and you have the hide of a lumbering antediluvian ruminant. Besides, you're too easy a mark."

Track grinned. "No, gorgeous, you just know a lost cause when you see it."

"Maybe," said Maggie. "But she's not what I expected."

"What did you expect?"

"I don't know—some breathless airhead who adores intellectual men, or a registered witch, or a pale, vacant-eyed psychic who solves murders by having visions of bloodstained car seats. Whatever. Just not this cheerful incubus."

"Aha!" said Track. "Now your real assessment comes out! 'Incubus'?"

"No," admitted Maggie, "not a good word. I guess I'm still under the spell of that costume . . ."

"Yeah," said Track, "me too."

". . . and those teeth. But I can tell things about people with very little conversation and no confessions. And I know she's the wrong woman for Liam."

"Yeah? Why?"

"Well, for one thing," said Maggie with a subtle trace of rising indignance, "she doesn't love him."

"How do you know that? All you've done is hiss and claw at each other for ten minutes."

"I watch. There are things I can see, things you could see if you looked—and I think you do look, and you do see—that are dead giveaways. I know the way Patti looks at you, even when she's mad at you, which is most of the time . . ."

"Ain't it the truth? I'm hard to live with."

". . . and I can see it in other people." She looked back at Anna, still enthralled by Doris. "I show it, too, when I'm with Sam."

"Yeah," said Track. "I noticed."

"But she doesn't show it. I can't imagine what she *would* look like if she were with a man she cared for. It's almost as if her facial nerves aren't wired for it. I guess that's the way Sam would say it."

"Well," said Track, "I see some strange things when Liam looks at *her.*"

"What, pray?"

"He looks like a man driving down an interstate, watching for a road sign. He's trying to find something."

Maggie looked at Track, suddenly serious and trusting Track's insight. "What's he looking for?"

"I don't know," said Track grimly. "I'm not sure he knows. And I'm not sure he wants to find it."

Patti slipped up behind Track and hugged him, then grabbed the garter he wore on his arm. "Come one, macho man, I want to dance."

"How can I refuse an offer like that? Can I snap your garter?"

"Depends on how much you value your ability to walk. Maggie's not the only one who takes martial-arts lessons." Track allowed himself to be led away, and Maggie looked for a partner. Sam was a terrible dancer; Maggie's feet had endured unspeakable savagery until she learned to keep track of Sam's lurching style. Liam was more graceful, but, like Sam, held her at an awkward distance. Both made her feel like a prisoner at a junior prom. She finally chose Liam, since Anna was ignoring him and she wanted to pump him about his mystery woman.

Sam watched them join the others, noting that the monk's robe was confining Liam's style. Sam pried Anna away from Doris Gilmer. He was not particularly curious about her and considered her, on the basis of her brief exchange with Maggie and her conversation about the ghost, rather narrow and sharp-edged. His real reason for asking her to dance was the scandalous dress, which promised an interesting sensory interlude.

They tried to keep up with the music, but it was no good, and they compromised by faking a conversation step. Sam was satisfied with the results. If he closed his eyes, he could imagine that he was dancing with a naked woman. "I learned to dance in high school," he said, to justify the conversation step.

"No, you didn't." No Ginger Rogers herself, she was still miles ahead of Sam.

"Go ahead," he said, "take cheap shots. You try tripping the light fantastic when your toes poke into the next county. Anyway, I'm vain about other things."

"What things?"

He thought a minute. "Good question. Actually, I'm shy and burdened by feelings of inferiority."

"Oh? Liam says you're arrogant and inhibited. Nice, but arrogant and inhibited."

"What do you think?"

"Inhibited, I guess, judging from the way you dance. Arrogant? I don't know. Are you?"

"No, not at all. Everybody thinks I'm arrogant, but they're all ignorant rednecks, common sods, trolls, and cretins."

"No, not arrogant! I like your wife."

"Really? So do I. But you sounded like natural enemies. Don't get me wrong—I love a good catfight, I just didn't sense much empathy."

She smiled, but her head was close to his shoulder and only Doris, dancing now with Herb Fisher, saw it. "I prefer men," she said after a calculated pause. "Most women don't have much to say that interests me."

"Not much on toilet paper and laundry soap?"

She laughed. "Oh, I'm not trying to be snide. I'm just more interested in the things that turn men on." Her eyes wandered for a moment. "That didn't come out quite right."

"I hear you," said Sam. Then, in defiance of reason: "Are you going to marry Liam?"

"He hasn't asked me. Not that it's your business."

"Will he?"

The music stopped and they walked back to the bar. "I don't know," she answered. "I really don't. I hope not."

"Why?" San was amazed at his own boldness. Since the news of Maggie's pregnancy his perspective of life had undergone a wholesale change, and he felt as if he were gazing down on Anna and Liam from a great height.

"Because I don't know what he wants from me," she said, equally amazed at her own frankness. "I don't know what he's looking for. It can't be a home and family if he's interested in me. That's not in my future, for sure."

"But you've known each other for some time, haven't you? Don't you have any plans, any understandings? Liam's too serious to dally with someone for years."

True, she thought. And once he had been terribly serious. He was in love, and his manner toward me was like an inane John Denver lyric. When he was so open and vulnerable I had only to delay in answering a letter to send him into despair. He is still serious, but now I don't know what it means. She wanted to tell Sam that his friend had become an oyster, shell closed tight, concealing a pearl. She wanted to tell him that Liam, for all his early passion, for all his patient devotion, had never bothered to wonder what *she* wanted in a man. If he knew, she wanted to ask Sam, could he change for her? But she didn't bother asking, she knew the answer.

"You're right," she said. "Liam never dallies. That's his problem. It's that damned intense *seriousness* that scares me. But look, this is too heavy a conversation for two strangers."

Sam turned red. "I'm sorry. I didn't mean to be nosy."

"I know. I talk too much. It's my great weakness—particularly when I'm talking about myself. Liam's a good friend, or I wouldn't be seeing him. I'm not very good at being married, and I guess he isn't either. That's two good reasons for keeping things the way they are."

A call went up for all the guests to assemble for a group photograph. Gordon, the third Supreme, was the official photographer.

He had spent much of the evening taking candid shots (the best proved to be of Track and Anna during the ghost conversation), and now it was time for the group shot. The shorter officers and their wives sat on the bar, the next rank stood in front, and the rest sat in chairs or knelt.

But a photograph shows only the surface of an event. It did not record Track's hand on Patti's bottom (and, since he put it there at the last safe moment, only the beginnings of her change in expression show in the department scrapbook). It could not record the unaccustomed pressure of Sam's arm around Maggie's waist and his comment, whispered in her ear just before the moment of truth, to the effect that it was a damned good thing the party had come when it did, since she wasn't going to be able to get into that dress much longer (which was the reason Maggie's eyes were closed in the picture, the reason for her smug smile). It could not record the distance between Liam and Anna as they posed, and it could not explain the distance in Liam's eyes, eyes that reflected a far light, a cold light.

"Okay, troops," said Captain Gordon, "say 'Skinner'!" He pressed the remote shutter and the camera flashed. The annual costume party was now locked in time, one of a thousand "remember-when"s kept in the scrapbooks of those who would, a year or two or ten from now, be sweltering under the white sun of Fort Bliss, or freezing in tanks or jeeps on the Fulda or the Imjin, or sweating out a promotion board or grumbling over a map exercise at Leavenworth. Or be only a memory, a bit of history substantiated by a folded flag and a page in the *Howitzer*, survived by a family that would somehow go on. And be forgotten by an America that always seemed to stop caring after a while. But on that night there were smiles, and those smiles, if not the separate invisible communications that lay beneath them, would be there in the scrapbook.

5

Stick, Stock, Stone Dead

Bolt and bar the shutter,
For the foul winds blow:
Our minds are at their best this night,
And I seem to know
That everything outside us is
Mad as the mist and snow.

—W. B. Yeats

16

*L*iam and Anna returned to the BOQ a little after midnight. Anna disappeared into the bedroom to put away the dress that was now a minor part of West Point's folklore, and Liam set about lighting the gas log in the fireplace. The bachelor officers' quarters at West Point (at least the older, preferred BOQ) was surely the last in the army with fireplaces, and Liam, a confirmed romantic, counted the days until the cold weather. Now, satisfied with the effect, he knelt on the floor and sorted through albums for appropriate mood music. After rejecting *Alexander Nevsky* as too bellicose and Sibelius according to the Berlin Philharmonic as too depressing (the connection of the Swan of Tuonela with the Land of the Dead was too suggestive for his current preoccupations), he narrowed the field down to *Peer Gynt* and an emergency album of what Maggie had called "PX music"—inert instrumental pieces designed to provide an aural background for large retail outlets. Anna's preferences argued for Grieg. Soon the "Morning" theme—it was after midnight, of course—filled the room.

Liam was a sparse drinker, but he had taken the trouble to stock up for Anna's sake; her Piscean capacities had shocked Liam at first, but he was a man who, to his own horror, could learn to live with anything. There was champagne in the refrigerator, but that was for later contingencies. He had bought a bottle of Remy Martin to addle her brain if required, but in consideration of the late hour and the mission facing him he decided to try Irish coffee instead of serious mind reform. She tended to drop off to sleep at inconvenient moments, and the Remy would hit her like a bar of soap in a sock to the base of the skull. Anyway, he thought, if this turns out the way I expect, I can kill the stuff myself.

He was almost finished preparing the coffee—a near disaster, since his ineptitude with food intended to any bartending duties more complex than mixing vodka and tonic—when Anna came out of the bedroom in a floor-length maroon nightgown. She made a delighted noise at the fire and curled up in front of it. Placing her bare feet near the fireplace, she reclined against the edge of the sofa, tilted her head back, eyes closed, and smiled. "I love it," she said to the ceiling. "This is elegant! Why didn't I come here before?"

He brought the coffee in on a silver tray inherited from his aunt, an item he had never used before; it was The Night. "You're hard to convince," he said. "I wanted you up here last summer."

"But there wouldn't have been a fire," she said, reasonably. "The fire makes it worthwhile. Coffee? Am I supposed to stay awake?"

"It would help. But it has additives, watch out."

She took a mug and sipped. "Great! You learned!"

"I thought it was the right thing. If you're still feeling ethnic after this, I have some Carolan liqueur to cap it off." Liam hated all liqueurs with a passion; Anna loved them all. He would change for the asking.

"I tasted it once," she said. "Interesting taste. Where did it get that name?"

Still wearing the monk's robe, he sat down beside her, with his own feet next to the fire. "O'Carolan was the last great bard of Ireland," Liam answered. "The little thatched house on the label is his cabin. I think it's still preserved as a national shrine or something."

"What is it about the Irish that makes them sing all those dreadful songs and live in such squalor? I don't mean to offend, of course—"

"Irishmen are not easily offended by Saxon ignorance," said Liam with a polite smile. "Nor quick to anger and take offense like the Italians—I don't mean to offend, of course—but you're half right. Only half right. Against those 'dreadful songs'—you mean, I suppose, the drunken ditties of the street singers that seem to sell so well. But there's also Yeats and Synge and Oscar Wilde . . ."

"Was he Irish?" asked Anna.

"Most assuredly. Are you a fan?"

"Not really. I had to read something depessing by him in

college. I think I've read something by Yeats, but I can't place what. Does 'Mad as the Mist' ring a bell?"

" 'Mad as the Mist and Snow.' But most people get their impressions of the Irish mentality from the Clancy Brothers and a few poets acceptable for high school anthologies. That isn't all that fair. It's like laughing at the moonshine and ignoring the . . ."

"The cream liqueur?"

"Exactly," said Liam.

"Well," said Anna, "you have to admit there's a theme of depression and hopelessness; I see it in you sometimes. I suppose you consider yourself Irish?"

"To my endless sorrow. It's in the genes. You know, Anna, the Irish are statistically more prone to schizophrenia than other ethnic groups. They say it has something to do with the influence of the church and the emphasis on guilt, but I think it goes back before that. There's a lot of it in the pre-Christian fragments, the Ossianic and Red Branch cycles and the older folk traditions. But the concept of sin is the real clincher, I guess."

Her eyes glittered over the coffee mug. "Irishmen have a thing about sin?"

"The popular view," said Liam, "is that we do it more and enjoy it less than any other race. Perhaps, on sober reflection—which usually translates to 'hangover' in Gaelic, with the connotation of waking up with one's eyes an inch from the sidewalk—it's a fundamental incompatibility between the pagan and Roman Catholic motives, both of which Irishmen cling to. The heathen devil makes us do it, Holy Mother Church makes us regret it the next morning. Life is not fair, as a famous president once observed."

Anna laughed. "What does the heathen devil tell you to do?"

"Mostly indulge the senses. In pagan times our favorite god was the Dagda. That's not his name, it's a descriptive: 'the Good.' But that doesn't mean he was good, it means he was good *at* things: he combined all the attributes of the other gods. He had a caldron that was always full of goodies; he was the all-bountiful, the father of gods."

"He sounds neat. Did he sin?"

"He was good at that, too, of course. Once he was so full of sins he flew in a cloud to the ocean by the cliffs of Moher and wrung them out of his soul. They became terrible winged harpies, the Dread Women, who still haunt the cliffs, or so 'tis said."

"Why women? He sounds like a male chauvinist pig."

"Well," said Liam, "I guess they personify the eternal feminine that lures to perfection—or to ruin, as the fit strikes. The real villains, and not just in Irish tradition, are often villainesses—the second wife of Lir, who changed her stepchildren into swans, or Mórrigan MacCaílltin, the worst of the Badb witches, who . . ."

Anna was getting bored, and had drained her coffee down to the whiskey. She rested her head on the edge of the sofa. When Liam looked at her again, her eyes were closed. He leaned over and kissed her on the tip of her nose, a gesture that conveyed affection, not lust. The gesture lied, of course, but it was time for caution. "Had enough analysis of folklore?"

Her eyes opened. "Sorry. It's late. I'm not bored."

"Can I get you anything?" She shook her head. The fire put coppery highlights on her hair. She was comfortable and about to go to sleep. Solveyg was lamenting piteously in the background; Liam hated this interpretation, one that made her sound like Brünnhilde. But he knew that the next band was *Hall of the Mountain King*. That would break the spell. Preparation was impossible; to speak now might be precipitous and abrupt, but in a few minutes his words would be accompanied by a rambunctious troll-ditty.

"Marry me."

For a moment her expression was what one would expect had Liam suggested a fast pelvic examination or brayed like a jackass. But she was awake now, at least. She closed her eyes and frowned, her face suddenly tired, not sleepy. Liam felt a cold fluid perfusing his veins.

"No. Let's quit for the night."

"I can't make sense of any of this except by marrying you. None at all."

"What's the matter with what you have?"

"What do I have?" said Liam, staring straight into her eyes. "I have your part-time attention. It eats away at me. I want to live with you. I can't do that informally, not at West Point. *I* can't do it anywhere. I want all this to make sense."

"I don't love you, Liam. I can't. You'd demand that."

"Would I? I've done all right without it so far."

She smiled sadly. "No, you haven't. We wouldn't be having this conversation if you had. I won't marry you. I'm not going to chalk up another failure and damage you in the process. I'm not

266

your Irish Wicked Witch of the West. You don't need me. You'd only end up frustrated and angry. There's a bitter, black thing in you, Liam. It's trying to master you. If you failed with me it would win. I'm not going to be responsible for that."

"You're not going to be responsible for me."

"You're right. I'm not."

"I mean," said Liam, "I'm the only one with the authority to choose my paths, so I'm the only one responsible."

"You don't mean that," she said irritably. "I'd just end up throwing that pious pledge back in your face someday and hate myself for it. No."

"I need you. but I won't beg."

"Please don't. You think you need me. You don't know. You're looking for something, and you have this crazy idea I can help you find it. I can't help you, Liam. You have to do it yourself. I won't be a part of it. If you want to make me into some kind of goddess-bitch, that's your business. You can cast me in your play, but I won't take the part. Let's go to bed. I'm exhausted."

Liam relented, burying his terrible, paralyzing sense of abandonment. He turned down the fire and took her hand and led her to the bedroom. By the time he had showered and undressed, she was asleep. He left her alone and sat in his study, awake in the torture chair. He drew one rune from the sack. He already knew what it would be.

Sam walked through the snow. It was pitch-black, only the faintest light came through dense clouds, but he felt the cold through the feet of his chain mail armor and he felt the flakes of snow as they brushed his face. He felt the cold, and then he found a great heavy cloak around his shoulders and the armor was gone, and in its place warm clothes of heavy wool, and a visored cap on his head. He felt the snow over the tops of his shoes, over his ankles, and he felt the blowing flakes collect around the collar of his cloak and melt down his neck in a cold trickle.

There were lights, and he recognized them: a line of windows, pale rectangles against the dark, dim and yellow, lit by candles. The snowflakes danced around them, fluttered in the miserly light. The heavy air carried the sound of singing and then a cheer from many voices. Sam stopped to listen; there was one voice from the hall, louder than the others. It was a song he knew slightly, but he could not remember where he had heard it:

> But now without the reveille,
> I've learned to close my eyes,
> And also can get up from tea,
> Without the word to "rise."
> I'm not at "rest" when I should talk,
> Don't flourish when I bow,
> Nor do I march when I should walk,
> I'm not a soldier now!

There was more cheering at this and the sound of the voices faded. Sam found his way out of the deep snow and stepped onto a hard, trodden path that led in front of the row of lighted house windows. He walked slowly, and heard the friendly crunch of boots on the road behind him. The gait was familiar, the quick, disciplined strides, the heel-first sound. *A cold night,* the voice said, and Sam replied, It is indeed, Ethan, my toes're near froze off. When will it stop?

Not before daylight. River's plumb solid, damn near drive a caisson across it. Matter of fact, caught young Clay down there this morning. Walked near a furlong out on it, on a bet, by heaven! A bet!

Sam laughed merrily, but the sound was muffled by the snow. A bet indeed. He'll make a dragoon, the villain! You can always tell by the bets they'll take.

Any bets on our Antique? said Ethan, serious now. *He looks older now, tireder than ever. Sad and dreamy. Looks like thirty, and what is he? Not twenty-one, by heaven!*

This is no place to be old, said Sam, and that's a fact. He'll be with us tomorrow at supper, and so will the Mansfields. Our Antique will play with Annabelle and charm us with French verbs! And Bridey's man, the corporal, he brought around a fat turkey, though the poor thing looked like he killed it with grapeshot! Will you join us?

Kind of you, said Ethan. *I'll inquire of the missus, it being a shame to let a bird slain in fierce battle die for nothing.* He laughed at this. *I'll ask our Antique to compose us a few couplets on the death of the turkey! Good night to you, and give my respects to 'Liza*

Sam turned into his quarters as Ethan Hitchcock strode away to his, and Bridey was there, white-aproned and turning stout now as Irish girls always seem to; but tonight Sam saw the fear in her eyes, and her face was streaked with tears. *It's herself again*, the girl said, *and she's in a state, a terrible state.*

Sam sighed as he entered the light of the hall. Snow fell from his great blue cloak. Don't be afraid, she'll tire herself soon. But the girl fell to her knees, crossed herself, and started to wail softly. She tried praying, and Sam turned away, irritated at her ignorant papist gibber and her light regard for dignity.

He sensed Eliza's presence on the stairs, up on the landing; he could always feel her before he saw her. Her presence was always there before you saw her. In that way she was like her father, stern old chin-whiskers with his black claw-hammer coat and the eyes that judged you in a glance and found you wanting.

He climbed the stairs, and the boards creaked. Indeed, she was there. Awake still?

Indeed yes, the voice said. *Oh, yes. Awake still. How can you ask?* She stood upright and proud, her thin white hands gripping one another with grisly strength, the veins blue against the procelain skin. *Have you celebrated tonight, husband?*

Yes, said Sam angrily, that I have. So must any man, Eliza, even a saint.

He saw her eyes then, and the fit was on them, worse than ever before; they were white, white and clouded as the snows that fell at dawn, seen through the window of a darkened room. The fit was there, like a fever, but cold. It must run its course. She was quite mad at times like this, not Eliza. She shined with a cold light, he thought, the polished stone face of hell itself, reflecting the light of heaven that it at once despised and craved.

I know you, she said, *I know you well enough, and I know what you've done, husband. Did it give you pleasure? What are whores for, but pleasure?*

No, said Sam, it wasn't that at all.

The child plays in the same nursery with the golden whore you made in your pride and your lust, clutching my back and moaning like an animal. You're damned, husband, he said you would be and you are. Damned.

No, said Sam. You're tired. Control yourself.

Get her out of my house, husband, get them both out, the whore and

269

her darkling spawn. But she is my own task, and I'll cleanse her of sin before the end. Just get them out and find damnation in your own good time, husband.

You forget yourself, Eliza.

I forget nothing, husband. Out! Get her out, chattering filthy foreign monkey, gibbering Roman whore! Get them both out, the Irish brat too! Then she was silent, as if suddenly in thrall of another, more distant, voice. Her eyes rolled back and her fingers loosened their grip. Her fit's on her again, thought Sam. Her little sickness.

He turned to leave and the hallway had grown, grown huge with stone columns and a high ceiling with corbeled vaults, a cavernous space lighted by candles; and Maggie was there.

She was dressed in her costume gown, and carried before her a great shallow bowl of silver. The children hid in her skirts, the blond curious trusting face and the dark boy hiding his face in her dress. There was a great fish in the bowl, a salmon he thought, silver and pale with a dark gray back and silver-violet scaled flanks. *This is ours,* she said with a pride that overflowed and warmed Sam, *and it comes from the well. I drank at the well, my darling,* she said, *and we can share it now. We have it, Sam, what we looked for: San Graal, sang raal, the beginning and end.*

Then, to his horror, he saw her eyes mist over. *Here now,* she said, and her eyes rolled back in her head; but she still spoke, and said: *Come, we'll share the celebration, husband! Any man must celebrate, even a saint!*

I want no celebration, said Sam, who knew it was a dream but could not make it stop, could only stand impotently horrified at the course he knew it would take.

Don't look, Sam, said Liam, who was there now, in his monk's robe, pushing past them out of the darkness in a wheelchair. *Don't look.*

You said it yourself, husband, said Maggie. *Any man must celebrate, even a saint. Come, husband, and look at the feast.*

Sam knew it was madness, hers to say and his to obey, but she was invincible in her madness and he was helpless in his. She walked toward him, her chin held high and her mad eyes shining with triumph, and held out the great silver bowl for Sam, and he saw what it held.

Sam woke up with a scream and Maggie, terrified, turned on the bedside lamp. He was cold and the sheets and pillowcases were soaked; his heart was racing. She put her arms around him and murmured, sleepily, "Sam, Sam, it's all right, it's all right." He looked over her shoulder at the clock. It was three thirty-two, Saturday morning, the third of November.

The room in the 47th Division had been cleared on Friday afternoon, Carson transferred to a new room to fill a bed left empty by a cadet who had resigned in October. The bare furniture remained behind, but the plebe had removed all uniforms and books and personal belongings. He had cleaned the room twice before it passed Andrea Linnell's inspection. Depsite the inconvenience of the move and the drudgery of the inspection, Carson was happy to see the last of the place.

About the time Sam was drifting into his uncomfortable series of dreams, the tracery of frost crystals began to spread its lacy way around the windowpanes in the empty room. It ran along the bottom edges at first, then up and around the tops and finally in the centers. The metal latch that held the sliding windows grew dull; then the crystals grew there, too, and after some time they were like a sparkling crown on each lock.

There was no ear to hear the sound, but it was there nonetheless: at first a thin, piping whine, pitched higher than the cry of a bat. Then it was joined by a series of lower pitches, down into the range of the ear's recognition, and the asychrony of phase as each new tone was added gave it a quavering, almost urgent sound. Then lower music still was added to the chorus of the empty room, and the voices edged outside the human capacity to hear once again, though the window panes heard and trembled at the song. It was a song, in its way, and in its wordless, unheard verses it gave voice to the cold, to the swirl of snow and the frost-plumes. Its highest tones were the voices of the winds that searched the valley from end to end, from High Tor to Beacon, searched through the black, skeleton fingers of the native oak on the rocky slopes of Storm King, wound its way through the boulders and high places, beat itself stubbornly against the granite blocks of Bartlett Hall and whirled around the gargoyles that guarded the clock tower of Pershing Barracks. Its middle chords spun forth into the night from the navigation bell on the rocks at the foot of Flirtation Walk, and

271

joined with the abrupt, insistent sound of the tugboats' horns as they pushed their great laden barges down the dark river between North Dock and Constitution Island. The bass tones were born of the endless groaning of the ice as it froze and broke up and froze, as the floes drifted in untidy armadas down the river from Albany to jam at the point and await the next night of cold.

The cold mist crept down the walls from the windows and collected on the floor. The music rose and fell, and when the song of the unseen voices reached a new crescendo, the loose window frames rattled, and paint, chilled by the cold and dislodged by the vibrations, flaked in tiny pieces and fell to the sill and the floor.

Liam had slept lightly, his mind kept racing by his failure with Anna. She slept soundly beside him, still in her plush nightgown, her knees drawn up and her arms, by coincidence, stretched out to Liam as if to mock his agony. Now he woke again. He heard the wind. It was strong for a night wind, it rose and fell in urgency. Come to the window, it said, come and see our strength, taste our power, come and hear our ancient song.

Carefully, so as not to wake Anna, he left the bed and walked to the window that faced the river and the far bank. There was a moon, and the starveling branches of the trees were alight with silver. He stood at the window and could not move away again, could not turn his head or close his eyes.

At the Lee Area house, Maggie and Sam held each other, Sam awake now and shaken, Maggie frightened too, and clinging to him. They rocked back and forth on the bed, sharing strength.

In the room in the 47th Division, the ragged flakes swirled around the points of cold light, danced in a slow circle—slow, then faster and faster, drawing into the vortex the shreds of cold fog from the floor and the windows. The song of the cold rose again, louder now.

Liam listened to the song of the winds and watched the tree branches. They were still, and so he knew the wind for what she was. I hear you, he said to himself, I hear you. Rune-caster, crone, Woman of the Hill. I hear you.

In the 47th Division room a pane of glass in the window, covered altogether in frost, cracked from corner to corner. And the room was quiet.

272

17

On Saturday, Liam spent a day of dangling conversations with Anna. Neither referred to the night before, but Liam's proposal hung in the air, a silent backdrop to the day's activities. They went for a drive across the river, over the Bear Mountain Bridge and up toward Cold Spring. Liam knew Cold Spring fairly well, and took her to a restaurant by the river, a restored inn that had hosted departmental luncheons in years past and afforded a superb view of Crow's Nest Mountain rising up abruptly from the far shore, with the buildings of West Point spread out on the flats to its south. The weather was clear and still, as still as it had been when Liam had heard the wind.

Anna tried hard to be upbeat and chatty, but she saw Liam's misery and her attempts gradually subsided into a long, distracted monologue about her work while Liam chewed his food glumly and nodded in occasional agreement. She knew that she had handled his proposal unskillfully, but she was at a loss to redeem herself. Sometimes it seemed impossible to spare Liam any pain; he led with his chin in every confrontation and, despite his politeness after each blow and his amazing resilience, every repetition left him corroded and a little more distant. It would have been easy just to tell him to forget her for his own good, but her natural inclination to avoid dramatic gestures and cut her own losses militated against this solution. Besides, Liam interested her—sometimes her interest was closer to morbid curiosity and a detached desire to see what he would do next, sometimes it was something she didn't understand herself. She had no intention of giving up her job or her freedom for Liam FitzDonnell. Her occasional joking about holding out for a yacht-owner with plenty of leisure time was only her way of reassuring Liam without making any commitments.

The passing of years caused the only pressure she felt to remarry, and Liam tactfully avoided reference to this, even at birthday time.

On the other hand, Liam, despite his years of courting Anna and his repeated proposals, had never formed a picture of what life would be like married to her. His ego whispered that he had asked her to marry him just so he could tell himself in later, even lonelier years, that at least he had made the gesture. He could summon no alternative explanation that made a shred of sense. His love of symmetry in thought and deed cried out for closure, for an end that—if nothing else—left him with his dignity and gave him some point for what would otherwise be wasted years. It was a cheap gesture, and he knew it. He had quit in disgust on Anna after this or that petty disappointment many times before, only to come back to her because his sense of fitness and completion was offended. Now, as they ate lunch and looked out at the Hudson, he had to wonder if that last empty ticket had finally been punched.

After returning to the BOQ before three o'clock Anna took her leave at once with a clumsy kiss and some vague, cheerful words about the next visit. Liam went to his room and changed into his jogging shorts, intending to do a few miles before dinner by way of getting tired enough for the night's work. It would not do, he reasoned, to lie awake in the haunted room. Instead of running, however, he propped up a pillow on the bed and lay quietly in his shorts and running shoes, reading a book on multivariate analysis; this occupied his mind with emotionally neutral discussions of gamma and beta matrices and profile analyses until dinner. It started to turn dark, but he kept the light off until it was too dim to read, then put away the book and stared at the ceiling.

When it was finally dinnertime, he stirred himself into the kitchen to make a sandwich of white bread and tinned corned beef and open a small can of mandarin oranges. He started the automatic coffee maker and watched the brown liquid trickle into the glass pot. As he tasted the coffee he regretted making it as strong as he had, but he drank it anyway. Let him come if I'm asleep or awake, he thought; he promised to leave the gate open.

After this modest dinner he pulled a gray athletic sweatshirt from his dresser and left the BOQ. It will do more good to run now anyway, he thought. I can take a shower when I come back and that will relax me. It always does. He ran at a slow pace past

274

Kosciuszko's monument and headed around the bend to Trophy Point. The way was clearly lit by streetlights and the traffic was light. He picked up the pace when he passed Thayer's statue and turned down the road on the steep hill past Eisenhower Hall. He took the route out of sheer obstinacy; when a runner takes a down-hill road, he is assuring himself of an uphill run later on, and the road from the low point at Ike Hall back up to the cemetery was a killer. He hated it when he thought of it beforehand, but forced himself nonetheless to run that way. It occurred to him that his best times, his toughest runs, followed a visit with Anna. I can master my body, he thought. It feels good to be in charge.

Halfway up the hill he felt his thighs go numb. When would he start to give out, next year? He breathed in time with his foot falls, counting breaths, ignoring the rawness of his throat as he gasped for air. He could have stopped, but didn't. It was only fifty yards or so more, then straight and level. He thought of Anna, nestled against the sofa with her feet next to the fire. This slowed him down. But the thought of her face when he had asked her to marry him spurred him to greater speed again, and, clearing the top of the hill, he turned with relief onto the flat in front of the old cadet chapel in the cemetery.

I wonder if he's in there? No, of course not; he died at Chapultepec, and they didn't ship bodies back in those days, God knows; well, maybe Nelson in the rum cask, but certainly not an overage captain. He'd be buried in Mexico. And Eliza and little Annabelle? Could be; maybe some of the graves went back that far, but he doubted it. Lord knows where they're buried. Maggie can find out. He was no longer aware of his legs moving. Now that he was past the first rush of pain that reminded him of his mortality the easy part came. Now he could run two or three miles without noticing it. Now the only drag would be a self-imposed limit born of a simple desire to have it over with.

He turned onto Lee Road instead of running up the long hill to Washington Gate. This was a night to be sleepy, not exhausted. There was a downslope to the bridge over Crow's Nest Brook next to Sam's quarters, and he pushed off to break the monotony. The thought struck him that Anna would have loved the view of the river from the Lee Area bluffs. But a tiny inner voice immediately whispered that he was full of shit, that Anna wouldn't care if she could look out her window at the fucking Alps or the near side of

275

eternity. Still, the thought of living there with Anna had done its job, and he ran harder to let one pain do its job driving out another.

He almost ran into Sam, who was jogging at a slower pace in the same direction. Sam hated running, and did only as much as he needed to pass the physical readiness test and maintain enough cardiovascular robustness to keep up with Maggie. Liam laughed silently. It was as Anna had said. We all work for what we need most.

He slowed beside Sam. "Having fun?"

"Shit, no. I'm running to and from Lee Gate exactly four times. That is damned near . . . exactly four miles. Four . . . point zero miles. Laugh if you . . . will, speed freak."

"I promise not to laugh, Sam," Liam replied, not without a gasp or two. "You have something to run home to. That shortens your trip."

Sam looked at him seriously, then turned his head and spat in the gutter. "You sound downbeat. Anna's gone already?"

"Yeah. She had to get back to Boston to finish a report be . . . before tomorrow."

"Enjoy her visit?"

"Her or me?"

"Choose your poison."

"Not good," said Liam. "But I won't burden you with my private tragedies. When are we gathering at the haunted house?"

"Ten, I think. That's when I told Saganian to be there. You can come . . . when you're ready. I guess things won't start popping until three in the morning or so."

They ran silently for the rest of the way to Lee Gate; Liam keeping pace with Sam, who was doing about an eight-minute mile. Liam was grateful for the chance to quit a pace that was really too fast for him at his age and frame of mind. Anna was driving him past a safe level of exertion. *I guess she'll have my heart pickled like Sam's ugly brain, one way or another. If it's not broken out of some neurotic shadow of romantic sentiment, it'll be scarred with infarcts wide enough to hide Hondas in. Sam is right; running more than four miles at a time is vanity and suicide. Of course,* he reflected, *there's a lot to be said for vanity and suicide. Maybe that's what I'm planning for tonight. Good timing. The gate is open.*

But Lee Gate was closed, and they shared the simpleminded

joggers' ritual of touching the painted iron gate and turning around for the run back. There was a short slope up to the gate, and they pushed off in the other direction, Liam out of habit when presented with a downhill stretch, Sam to knock a few seconds off his modest time. But the new pace turned suddenly and unexpectedly into a sprint past the first quarters on the road. "To the streetlight!" Liam gasped, and he saw Sam abandon his steady chug and start to pump hard, intent on the finish line.

Liam noted that while Sam was not a long-distance man he was a fair sprinter, and Liam had to push hard to keep up. They passed the light with Liam a few feet ahead. He laughed while Sam cursed hoarsely and leaned for a moment against a parked car. "Come on," Sam said, "I've got to get back and reassure Maggie that she's still going to the party tonight."

Liam kept jogging in place. "It may not be a party, Sam. Remember what I told you."

Sam leaned back against the car. "I won't forget. I had one of those dreams last night."

Liam nodded. "So you understand."

"Not entirely. I know there's something terrible behind all this. Do you know what we're dealing with?"

"Come on," said Liam. "I don't want to stiffen up. I have to go all the way back to the Q." They started jogging, slowly now, past the streetlights. "No, I don't know what we're dealing with, not by a long shot. What happened last night?"

"Well," said Sam, "I really don't want to go into it at great length . . ."

"I know," said Liam. "I understand."

"But for a while I was somebody else. It wasn't a nightmare; it was for real."

"Did you see her?"

Sam looked at Liam sharply, then stared ahead again. "The woman? The one in the blue dress?"

"You know who she is, Sam."

Sam didn't answer for a moment. "Yes, I know who she is. I knew last night. I knew who she was before I saw her."

"And what did you think?"

"She's crazy, Liam."

Liam took a deep breath. "Yes. She's crazy. That's a clinical term. She's capable of anything."

"We can't change anything that happened, Liam. It does no good to fight it. I have no rational explanation for the hex on that room, but we can't change it. Anyway, you're right. Maggie stays outside." Sam slowed and stopped, and Liam stopped with him. "Liam, she killed the child. I don't know why, but she killed it. In the dream, it was my baby, Maggie's. I'll never forget it. I woke up screaming."

"I'm sorry, Sam. This isn't a time for you and Maggie to be doing this. What if she sees the thing and starts to have dreams in her condition? Did you tell her about the dream?"

"Christ no, Liam! That might start her off on her own! She's fractious enough what with the baby and the excitement. 'Morbid suggestion'—that was your term."

"Maybe it's worth it to keep her away from the—"

"Liam, I want her safe at home. But I can't stand there and tell her I saw our baby reduced to a charred little corpse in a silver dish!"

"Jesus . . ."

"Maybe you resonate to good shit like that, but I stick at some things. I may have my hands full watching her, but by God she's not going into the room."

"Sam, *you* didn't go into that room."

They looked at each other. Sam was scared, Liam could see that, but he wasn't sure Sam's say-so could make Maggie stay at home. Were it Anna, a say-so might work, for Anna was no daredevil, but Maggie was a force to be reckoned with.

"I'm worried about you, too," said Sam. "You watch out. You were in the dream last night, and you were in a wheelchair."

"That's great news. Could you expand a little?"

Sam reluctantly told him the part of the dream that had been set in the great hall.

"You know what that was, don't you?" asked Liam.

"Oh, hell yes. Didn't I proofread Maggie's damned dissertation until my eyes gave out? The Grail Castle, the Grail Procession. More of your morbid suggestion. But I don't laugh at dreams anymore. You watch it."

"I will," said Liam. "Come on—I have to get ready for tonight, and it's a good distance back to the BOQ." Liam started to run. Sam ran beside him, until he reached his quarters, where he turned off with a wave. It was nearly eight; Maggie was waiting.

Liam was back in his room by twenty after. He took a long, in-dulgent shower, letting the hot water relax his tired muscles and clear his mind. He had plenty of time. Ahead of him was the prospect of sleeping in a strange bed, in a very strange room. It was no more than he did any night.

After drying off, he put on a uniform and packed a warm-up suit to sleep in, along with heavy socks in case it got cold—that innocent thought struck him as exquisitely funny. I must be crazy too, he thought. Just like crazy old Eliza, daughter of crazy old— what did Mag say his name was? Eli? No, Elihu! Christ, Elihu. I can see his face now; probably looked like he suffered from an intestinal blockage. He must have preached a good hellfire-and-damnation. You could see it in her face.

He absently poured a last cup of coffee, but immediately poured it out and turned off the coffee maker. Then, having turned off the kitchen light, he went into the study with its great ornate desk and the shelves of books. He carefully removed a plaque from the wall and sat in the baron's chair.

It wasn't a fancy plaque. It had been made in a shop in Hue that catered to the whims of Americans: polished dark wood with a garish replica in the center of a black shield with the white head of an eagle, mouth open in a scream of triumph. There was a smaller unit crest above it, and underneath, a brass plate:

1LT LIAM JAMES FITZDONNELL
1st PLATOON, C COMPANY, 1–502 INFANTRY (ABN)
101st AIRBORNE
APRIL, 1967–FEBRUARY 1968

On the back was a yellowing square of paper. The ink was faded, the blue lines almost gone. A simple message:

Good luck 12—we'll be thinking about you!

And beneath it, crowded together, eleven names. All that had been left to sign it.

He put it aside and pulled Barstow's letter out of its cubbyhole.

279

It was addressed to Stu Broadnax, but the tactical officer had given it to Liam on Friday as soon as he had read it. Liam examined it carefully one more time, then left it, open, in the center of the desk.

Somebody will find it, he thought. Maybe.

The desk lamp cast long shadows on the walls. As he looked in silence at the rows of books, stacks of papers—journal articles, drafts of research reports, lesson plans—no movement, no flicker of his eyes betrayed his thoughts.

Then he covered his face with his hands and whispered: "Oh, screw it." With deliberate fury he pulled books from the shelves and threw them against the far wall, volume after volume, pages fluttering like the wings of white birds, like the wings of seraphs in a prophet's vision of Yahweh on his throne. He clutched stacks of papers and threw them too, for good measure, and they scattered on the floor and the desktop and on the great carved chair. Finally, he pulled open the secret drawer and drew out the sack of rune stones, raised the window and threw them out into the night. One struck the window frame and bounced back. Liam picked it up and aimed more carefully. Away it went. He heard the faint sound as it landed in the woods far below.

Saganian had arrived first and started checking out the instruments, his evening ritual now made a little harder by the stiffness of his bandaged hands. They itched like hell, but it did no good to scratch; the scabs cracked and it was worse than ever. Anyway, he consoled himself, I think I've got it all working right, for once. It ought to be—I've fixed everything at least once since this crazy project started. The room had been chilly when he checked out the video and still cameras in the room. The cold had startled him, since he knew from experience what it signaled. He was relieved to find only a broken pane of glass in the window. After patching it with tape and cardboard, he turned up the heat—Andrea Linnell had turned it off to save energy—and soon the room was comfortable again. But he wasted no time in it once the cameras were checked out.

Track arrived at ten, and Sam and Maggie followed about five minutes later. Saganian took great pleasure in explaining all the technology to Maggie while Sam busied himself with administrative chores. "I'm not sure I can stay awake all night," said Maggie.

"Don't worry," said Sam, "we have a spare bunk back in the other alcove. We take turns napping. You can use it when you get bored. We'll wake you up if anything happens."

"You'd better! This is a once-in-a-lifetime chance."

At this moment Liam arrived, dressed in his greens and a black uniform sweater and carrying a warm-up suit rolled neatly under his arm. "Aha!" said Maggie, "the great ghost-hunter."

"In a very short time," said Liam mildly, "I hope to be the great sleeper. With any luck at all, this is going to be the first good night's sleep I've had since Sunday."

"Yeah," said Track. "I guess you were up last night. Did Anna leave already?"

"Uh-huh. She had to get a briefing ready for Monday. We had a nice lunch across the river."

"Will she be back?" asked Maggie.

"Good question. Well, I'm ready to turn in. Let's get the torture over with."

"The torture?" said Maggie. "Now what?"

"Oh, we have to hook him up," said Sam. "You can watch through the TV monitor."

"Through the TV monitor? Why can't I help?"

"I need you to let me know if there's any temperature change while we're in the room," Sam lied. "All you have to do is watch these green lines on the monitor. Watch them, now—see, they scroll across the screen. Now watch when they get to the end." The eight snaking lines completed their course and stopped for half a second, then the computer beeped and a line of numbers flashed in the lower left corner of the screen and the printer chirped briefly. "Now, that records the average temperature for the complete analysis epoch—that's the time it takes all the lines to go across the screen. When it beeps and displays the number, I want you to call it out to us in the next room."

"Okay. Do I do anything else?"

"No, that'll be just fine. Don't touch the keyboard."

"Okay, darling. By the way, if you're having me do this just to keep me out of the way, you're in mortal danger."

"Don't worry," said Sam. "Just call out the temperature averages."

281

Sam, Saganian, and Liam went into the haunted room; Track and Salinger stayed with Maggie. Maggie knew at once that either of the officers could have read off the numbers as well as she, and gritted her teeth. Sam would suffer later, but for the time being, she was going to be the best goddamned number-reader at the U.S. Military Academy.

Liam hung his hat over the video lens and stripped to his shorts, then put on the warm-up suit. Saganian had put sheets and two blankets on the bunk in Barstow's old alcove, and Liam lay back under them with his head on the pillow.

Sam looked at him doubtfully. "I don't suppose it's worthwhile asking you if you really want to go through with this nonsense."

"Don't be absurd," said Liam. "Why ask me now that I'm tied up here waiting to awake beneath a slowly swinging pendulum?"

"Jesus, Liam! Don't drift off into dreamland with that kind of an attitude."

Liam smiled slowly, really tired now. "What should be on my mind, Sam, laying me down to sleep in this place? My income tax?"

"Think about personality theory, Liam. Plan your next lecture on the topic. Think silently, though, or you'll put all of us to sleep."

"Go fuck yourself."

Indeed, Liam was asleep within twenty minutes. Maggie marveled. She had no way of knowing he had not slept well for a week. Exhaustion had claimed him, not cool detachment. She stuck with the quiet conversation until about midnight, then excused herself and lay down on the spare bunk, which was separated from the equipment alcove by a wooden partition. The strange feel of the hard single bed and the rough blanket kept her up, but after half an hour of pleasant warmth she yielded herself up to dreamless sleep.

"Sorry I missed the excitement on Thursday night," Sam said softly, so as not to disturb Maggie or Liam. "I always get the dregs of adventure."

"Cheer up, sir," said Saganian. "At least you still got skin on your hands."

"Okay, what the hell you people got the lights on in here for?

I ain't written anybody up all day." It was Stu Broadnax, grinning under the visor of a camouflage fatigue cap.

"It's true," said Sam. "Tac officers never sleep. Come to see the final act?"

"Shit," said Track, "getting Stu out after bedtime's an unnatural act, final or not. But hark, what welcome parcels of steaming fluid do I spy in your hands?"

"Mess hall made some coffee," Broadnax explained. "I figured you could use some. Where's Colonel Fitz?"

"Sawing timber next door," said Track. "But keep the noise down, Maggie's asleep." Broadnax passed around the coffee and they sat slurping noisily as men do around the flickering light of a campfire or a bank of cathode ray tubes. The lights were dim for ease in reading the displays, and the effect was almost cozy.

"Beats me how he can sleep in there," said the tac. "You don't know it, but General Harrington passed the word to convert it into a storage room again. That's going to be tough on us. We're full now, no spare bunks, no spare room."

"What happens if Barstow decides to come back?" asked Sam.

"They wouldn't take him back after going AWOL," said Salinger.

"Barstow isn't coming back," said Broadnax between sips.

"How do you know?' asked Sam. "Did he call?"

"No, I got a letter. Didn't Liam tell you?" The tac glanced foolishly at the blank wall that stood between him and Liam.

"Hell, no," said Track. "A letter? When?"

"Friday. I called Colonel FitzDonnell, and he came over and read it. Still has it, I think." Broadnax looked at Track, then back at Sam. "He didn't tell you?"

"What was in the letter?" said Sam.

"Oh, Barstow just sent a note to me saying he was sorry he had taken off without saying good-bye, that he'd been staying with a relative in Maryland and was on the way home. He said he wasn't coming back on account of what he'd seen in the room the night he left, and that he was still having dreams and would I please forward any personal articles he'd left behind."

"What did he see in the room?" asked Sam. Track looked at him closely. His fists were clenched.

"Oh, a bunch of walla walla about some guy with his face shot away, and blood all over the floor. Sounds a—"

"Oh, that's what Carson saw on Thursday," said Saganian. "He called it 'the bloody man.' "

"Why the hell don't I know about this?" said Sam, his voice rising.

Salinger recoiled. "I thought Colonel Fitz told you—"

"He didn't tell me about any damned bloody men. Of course, what the hell, every room has bloody men walking around with missing faces, no problem. Don't bother Bondurant about it. Now, if you have a minute to spare, how about catching me up on this continuing drama?"

"Oh, it started out about the same as Tuesday," said Saganian. "Fog, some movement, the flash went off by accident. When Colonel Fitz went into the room, Carson was standing up. I saw him through the monitor—Carson, I mean. He stood there looking at something, and said 'Yes.' "

"You mean he was talking to the ghost?" said Track. "Nobody's done that before."

"Well, Carson woke up and saw it. Colonel Fitz sat with him for a few minutes and they talked. I didn't hear all of it. Carson talked about a 'bloody man' who had his face shot away, a lot of nasty stuff about how you could see his teeth, and how there was blood on the floor." Sam remembered the spattering of heat sources in the thermal picture, mixed with the cold water and the tracks.

Sam leaned forward. "What did Colonel FitzDonnell do? Did he seem surprised?"

"No, sir, he just sort of sat there and comforted the guy, calmed him down. Asked him once about a hunting knife."

"A what?" said Sam. "A hunting knife?"

"Yeah. Carson said the ghost, the bloody one, had something taped somewhere, and Colonel Fitz said, or asked him, 'a hunting knife?' And Carson said yeah, that was it. Come to think of it, he sounded surprised."

"You said Carson said 'Yes' to the ghost," said Sam. "That's a good answer. What was the question?"

"I don't know, sir. The colonel asked him when everything settled down. I didn't understand what Carson was talking about. He sounded sort of in a daze. He said the bloody man told him to 'Tell Leemy the gate is open.' Is that it? No, maybe it was 'Tell Leemy I'll leave the gate open.' "

There was a brief silence as Track and Sam looked at each other. Finally Track said, "Oh, shit."

"I don't like this," said Sam.

"What's going on?" asked Salinger.

"I haven't liked it from the start, ever since that hypnosis, when Tetzel's voice changed, that 'old buddy' business, all that 'torch one two torch one two' nonsense."

"What are you talking about?" asked Broadnax. Sam told him about the hypnotic regression and Tetzel's strange outburst. "That's been in the back of my mind ever since. I still don't know what 'torch one two' is all about."

"Sounds like a radio call sign," volunteered Salinger.

Track looked at Broadnax. " 'Leemy' was Colonel Fitz's cadet nickname."

"How would Carson know that? Or Tetzel?"

"Maybe they didn't," said Sam.

"Oh, shit," said Track again.

"I just ran out of theories," said Sam. "Time for a paradigm shift."

"Fuck the paradigm shift," said Track, shaking his head. "Do we wake him up and drag his ass out of there?"

"On what grounds?" said Sam. "Because we voted and decided he's walking into an occult ambush? He knew what he was doing, the son of a bitch." He told them about the boot marks.

Track chewed his lip. "Well, nobody's been hurt yet, except by bad luck or plain foolishness."

"Which was which?" asked Salinger.

Sam ignored him. "Let's just be very alert and get ready to bust in there if it looks like anything new happening."

"Sir, I've heard that before."

"Yeah, I know, Sarge. But we have a whole panel of experts here tonight. Let's just wait it out and see what develops."

Nothing developed. By three-thirty, Liam was in a deep sleep stage for a second time after two brief periods of paradoxical sleep lasting less that twenty minutes and separated by an hour. His heart rate was a runner's—sixty-one—and his EEG was full of alpha.

"Well," said Salinger, "maybe the last night's going to be a fizzle after all."

"It wouldn't dare!"

Sam turned in his chair. "Good morning, Maggie my love. Sleep well?"

"Yes, beautifully and without screaming dreams, I'm pleased to say. Nothing yet?"

"Nothing," said Track. "He snoozes like a fallen tree."

Maggie sat beside Sam. "Isn't this prime time?"

"Pretty near," Track replied. "If he's coming he'd better do it soon."

They waited, watching the EEG and temperature lines. There was nothing. Saganian saw a few peaks on the sound analyzer, but heard nothing through the earphones.

"What can we do to stir him up?" asked Salinger.

"I wouldn't try the camera," said Saganian. "That gets his goat."

They waited until three forty-five. Liam came out of deep sleep and into REM again, but the temperature stayed at sixty-five degrees. There were a few audio bursts on the analyzer, but Saganian traced them to the ancient steam heater's asthmatic fits.

"Maybe he could use a little music," Track said. "What about a chorus of 'Benny Havens, Oh'?"

"How about the theme from *Jaws*?" said Maggie.

"I don't want to disturb you, troops," Sam said, "but I believe we have a visitor." They all looked at the EEG traces. Liam was in an active state with heavy beta.

"Temperature's down to fifty-six," said Salinger. "And it's falling fast."

"Jee-sus!" said Track. "Look at that heart rate! Eighty-one, with an upslope."

Saganian had put on the headphones. "I got a noise, sir. I don't know if it's her, though, the kid. The RTA pattern has the right peaks, but low decibels."

"Is that the seizure shape?" asked Maggie. It was. The EEG channels were both surging in the dome-and-spike pattern.

Track grinned and scratched his head. "Don't waste any time once he's started, does he?"

Sam panned with the video. The moon was full tonight, illuminating the far wall and brightening everything up enough to see the dim shape of the bed and the indistinct form of Liam under the blanket.

"Keep calling out the temperature and heart rate averages,"

said Sam to no one in particular. "I'm going to give my full attention to the video."

"I can hear her now, sir," said Saganian. "Clear as a bell. Never heard her this loud! Shit, she's up to forty dBs!"

"Heart rate's eighty-eight," said Track.

Maggie knew how to read the computer display. "Sam, it's fifty-one degrees, and the lines are still going down. No, I take it back—one of the columns is down to forty-eight."

"That's the thermistor on the floor," said Saganian.

"See anything on the screen, Sam?" Track sounded alarmed. This worried Maggie. Track was never scared.

"Negative. Maybe it's too bright with the moonlight coming through the window. It was faint on Thursday."

"Forty-six on the floor, Sam; forty-eight on the others. Are you going to do anything?"

"Nothing yet, Maggie. Just keep watching the temp."

"Heart rate's level at ninety-two," said Track. "We have some wild spikes on the EEG."

"He's tossing around," said Sam. "Those spikes are the electrodes getting moved. We'll lose EEG pretty fast if he doesn't settle down," Sam looked at Track and frowned. "That doesn't make sense. He was in REM. In REM the skeletal muscles are relaxed. He must be awake."

"The seizure activity is gone, sir," said Salinger. "He's back to beta, like before. Could the movement be a fit?"

"No. The waveform was petit mal, not grand mal. A seizure that would start him into tonic-clonic epilepsy would look like an electrical storm, great high-frequency and high-amplitude spikes."

"Forty-two on the floor, Sam, the others are forty-five. Still going down."

"Damn! What's his heart rate?"

"Steady—no, down again, Sam, down to eighty-eight."

"Okay. Maggie, just tell me if the room temperature goes down below . . ."

"Oh, shit!" said Salinger. "The EEG's gone! A big spike, and now we have garbage!"

"What happened?"

"I don't know, Maggie. The video's foggy again. Maybe the moon's behind a cloud."

"Sir," said Salinger, "it did that on Thursday night, went dim like that. When we went in the room, the lens was covered with frost."

Track stared at Sam. "What do you think, partner?"

Sam looked at the screen and drummed his fingers on the table.

"Oh, wow!"

They all looked abruptly at Salinger. "Look, his heart just sent up a terrific spike, and now it's just garbage, a jagged mess!"

"Oh, Sam!" said Maggie softly. "Did he have a heart attack?"

"No, God damn it, he took off the sensor! Let's go, enough of this!" Sam pushed his chair back and dived out the door, Track behind him. He turned and yelled over his shoulder, "Maggie, you stay in there, no matter what! Hear me?" She nodded.

He started for the doorknob, but saw just in time that it was wreathed in fog and coated with hoar frost. He pulled his sleeve down over his hand and tried to turn the knob. It was frozen fast. "I can't turn it!" he yelled to Track. "It's jammed and frozen shut! Get some hot water!"

"Hot water my ass!" said Track, "just get outa my way!" Sam did. Track hit the door sideways with a good windup, and it burst open. He pitched through from momentum and fell on his face. Sam stood in the doorway and watched Liam.

He had pulled off the EEG electrodes and the finger pulse crystal and stood by the bed, his back to Sam. The flakes of luminance whirled around him, lit now with a dim yellow glow as if reflecting firelight. Sam tried to call to him, but the words stopped in his throat. Liam's feet were invisible. The part of his legs below the knees had disappeared into the floor, as if he were wading in a pool.

The flakes spun faster and now glowed a bright orange. The sound of the child's screams was loud enough now for even Sam to hear. He felt Maggie behind him, her arms around him.

"Oh, Sam," she said. "Oh, Sam." Track heard her and looked up from the floor. To his horror her shoulders slumped and her eyes rolled back until only the whites showed under her eyelids.

Liam never looked back. He walked straight ahead, through the wall and out of sight.

18

*L*iam was tired; his lungs burned from the run, his legs were leaden. The run was longer now, harder than ever before. He passed streetlight after streetlight, each time feeling the darkness fade behind him as he entered their glow and feeling it surround him again as he left the fragile patches of yellow light and sharp black shadows. He knew he should pace himself or he would run out of wind, run out of strength before he came to Cullum Hall. He had a short uphill beat in front of him now, as he passed under Mahan Hall and headed for the library corner. This was a grim stretch, a lung-ripper, the last challenge before the half-block sprint to the BOQ. It was cold tonight, and as he ran he could feel the snowflakes brush gently against his face. He was afraid he would slip on the hill, but his shoes dug into snow that was accumulating too fast to be plowed off the roads. It will be deeper still, he thought, before I get home. The idea frightened him, though he could not have said why.

Halfway up the hill, he knew he would never make it. His heart pounded, his face was flushed and hot despite the snow, and as he slowed the flakes began to melt down inside the collar of his nylon jacket. He tried harder than ever to keep up the pace, but before he reached the top of the hill he slowed to a walk. He could hear the snow crunch under his shoes, and he wanted to stop and throw up in the gutter. His vision was blurred, the streetlights seemed dimmer, somehow, and he forced himself to keep walking.

("Temperature's down to fifty-six," said Salinger. "And it's falling fast.")

Now, strangely, the streetlights were gone. It was darker than he had ever seen a night, black as the pit from pole to pole. There was only a dim glow from the sky, barely enough to tell sky from trees. The shape of the public storehouse was to his left now; he had his bearings again. There, to his left, he could see the lights—just two windowlights, really, of the South Barracks, and he picked out the track of the road that ran in front of the academy building and the mess hall. Its snow was darkened even under the new fall, by the mud and manure of wagon drays. If he followed it he could keep up his pace without exhausting himself in the snow.

As he turned left and ran along the deserted road, he could see the first terrifying glow from behind the mess hall. It was enough to make him run again, though he was soaked with sweat now under the heavy wool cloak and the wool coat with its stiff collar. The snow was in his shoes, his stockings were wet, and he could feel the water pressed under his feet with every step. All at once he heard the shouts from the fire, the cries of men and women and the neighing of a horse as it strained to move a wagon in the snow. He ran faster, and the muscles in his legs ached. How could he keep running? It's Mansfield's, he thought. Yes, from this angle, it has to be Mansfield's! God, it's Mansfield's, please let it be Mansfield's. The thought was unworthy, the prayer without grace. And he knew by now that he was lying to himself. It was not Mansfield's. It was his.

He stumbled and fell on the road, his knee scraping against the frozen mud, and he felt pain like a bolt of devil's lightning down to his foot, breath-stopping pain like the agony he still remembered when he was struck down from the log breastworks at the Horseshoe, and the Creek with a red cloth wrapped around his head fell with him, stone dead. As he lay in agony later, and the flies gorged at his wound, Old Hickory had said to him, *Be brave, son, by the Eternal, and you'll see a fine day tomorrer*. He lay face down and cursed his weakness as he remembered how he had been brave then, so long ago when he was scarce more than a boy, more fit to carry schoolbooks than the epaulet. But for all his youth he had burned with righteous strength when he pulled the long bayonet out of the Indian and knew the joy of his manhood in that last moment before the musket ball struck him down like a blacksmith's hammer. He had been brave then, by the Eternal, and had seen many a fine tomorrow. And now he lay in the ice and mud of the road like a cur crushed by a coachwheel and cursed. Get up, cur. You were brave then, be brave now. And slowly, with great pain, with more courage than he thought he had, Liam crawled to his knees and then actually to his feet, though the pain in his leg took his breath away.

("Je-sus," said Track. "Look at that heart rate! Eighty-one, with an upslope!")

He started to run again, lurching at first, slipping with every other step in the icy muck, each stumble clawing at his hurt leg with steel nails, needles of ice. A form ran toward him, up the road behind the mess hall, and others came out, one with a lantern. *The wagon's coming,* one cried out, *load water buckets. Not much left,* shouted another, *the cistern's iced over. Can't get to it to break it.*

The kitchen fire, screamed the first, *melt snow; there's not enough water, she's damned well afire from top to bottom.*

Who's there, cried Liam, what house?

Who's that? shouted the first who had come for the water. *That you Cap'n? Praise God, it's himself. Yer own house, Cap'n, yer own, an' lucky yer back,* said the corporal, Bridey's corporal who had brought them a wild tom that morning for supper.

Annabelle, said Liam in a soft voice, hoping he would not be heard or answered.

She's in there, Cap'n, her an' the missus, upstairs. My Bridey, she jumped, an' threw Johnny out afore, into the snow. The missus, she won't answer. Praise God an' ye came back. Run, no one will go to them with the fire.

And Liam did run then, a wild scramble over the frozen ruts, and when he rounded the corner of the mess hall and looked up the row, there was his house, alight from top to bottom, and a crowd around it, lit by the glow and running around like madmen. There was Worth, wrapped in a buffalo robe against the cold, and Davies, holding his wife as she sobbed, standing there off the road in snow that was over their ankles. There was Hitchcock, shouting at cadets to fetch the buckets faster as if he were drilling them on the Plain on a spring day instead of forming a water-line with dwindling water in a snowstorm. The line of cadets was hard at work, but there was little enough water. Someone had managed to break the ice in Douglas's well, but the water was far down, the bucket kept jamming in the ice that remained, and a lot spilled as they pulled it free. In the line of cadets he saw the Antique, who loved the golden Annabelle and nothing else in this place he called his place of trial, else it were the books he could not have with him. The cadet looked at Liam, his dark hair wet with labor and the heat of the flames, his face puffy and his small eyes beseeching Liam without a word spoken. Their eyes met, and Liam saw a darkness in the cadet's soul, and he knew that this night's work might call forth that darkness in himself.

Then Bridey was there, and she grabbed his sleeve and said: *It was herself,* a graidhe, *the fit was on her.* Bridey spoke in a whisper of shame and fear, her face, once pretty enough, now common and drawn with labor and care and already plump as only an Irish girl's pretty face turns plump in a few years, her face stained with soot and streaked with tears, her eyes squinting and watering from the smoke. *It was the fit, Nije, the fit again, you saw it yourself before you slammed out, worse than ever.*

Liam grabbed her by the shoulders. Annabelle! Damn you, stupid cow, Annabelle!

Bridey looked at him in stupid fear and hurt. *Upstairs, Nije,* she whispered. *Upstairs. God forgive her, she locked the child in her room and set the house ablaze.*

Then Ethan was there. *Nije, there ain't enough water! River's near froze, wells are froze, we've used the cooking water, there's no more!*

Liam looked at the house. Heat blasted his face, and the snowflakes melted as they touched it until his skin streamed water. The fire was hot, hot as the pit of hell, that hell her father spoke of with such learned eloquence, and it sucked the air from around them. The snowflakes next to the broken downstairs windows were lit by the fire and whirled in the wind that rushed through the broken panes, a blizzard sucked by the consuming greed of the fire into its heart.

Then he heard Annabelle; the smoke had reached her, perhaps, or the fire was licking under the door. Her scream stopped them all, cadets and officers and soldiers, for a moment of stunned horror. Liam looked at the Antique. His were the eyes of a man who sees death in its ultimate corruption, sees death and decay devour the sun.

Liam stood in front of the door, bracketed by windows of fire. No one could hope to go in there and live. He felt the Antique's eyes on him, and he knew fear.

("I can hear her now, sir," said Saganian. "Clear as a bell.")

Liam now knew more fear than most men face in a lifetime of this world.

("Heart rate's eighty-eight," said Track.)

Corey Fletcher was suddenly beside him, wearing those disreputable tiger fatigues despite the cold, but looking strong and fit, his load-carrying equipment rigged to perfection and his beloved damned hunting knife taped with army green tape to the shoulder of the left suspender. The yellow snowflakes whirled around his head. God, Corey.

Tough time, Leemy, said Corey. *A tough spot. Late again. But you have to show them you've got balls. He needs you, Leemy. The old duty concept.*

I'm afraid, Corey, said Liam, trying not to look at Corey's pitiful remnant of a face, at the bone fragments and torn flesh, at the teeth that glistened in the light of the fire where the skin was gone, the mandible torn away. Corey's eyes glistened with a pale light, a cold light.

Well, hell yes you're afraid. You were never a fool, Leemy. A little spaced sometimes, and you were never on time for a damned thing except your graduation. But he needs you.

You needed me, Corey, said Liam.

No sweat, buddy, nothing you or anybody could do. He needs you now. It's quiet, Leemy, there's no pain once you're through. The gate's open, old buddy, it's a breeze. And you said you would.

I know, Corey, he said. The old duty concept. And Liam smiled at Corey and as he did tasted the salt tears in the corners of his mouth. But Corey was gone except for the blood on the snow, and Ethan was there. *There's nothing to do, Nije. Step back, by God, or you'll be buried if the thing falls.*

("Heart rate's level at seventy-two.")

He needs you, Leemy. The gate is open.

Be brave, boy, and by the Eternal there'll be a fine day tomorrer.

Liam pulled off his visored cap, and the electrodes came away with it . . .

("Oh, shit!" said Salinger. "The EEG's gone! A big spike, and now we have garbage!")

. . . and he looked at the gold ring on his finger. The fire would melt it, and it was the ring that had come from Eliza, before the darkness came, or before it made itself known since he guessed it had always been there. He slipped it off and handed it to Ethan, bewildered Ethan . . .

("Look, his heart just sent up a terrific spike, and now it's just garbage, a jagged mess!")

293

. . . who looked at it and then at Liam as if he had gone out of his senses . . .

("No, God damn it, he took off the sensor!")

. . . but then he understood. *No Nije, don't you be a damn fool, you can't help them!*

But Liam smiled. This time I have the courage, Ethan. It's given to me to live again, and in living again I choose to die. But Ethan either did not hear Liam or, more probably, did not understand him. Liam put his hand on Ethan's shoulder for a moment. Then he looked at the Antique.

("Oh, Sam," she said. "Oh, Sam.")

Then he turned and walked through the door, into the flames, and when he opened the door the hungry fire drew the cold wind to its heart and the fiery snowflakes were pulled in a swirling maelstrom through the door behind him.

The wool of his cloak and uniform were soaked, and this protected him for the space of a minute or so. Even so, the heat was near unbearable on his face, and he drew the cloak up over his head to protect it and moved to the stairs by feel, for it was his house and he knew the way step by step. But he stumbled over the first step anyway, and his leg screamed again from the old pain. It was nothing compared to the fire, he told himself, and it can be mastered. Nevertheless it was hard to climb the stairs, choking on the smoke and the steam from the wet wool, and he burned his hands.

He could no longer hear Annabelle, the golden child, could only hear the roar of the firestorm, the crackle of wood and the popping of the pine tar as the fire hit it. He kept his shoulder to the wall and felt his way along blindly, in real pain now, the heat of the fire searing his lungs. He had no idea now how far he had come down the hall, and looked through a gap in the cloak. He saw her in the hall, standing and proud, proud as a queen whose last jewel is pride. The fire had not taken hold along this part of the hall, and although she was nearly blinded by the smoke and the heat, she saw him.

She smiled a terrible smile at him, and her eyes reflected the light of the hellfire that awaits those who flout His merciless commandments. There were no words this time. But her message was clear. You came this time. Finally you came.

Yes, Eliza. This time I did. The gate is open.

For you, her eyes said, proud eyes. For a moment the fit was gone from them, cleansed out of her. But then the strange look came over her proud face again, the fey look that was worse than ever in the glare of the fires of hell. *Not for me, husband. Not for me.* She smiled at Liam, and his heart broke; she was lost again, this time forever. And she looked with squinting, seared eyes at the window beside her, and with her small fist she smashed a pane of glass.

The wind rushed in and the fire flared white-hot. The fire below them, finally burning through the beams, had also done its work, and sparks and flame rushed up from below. Liam was blinded and his exposed hands felt the terrible pain first. He felt the floor give way under him and heard Eliza scream as a roof beam fell between them.

Then the pain was gone, mercifully gone, and Eliza's last cry was gone, and he heard only the song of the winds, the song of the cold, with its dance of chords. *Come with us*, they said, *come and find peace.* Liam fell, and the song of the winds led him as he rushed headlong through darkness. The song was louder and louder, and he knew he had heard it before, but did not know where. The song filled him, passed through him and around him, he knew he was part of the song.

He fell for the passing of a second, he fell for a thousand years. Time was no longer a part of what surrounded him, and the very idea of this-before-that departed from him. It was light, but it was not his eyes that saw it; nor did he hear, for the song of the winds, the song of the cold, were suffused through every part of him. Then suddenly it was quiet, and the brilliant light filled the stillness.

He stood on his feet again in the middle of a stony desolation, a landscape empty of everything but the great tree. It had grown, he saw, since he saw it last, and it was covered from the lowest branches to the very top with flowers of the purest white. The sun was overhead, white light, brilliant light, pure light that did not burn.

There now, said the Old Man who tended the garden—*There now, boy. You showed 'em, sure enough! That was brave, indeed.*

Liam smiled at the Old Man, who looked older than ever in his labor-stained, faded khakis and battered work shoes. Brave? Maybe only you know, Father. How did I find the courage to go through the gate?

Oh, have a care, boy! said the Old Man, genuinely horrified. *He went through the gate, not you. You got off at the last exit before the toll.* Then he laughed, a kindly, gentle laugh. *I like that,* he said. *Getting to be a wit now, in my old age.*

And her, Father?

Well, he said sadly, *it's as I said: Mercy is without limit but wisdom's in short supply.* And the Old Man looked up at the tree that Liam had once planted, looked up with real awe. Liam's gaze followed him, and he was dazzled by the white, purifying brilliance of the sun.

As they watched, the tree seemed to come alive. Each flower's petals opened wide, and out of each flew a pure white bird. The sky was filled with them, and their wings in concert were the wings of the storm. They circled and rose, up into the brightness, until Liam could no longer pick them out against the blinding light.

Then he felt the Old Man beside him; he looked and saw a sadness in the ancient eyes. *Don't forget, boy,* said the Old Man: *Once your roots were watered by the spring.*

Liam felt a crushing pain in his side, a hammer blow that left him breathless, knocked him senseless. A burst of colors surrounded him. Then darkness.

"Oh, Sam," said Maggie. "Oh, Sam."

Liam was gone, and Sam felt the rage explode from the room, carried on the dark wings of the cold. He staggered back and heard Track curse, as if from far away. The light was dimmed, and he reached for Maggie. The fury had passed him, never seeing him, and he knew it was seeking her. He panicked when he saw no sign of her, only Saganian slumped against the far wall with his arm flung across his face, and Broadnax, bent over at the waist as if leaning into a hurricane. The snow was everywhere, he was nearly blinded, and his hands were numb.

He found her hand and pulled her to him out of a swirling cloud; he heard her call, but her voice seemed far away, quavering and queerly modulated as if down a tunnel. Then he saw her, looked full in her eyes, and saw the madness.

She stared at him proudly, cold pale eyes and porcelain face, the white lace of her collar scorched and blackened by the smoke. But her eyes were steady, merciless, the eyes of a predator bird; the rage was quiet, refined to a perfection over the endless seasons. There were no words to say, there was no form to the fury; it transcended mere words, flowed swiftly on its soundless grammar of hate.

Sam grabbed for her, as if to tear Maggie out bodily, but then he stopped and opened his mouth as if to cry out. Her face blackened, the lace curled and was consumed to a sooty trace, smoke enveloped her and his last sight of her was of a whirling gray explosion of ash that circled on the cold wind, mixed with the snow, and slowly vanished.

"Oh, Sam." Maggie came to him and they held each other in the cold hallway as the last of the fragments dissipated and the warmth slowly returned.

"What happened?" asked Broadnax, leaning against the top of the stair rail now. "Are you all right?"

"He just walked through the wall," said Saganian, sitting now against the floorboards on the far side of the hall, "right through the fucking wall. Did you feel that wind? What the hell *was* that? A deuce-and-a-half truck?"

Track was back on his feet and into the hall. "Mag, you okay? You looked . . ."

"Yes, Track. I'm fine. Fine." She looked up at Sam and he pulled her head against his shoulder.

"Shouldn't we *do* something?" Saganian asked. "Colonel Fitz is gone, right through the wall. We have to do something."

"Like what?" asked Broadnax and Salinger at once. No one offered a suggestion. There was an awkward silence. It dawned on Sam that none of them had seen what he had seen, what Maggie had seen, in the hall.

"What the hell are we supposed to—" Broadnax was interrupted by a shrill scream from somewhere in the barracks.

They all listened. A door slammed somewhere in the next

297

division, followed by a babble of voices. "*Now* what?" Track asked no one in particular.

They heard someone push open the main door on the 47th Division stoop and pound up the stairs. No one spoke. Maggie held Sam's arm as Tetzel came into sight. He was red-faced and dressed in his gray bathrobe and rubber clogs.

He saw Track. "Sir, Colonel FitzDonnell's in Andrea's room." He was out of breath. "He's hurt. I think he broke something. What's he doing over there?"

"Even if I guessed at that," said Sam, "you wouldn't believe me. Get on the horn and call an ambulance." Tetzel flattened himself against the wall as they streamed past him and down the stairs.

There was a crowd of cadets outside Andrea Linnell's room, gawking at Liam. When Sam and Track arrived he was on the floor, doubled up in pain and barely conscious. Kneeling beside him, Sam raised one of Liam's eyelids. He was conscious, his pupil somewhat pinpointed. "Liam," he said, "what the hell happened?"

Liam opened his eyes and looked briefly at Sam, then rested his head on the floor. "I got off, Sam," he said quietly, like a child just falling off to sleep, "I got off at the last exit before the toll."

Sam looked at Andrea. "How did he get in here?"

"Sir, I don't know! I was asleep and heard this terrific crash, and then someone moaning. I wasn't awake enough to see straight, but there was enough light for me to see somebody on the floor. I guess I screamed loud enough to wake the dead . . ."

"Yeah," said Sam, "I know." He looked up at the ceiling; there was no damage, no way Liam could have fallen through. "Where do you hurt?" he asked Liam.

Liam grabbed Sam by the sleeve. Sam recoiled. It occurred to him that Liam was touched by death, and he shuddered at the thought. But then he forced himself to put his hand on Liam's shoulder. "Can you talk?"

Liam nodded. "Hip may be broken; I landed on my side when I came back, or maybe on one leg and then fell on my side. My hip took the whole weight. I'm cold."

Sam looked up at Andrea. "Let me borrow your green girl." She untangled it from her sheets and blanket, and Sam put it over Liam.

Liam looked dreamily up at Sam again. "Maggie."

Sam looked over his shoulder. "Is Maggie here yet?"

Maggie joined them on the floor. Liam reached up with a painful effort and put his hand on the back of her head and drew her down to him. "Maggie, listen; you have to know." She nodded; she was through being scared.

Liam spoke so softly that Sam and Track could not hear more than a few of his words. "Maggie, he needed me. He had to have another chance. He had to die at the right time. He used me to do it. I knew he had to find something, he needed me. I didn't know why."

She nodded. "Did he . . ."

He smiled at her. "Yes. I carried him there, almost all the way. It was what the Old Man said—I got off at the last exit, Maggie, the last exit before the toll."

"What?"

"He said it, the Old Man . . ."

"What old man?"

"The Old Man who tends the tree. There were flowers, Maggie. You should have seen it. The flowers opened, and the birds flew out, perfect white birds without a spot on any of them; they flew into the sun, all of them, and him with them . . ."

"The old man?"

"No, Maggie; him, the one who wanted me. The Old Man stays at the gate."

"Was that the gate, Liam?" she said. "The one he left open?"

He nodded. "He knew. He needed me to be brave. Oh, Maggie; so much sadness, so many years he blamed himself. He would have died the first time and not saved her . . ."

"I know," said Maggie.

"But he lived until every moment was a burden. He had to live again and die again through me."

"Jesus," said Track, "look at his hands." Maggie looked at the hand that was holding her arm. It was covered with blisters, the skin was an angry red around them. Liam looked too, as if he had just noticed them.

"The fire?" asked Maggie.

Liam nodded again. "He couldn't save her. He tried, she almost came to him; but in the end there was too much bitterness,

299

she was beyond him, beyond herself. It grew in her, like a shadow, like a cold fever. It wouldn't let her smile. She didn't come with him.

"She tried," said Maggie. "She couldn't."

He rested his head on the floor again. "I'm tired. I went a long way. It was the wind. I heard it last night, while Anna was asleep. I knew then." He closed his eyes, then opened them again, just a little. "Maggie . . ."

"Yes?"

"Tell Dana . . ." He smiled at something. "Tell Dana Raymond is thriving. He sneaks them in." Maggie laughed and asked him what on earth Raymond had to do with it, but Liam was gone, asleep or unconscious.

"I don't know what you all are doing over here," said the ambulance driver, a specialist five in hospital whites, "but I hope you're going to stop. I'm wearing a path over here. I've been here three years, and this is the first time I've seen so many people getting fucked up in one place."

"Don't worry," said Sam. "It's over."

The driver picked up one end of the stretcher and Track grabbed the other. Liam was still unconscious, and had made no sound when they lifted him from the floor. The medic had slit Liam's nylon running suit to see if the hip had a compound fracture. There were the beginnings of a gigantic bruise, but no external sign of a broken bone. Track had told the medic to watch out for the blisters, and the man had stared wide-eyed at Liam's hands, but asked no questions. Track rode the ambulance with Liam, and Sam and Maggie followed in their car. George Salinger was left behind with instructions to tell the OC to hold his report until Sam had a chance to talk to him, or at least keep his speculations to a bare minumum, and suggested the OC be instructed to call Colonel Pretorius.

"At four-thirty in the morning?" George had asked.

"At four-thirty," Sam had insisted. "We share good news around here. If he bitches, tell him we may have solved his ghost problem. I guarantee he'll be thrilled."

By chance the doctor on duty in the emergency room was an

orthopedic specialist used to dealing with cadet knee injuries, and, in a stroke of doubly good fortune, he was not an excitable man. He examined Liam as he was being rolled down the hall, and Track sat in the waiting room drumming his fingers, then called Patti and told her briefly what had happened. Sam and Maggie came in about five minutes later, and they sat together trying to make some sense of the thing. Maggie told them what Liam had said.

"What did he mean about the 'last exit before the toll'?" Sam asked. "Did he have all his oars in the water?"

"I think he means Adonijah entered him somehow and used Liam's—his psyche or something—to relive the night that lodged his soul in that place, and somehow escaped through Liam. Adonijah followed his Annabelle, finally, but Liam couldn't go all the way."

"What do you mean, 'couldn't go all the way'? You mean he couldn't die?"

"That's what Liam believes, Sam. I think that's what he was trying to say."

"But what was Adonijah trying to relive?"

"Want a guess?"

"In the absence of something intelligent, I'll accept a guess."

"When the fire came, Adonijah thought it was hopeless to try to save Annabelle and his wife; maybe he was just too afraid. Whatever the reason, he found that living was too much to bear for as long as he did."

"Hancock's opinion about Adonijah knowingly going to his death in Mexico . . ."

"Yes, but it didn't work; he was stuck there. He was held there, at the point in time and space where he failed. And Liam helped him out."

"Who's in charge here?" It was the duty physician who had disappeared with Liam. "I need to get some details from somebody who has some idea what's going on."

"I'll do it," said Sam. "Can we go somewhere private?"

Sam accompanied the duty physician to a private examining room. He explained that they had been directed by the commandant to investigate the ghost reports.

"Are you a psychologist?" the doctor asked.

"No," Sam said craftily, "a biophysicist. FitzDonnell's a clinical psychologist."

301

"I knew one of you had to be. Go on."

"Well," Sam explained patiently, "he somehow passed through the wall without leaving a mark and, after what was either a wild ride on the back of a troubled spirit from a fire in 1830 to the edge of death and back, or one hell of a vivid series of hallucinations, he materialized in the next section of the barracks on the floor of a cadet room with a damaged hip and blistered hands."

The doctor sat back and regarded Sam with a blank look. "Where did he get the blisters?"

"I believe he had a vivid experience, hallucinatory or not, of being in a fire and dying of the experience. I'm not much on psychophysiological disorders, but I'd venture to guess they're some sort of somatoform reaction. Like blisters induced under hypnosis. They mimic the burns that he would ordinarily have received."

"You're certain he had no contact with chemicals or anything that could have caused—"

"Hell no, I don't know if he had contact with chemicals! I'm trying to tell you, sitting here befuddled and scared, that this man passed entirely out of my world into some never-never land for over a minute and landed in another room having passed through a fire wall and a very solid floor without leaving a scratch. He could have been on the moons of Barsoom for all I know. Chemicals!"

"The moons of *what?*"

"Never mind. Look. If you want a good answer, I can't give it to you, and I don't know for certain if anybody can. I'm out of my depth. If I hadn't seen him walk through a wall, if I hadn't worked this project for a week and seen the unaccountable shit that goes on in that room, I'd say he was an exceptionally intro-spective, introverted intellectual who had a brief psychotic break, hallucinated his morbid fantasies, and has a bad case of conversion hysteria. Matter of fact," he added with a grimace, "I've got colo-nels and generals who are going to be sitting on the edges of their leather-covered swivel chairs tomorrow, bright and early, waiting for me to say just that. But I'm also up to my ass in data that suggest what happened in that room this last week is nobody's imagination, and I have four witnesses who saw a man go from one room on one floor to another room on another floor without leaving a mark or opening a single door."

They stared at each other. Finally the doctor said: "What am I supposed to write in my report?"

302

"Beats the piss out of me," said Sam. "But when you decide, how about giving the OC a call over in Central Guard Room. He can probably use some ideas, too."

Sam, Track, and Maggie stayed at the emergency room. Patti arrived there at five o'clock, after putting Dana and her brother with a sleepy and confused neighbor. By seven o'clock, Liam was in a room upstairs and wide awake. They crowded in as a group, and Liam fought the urge to hide under his sheets.

"It lives!" said Track. "How you feeling, buddy?"

"Like I was just dragged down a mile of gravel road," said Liam, "with one end of a tow chain attached to the pintle of a tank with a fuel leak and the other end to my tongue." He lifted his bandaged hands. "Tell Saganian I know how it feels," Liam looked tired, but he was excited and apparently none the worse for whatever road he had traveled.

"Do you remember what happened?" asked Maggie.

He smiled at her. "Yes, I remember. The tree and the birds. I know what it looks like, Maggie."

"Know what *what* looks like?" asked Patti.

"It's a long story. Sam," he said, suddenly serious, "I couldn't tell you. I had to do it."

"Why? What if you hadn't taken the exit?"

"*What* exit?" said Patti.

"Well. I guess you'd have had quite a meeting with the com, among other things. I'd have been the lucky one; no report to fill out."

"You're still an asshole," said Track. "You're the only one I know who can come back from the dead without being improved by the experience."

"Back from the dead?" Patti squawked. "Is somebody going to tell me what is going on?"

"Sure, darlin'," said Track. "Let's go get some breakfast and I'll fill you in. As much as anybody can fill anybody in. You three have a good time trading war stories. See you at college."

Liam smiled gently at Sam. "What are you going to tell them?"

"I'll talk to the com this morning, without the others. I think we should keep this one quiet and just close up the room."

"Maybe you won't need to, Sam. He left. He didn't take the exit. He won't be back."

"Close it," said Maggie.

"I agree," Sam said, not noticing Maggie's quiet vehemence. "Maybe some other year. I don't think we could trust the place to cadets for a long time. You're expendable; beanheads are protected by law."

6

June

Her brain allows one half-formed thought to pass:
"Well now that's done: and I'm glad it's over."

—T. S. Eliot
The Waste Land

19

Sam and his crew removed the equipment from the division on Sunday afternoon, and a team from the Directorate of Engineering and Housing arrived on Monday to patch the wall where the cables had passed through and to install shelves in the room. Colonel Street had designated the plebes' room a storage area again, and prepared sealed instructions for his successor as regimental commander explaining why the place should remain unoccupied. The workmen, old civilian carpenters who had been at West Point for years, had heard rumors already of the week's events. It turned out to be the fastest work they had done in many months, and the last shelf was firmly in place and painted by close of business on Tuesday.

Sam and Track met on Monday morning with the commandant. None of the three discussed the meeting afterward, and when a reporter from *Newsweek* laid siege to the public affairs office that Thursday after the appearance of an *Army Times* piece, he was met with a solid wall of polite denial. The story was dropped except for a snide byline in *Krasnaya Zvyezda* that quoted *Army Times* and suggested that such nonsense was the natural result of Freudian bourgeois idealism and the babble of voices, described to onomatopoetic perfection by the term *raznoboi*, in Western psychology and science. Liam was much amused.

The corps remembered the events in the old North Barracks for much longer. That year's Hundredth Night Show, an annual event celebrating the change in number of days to graduation from three digits to two, featured the ghost in an extended musical number. One bright soul suggested dedicating that year's volume of the *Howitzer* to the "Spirit of the Corps." Nothing came of it in the end.

In February, Andrea Linnell broke her long engagement to a hometown man and John Tetzel managed to reserve a time slot for their wedding in the Cadet Chapel for the day after graduation. Major Broadnax had Andrea transferred to another regiment for the balance of the year to avoid any duty conflicts, since it seemed an uncomfortable breach of good order and discipline to let a company commander be engaged to one of his platoon leaders.

Steven Barstow's personal belongings were mailed to his home; he enrolled in a college close to home, and never returned to West Point. Eliot Carson would stay to graduate, but never visited his old room again. He was not disposed to discuss the ghost until years later, when he was a tactical officer himself; nor did he laugh at the sketch in the Hundredth Night Show.

Liam was out of the hospital in four days, but cartilage had been damaged in his fall and he was obliged to hobble about on crutches for several weeks. He seemed unchanged, to the satisfaction of some and the distress of others, but was silent on the circumstances of his injury. The matter was talked about in the department for some weeks, but eventually everyone learned not to press Liam or Sam for details. Everyone but Maggie was surprised when Liam, reversing the decision of his great-grandfather, began in February to take instruction in the Catholic faith. He discussed his reasons with the priest at the Chapel of the Holy Trinity. They were never revealed, nor much discussed; by that time, people had largely ceased to wonder about Liam. Maggie asked him about it that spring, before the end of the academic term, when they were at the farewell party and alone for a moment outside. "A little bird told me," he said, and they laughed.

On the second of April, Maggie received a letter from a law firm in Newburgh announcing the death of Mrs. Elizabeth Cleary O'Grady, and stating that a recent revision in Mrs. O'Grady's will had stipulated the transmittal of certain documents from a safety deposit box in the Marine Midland Bank into the care of Mrs. Samuel Bondurant of West Point, New York. The papers were sealed in a manila envelope with Maggie's name on the front, lettered in Betty's fastidious hand. Their last meeting had been eerily strained. Maggie had simply handed the old librarian the

Upton memoir without comment, along with the Cleary Bible. Mrs. O'Grady had nodded and thanked her. Maggie had not visited the library again in the months that followed, and the news of Betty O'Grady's death came as a surprise.

Inside the envelope were a letter from Betty and a much older, handwritten letter protected by two pieces of stiff cardboard. The librarian had written:

Dear Mrs. Bondurant:

I regret that our acquaintance could not have been more cordial. The fault was mine. As a younger woman, I allowed my pride to get the best of my duty and my good judgment in the matter of the missing book.

You will, of course, have discovered the reason for my unsuccessful attempt to remove John Upton's memoir from the library. My family was a part of Highland Falls for many, many years, and we were sensitive enough of our position to fret over our family secret long after it had ceased to be a matter for concern to anyone but us. I am, as you may also have concluded, the last of the Clearys. My only living relative is my late brother John Cleary's wife, who lives in Tompkins Cove. And she, of course, is not a Cleary.

I removed the book from the library shelf in the late 1960s, when the historian was doing a project on the ghost. I had noted the unfortunate and embarrassing disclosures, which were unsuspected, I think, by Colonel Upton, when Bernice did her paper. My father, John Cleary, Jr., knew Colonel Upton and, along with my garrulous great-grandmother Bridget Hardesty Cleary, gave him a number of stories that he included in both his memoir and the official history of West Point folklore. I have never decided whether that remarkable lady was enfeebled by age when she blurted the dates of John, Sr.'s, birth, or if she had just decided with Emerald Isle wit to visit the problem on her descendants. By the time you read this, perhaps I shall have had the opportunity to satisfy myself on the matter.

The enclosed letter is something of a family heirloom; since it no longer has a family to go with it, I pass it on to you. It may have some value. Happily, my late husband was unable to lay hands on it. It came, of course, from Captain Proctor's papers, which came into John Cleary's hands when the old soldier departed for Mexico in 1847.

I have heard a number of stories about what happened in the cadet barracks. I wish to know no more, unless it be on the other side of this life, a life in which I have seen all my close friends die one by one and found myself alone with memories and secrets that can no longer be shared with anyone who would care—except you, Mrs. Bondurant, whose curiosity and righteous indignation shamed me. Accept this small gift in my memory, and in the memory of my great-grandfather, Adonijah Proctor.

Elizabeth Cleary O'Grady

Maggie sat quietly for some time, staring at the last words. She had opened the envelope in the evening, while Sam sat on the sofa beside her reading the *Times*.

"What's the matter, Mag? Did she smear the pages with cyanide?"

She handed him Betty's letter. "Damn! Old Nije must have been the father, not Corporal Cleary. That explains a lot. Makes my dream a little clearer, anyway. Damn. No wonder Eliza was a terror."

"She was indeed."

"I remember her," said Sam, "standing on the stairs. '*The child plays in the same nursery with the golden whore you made in your pride and lust.*' I wondered what she was talking about."

Maggie was not listening. She read the old yellow page slowly and shook her head. "Ye Gods. It was him."

"Whom?"

She handed him the letter silently.

New York
March 10th, 1831

Sir

In consequence of my lack of prospects in my native country, it is my intention to remove forthwith to Paris,

310

as I proposed before, in search of appointment in the Polish Army, in behalf of which plan I have petitioned the assistance of Col. Thayer. Having no other "hopes" I must rely upon the goodwill of the whole academy and the slender means proffered by the publication of my work so graciously sponsored by Col. Thayer.

Illuminating the fatigues of cadet life and the niggardly rudeness of my "father" are only the kindness shown me by you and Capt. H. and the brief delight of our golden Annabel. Without her the academy is a place of shades.

Most respectfully
Yr. Obt St
Edgar A. Poe

Sam read the letter twice, slowly. "That was the 'Antique.' The cadet we talked about in my dream, the one in the snow."

"Liam mentioned him when he told me about his own dreams. He sort of smiled, as I remember. I guess he knew."

"This," said Sam, "is pissing me off. Every time I'm ready to find a rational explanation . . ."

"Give it up, darling, what we have here is a true paranormal experience."

"Let's find some other name."

"Oh, stop being so damned stuffy. Maybe you were right after all—maybe we just have to classify these things as part of the natural order of things, not supernatural. Does that make you feel any better?"

"Oh, lots! Now I just have to explain to myself how slow DC potentials coursing across the surface of the cortex can somehow translate themselves into signals transmitted around a room. No, further than that. They made it all the way back to the BOQ and Lee Road. That's where we had the dreams."

"Couldn't it be that while you and Liam were in the barracks, during the manifestations . . ."

"Don't be lurid."

". . . the signals were stored in your brains for replay, like a video cassette?"

"Sure, Maggie—*if* you grant about half a dozen absolutely lunative premises, it all makes elegant sense."

Maggie stuck out her tongue.

"Liam's off crutches, by the way, and—speaking of lunatic premises—he's off on leave. He went to Washington, D.C., this morning, and tomorrow he's off to brave a visit to Boston."

"Has he seen her since Walpurgisnacht?"

"No. Doris Gilmer, of all people, phoned her at that computer company she works for on Monday morning after Liam went into the hospital. She sent him a get-well card."

"How touching."

"I can't imagine what Liam sees in her," said Sam.

"A good question," said Maggie, "and one I've thought about a lot. Maybe there's just something unknowable in him that somehow resonates to her. Maybe he finally found out what it is, or was."

"I think Liam ccould be a big success writing morbid poetry or disgusting short stories, like Poe."

"What a thing to say, Sam!"

"Probably wrong, though. Unlike Poe, Liam's a grad. He thinks like a grad. I'll bet Edgar Allan Poe never jogged once in his entire life."

"Find him?" The bearded man next to Liam gestured at the wall. He had kept silence as Liam searched up and down the columns of names on the granite slabs. Liam wore his greens and leaned on a cane; the bearded man wore a faded field jacket with the left sleeve tucked in.

Liam looked at his unsuspected companion, startled. Then he smiled slowly and shifted his weight to his uninjured hip. "Yes, finally. I knew the day."

"You were there? That's a bitch. I know."

"Yes." Liam turned back to the wall. Corey was there, just under Mike Absher, his platoon sergeant; Flores, who carried his radio, was two names higher. If you stepped back, the names faded into blurred shades of gray, but this close it was personal, no matter whose names you saw.

"Anyone special?" asked the bearded man.

Liam smiled again; the man needed him, needed not to be alone. "Yes," said Liam. "A friend. My platoon was trying to get close enough to extract him, but we froze, I guess, then I was hit. I couldn't help him."

The man glanced at Liam's cane, then at his uniform. "How come you stayed in, man? I couldn't have."

Liam laughed. "The old duty concept." The bearded man looked at him and nodded. Liam put his hand on the shoulder of the old field jacket, the one that still had a real shoulder in it, and the man looked back at the wall.

The man shook his head. "A real bitch."

Anna was in a mild quandary. Liam had not written or called since she had left West Point, and she had tentatively removed him from her list of devotees. Then, without warning, he was coming. She had prepared all the enthusiasm she could manage on the spur of the moment. He had seemingly abandoned her before, only to reappear months later as if nothing had happened. Anna could allow herself a certain smugness. She did not consider herself a mean or manipulative person, but Liam's dogged faith in her provided an anchor point of sorts.

Now he was coming to her, and the cane was obviously no decorative accessory. He looked thinner than in November, but somehow younger. When he kissed her, she sensed still another change. The kiss was a warm gesture, full of typical Liamish grace. But the tension she always felt in him at first was not there. She could not have described it that way; she only knew that something was changed. Being above all a creature of habit, Anna was not comfortable with change. Liam had been predictable, hence easy to deal with. Now, in the shuttle terminal, Anna found herself off balance.

"I like your hair," said Liam. "You're more authentic as a brunette."

"You told me that in October," said Anna. "I've kept it that way just for you."

"Bullshit. I do like it, though."

"I'm flattered. Let's go pick up your bags."

"No bags, this time. I'm flying back this evening."

313

She frowned. "I thought you were here for the weekend. I made reservations at . . ."

He shook his head. "This is just a quick visit. I have an interview in New York on Monday, and a lot to prepare for. I should have told you. I'm sorry. I'm getting forgetful in my old age."

"Old age! You look years younger. What happened?"

"A lot of sitting time, I guess. I just got off crutches this week."

They walked toward the escalator and the hourly parking lot. "It's a long story. I came here to tell you part of it, I guess. It won't take long."

"I've been dying to hear about it. Your friend—Doris, is it?—called me and said you and Sam what's-his-name had exorcised the ghost or something. I hoped you'd tell me about it before now."

"I've been busy," he said dryly. "Anyway, I needed a lot of time to put my thoughts together."

Anna looked up at him, then straight ahead. They walked through the parking lot in silence. Here we go again, she thought, La Perugino gets another proposal. This time, I refuse him and *he* walks out, or he wouldn't have made this an afternoon visit with no suitcases. This will require great tact, far more than last time. I owe him more . . . No, she corrected herself, I owe him nothing. He has no debts to call in.

Liam was not in a chatty mood. He recommended they go out for lunch; they ate in a delicatessen Anna favored, and he recounted the essentials of the final night in the haunted room. He skipped the details of his dreams and stuck to the same facts Sam would have trotted out: the instrumentation results, the accumulated data, and his injury. She feigned interest. Her mind was occupied by the insistent alarums of her sixth sense.

But Liam's description was distant and lackluster as well. The discussion went on in this vein for some minutes, until Anna finally gave up and talked about her job and her plans to move up the Analog ladder when her boss retired in August. Liam listened politely; there was no vacuum Anna could not fill with her own plans.

After lunch they walked. There was a small park near the delicatessen, and they finally gave up the stroll and sat on a stone bench. "Liam, why are you here?"

"I had something to tell you."

"All right," she said. "Tell me." She avoided looking at him, and studied the passing traffic.

"First, I'm retiring from the army. With my prior enlisted service, I have twenty years in on one July."

"I thought you were going to stay at West Point until you dropped dead. Don't you have tenure?"

"Yes. I could stay for thirty. But I can't do it. I've run out of contributions."

"You'll never run out of contributions," she said. "And you're so willing to be used, you'd be writing proposals to the army the day before you reached your thirtieth year. What are you going to do? You're forty-three!"

"I won't know that until after the interview on Monday. But that's not what I came to say."

"I haven't changed my mind," said Anna. "I'm not giving up *my* job."

"Yeah, I know. I didn't come to say that, either."

"Then what?"

"You're going to have a tough time understanding this. If you were in my place, you'd just stop talking and leave me to rot, wondering what happened. I can't act that way. I was raised on the classics; I like a beginning and an end, and I like to know there are no questions."

"What was I raised on?"

"I don't know," he said sadly. "*The Flintstones*, I guess. I admit no particular insight into what goes on in your mind. I'm down here for my satisfaction: if it pleases you to hear me out, fine; if not, I guess it's no more than a few wasted minutes."

"Okay. I'm listening." And she was listening. This was the other Liam, the one who had always peered at her from behind the other face, that other man who was hers to please or torment as the fit took her. Something had peeled away the old manners, the old deferential affection and tolerance. She had thought once that nothing short of the grave could change Liam.

He took a breath. "I won't replay any old romantic notions. If you don't have them memorized by now, they'll never mean anything anyway. You've never understood why I loved you. You never asked, either, but if you had I'd have been damned hard pressed to explain it. Now, just to tie up all the loose ends, I'll try.

315

"You had to be there. I had to have an Anna Perugino. You were unlucky enough to be picked for the detail . . ."

"I'm not unlucky."

". . . and that's not my fault or yours. You were there when I was at a crossroads. I didn't know where to turn. I could have married the army and lived and died that way. Or I could have resigned and found another life. But I'd reached a point a lot of us reach after ten or fifteen years of service. The army takes a lot out of you. It leaves a lot of people burned out before they're forty. Sometimes it seems there's a do-or-die point every damned year: some assignment you have to have to get your ticket punched; a selection board for promotion or a school. Every damned year, something can go wrong that screws up the rest of your life. And there's the constant moving, the strain on your family, the shoe-string pay. And all of this so you can go off when war comes and get your ass shot off. It makes you tired; it takes a lot of stamina to be able to put up with it, it takes a lot of confidence and a lot of optimism and a good measure of luck, blind luck. To be really good in the army, you have to be fantastic, indestructible, nimble-witted, silver-tongued, and thick-skinned.

"You were there when I came to the place where I had to decide. I could be Liam FitzDonnell, Major General, U.S. Army (Retired), when my luck ran out late or Liam FitzDonnell, Colonel, U.S. Army (Retired), selling insurance in Killeen, Texas, if it ran out early. I could have been an old man with hypertension and deaf ears and a second life that meant nothing. But you were there—yeah, Perugino, you. And that made all the difference.

"I wanted to be something for you. You couldn't have cared less whether I made it to colonel or commander-in-chief of Walt Disney World."

"Why me?" she asked. "You were supposed to answer that question, remember?"

"Oh, yes. Why you? Because it wasn't you. It was something in myself I had to come to terms with before I got too old to play the game anymore. It was there when I met you, yammering and kicking, begging to be let out. I was going to offer it to you, you were going to take care of it, nurture it. You were beautiful and bright and—by my standards at the time—sophisticated. On second thought, maybe it wasn't that I was going to offer something to you. Maybe I just wanted you to help me create some kind of reflection, an image of myself. Yes, you were to be a canvas, a canvas on which I could paint the Liam I wanted to be before I died."

"But a canvas is blank," she said with a toothy smile under demurely closed eyes. "Am I blank?"

"Of course not," said Liam with a soft laugh. "If you'd been a blank canvas, we'd already be divorced."

Anna laughed at that, too, but hesitantly, as if she weren't quite certain if she should be angry instead. "But is the painting finished? And, if so, am I finished too?"

He smiled his slow, reflective smile. "You never really let me get started," he replied. "And now I have to begin somewhere else. The painting's still got to be done, and that's going to take a long time, maybe longer than anyone has a right to expect. You can't help me anymore. I have to do the rest myself. And you," he added, "have to do your own self-portrait."

"I'm happy with me now," she said. "I have what I want."

"Whom the gods would disappoint," said Liam, "they first make optimistic. Maybe you do. I'll ask you again when you're farther down the road. But in the meantime, I have other roads to travel."

"What roads? You still haven't told me what you're going to do."

"As far as that goes," said Liam, "this one will do. When I walk away from this park down this gravel path, I know it's a road of sorts, and as long as I know what I'm looking for, it can carry me there. But that's an evasive answer. For now, the road leads back to the airport." They walked along the path and back to Anna's car and he told her about his interview and the years of analysis and supervised clinical work that lay ahead of him before he could replace the Old Man at the tree and do his work with others. She allowed that he probably knew what he was doing.

"But how will you know when you've found Liam?" she asked, finally, as he filled out his boarding pass.

"I don't want to sound trite," he said, "but the object is the search, not the finding. Look, I'm widely regarded as a nut by my associates. Most of them have reasonable goals and standards for their lives. I set different goals for mine. You helped me get that way. You didn't intend to, and I know you don't understand how. But you did, and I'll never forget it. Now, I have to get to the gate. I hate elaborate good-byes."

"Look," she said, "call me up if you're passing through Boston. You can keep in touch."

Suddenly tired, Liam looked at her. It seemed to him for a moment that he had been so indirect and abstruse that Anna had really not understood him, not a word. But then he saw her eyes, and they no longer hid Anna from him. He saw into her, past that impenetrable opacity of hers that had kept him at bay for years. She was undone, unprepared for what he had brought to her out of three months of silence. It was a scenario she had never foreseen, and the veil of privacy fell away; behind it was an ordinary girl who was unexpectedly hurt by someone who, until an hour or so ago, could not possibly have hurt her. Liam looked into new, unsuspected depths.

He put down the boarding pass and drew Anna to him, held her in his arms and for the first time in all the years he had known her offered his love and felt it accepted. Passengers moved in on both sides of them to fill out their boarding passes. Liam and Anna ignored them. Then he felt her pull away, gently; and when she had stepped back he saw the veil in place again. She was composed once more, the lapse was covered.

Liam last saw her from beyond the security gate, walking away with that awkward, unaffected stride that he had seen so long ago. She pushed through the glass doors and left the terminal. It was past, he thought, beyond redemption; the last exit before the toll.

20

*A*pril is the cruelest month, saith the poet, but June, saith the Military Personnel Center, is the busiest. Orders are cut in the winter and much of the army is either in transit or clearing government quarters by the start of summer. The effect is particularly noticeable at West Point, where officers of the staff and faculty are invariably assigned at the beginning of the summer to prepare for their first academic year and depart at the end of their third or fourth, when the cadets have left and there is the suggestion of the end of a cycle. Moving vans maneuver through the quarters at Stony Lonesome and New Brick, Lee Area and Dunover Court; harassed wives and cynical, obstinate loading crews fight their battles over wardrobe crates and dish packs and how to fold a baby's crib to fit in the smallest possible space. Against this Hieronymus Bosch mural of madness, we say good-bye.

Our good-byes are said in the department's conference room with officers and wives and office staff crowded together to hear sentimental reminiscences and watch the awarding of medals for meritorious service. On this afternoon, Track Dortmunder makes his official farewell; this summer he will join the 11th Armored Cavalry in Fulda, Germany. Doris Gilmer is bound for the Presidio of Monterey. And there is a baby cup for Sam and Maggie from the Association of Graduates gift shop, engraved with the name of Elizabeth M. Bondurant; Sam accepts it with grace, and Elizabeth shows her gratitude by poking a wet finger in Sam's eye.

Track's medal is affixed by the Dean. There is loud, enthusiastic applause; Track is much loved and Sam is not the only one who will miss his bluntness and caring insights. Liam glances at Sam and Maggie just in time to see them exchange a few soft words. They are smiling, and Liam wonders what they share at this moment.

In fact Sam, who has taken Elizabeth, has whispered to Maggie: "She's wet."

"Really? Isn't it lucky you're holding her?"

"God damn it, Maggie, the sleeve of my greens is getting wet. I have to wear this uniform the rest of the day."

"It is a stroke of fortune, then! You have on a dark outfit, and it won't show! I, on the other hand, am wearing a pastel blue blouse that would certainly show the dampness, and of course I could hardly be expected to take it off."

"Thanks."

She smiles sunnily at him and whispers: "Let it be a challenge."

Now it is Liam's turn, and we stand at attention while a citation is read for award of the Legion of Merit.

Liam smiles his slow, private smile. "I have no statement as elegant as Track's, nor any trophy or accomplishment for these years as valued as the one Sam shares with Maggie.

"This is the end of my time," he says, blushing. "I don't have a swan song, only a few lines of verse from a poem by my favorite countryman, William Butler Yeats—now that I've said it, all you clods and Saxon swine know how to pronounce it. And here it is, in all its typically Liamish inscrutability:

> *Bred to a harder thing*
> *Than Triumph, turn away*
> *And like a laughing string*
> *Whereon mad fingers play*
> *Amid a place of stone,*
> *Be secret and exult,*
> *Because of all things known*
> *That is most difficult.*

"I bid you farewell."

"Wasn't that just like the asshole," said Track, "to quote Yeats and cite him and then quote Douglas MacArthur without a footnote."

320

"I'll forgive him," said Maggie. "It was his moment. 'Amid a place of stone,' indeed! He had to have just one last private joke."

"You seem to be the only one to pick it up," said Sam. "But then you weren't standing there with a sleeve soaked in baby urine. You had time to be literary."

They walked out of the heavy oak doors of Thayer Hall and crossed the street to the library corner. Patton's great bronze statue regarded them sternly as they shut the doors of the car and Sam, out of deference to Elizabeth's surly temper in the heat, turned on the ignition and started the air conditioning.

"I'll miss him," said Maggie.

"So will I."

"It isn't the same. I can't imagine the place without him."

Sam knew what Maggie meant. It was the cost of staying in one place when your friends were forever moving on. But it wasn't the same. "Don't worry, darling," he said as he watched her stare straight ahead out of the window. "Pretty soon you get used to ghosts."

She was alone, and the solitude did not make her anger less, did not wipe away the betrayal. Her cold anger swelled and sought out all the corners of the room, spreading from the low places and seeking the lifeless things. The frost of her anger, the cold mist of her curse, touched the room in spite of the heat of the day.

In that minute passage of time when Liam had passed through the wall and down his own path to redemption, she had burst from the room, and Maggie and Sam alone, because of the life they shared, had seen her; Maggie had become her and had felt the cold, the rage, the inarticulate pulsing cold fury that came unbidden long after the delicate vessel of flesh was ashes. The aura came to her now in the room as it had when real blood coursed through her; the sparkling warning, the oblivion, then afterward the rage. It had been strong enough to hold them in that place, strong enough until the new force came, full of life. And then they were gone, and only she remained.

Maggie and Sam, by mutual agreement, never spoke of it. To speak of it, of her, was to give it a name, and the name was forbidden. For Sam's sake, and for their child's, it was forbidden.

In that instant, wrapped in a cloud of darkness and cold, the rage had come against Maggie from the room, against the life she carried. But the rage was too cold, too ancient to prevail. Maggie had felt the aura, sparkling and terrible, and the room had been gone and she had seen Sam through those ancient eyes. Maggie had traveled her own road, and found her own exit in Sam's touch.

In the room, a pane of the window split with a harsh ring of shattered glass, split from corner to corner.

c.1

F
ONE   O'Neill, Timothy R.
        Shades of gray

$17.30

DATE			
JAN 2 8 1988			
FEB 2 3 1988			